BLACK HOLE OR BUST

Trapped in a suicidal plunge into the maw of a black hole, Lucky thrashed in the cockpit of his tiny vehicle. He hurled imprecations at the ruined communications ports. He flailed, kicked, punched at everything and anything within reach. But it was only when he removed his helmet that the craft reacted.

"Warning. Cockpit life-support gases are nearing depletion. Expiration estimate without helmet: one hundred and eighty seconds. Singularity event horizon ETA: two thousand, three hundred and fifty-nine seconds. Evaluation: life-support termination. Expiration of vehicle occupant. Breach of contract. Reminder: no refunds."

By Jack McKinney
Published by Ballantine Books:

THE ROBOTECH SERIES:
GENESIS #1
BATTLE CRY #2
HOMECOMING #3
BATTLEHYMN #4
FORCE OF ARMS #5
DOOMSDAY #6
SOUTHERN CROSS #7
METAL FIRE #8
THE FINAL NIGHTMARE #9
INVID INVASION #10
METAMORPHOSIS #11
SYMPHONY OF LIGHT #12

THE SENTINELS SERIES:
THE DEVIL'S HAND #1
DARK POWERS #2
DEATH DANCE #3
WORLD KILLERS #4
RUBICON #5

ROBOTECH #18: THE END OF THE CIRCLE

KADUNA MEMORIES

The Black Hole Travel Agency:
　　Book One: Event Horizon
　　Book Two: Artifact of the System*

* Forthcoming

EVENT HORIZON

The Black Hole Travel Agency,
Book One

Jack McKinney

A Del Rey Book
BALLANTINE BOOKS · NEW YORK

To ace *tololoche* thumper Steve Luceno,
with a brother's love

The center cannot hold,
The world feels like a con.
"Just Say No" emblazoned on your brain;
What's Really Going On?

"Expletive You and the Horse You Rode in On"
by Bruised Dessert, c. 1991

ACKNOWLEDGMENTS

Much thanks to Mr. Junsaku Moko and
Richard Hansen for help with the Japanese
neologisms; and to Howard, Robin, and the gang
for easing the Route 95 commute. And special thanks to
Skip Youngquest for his slant on the
RGO.
I am likewise indebted to
O. B. Hardison Jr.'s
thought-provoking *Disappearing
Through the Skylight*.

PART ONE

Somewhere Out There

ONE

WORD ALONG THE Trough was that Avonne had been shortchanged by the Big Bang; that where most worlds had been granted an awesome if not always hospitable mix of gases, ground swells, and gravities, tiny Avonne was little more than a misshapen sphere of forlorn rock with neither an envelope nor a sea to call its own.

Moonless and crazily tipped on its axis, the planet knew only the briefest of warm spells and passed most of its eccentric year in seeming exile from the red giant that had birthed it in far better times. Indeed, scarcely a meteor had visited the place in close to two hundred and forty million revolutions now, and what with its poverty of scenic overlooks, important people, and decent night life, Avonne had been voted "least desirable stopover" for twenty standard-years running by the editorial staff of *Tourist Trap*, the Black Hole Travel Agency's in-house quarterly.

All the more puzzling that an Adit should have been opened on Avonne, but such was the case. An array of unadorned portals dubbed "rectangles with fallen arches" by *Tourist Trap*'s chief architecture critic, the planet's contiguity-gates to the Trough didn't make for much of an Adit; but thanks to them Avonne saw more than its share of offworld wonders—even if most of what appeared were consumer goods of one exotic sort or another, invariably in mass transit to worlds where such things mattered.

So it was of some interest, then, to on-duty ingress control officer Goran Lennix that thirteen HuZZah should suddenly materialize on Avonne among a consignment of shape-memory meditation coffins bound ultimately for a first-class departure lounge in real-time way station Sierra.

Well, thirteen HuZZah and one human, to be exact—the latter being a leggy female with a mane of rust-colored hair and a tour guide holo-ID affixed to the the breast pocket of a magenta jumpsuit. SHEENA HEC'K, the badge displayed, representing Singularity Flings, a Foxal-based packager of solar-sensual getaways. A handsome creature, if you liked the species, although a bit too tall and broad-shouldered for Goran's taste.

The guide towered over her brood of similarly tagged egg-shaped HuZZah, who, for reasons yet to be determined, were clothed in oversized tunics emblazoned with fanciful depictions of tropical fruits and vegetables, and what could only be described as party hats.

"I take it we're not on Foxal." This from sinewy Sheena after a moment of bewilderment, eyeballing Goran from the carpeted ramp fronting the arrival gate.

"About as far as you can get," the control officer replied in the same lingua franca, chuckling to himself as his calculated response sent a ripple of distress through the HuZZah group.

Visibly shaken, the tallest among them was already waddling down from the Adit on stubby legs, doffing the conical hat, tugging at the tight-fitting sleeve of the guide's wearever.

"Not Foxal? Did he say not Foxal?"

Sheena Hec'k put her fists on her hips and directed a bemused gaze down the length of the concourse, then turned to lay a calming hand on the HuZZah's now bare crown.

"Nothing to worry about, Hamm. A minor glitch. I promise, we'll be on Foxal before you know it." She swung a toothy smile to the rest of the group. "Does everyone recall our agreement about remaining centered and not allowing any small setbacks to bother us? We're on vacation, remember; we don't want to see a repeat of what happened on Nmuth Four, do we?"

The ovoids spent a nervous minute regarding one another before jiggling a communal no.

"Then just keep thinking about Foxal; bright sunshine, pristine beaches, warm ocean waves . . ." The group huddled and squealed. "Room service, nightly sweets, herbal wraps . . . and complete tranquillity, let's not forget tranquillity."

The HuZZah relaxed somewhat, the shaking gradually winding down to rhythmical shimmies, and Sheena commenced a sort of lilting song, encouraging everyone to join in.

Disengaging two of his retrofitted limbs from the horseshoe of instruments in which he was housed, Goran popped and retracted the interface umbilicals that wedded him to various commo devices and inclined his sensor-studded head in the direction of the group. He understood just enough low HuZZah to comprehend the lyrics of the sing-along.

"*Keep a finger in your socket, keep a smile on your face; turn your pocket to the sun, wrap yourself in your embrace . . .*"

Sheena was leading them into one of the transit lounges now, snaking her way down the ramp in an interpretive dance, complete with hand movements and pelvic thrusts. "That's it, that's it." She allowed the group to take over as she backed out of the lounge toward Goran's station, throwing him a sidelong look of exasperation when she got near enough. "For God's sake, where in the Trough are we?"

"Avonne," Goran said, releasing it like the punch line to a bad joke—which Avonne certainly was—and receiving just the predicted wince. A grin assembled itself beneath his fleshy snout. "A minor glitch, isn't that what you called it?"

The guide took her eyes off the group just long enough to sneer at him over the top of the instrument station. "If that's not a mouth you're wearing, quit using it like one. Trough travel isn't supposed to have glitches—minor or otherwise."

Goran let his eyes roll in opposite directions. "I'm as surprised as you are."

"Then don't just sit there with your umbilicals retracted. Find out what went wrong and fix it. I don't know how long I can keep this group under control."

The ovoids sang: "*Mistress HuZZah had the means; the HuZZah made, she cooked the genes . . .*"

Their attention attracted by the song, some of the passengers in the Adit concourse and departure lounges were smiling, clapping in time, mimicking the ovoids' hula-hip gyrations.

Goran studied the undulating hand motions and silly kicks before reinserting himself into the interface desk. Sheena wasn't sure just where the control officer left off and the instrumentality began.

"I don't understand it," Goran told her a moment later. "According to way station Sierra, you and your group have arrived at your intended destination."

The guide stared at him as though he were data-dazzled. "Who—outside of a couple of demented dust demons, maybe—would choose Avonne as a destination?"

Goran wriggled his proboscis. "I chose Avonne. Of course, the transfer came with company perks—paid vacation leave, health coverage for my family, extra limbs—"

"I don't remember asking for your bio." Sheena's softboot tapped while she glared at him.

"I'm only saying—"

"Escort Hec'k!" The HuZZah named Hamm had appeared at the transit-lounge doorway and was gesticulating with short arms. "You promised we'd be properly cared for. You said nothing could go wrong."

"And nothing has." Sheena hurried over to him, full of professional concern.

Hamm held up tiny hands. "Don't you dare pat me."

"Come on, Hamm: *'Put a finger on your crown, keep the world in its place . . .'* " Sheena pirouetted under her own forefinger, broadening the forced smile. Several travelers, obvious veterans of Foxal or Nmuth Four beach packages booked through Singularity Flings, stopped to join in—although Goran did notice three humans in mimetic coats and broad-spectrum goggles hurry by the transit lounge with barely a curious look.

Reluctantly, Hamm fell back into the dance line, and Sheena whirled on Goran. "Do I have to menu what can happen here if we don't get this group to Foxal?"

Goran's shoulders heaved under the station harness. "I'll see what I can do. But don't blame me if I can't arrange for an immediate fade. By all accounts you're where you're supposed to be."

Sheena's laugh was more a shriek. "Then where's our luggage?"

Goran glanced at the arrival gate, where the shaped-memory meditation coffins were awaiting transfer clearance. Manufactured by Halo, Inc., a Black Hole subsidiary, the coffins were designed for use as either sleep caches or sensory-deprivation chambers, and featured such upgrade options as Full Chakra Massage, Auramatic Snooze Alarm, and Snapping Gyro—for those who preferred the masochistic route to on-the-go flow or transitory enlightenment.

"Lost baggage. That's something to consider," the control officer was willing to admit.

"And just what am I supposed to do with thirteen HuZZah on Avonne, anyway—take them pumice skiing? They paid for relaxation, not abrasions."

Goran's free limb undulated in a placating gesture. "Things could be worse, you know. You could have ended up on Collaxis."

"Why Collaxis? What's going on there?"

"Unexpected primary flare fit."

Sheena sucked in her breath. "How many dead?"

"The entire planet."

Sheena felt faint. "Just arrange for our fade, will you?"

Goran turned peevish again. "Well, I'm just warning you not to expect any meal or lodging vouchers if you're forced to remain here for a time. You'll have to take that up with Singularity Flings, not Black Hole."

"Damn these discount package tours," Sheena was muttering to herself. "It's always some—"

"We're here to collect our shipment," a basso voice interrupted.

Sheena and Goran turned at the same instant, the source of the voice being a hundred and fifty kilos of hulking, claw-handed Yggdraasian, with a face that had surely stopped a few surface-effect vehicles in its time—head-on, by the look of the creature's flattened nose and lumpy forehead escarpment.

Behind the voice stood lesser and yet greater versions of Yggdraasian muscle, some fashionably exoskeletoned in vanity plate—battle-scarred armor, enlivened in places by patches of what Sheena took to be dried blood. She was certain she'd seen one or two of the faces on "wanted" displays in Adit terminals up and down the Trough.

"We're here to collect our shipment," the voice repeated, leaning a scent into Goran's workspace that started his snout twitching.

A sudden quiet had descended over the immediate area, save for the transit lounge, where the HuZZah were trying hard to put a happy face on things. Goran noted that the Yggdraasians had even won a fleeting glance from the three humans sporting the all-sights and copycoats, who had seated themselves a short distance down the concourse.

The ingress control officer quickly indicated an input port on the station deck. "Insert your receipt, please."

The Yggdraasian dug an info-crystal from his vest pocket and drove it into the port, simultaneously favoring Sheena with a narrow-eyed appraisal. A regular stare-master. "You from Foxal?"

Sheena folded her arms, nodding.

"Not all of you though, right?"

"My father was . . . from somewhere else."

The Yggdraasian used his spiked chin implants to motion toward the transit lounge. "So what's with the chub group?"

"Escorting them to Foxal. Five days of ultraviolet bombardment."

The Yggdraasian's one good eye focused on Sheena's ID badge. "Black Hole guide?"

"When I can get the work."

The hulk snorted, turning away from her to tap a claw on what might have been the workstation desk or some anatomically flattened portion of Goran. "About that shipment, Pit Boss . . ."

Goran offered up a blank look. "Uh, I don't imagine you're here for the meditation coffins. Sir."

The Yggdraasian rearranged his bulk and lowered his voice. "Do we look like we'd be?"

Sheena could hear Goran's gulp from ten feet away. "It's just that there seems to be a bit of a mixup—a minor glitch, you might say."

The Yggdraasian straightened. "Meaning?"

"It seems irregular, I know, but, well, the transfer codes match up, and, uh—"

"Out with it!"

Goran shot a limb over his shoulder and in a rush said, "These HuZZah *are* your shipment!"

Sheena traded dumbfounded looks with the Yggdraasian before swinging to Goran. "You've done too much time on the machine, pal. We're nobody's 'shipment.' "

"What kind of operation you running here?" the Yggdraasian bellowed, apparently concurring with Sheena's assessment.

Goran shook his head, snout swaying over the controls. "I assure you, sir, Black Hole has a unblemished record—"

"Then where's our stuff?" came from someone at the voice's elbow. Another added, " 'The reliable name in Trough travel,' my sphincter."

Sheena blew out her breath. "No way I'm allowing my group to get mixed up in this." She wasn't three steps to the transit lounge when the lead Yggdraasian called to her.

"Where do you think you're headed?"

She spun on her heel, intent on toughing it out. "Like I told you, Foxal—"

Two of the lesser Yggdraasians were up in her face in a flash, wagging outsized claws. "Play the safe odds and stay out of this," one of them cautioned. "I know you're a protected species, but look at it this way: You're endangering the only life you've got.''

Sheena bit back an insult. But when it was obvious the pair were making straight for the HuZZah, she steeled herself and hurried after them. ''Look, be reasonable, okay? Let me at least explain to them what's going on before—*aargh*—''

''That's it, you're extinct,'' said the one who'd just about picked her nose, vising a pincer on her throat, cocking the other one back.

Sheena was ready to skull butt him, maybe take a bite out of his nose, when the lead Ygg intervened, waving his minion off. ''Don't bother with the caretaker. I'm more interested in our *shipment*.''

The second Ygg was already herding the now silent and wobbly HuZZah out of the lounge, onto the concourse. ''Just keep singing,'' Sheena shouted, bouncing up on her toes, patting her head and rubbing her stomach. ''Keep calm, keep calm!''

The voice laughed as he muscled past her to inspect her baker's dozen of frightened ovoids. ''Contact Sysops security,'' Sheena told Goran on the sly. And just what had the Yggdraasians been expecting from the Adit? she had time to wonder. Black-market genetics? Transmog drugs? Political prisoners? Weapons?

''So your tentacles tell you the shipping codes match up,'' the voice was saying to Goran. ''Then I guess we get to do what we want with this bunch.''

Sheena wended her way to the edge of the circle the Yggdraasians had formed around the HuZZah. Poor Hamm had been singled out and positioned up front. ''You want a hostage, you've got me.'' Sheena stepping out to shield him, adopting a martyr's stance while she was at it.

The hulk laughed and dragged her aside. ''What's Black Hole care about a part-time guide? Guides they've got plenty of. But paying clients,'' eyeing Hamm in an evil way, ''that's another story. Clients mean revenue, and revenue's what keeps the universe in flux. That's Black Hole's bottom line, wouldn't you say—*HuZZah!*'' suddenly whirling on Hamm.

Sheena saw it coming and shut her eyes. When she could bring herself to look, she saw that Hamm's shiny carapace, where it showed above and below the garish tunic, was crazed foot to crown. Paralyzed by fear, the HuZZah let out a high-pitched whine, then tipped forward and hit the concourse with a sickening crack.

Everyone waited. You could have heard an electron spin.

Seconds later, Hamm's carapace broke open and three HuZZah—already of fair size—emerged from the ruins.

The phenomenon was most often referred to as "spontaneous replication"—typically but not always brought about in response to stress. "Trauma birth," as it was also called, had been known to cause problems for anyone addled enough to have dealings with the species, and had resulted in population explosions of unequaled magnitude on HuZZah home-system worlds.

Nmuth Four, in fact, was still in the midst of resettling the eight thousand HuZZah birthed in its Adit terminal by some prankster's noise bomb.

But you'd think the Yggdraasians had never had so much fun. "Guess you're going to have to report that you overbooked the tour, huh, Hec'k?" their leader managed between fits of manic laughter.

Sheena didn't reply, caught up as she was in calculating the insurance nightmare Singularity Flings was in for.

Goran took the next volley: "Now, wire head, you think you can get your tracers to find out what happened to our shipment, or am I going to have to scramble another one of these yokels?"

The threat alone was enough to tip two more HuZZah to the floor, eight replicants rolling from the wreckage.

"I'm trying, I'm trying!" Goran shouted, limbs and umbilicals flailing about in an attempt to access data on the misplaced shipment.

By now a sizable crowd had gathered round, a few concerned travelers attempting to lead the HuZZah back into song while the rest were wagering on a final ovoid tally. Growing larger by the moment, Hamm's three replicants were running mad circles around Sheena's feet, threatening lawsuits of the highest order. The other eight had scattered into the crowd. The voice, meanwhile, had selected two more HuZZah as potential candidates for his sadistic little shell game.

Sheena pushed up her sleeves, shook the tension from her arms, and once more shoved her way through the circle of onlookers. Arriving at the center, she gritted her teeth and threw the punch that started the panic . . .

A safe distance away, the woman in all-sights and copycoat asked, "Shouldn't we lend a hand?"

"This has nothing to do with us," one of her companions answered above the din. "Sysops security can handle it."

"Anyway, Cups," from the second man, "you don't really want to draw undue attention, do you?"

"That's Cup," the woman told him, anger showing in her amber eyes and at the perfect corners of a perfect mouth.

The man smirked, making no pretense about ogling the swell of the woman's breasts under the mimetic fabric of the copycoat. "Not from where I'm standing, steel meal."

TWO

CUP WASN'T HER real name, any more than Silvercup was, or any other she'd answered to these several micro-lifetimes now. On Aart's World, where they'd found her work as an organ-bank biotechnician, the name was S'ss't. Then more recently, on the *Hero's Tomb*, a lightsail salvage ship out of Pasals Cluster, it was dBow.

To date she was a step ahead of her enemies and the techno-assassins they dispatched and deployed—an elite, machine-trained breed of heartless executioners. In this she had been forced to rely on the intelligence of her would-be allies, to submit to their control and guidance, to comply with the modifications they demanded. For they saw her as not only vulnerable, but invaluable to the criminal case they were mounting as well. And so the job changes, the jumping about in real-time or the Trough, the applications of tissue that masked her metalflesh self, the endless succession of identities.

But names or appearances scarcely mattered any longer. "Silvercup" even had a pleasingly visual appropriateness. How she gleamed under the falseflesh and copycoat! The name had been bestowed on her by a former friend, now a sworn enemy. Ka Shamok. A sworn enemy of the Trough, if the truth be known—an enemy of the shadowy entities who had brought it into being.

Now if only her male marshals could keep from calling her "Cups," as if delighting in their object fascination for the female breast—even when hers were ill-equipped to nurture or in any other way gratify.

"Let's go, Cups," the one called Lister said, tugging her away from the curious scene unfolding in the Adit concourse on Avonne. There was little point in offering resistance; Lister could overcome her will by activating the containment field remote he wore on his belt.

It was difficult to imagine HuZZah inviting confrontation with an Yggdraasian, let alone a gang of the outsized creatures. But perhaps it was the ovoids' mind-numbing song that had brought the melee about. Silvercup wished now she'd been paying closer attention.

Thick-soled boots gave Lister added height, though he still had to raise his eyes to look into hers, and there, behind the lenses, she could detect the leer he assumed the goggles hid. An element of arousal was always present when he spoke directly to her. Lister was afraid to confess his attraction for her—an attraction he plainly considered aberrant. Lister, the confused human he was.

It was Lister who insisted on the three of them wearing the broad-spectrum all-sights. The goggles extended the range of human vision. Compensation, no doubt, for what she could see innately and he couldn't—a kind of enforced spectral equality.

Price was her other custodian, stockier and somewhat more intelligent than his partner, and not nearly so enslaved to infantile thinking, although far from evolved to any real degree. Price affected a limp. Symbolic of what—his impotence in her presence? Perhaps some wound waiting to happen?

She had become their assignment shortly after her arrest by Black Hole Sysops security—the so-called White Dwarves. Since then Lister and Price were forever showing up at untimely moments to spirit her off to some secret location, some false life. *You've just got time to grab your silicon spray, Cups,* as one of the jokes went, *and your gallenium arsenide vitamins.*

But better those midnight flights into the unknown than the series of safe houses she'd known earlier on. She was at least out in the real world. And when the trial finally ended . . . Well, who could say, perhaps she would be free to carry out the mission she had been birthed and tasked to oversee: to search out Black Hole's Founders, the Sysops, and reverse the hold they had clamped on the whole of the galactic arm.

Her parent system was the Fealty, a condominium of silicon intelligences, which rendered her—certainly in the minds of those who favored Trough-speak—something of a *made-man.* The Fealty had risen from the chaos of the Nanite Plagues which had destabilized the machine technologies of the Prior Times and was currently ensconced on Sweetspot, terminus of the outlaw Adits, the Inroads that provided routes of escape for liberation-

bent SIs and machine minds. It was there, in Sweetspot's ironically christened capital, Computopia, that the Monitor resided.
Silvercup's control.

"Thinking about the good ol' days?" Lister asked, noting her
sudden quiet. He laughed then, adding, "That's behind you,
Cups—just about where some horny robot'd like to be."

A courtesy monitor at the departure gate informed them that
they would have the Adit to themselves. Plenty of room to
stretch out for what amounted to instantaneous teleportation. A
quantum leap into one of the singularities that powered the Adits;
an emergence at the far end of some space-time conduit the
tamed black mass maintained. A reassembly, really—the re-
trieval of a mathematical code. Instructions for a new you, identical to the old you.

They stepped up into the curved-top portal and faded.

"Sierra," Price said not a breath later as they materialized in
one of the way station's numerous gates.

Silvercup conjured a look of surprise. "Sierra? Don't tell me
I'm being relocated to a habitat?"

Lister steered her by the elbow toward egress control, offering
his high forehead to the ID and ticketing scanners. "Maybe
someday, Cups, but not this time. We're in transit is all."

A sphere whose manifold concourses were lined with arrival
and departure gates, way station Sierra was one of the few stops
along the galactic arm opened to both Trough and real-time
travel, with docking facilities for hundreds of vessels—some
traversing the vast distances of the continuum by means of conventional power, their half-crazed captains determined to discover frontier worlds suitable for inclusion in the Trough.

Dozens of shipping and transport companies were represented,
but Black Hole Travel Agency had recently acquired the con-
glomerate that built the station, and many of the hotels, restaurants, and concession stands were now Agency-franchised or
wholly owned and operated by BHTA subsidiaries.

Silvercup was curious to learn what Witness Security had
planned for her, but she waited to ask until they were safely
tucked away in a transit lounge. Price had already ordered drinks.

"Was there some conspiracy aboard the *Hero's Tomb*? Is that
why I'm being moved again?"

Lister waved a hand at what he misconstrued as concern.
"The trick's not to wait for a problem. We relocate you even
when things couldn't be better. That way we keep everyone
guessing." He motioned with his chin. "Even you."

The friendlies, her guardians since the arrest, had originally gotten her on a technicality, invoking the Laws of Cybernetics to force the confession they needed—the testimony that was ballast for Black Hole's case against Ka Shamok's cell of insurgents. Never against Ka Shamok himself, who typically remained far removed from the consequences of his machinations. But the interrogation of her neural circuits had presented the courts with something of a conundrum: Wasn't she in fact harming her former allies in crime by testifying against them? Condemning them, as a consequence, to death or worse?

She'd let the lawyers argue for precedents and such; and in the end they'd won her testimony through an appeal to a kind of utilitarian, greatest-good-for-the-greatest-number logic. Or so they thought. It was important above all that they remain ignorant about precisely what the Fealty had fashioned and infiltrated into their midst.

When the drinks arrived, she clinked her glass against Price's and raised it to the falseflesh adhering to her lips. "Proud of me?"

Price allowed a mild smile. "You're learning."

"It's what I'm meant to do."

The comment only drew a derisive snort from Lister. "Too bad no one learned you how to choose your friends," setting his own glass down and passing an implant-hardened hand over his mouth.

"What sort of life will I have—this time?"

Lister slid the goggles up onto his brow and knuckled his restless eyes. "A perfect setup. Run by some trusted people on Gilgit."

She was genuinely surprised now. Gilgit was a low-tech human world with a downside Adit similar to that on Avonne. But unlike Avonne, Gilgit was classified a tertiary planet. Most of Gilgit wasn't even aware of its status as a Trough world; that knowledge was limited to the operators of the Black Hole franchise and the relative few who came and went via the gate.

Silvercup touched her shorn hair, dyed black after the vat-dipping that had left her sheathed in pliant brown skin. "That explains my new look."

"The White Dwarves don't figure Gilgit's ready for met-alflesh, Silvercup." Referring to the Sysops security personnel, Price was careful to keep his voice down. "Gilgit. Hell, they still grow food out there."

Lister gulped his drink. "That's where you come in, sweet

steel. Some people put out a call for a number cruncher to count soil-grown beans in some nowhere patch of farmland.''

Farmland: she liked the sound of it. ''The lowest of my low profiles.''

''Hey,'' Lister put an arm around her shoulders, ''don't you know you're our most precious piece of paraphernalia?''

Only no one was there to meet them on Gilgit, where Black Hole's local franchise operated out of the back of a hover-parts store in a city of fair size. The franchise staffers hadn't received word about a rendezvous, so Lister suggested they hit the streets for a quick look-see. Price was worried about not blending in, but Lister loved a challenge. It was a human world, after all, and they'd both been briefed on local customs and such. Lose the all-sights and they could pass for indigs, he insisted. Besides, what good were the mimetic coats if they couldn't trust them for a bit of copy cover?

The front door of the parts store opened on a wide boulevard, busy with pedestrian and vehicular traffic. Silvercup assessed her new surroundings, sampling the air and cataloguing the faces of passersby. Gilgit was civilized enough to have hovercraft, but even those were driven by crude, fuel-burning engines. The indigs seemed to be of a single human racial stock: lean, fine-boned, dark-complected.

They walked for a city block before a battered-looking craft alighted alongside them. The hover's doors hissed open and the driver, a man of moderate height with a shock of curly black hair, climbed out. His three passengers, a man and two women, remained seated inside.

The man hurried over, digging into the pocket of utility coveralls for a plastic-encased ID. ''Sorry we're late,'' he said, extending a hand to Lister while Price was studying the print document. ''I'm Rikker. But I guess you know that already. And this,'' turning to Silvercup, ''this must be our new employee.''

Her eyes picked out minute traces of facial scar tissue from hastily done laser work, and her mind assembled a portrait of the man before the reconstructive work had been completed. But she needed to be sure, so she extended her own hand to him, saying: ''Lin DeMor, Rikker.'' Her fingernail scratching just enough cells from his pink palm to provide a specimen she could analyze.

Price handed back Rikker's ID and sniffed. ''Guess I don't have to remind you to take good care of her.''

Rikker grinned. "Trust me, we'll do that."

"What's the program?" Lister wanted to know.

Rikker shrugged. "Standard procedure: Take her out to the farm, find her something to do, wait to hear from HQ."

Lister looked over at her and laughed. "You on a farm, Cups. Somehow I don't see this lasting."

Price was about to say something when Silvercup broke in. "This isn't Rikker," she said evenly. "I've just run a DNA profile," rubbing her fingertips together as her escorts turned to her in alarm. "The name is Cleat." She motioned to the imposter, who was maintaining the grin nevertheless. "He answers to Ka Shamok. We knew each other before he had his hair curled and his face rebuilt."

Cleat took a backward step. "And you fed me to the Dwarves, you freakin' mutant!" His weapon came out, but Lister and Price had a split second of lead time. So, unfortunately, did Cleat's three passengers, who were suddenly showing directed-energy weapons of archaic design.

"We told you you'd never testify!" someone said before a short-lived star flared on the street corner.

Everyone had fired at the same moment, but it was Cleat's plasma weapon that gave rise to the explosion. One of Lister's shots had apparently found the weapon's containment chamber, loosing a block-wide globe of starfire that not only atomized Lister, Price, Cleat, and the hover itself, but several wheeled vehicles and perhaps two dozen innocent Gilgit bystanders as well.

With Price had gone the twin-pack containment field that had restricted the range and speed of her movements, and so Silvercup had phased from the scene in time to escape any crippling damage. An errant charge, though, had holed the midsection of the copycoat and seared away most of the falseflesh adhering to her right side, from armpit to hip.

She stepped over a half-dozen lifeless bodies as she hastened back to the parts store, moving against a crippled swell of shoppers, strollers, and office workers, blinded and deafened by the explosion. Others, unharmed, were rushing toward the ruined site, too dazed to take much note of a tall brown woman with gleaming metal where a rib cage should have been.

Security curtains were lowering over the door and windows of the parts store, so Silvercup phased again, moving faster than the human eye could follow, and halted just short of the back-room

Adit gate, which was concealed at the rear of a vane-alignment
bay. The franchise Pit Bosses were in the front room supervising
the shutdown. The hope was that no one would implicate the
shop in the fusion event that had slagged a good portion of the
street.

Silvercup bit the tip from her right forefinger and inserted the
exposed joint into the Adit's control port, ticketing herself back
to Sierra.

She hastened into the sunken portal and faded.

And a moment later was hurrying out of a way-station arrival
gate, clutching at the tattered remains of her copycoat—gone
deep red where misted by Lister's blood—tugging the mimetic
fabric down over metalfleshed breasts and bare midriff.

She phased through ingress control and began to search for a
departure gate she might slip into undetected. But way station
Sierra wasn't Gilgit; eventually she would have to stand still for
the fade itself and some Pit Boss would undoubtedly spot her.
Good chance Gilgit's franchise operators had already alerted
Sysop security of an unauthorized fade.

No, this time escape was going to require a lot more than a
smart finger. And suddenly she was not only running from Ka
Shamok's scattered band of chaosists, but the Witness Security
Program itself, for it was obvious that WitSec's plans for her
continued well-being had been compromised. What she needed
now was a credit spike, a change of clothes. A new identity.

She phased to a first-class lounge elsewhere in the moonlet-
size sphere, where service techs were busy installing a bank of
Halo meditation coffins. Scanning the lounge's telecaster commo
stations, she spied a being as rough-skinned as she was smooth,
as vegetal-looking as she was metallic—a Nall, apparently waiting for his luggage to be moved out of the Adit. He was close to
her height, wealthy by the look of him, and so engrossed in his
conversation, so caught up in his own importance, that he took
no notice of her as she phased into the lounge and made off with
the expensive carrycase an overworked porter from Black Hole
Teamster Alliance had delivered to his side.

Just for good measure, she lifted the Nall's coat on her way
out. Then, donning it, she phased back into the concourse and
disappeared into the crowd.

Sometime later, the Nall was still waiting for his bag to arrive.
Ridding himself finally of the telecaster headband, he began to
launch invectives at the porters. It was only when they had

begun to amble off on spidery legs to complain to their union rep that the Nall realized his coat was missing as well.

Panic contorting his features, he hurried into the crowded concourse. A short distance down the hall he stormed into the way-station office of the Black Hole Travel Agency and, pounding a gnarled fist on the alloy countertop, demanded to know who, if anyone, was in charge there.

THREE

IN COMMON WITH crowd-pleasing circus acts and dare-devil stunt doubles, the founders of the Black Hole Travel Agency had nothing but disdain for the cautious approach, the safety net. Risk was their motivation, the potential for disaster, regardless of who or how many might take the plunge with them—leanings which also invited comparison with certain species of investment banker, corporate lawyer, and tax consultant.

So what that their gross manipulations had less to do with the flow of data than with that of light itself? In the end it all came down to laws and regulations, both system-innate and consciously enacted, and the ways and means to circumvent them. In a very real sense, marketing the space-time continuum for travel, opening the Trough, and fabricating the Adits that accessed it had required little more than a thorough understanding of loopholes.

Yoo Sobek, recently promoted to a position as an Agency Probe—he'd served as a lowly auditor before that—saw nothing intrinsically wrong with making the most of loopholes. That they existed at all meant they were there to be exploited. But there were indications of late that some agency other than Black Hole was exploiting those same loopholes to its own advantage. And that was not to be tolerated.

"I'd just discovered that my coat and attaché were missing when I entered the office of Black Hole's representative on Sierra and inquired after the person in charge. So naturally I was upset."

"Inquired," Sobek said.

The Nall cleared his throat and shot back a look of indignation. "Exactly that. Only to be told, in no uncertain terms, to—"

"Yes, we've been over that." Sobek cut him off with a flurry of hand movements.

The two, Probe and Nall, faced each other across a thick slab of alloy desk in the mass-transit lounge of Aart's World's downside Adit franchise. Sobek sat with his back to the open teleport gate, as in-transit inanimates—supplies, consumer goods, luxury items—materialized and faded from view.

"This of course was *after* you'd threatened the porters," Sobek continued.

The Nall's barklike hackles went up. "And why shouldn't I threaten them? I'd been waiting over an hour for my attaché. Then they have the nerve to ignore me."

"Because one of them claimed to have already delivered your attaché."

"So they maintain. But I assure you I never received it. And I'm certain one of those creatures made off with my coat."

Sobek conjured an image of the Nall's double-sleeved coat draped over the humped back of one of Sierra's six-legged porters. "It seems rather unlikely, doesn't it?"

The Nall bristled, obviously undaunted by the human conjugation Sobek had adopted for the meet—brown eyes and a mop of black hair today. "I don't care how unlikely it 'seems.' My coat and attaché are missing, and I demand that Black Hole locate them immediately or compensate me for my losses."

It was really a matter for Temporal Adjustments, with whom the Nall had already spoken; but the T.A. division chief had requested a Probe because of the exorbitant size of the claim. And yet the Nall refused to clarify whether that amount was based on the value of the items, or something either of them may have contained.

Sobek had traveled to Aart's World from clear across the arm to question the claimant firsthand, but the Nall refused to be moved by mere conciliatory offerings.

The Nall was drumming thick digits on the platform desk, waiting for Sobek to say something. "I'm a recurrent relocator with Black Hole Travel, and I happen to know that attachés don't travel the Trough without someone directing them—even on mass transit. Find my things, Probe. I don't enjoy mysteries."

Sobek inhaled deeply for equal effect. "Nor I."

Although these past three troubleshooting Adit jumps had brought little else, he told himself. Commencing with an incident on Avonne that was probably going to result in the planet being closed to Trough travel for some time to come, or at least until all the newborn HuZZah were rounded up and faded to some spacious world where they could spontaneously replicate to their hearts' content.

Sobek had assumed Yggdraasian form for that visit, since it was the Yggs who had filed a claim. The HuZZah, too, would need to be compensated for the technical blunder that had robbed them of their vacation fling on Foxal, but that could wait until all the strays were accounted for.

Then there was the guide, Sheena Hec'k, whose two-fisted approach to problem solving had led to a terminal-wide brawl. Hec'k had a reputation for thoroughness and attention to detail, but she was known to be somewhat short-tempered, and the HuZZah incident was going to work against her. Sobek ventured she would be demoted, confined to running human group tours to and from tertiary worlds, or to chaperoning abductees.

As to the origin of the blunder that landed the HuZZah on Avonne, that had yet to be ascertained. However, the Yggs' misplaced shipment had been tracked to a seldom-used Adit on Bzarba, at the far end of the arm. Ordnance comprised the bulk of the shipment: neutron bombs, biochemical weapons, directed-energy rifles. Avonne's small contingent of Yggdraasians was apparently a splinter group of a mercenary alliance operation out of Pasals Cluster.

Black Hole Teleportation Authority denied it had had any hand in procuring the weapons for the mercs; the Agency had merely supplied the medium for their exchange. And in this, as always, Black Hole remained impartial. The Adits, after all, were there to use. The Agency was frequently criticized for profiting through the spread of interspecies hatred and galactic unrest, but in this Black Hole's policy was clear: There was no ethical wrongdoing in the movement of warships, arms, or armies; evil arose from the use made of those devices.

Sobek's second stop had been on Gilgit, where matters were complicated by the planet's tertiary classification: Adit-equipped but only recently opened to Trough travel. The privileged few whisked in and out walked unknown among the resident population, going about their business without having an impact on the planet's sociopolitical development—the reason why a sudden unexplained fusion event on a downtown city street corner posed such a cover-up nightmare.

Eyewitnesses reported that shortly before the event, a confrontation had taken place between the driver of a beat-up hovercraft and three pedestrians in odd-looking suits, who—a few witnesses recalled—had emerged moments earlier from a parts shop not a block away from what was destined to be the epicenter of the slagfest.

On Sobek's recommendation the parts-shop Adit had been shut down, the former franchisers faded—save for a Gilgit couple who had been mem-wiped and left to fend for themselves. Regrettable, to be sure, but hardly the sentence leveled against the planet Rize after similar breaches in operational procedure by its Adit franchisers. The Founders—perhaps to prove they still had what it took—had ordered their Red Giants to terminate the Rize system's primary.

Sobek's actions on Gilgit were prompted by the discovery that one of those believed killed in the explosion was a silicon intelligence, metalflesh female. Worse still, the gleamer—so it emerged—had been enrolled in a WitSec Program after testifying at a Sysops espionage trial.

And now a missing coat and attaché.

Stolen from under the sniffer of an executive employed by Black Hole's principal corporate rival in Trough tourism, Eternity Tours, Unlimited. A development that wouldn't have warranted undue concern were it not for the fact that Gilgit's Pit Bosses had initially reported an unauthorized egress from the Adit gate following the explosion. And along with it, Sobek's suspicion that Silvercup, as the metalflesh was known, might well have phased her way to safety.

Gilgit's franchisers were now willing to accept that the power flux they took for a departure could have been caused by the fusion blast, but Sobek's instincts told him differently. He gave the metalflesh five minutes to get from the street to the departure gate, another five to get from one of Sierra's Adits to the way station's first-class lounge . . .

And so the Probe had to ask himself if there wasn't some link between the Nall's missing coat and attaché and a possibly self-relocated witness.

"You say you had your coat in plain sight and suddenly it wasn't there."

The Nall nodded stiffly. "I was on the telecaster to a client in Pasals Cluster—"

"Pasals Cluster?" Sobek flicked open a recording device to glance at the notes he'd filed on the Yggdraasians' misplaced arms shipment. He had no real need of the recorder, of course, but had found that devices of any sort lent at least a veneer of authenticity to his primate conjugations.

The Yggdraasian mercenary group called Pasals Cluster home.

"Yes, a business call," the Nall was saying. "In any case, when I realized the coat was missing I naturally assumed that one of the porters had put it aside for safekeeping."

Sobek's eyes returned briefly to the recorder. The device's disk-shaped lid was damaged from wear and tear and he had to keep a finger wedged under the thing to keep it open. "The coat you described to our Temporal Adjustments division," he said at last, "doesn't equate with the value you've affixed to it."

The Nall took longer to reply than was necessary. "It has sentimental value. Find it, if you think I'm asking too much in compensation."

Sobek was still reviewing his mental notes long after the interview ended. Bad enough that his promotion to Probe should coincide with a series of unexplained glitches along the Aditway, some disruption loosed in the Trough—off-course tourist groups, misplaced ordnance shipments, ill-informed security marshals—without the added nuisance of a mysteriously disappeared coat that had obviously contained something of great importance to Black Hole's chief competitor in Trough travel.

Clues to the existence of some disruptive force at work. Clues to a mystery, when he had nothing but disdain for the format. Facts were all that mattered to a Probe, black and white the only colors to which they were trained to respond. Probes looked outside themselves for answers. There were the real and the imagined, the truth and the lie, the manifest and the invisible, without middle ground, shadowed places, twilight zones. Mysteries invariably entailed looking inside oneself, at the gray and the partially realized, and this, for Sobek—ostensibly for all Probes—meant a journey through a land of misgiving.

Vague notions, however, were not something he could bring to the attention of his Trough Administration superiors—not unless he wanted to risk being diagnosed glitched as well. Resulting perhaps in a demotion to auditor, a return to running accounting checks of Adit franchises on tertiary worlds like Gilgit, or airless stopovers like Avonne.

Taking a quick spin through his recorded notes, he popped the plug from his cranial port and zeroed the recorder, only to have the lid snap off in his hand as he was thumbing it closed.

He allowed a sigh to escape the human part of him, then a whispered curse as he turned the lightweight disk about in his reshaped hands, puzzling over its atom-stacked relief of eight interlocked rings—a logo of some sort—and wondering just where and when he had picked up the thing to begin with.

Yet another sign of disruption, he thought, eyeing the now lidless device.

Absently, he gave the lid a discus toss in the direction of a slagger to one side of the desk, turning to other tasks just short of the ricochet that sent the lid careening from slagger rim to counter edge before vanishing into the enabled mass-transit Adit behind his back . . .

PART TWO

Theme-Parked

FOUR

LUCKY JUNKNOWITZ, DOWN in Orlando for the day to investigate a complaint filed by Matsu-Universal Studio's Character Actors Guild against the nonunion themers of AdLand, and trying his damnedest to keep cool under a relentless April sun, decided he had no recourse but to get tough with the six-foot actor in the pink-and-white bunny suit holding the bass drum.

As an on-site inspector for the Theme Park Advisory Group, a New York–based oversight panel set up to monitor and regulate recreational propaganda, it was well within Lucky's provenance to do so. Still, a former themer himself, he had his reservations.

"How 'bout we do it like this," Lucky putting some volume behind it this time in case the bunny started banging the drum again, "I turn my back and the one who took King Kong's love interest just shouts out where she's being held."

AdLand's assembled themers adopted poses of the sort they used on tourists—bewildered, chagrined, self-convicted—then, for Lucky's amusement, began emptying their pockets, peering eagerly into costume paws and outsized heads, patting one another down, searching under the open-air amphitheater's fiberglass benchseats. Lucky had never heard of the Ann Darrow character until that morning, but execs at Universal had told him she was crucial to the park's *Kongfrontation* experience, which itself was second in popularity only to *Schwarzenegger: The Ride!*

Behind the amphitheater rose faux Monument Valley monoliths fashioned from plasteel and textured sandcrete, pre-Turn interbust jeeps and sedans perched precariously up top—the high point of Chrysler Motors' continuous-loader *Car Tours*. Elsewhere in the park you could visit the Clio Awards Hall of Fame, or roller coaster through any number of thrill rides sprung from the Golden Days of televised advertising. AdLand's half-dozen restaurants were mock-ups of supermarket interiors and game-show studios. Its snak bars were kitchens crowded with examples of pre-Turn frozen food, Tupperware, detergents, and plastic wraps; living rooms sporting stain-resistant carpets and La-Z-Boy recliners; or bedrooms featuring adjustable beds, sound-activated Clapper remotes, CFC-spewing air conditioners . . .

The entire park bore witness to decades of rampant non-eco consumerism, but it was less an indictment than a nostalgic vision, given a fanciful turn by character actors cast as the very television creations that had hooked the world on junk.

"What makes you think we've got your Ann Darrow, Lucky?" asked Joe Isuzu, a car dealer known principally for his comic way with half-truths. "If I remember right, Ann told me she was fed up working with the big ape and was going to ask E.T. to help her phone her agent. Last we heard, she landed a job at MGM, playing Breathless Mahoney or somebody." Joe spread his arms and grinned. "I can guarantee it."

Heads—human and otherwise—nodded across the arc of seats, the themers murmuring agreement, the Energizer Bunny beating on his bass drum.

"Honey, I shrunk the monkey!" someone up top chimed in.

Lucky, lost in a moment of *why-me* introspection, sucked at his teeth while everyone carried on. A bad day only getting worse. Beginning with a backup in the hotel room's low-flow toilet, and a glitch in the kitchenette McTrasher that had nearly cost him his hand. Then of course the e-mail message from Bulaful, the Nuba tribal shaman who'd been promising all manner of evil things for Lucky because of what had gone down at the Aboriginal Olympics a few months back.

Lucky swallowed a flitworm tablet to deal with a nascent headache and tipped his head back to dropper Peerless UV sunscreen into his eyes. He heard someone in the crowd mutter, "A little dab'll do ya." Sweat trickled off the top of his nose as he glanced at his watch.

AdLand was due to open in fifteen minutes, although he didn't guess the park was going to see much business today. Most of the tourists on the monorail he'd ridden in from Disney World's Fantasia Hotel had exited at The World of Coca-Cola and IBM's recently opened Data Haven. Sure, he'd seen a few orbital-engine buses arriving in AdLand's parking lot—the 'crete so cooked it was like some desert straight out of *Lawrence of Arabia*—maybe two hundred people who'd peddled in on bicycles lined up at the entry gates. But with the ten A.M. temp creeping toward one hundred degrees Lucky figured the place would be dead by noon.

Families out front were already depleting their credit on citrus-flavored shaved ice, rhubarb ice cream, paper parasols, or solar-driven personal fans you could clip to the brim of your themer cap. But how many moms and dads were going to be willing to write off three hundred dollars for a day of stomach-turning rides and consumer hard sell from characters born in thirty-second spots on the old CRTube?

AdLand was still waiting on a chlorine permit from the Bureau of Tobacco, Firearms, and Hazardous Emissions to install a much-needed swimming pool.

"Look, I know this place's employee-owned and you guys are hungry for the overflow business," Lucky grabbing hold of the rabbit's drumsticks and tossing them aside, "but you're heat-stroked if you think Universal's going to shut down King Kong just 'cause you've got their Ann Darrow." He gestured in the direction of the cinematic theme park. "My bet's they're already warming up Ann's understudy."

A few rows short of the top the Marlboro Man stood up, hands cupped to his mouth. "Maybe you oughta mosey on over to Six Flags, Lucky. See if Batman or Bugs made off with the big ape's girlfriend."

Frowning, Lucky plucked his shirt away from his shoulders. "Some of you people got cited last month for taking your jobs too seriously. You wanna make matters worse, is that it?" He directed a look at Tony the Tiger, then Speedy Alka-Seltzer; moved on to the Pillsbury Doughboy, Mr. Peanut, Spuds McKenzie, and a couple of the California Raisins, who were conversing in Spanish.

A supermarket clerk in bow tie and glasses made a peevish sound. "We were *just* trying to stay in character, Mr. Junknow-itz."

"Nuh-uh . . . Whipple," Lucky recalling the character when he spotted the roll of toilet paper stuffed into the pocket of the white coat. "The idea isn't to *sell*. You're s'pose to make everybody realize how lame it was to be taken in by cutesy slogans and jingles. I shouldn't have to tell you this."

Overplayed *oohs* and *aahs* went up from the lower tier seats, the cast turning on one another looks of feigned enlightenment. Lucky's hands made fanning motions.

"All right, all right, so you guys aren't in the mood for a lecture."

"Sure we are," earnestly from Commander Eco, former animated spokesperson for Triple M's prototype line of biodegradable trash bags. "Think we'd really want to mess with the Theme Park Advisory Group?"

"*Weltanschauung* Protection Agency," Mr. MacGreensleeves added, yet another environmental spokesperson from a bygone era.

"Fine way for a former Goofy to behave," someone pointed out.

"Yeah, what's his beef?" asked the little old lady down front.

The Marlboro Man loosed a loud laugh. "Doncha know Lucky's gone over to the other side, gang? Got himself hooked up with the people that make policy for all us themers now."

"Lucky gets to have his own personal hotel room."

"Lucky is a themer . . ." someone began.

"Lucky is an inspector . . ." another picked up.

"Lucky is two," both voices finished, "two things in one!"

"Ninety-nine and forty-four one-hundredths percent pure, that Lucky Junknowitz."

Accustomed to ridicule, Lucky took the comments in stride. It was true he'd done a Goofy stint at Disney World, but that was years back, another lifetime.

"Yeah, well, I sure don't get this kind of abuse over at Disney," he told everyone. "Or at MGM, or at Time-Warner. So how come I've gotta hear it from a bunch of what-was products who can't even draw a decent crowd?"

A brief but sullen silence fell over the group.

" 'Cause the Mickey, the Ronald, the Donald and the rest of those Teamster diznoids make a decent living, is why."

"Better th'n the avvverage, *themer* . . ."

It was the Coppertone Girl who had spoken to it, the only actor who looked at all comfortable with the heat. Although rumor circulating around the home office had it that Ms. Coppertone's days were numbered, there being some concern that young visitors to AdLand might get the mistaken impression that sun worship was an acceptable practice—even if the actor's "tan" was cosmetically applied.

"So get yourselves organized," Lucky said after a grunting cheer had died down. "Elect a rep and petition the guild for membership. What about you, El Exigente? You're awfully quiet today."

The Demanding One pushed his campesino hat back on his head, gave his chin a kind of Ricardo Montalban lift. "Management's against us unionizing, Lucky. We've been trying to get the guild to hear our case for six months now and nothing." He rapped a knuckle against Speedy Alka-Seltzer's head. "You know how hot it gets inside these things?"

Lucky recalled days in the Goofy suit, posing with a gaggle of kids from Oklahoma or somewhere, when he'd come close to passing out from the heat. "Yeah, but you get breaks, right?"

"Sure we get breaks. But half of us are working double shifts just to make ends meet."

"And most of what we bring home goes right back to management for lodging and food," the Marlboro Man added. "We're gettin' a mite desperate here, pardner." He threw Lucky an imploring look.

Lucky'd heard the same thing from the themers over at IBM on his last trip down to Orlando. From Modem, Hard Drive, Floppy Disk . . . "It's what happens when you go up against the big guys."

"That's why we decided to take matters into our own hands," Mr. Whipple said.

Lucky looked around, wary all at once. "I hope you're not telling me you abducted Ann Darrow just to get your case heard. . ."

Punchy, wearing an electric blue Hawaiian shirt, folded his arms. "It got you here, didn't it?"

Lucky's eyes narrowed some more. "All right, where is she?"

A minute of group fidgeting followed before someone said, "Ah, Lucky deserves a break today," and two actors fifth-row center began helping a third out of a somewhat long-nosed head. And suddenly Lucky was staring at the missing Ann Darrow—a frail-looking young woman with fine blond hair plastered to her forehead and temples—who'd been concealed inside the head of Pop from the notorious Kellogg's trio.

"I'm sorry for not speaking up sooner. . ." the woman said sheepishly, drawing on her Fay Wray innocence-training.

"Sure thing," Lucky said, sensing that the wide-eyed Ann was more co-conspirator than abductee. "What s'matter, getting snatched three times a day by the big ape wasn't enough for you? You need to double your pleasure, double your fun?''

Ann pouted. "I just wanted to help out.''

"So you agreed to be taken?''

"We planned to issue our demands once we knew that our action was having an effect on attendance at Universal,'' Mr. Whipple said quietly, looking over at Ann. "Anyway, we figured Nora—er, Ann could be our bargaining chip with the Character Actors Guild.''

"I did it for Crackle,'' Ann said, taking the actor's white-gloved hand. "We're engaged. Since Tuesday, right, sweetie?''

Crackle nodded and flashed Lucky a thumbs-up.

"Themer terrorism,'' Commander Eco shouted, raising a rallying fist. "AdLand First!''

Lucky shook his head as the actors revved up, muttering, "Beauty and the breakfast cereal.''

Lucky had Ann the cooperative captive back to Matsu-Universal in time for the two o'clock show, earning himself brownie points with Universal's execs, who were yanking their hair after what had transpired at the early performance. Seemed that Ann's understudy had developed a sudden case of mittophobia—fear of the mechanical ape hand—and had refused to allow herself to be tied to the temple stakes outside the great wall, much less be scooped up and disappear into the park's facsimile of a climax rain forest. Desperate by then, the show's director had substituted an extra borrowed from another attraction, the *8.3 Earthquake,* who began screaming just that as the giant hand was closing over her, so thoroughly confusing the audience that people in the front rows were already ducking and covering by the third scream. In the mild panic that ensued, several themers cast as Skull Island villagers were trampled, and a good portion of the viewing stands had been left in ruin.

Before leaving for the airport, Lucky had also arranged a meeting between AdLand's actors and a rep from the local chapter of the Character Actors Guild. The limo driver that delivered him and three others to Disney International for the shuttle flight to New York wanted everyone to know that the stretch was powered by krypton batteries and that its solid tires had been fashioned from recycled rubber.

"Thank you for listening,'' the synthesized voice announced as everyone was exiting the car. "And don't miss AdLand,

Orlando's newest theme park, on this or on some future trip.''

Lucky had doubts AdLand would even exist a month from now. Allowing the themers to join CAG might put an end to some of the park's internal problems, but beyond that AdLand's founders, Chiatt/Della Femina/Eurocom, S.A., had yet to arrive at a socially redeemable park philosophy that was going to keep the Advisory Group off their backs. AdLand wasn't a SonyLand or a World of Coca-Cola, where every 'toon or comic-book hero had an antidrug, safe-sex, or self-esteem message to run on you.

But neither was it the Gaian DaiseyLand, where character actors costumed as black, white, and gray daisies sent you away feeling like some low-down no-good virus. The thrust of the park being that Momma Earth could care less about the ozone shield or who sat at the top of the evolutionary ladder—oxygen or carbon-dioxide breathers, methane breathers for all She was concerned—just so long as the planetary furnaces were in good working order. Problem with all that life up top? Then Momma'd just throw a regular tectonic blowout and start from scratch: boil away the oceans, scrub the atmosphere clean with some volcanic fire and ash, get all those landmasses back together . . .

AdLand, though, wouldn't be the first park in Orlando that had failed to find a niche. First to go, decades earlier, about the time of the Turn, was SeaWorld, pronounced decidedly non-eco by species-rights advocates. Busch Gardens folded soon after, although the chain had since taken root overseas, French and German tourists eager for a peek at the way things were before a Unified Europe had homogenized the customs of half a dozen nationalities.

Then there were the safari parks and zoos, done in by a coalition of Right to Lifers and Deep Ecologists. The best you could do now—short of hopping a hypersonic to a wildlife reserve in East Africa, Brazil, or Australia—was to endure some imagineer's version of a Serengeti or a Mato Grosso, suspend disbelief while you were electro-carted through holographic displays past one after another animatronic beast, everything from dinosaurs to yet-to-come transgenics represented, the emphasis heavy on how many species Earth had already lost, extinguished by humankind in its quest for evolutionary dominance.

Anyone with an idea and a line on a billion world dollars could license a theme and open a park, but it was the UN-commissioned Advisory Group that decided policy. Just as the Television Advisory Group determined what was fit for broadcast, and the Art Advisory Group handed down its rulings on literature, film, painting, and music.

The themers who staffed Xingu Park in the heart of what remained of Brazil's Amazon forest, then, might be instructed to downplay the role hallucinogens had in shaping the worldview of their ancestors, and scoff at the notion that kidnapping and head-hunting had been common practice for settling interclan disputes. And the themers at Raja's Water World near Surajkund in northwestern India were expected to deny that a caste system had once held sway over the subcontinent, or that the cow—now something of a modern evil—had been thought sacred.

Problems usually stemmed from some themer's failure to adhere to park doctrine. So Lucky might have to come down, say, on a highlander at Stone Age Village in Papua for reverting to burning real logs instead of wax-and-sawdust in the communal fires, or drawing real blood during the tribal warfare reenactments. And naturally there were problems with unauthorized trinket or icon sales, overcharging for photo ops, lewd posing, and the like.

The aim was to instruct and educate the younger generations in how best to conduct themselves during their stay on Earth. What did it matter that history was being rewritten when the Future of humankind was at stake?

Lucky, these past few years, whether off on assignment in Jellystone Park or walking the sidewalks of his own inner-city neighborhood, cam shafted by security lenses and surrounded by mobile trash cans, courtesy monitors, and environmentally correct street gangs, had actually come to see his own life as a kind of theme park, having its own rides and attractions, its own cast of character actors, its own rules and regulations, its own sense of government-sponsored unreality.

The kid in the adjoining shuttle seat introduced himself as Diss. He was a short, wiry black—a Charismatic Muslim, perhaps—sporting burgundy fez and Janus buzz, which left the back of his strategically shaved head resembling a face, complete with eyebrows, mouth, and goatee. Over spandex unitard shorts he wore a sonic vest, which he had accessorized in urban street chic with transparent shock-absorber sneaks, wristbands, and knee pads. Said, when Lucky'd asked, that he was just returning to New York from the Air Dancing regionals at Epcot II.

"Placed first in my division," Diss confessed, without sounding happy about it.

But Lucky was impressed. Air dancing, the latest in street sport, involved the use of a magnetic board to ride the juiced recharge lanes of the commuter highway system. Japanese *shinjinrui*, the fast-lane Twenty-One crowd, had introduced the boards to Harlem a few years back and the sport had taken hold. But a skilled rider could do more than simply levitate a board; he or she could conjure a kind of song from the interaction between board and recharge strip, and thus dance to a personal score—a so-called juice song.

"A first place, huh?" Lucky said. "Congrats."

Diss just fixed him with a dubious look and snorted. "For what, man? The custom board they prized me? One I cut myself'll fly twice as high and outsing anything store-bought, you understand what I'm saying?"

Lucky did. Just the same, a first in the regionals meant Diss would go on to the finals, didn't it?

Diss laughed, shaking his head. "Who gives an ad-lib 'bout trophying on a *track*, man? I mean, where's the sizzle in that? Where's the buses and shit, where's the obstacles, the challenge, the fix? Fucking Sports Council or some shit decides to mainstream dancin' . . . legitimize it. Jus' like they did with graffiti, elevator action, 'scraper scaling. You think anybody who's committed wants a sanctioned graffiti wall, a chance to dance, dangle, or helicopter on an elevator in some safe chute, a fake building wall to toe up?"

Diss made a spitting sound. "Done just like always: coopted us. Drive out the radical by making everything clean, and safe, and socially relevant. Turn us right into media heroes for technotourists, make us all rich enough so we can forget where we came from and get all complacent and shit. A guy's into cardiofunk radical rap; prize him some record award. Cyberwizards into phreaking; give 'em their own network, get 'em running penetrations against each other instead of peeking and poking into government dumps. Depower 'em's what I'm saying." He looked Lucky up and down. "You oughta know. Your generation let it happen."

Lucky fingertipped his chest. "Me? What'd I let happen? I was born at the Turn, Diss. It was all in place way before I came along."

"Yeah, well, you look older," Diss taking another look.

"Thank's a bunch."

"*Inshallah*, amigo. I'm just saying it's no contest when the idea's to give you your fifteen seconds in the lens, turn up your volume, then kick your ass off the lot. Bad enough we can't sing what we want, watch what we want, paint what we want, drive what we want, without having to surrender the Street, too.

"Powers that be patting each other on the back 'cause they figure they cooled the planet, patched up the hole, when it was all about maintaining power, anyway. And now they wanna tell me how to run my life. Like they own the world now. Social engineers, population managers deciding what's right for everyone. Meanwhile, you can't take a leak without asking somebody's permission to do it."

For several minutes Lucky had been aware that the young kid across the aisle had a cam trained on them, and thought to point this out to Diss. The hand-held was perhaps one of forty on board the aircraft, not counting the happy-face cabin security cams themselves.

Diss looked over at the camera and grimaced for the telephoto lens. "I don't care who hears me. Go ahead," talking to the young kid now, "report me to an Urgent Care Center, you little spy."

Diss turned back to Lucky when the kid's Mouse-eared parents intervened and made their son switch off the camera. "Here's some close-up truth, you want it—some of that *cinéma verité*. It's still the same old split: Those who get to stuff their faces and the ones who have to clean up after them. You're either featured player or you're extra; you're what-is or what-was, no other way round it.

"People at the top, all these committee chairpersons and advisory group leaders, making films and writing books that show just how fucked up their personal lives are so all us extras can think, Hell, blood, glad we're not with them, huh, be thankful for what little we got. Make the rest of us think we're all going to live longer 'cause we eat less—like they got the idea for these long-life cutback lim-intake diets from *us*. Like when my grandmom was throwing all her tin cans and bottles into the building well or the empty lot next door she was really just composting, huh?" He shook his head. "Every time I see one of these celebs or politicos come on the tube, I think, Here it comes, the MOS—the Moment of *Sincerity*. The Moment of *Shit*, I call it."

Several passengers seated nearby were listening in. Lucky noticed one of them doing furious input at a smart-paper laptop. The mood in the cabin had turned ugly from the moment it was announced that the captain for that day's shuttle flight was Commander Dopey.

"So why'd you bother to compete in the regionals?" Lucky asked Diss, wondering if he could steer the conversation onto even ground.

Diss shrugged. "For this," gesturing broadly. " 'Cause I wanted to see what traveling was about."

Lucky waited a moment before asking: "And?"

Diss closed his eyes and reclined his seat. "And who needs it. One place is just like the rest."

Lucky left Diss to the sounds of his sonic and staggered down the aisle to the vending machines as the captain was announcing D.C. out the left-side portholes. Upright but swaying, he sucked down a soda and continued on to the lavatories. See, he wanted to tell Diss, it just wasn't true you needed permission to take a leak. But even as he was thinking it, the lavatory door screen asked what he'd like to do, offering up a menu that covered everything from using the toilet to applying alcohol-free hypoallergenic cologne. The little room was, however, the one cam-free zone in the entire plane.

An outgrowth of a period when nations and special-interest groups were lifting surveillance and communications sats into orbit every other day, and prime-time shows paid thousands for candid shots of people caught in natural or unnatural acts, cams and monitors were ubiquitous features of the post-Turn landscape, participants in daily life. It was the rare moment, in fact, when at least one lens, either privately owned or a staple of the decor, wasn't trained on you. You could find them on every street corner, in every shop, in every quarter of the night sky.

But if cams were intrusive, if they had redefined privacy, they had also been a major force in countering crime and violence. Install a home battery of cameras and you could go without locking your doors; park in cam-equipped lots or on a monitored street and you didn't have to worry about your car. The cam—especially the new line of video goggles—had become both watchdog and bodyguard, home security system and antitheft device.

Cams had also turned every five-year-old into a potential surveillance operative.

Lucky shared Diss's distaste for them, even though at one time he'd seen himself pursuing movie-making as a career. Instead he'd become a themer—what was once known as a walkabout.

"Definitely a themer's face," he said just now to the reflection in the lavatory mirror, giving his head a turn in both directions. "Definitely a themer's body."

At twenty-five, he was tall and somewhat gangly, with long fingers and feet large enough for him to be constantly tripping over. His hair was brown and disobedient, his eyes a bit heavy-lidded, his front teeth large and slightly gapped. His ears might have been good candidates for biocosmetic surgery, save in an era where courses in self-esteem began in preschool and clinics did more business returning people to their pre-op appearances than they did in elective reconstruction. Worse still, a day of Florida sunshine had summoned a figure eight of freckles that spanned his face from cheek to cheek.

He was born at what had come to be considered the turn-around point for the planet—the Turn—when geopolitical walls were tumbling down and humankind was taking a hard look at the world's dwindling forests, polluted seas, and ravaged skies. Global warming had brought every nation from China to Chile into the same game, and the stakes were higher than they'd been since the first group of true *homo sapiens* had huddled around their first fire wondering just what they were going to do with themselves for the next several million years.

Lucky was only a kid when the first Fresh Air Event had been organized and something like twenty million cars were left parked at home. The day didn't mean much to a four-year-old with three new teeth, but he could remember his parents talking about how wonderful it was to see the streets empty, the high-ways quiet—even for twenty-four hours. He had better recall of the day millions of television sets were voluntarily switched off. Some viewed the day as a logical extension of the Fresh Air Event, and the networks responded by withholding a full eve-ning's worth of programs the following week.

But by then "Planetists" of all denominations were on a roll. Fast-food restaurants were boycotted; protests were staged at logging concerns and chemical plants. The Glen Canyon Dam was destroyed by a group of well-armed Monkey Wrench eco-terrorists. There was a day devoted to roadside cleanups; another to living without electricity; and dozens of like days, still com-memorated annually, devoted to a humbler approach to living.

Not that the Turn had been ushered in easily or overnight. Right up to the end individuals and corporations were saying, Hey, we live here, too, and maybe we're not neat freaks like the rest of you, but that doesn't mean we won't get around to pick-ing up after ourselves in our own good time . . .

Conflicts erupted weekly, but Lucky remembered the small changes best. The day his dad, a suburban working stiff, had

garaged his pride-and-joy sports car and bought a Toyota Eco—
an electric runabout that needed weekly recharging. He remembered the timer his dad installed in the shower. The day the
washer, dryer, and air conditioners were dragged out to the
garage, which over the years was to become a kind of dump for
personal appliances, scrap metal, and plastic. Laundry from then
on was done at the neighborhood coop 'mat, and the car got less
and less use—radically reconfiguring Lucky's fantasies of high
school good times and the thrill of coming of age.

Suddenly, in fact, there was less of everything about: fewer
items on the supermarket shelves, fewer paper plates and rubber
balloons, fewer mail-order catalogues, home fires, barbecues,
movies, and family vacations. Fewer cemeteries and golf
courses. Fewer shirts and pairs of sneaks in Lucky's clothes
closet.

And just as suddenly Lucky's mother was working at home—
telecommuting to the office, except for one day a week, and
spending hours at the same computer his father used to catch up
on the daily news and download mystery novels from an
electronic-publishing warehouse. The computer had also become
their link with the bank, the post office, the drug store, and the
supermarket, which dispatched monthly deliveries of bulk foods
in electric cykes equipped with sidecars.

At the same time, those people who weren't rushing off to tag
birds, plant trees, or teach economic theory to Thai highlanders
were busy making room for extended families. Homes were
parceled into private spaces to accommodate boomeranging sons
and daughters, newlyweds, in-laws, and grandchildren. Once
well-tended leaf-blown suburban lawns were converted to vegetable gardens and tree nurseries.

Thousands of businesses went under: advertising firms, travel
agencies, manufacturing companies that couldn't adhere to strin-
gent new ecological guidelines. And everyone began to recognize the monster human history had fashioned. The world had
been set up to produce and consume and grow fat on itself, and
as that began to change there was no choice but to surrender to
a new ideal of who we were and what we were all about.

As unemployment soared, Western nations' governments
mounted the most massive civilian conservation corps the world
had ever seen, and so the maglev rails and transoceanic fiber-
optic lines had been laid, the confinement fusion and recycling
plants built, the homeless fed and sheltered, the beaches, river-
banks, and reservoirs swept clear of debris and litter. In Africa,

armies were mobilized to reclaim the desert, while in Asia, the Green Spirit gripped the governments of the Soviet Union and China.

You didn't hear so much about moon bases, regional conflicts, or famines anymore; what you heard instead was talk about biomass crashes and species triage, turning the SDI lasers loose on airborne CFCs, peppering the stratosphere with rail-gun-launched bullets of frozen ozone, covering the oceans with Styrofoam chips or replenishing the algae through iron dumping . . . But something must have worked, because by the year Lucky graduated junior high school, where his generation's three Rs were Reduce, Reuse, and Recycle, the global temperature had leveled off and Bangladesh, the Maldives, and the Nile Delta were still above sea level. People were still saying, Wait till every Chinese and Indonesian demands a car and refrigerator, we'll be right back in the same mess. But the answer was simply to keep that from ever happening.

And it was probably about that time that the people in power, high on their apparent success, had begun to make plans for managing the sociopolitical and moral climate as they had the environment.

Lucky, already thinking about the action films he was someday going to direct—when he wasn't dreaming of getting laid—didn't see it coming. And neither did most of the population, which after years of carpooling, recycling, and curfews had grown used to the idea of surrendering civil liberties for the prospect of an assured Future. But one morning, it seemed, Lucky woke to discover that the guarantee of the pursuit of happiness had gone the way of the Bengal tiger. All at once there were a score of new laws to abide by, and dozens of new councils and agencies, committees and advisory groups to answer to. Everything from song lyrics to childbirth was suddenly under the authority of a handful of people no one could remember—or would admit to—having elected to power. And, well, at times maybe it did feel like you couldn't take a leak without getting someone's permission . . .

Diss was still zoned on whatever his vest was playing when Lucky returned to his seat. The kid across the aisle had his cam out again and was attempting to shoot up the short skirt of a Tinkerbell-costumed safety steward who was crouched over a popcorn spill near the cabin's forward bulkhead.

Lucky ripped open the Velcro pocket of his jacket and retrieved his computer. Turning his fingers to finishing up the after-mission report he'd begun earlier on, he entered his recommendation that no punitive action be taken against AdLand's character actors for their part in the staged abduction, but suggested that the Advisory Group might wish to address the larger concern of "themer terrorism" raised by the incident.

Retrieving his e-mail, Lucky found yet another message from Bulaful, the Sudanese shaman, who was now promising a one-way trip to some crocodile-infested Nuba twilight zone unless Lucky compensated the tribe for the collective loss of face they'd suffered at the Aboriginal Olympics.

Nuff's anuff, Lucky decided, plucking the Motorola Globalnet from his belt and punching for the service that forwarded his electronic mail. Thing to do was find out where Bulaful was calling from and put a swift end to it. Which was precisely what he told the woman at customer relations, who, after a moment of cross-checking, reported that the service had no record of Bulaful's calls—neither the one Lucky had received at the Fantasia nor this latest.

The shaman's messages having apparently arrived by means of some alternative technology.

FIVE

LUCKY AND THE family that owned the kid with the camera shared a *collectivo* up to La Bronx from New York's Kennedy-Monroe Airport. The driver was a bright-smiled Masai woman in beaded headband and chokers, large brass rings dangling from earlobes that grazed her brown shoulders. Bone fetishes done up in batik cloth and cowrie shells adorned the van's dashboard.

It had rained sometime earlier and the streets were still slick, but the temperature was a balmy seventy-four degrees, not bad for an early-April evening. Lucky rode with his face pressed to the tinted glass of a bubble window, watching bicyclists on hubless maglev machines navigate the puddles. He wondered about all the filtration masks he was seeing, until his looking at his watch reminded him that Tuesday was a Yellow Permit day, bikes, trikes, and light-component a-cells—as the roadway-powered electric vehicles were known—forced to share the road with petro-pig interbusts.

Difficult to imagine a time when someone would actually climb into a gasoline burner and drive for an hour, only to spend half an hour riding a stationary exercise bike. But then the pre-Turn world was filled with such contradictions.

"Bet you were asking yourself what my son was up to," the young lensman's father said suddenly. "Back on the plane, I mean. Pointing that camera of his."

"No, I wasn't," Lucky turning away from the window to regard the man in the dim glow of the *collectivo*'s fiber-optic light-distribution system. Dark-haired, sharp-featured, something chameleonlike in the way his expressions shifted.

"Making a film," he went on regardless. "School project for a course in Transactional Dynamics. Isn't that right, Nader?"

Lucky found the camera aimed at him when he swung around

44

in time to catch the kid's nod. Mom, whispering, was apparently directing the shot.

"Nader Junior, actually." continued the father. "Parents named me after Ralph. Things being what they are, I thought it was a good one to pass on."

"Very green of you," Lucky said.

"Working title for the documentary's *The Role of the Action Figure in Modern Sports Mythology*. Very high-concept. Reason why he was so interested in that character you were sitting with on the shuttle."

Lucky nodded uncertainly. "When I was his age I nurtured a tree."

"You what?"

"Nurtured a tree. For my Biological Peace Corps project. We all had to."

"Nature, huh?"

"What-was," Lucky told him, glancing again at Nader and showing a slow grin as he recalled the airline safety attendant in the short skirt. "Action figures, huh? You might wanna keep an eye on him."

Nader Senior looked over at this son. "Oh, I do that. Fact we just had one of those smart-chip locator eyedees installed in his thigh. Can't be too careful. Kids'll stray."

Lucky had his doubts, but left them unspoken. "That's not what I meant. I saw him trying for an American shot on the plane."

"You talking about the Tinkerbell steward?"

"That's the one."

The man offered an infectious grin. "Hell, I told him to shoot that."

As it emerged, Lucky and the elder Nader had something in common in that Nader, years back, had done a character-actor stint as Emilio Estevez in a well-known Manhattan restaurant called The Beverly Hills.

Lucky's days as a themer, a Walkabout, had begun almost right out of high school, after his parents sold the house and moved to a retirement community in southern Mexico and the Life Guidance Committee had handed down their ruling on his future. He was told that while his student vids did indeed exhibit a certain flair—particularly the eco-allegorical occult thriller featuring Paul Bunyan as a crazed woodsman and Chico Mendes as the man who topples him—his overall grade-point average was too low to earn him a government scholarship. The committee further suggested that a few years of voluntary service might offset the lackluster GPA, and had offered several choices: He might do famine relief in Africa, or drug counseling in South America; then there were the homeless in the Soviet Union, the world-weary in Japan, Asia's godless, Antarctica's self-exiles . . .

But Lucky had a surprise in store—one he hoped would demonstrate just how the System could be made to bite its own tail. The stated purpose of the Life Guidance Committee was to simplify an individual's future by eliminating the overwhelming, often intimidating aspects of overchoice, thereby allowing said individual to retain a proper perspective on issues of global import—a bit like being imprisoned, where your meals and lodging were seen to and the only things you had to work on were your social skills.

So Lucky made the simplest choice possible: He became Goofy.

For a short while, at any rate. By nature a *freeter*, as the Japanese said—one who moved from job to job, rarely if ever working for a major company—Lucky moved on, abandoning a career that might have led to a shot at playing the Donald, the Ronald, the Mickey, to work for a casting agency that placed character actors in theme parks around the world. Turnover being more rapid in those days, current cases of character burnout and Themer Identification Crisis notwithstanding, simply because the world was changing so quickly. Microstates forming and dissolving, nations adopting new names, indigenous groups uprooting, scattering, relocating. Themer work in East African parks opened up for disenfranchised black Americans after the Masai gave up competing with elephants and raising camels and accepted job offers from Japanese cattle ranchers in Brazil. American Indians found work portraying Eskimos and Aztecs at parks in Korea and Taiwan. Angkor Wat Sound and Light was staffed chiefly with Tibetans, some of whom summered in Peru, where they were cast as Incas at Machu Picchu.

Familiarity with the terrain and a natural way with role players were what finally brought him into contact with Marshall Stack, a promoter who had handled concerts and sporting events before the Turn—before decibel monitors had taken the punch out of rock 'n' roll; motiontronics, the contact out of contact sport.

What Stack had in mind, he'd explained to Lucky, was a kind of special olympics, an *Aboriginal* Olympics, that would not only return some of the pizazz to arena events but serve the eco-cause of acquainting people with a diverse sampling of rites and customs practiced by cultures on the verge of extinction. Stack had already given thought to the individual contests—river archery, pole climbing, bungee cording, wrestling, machete wielding, snuff snorting, projectile vomiting—and had already struck a deal with the owner of a venue in Burkina Faso, the former Upper Volta, in West Africa. If the show did even half the draw Stack was anticipating, there'd be no stopping them from taking it on the road. All Stack lacked were contestants, which was where Lucky and the placement agency's software came in.

Lucky never could figure how Stack had weaseled an okay out of the Cultural Traditions Protection Agency. But then the Oaugadoudou arena Stack had secured wasn't exactly centrally located. Still, advance sales were promising, especially among the moneyed in LA, New York, Tokyo, and Berlin, and on opening day the show played to nearly a full house.

Lucky had culled participants from all over: Kalimantan, Papua, Ruwenzori, Shaka-Zulu, Siberia, the Amazon. But the single event that captured the most interest was the tag-team wrestling bout which pitted the Xaipopo, from the Xingu Reservation, against the Nuba of Sudan. Rumored to be a grudge match of long standing.

Favored by the odds makers, the Xaipopo wore arm and leg bands fashioned from red and yellow feathers and slicked their long hair into fantastic shapes with red-ochre paste. Their trainer was a Jivaro named Barsana, whom Lucky had located in Chicago, where Barsana was doing a brisk business in freeze-dried foods.

The Nuba had shaved skulls and ash-whitened bodies, and frequently wrestled with calabash gourds lashed to their backs—no small handicap. Bulaful, their shaman/trainer, wore a long checkered skirt, goat's-hair anklets, and a wrapping of red, white, and black cummerbunds that reached as high as his armpits. He concealed his face behind a beaded curtain that fell from the brim of a pith helmet bedecked with eagle feathers and ostrich plumes.

What Bulaful didn't realize, however—or perhaps failed to acknowledge—was that his wrestlers were expected to throw the match. And when that didn't happen after six rounds of reverses, double-reverses, body slams, and splashes—during all of which The Nuba scored heavily against the favorites—Stack had the refs surreptitiously fill the Nuba's gourds with coins liberated from the arena vending machines, so that by the time the seventh round commenced the ash-covered wrestlers could barely stay on their feet, and after a few minutes of staggering about the ring, were easily pinned by their Xaipopo opponents.

The deception wasn't lost on the largely African and Arab audience. But even a riot which had to be put down with water cannons and Crowd Control, a pre-Turn gas developed by Dow Chemical, failed to reverse the judges' decision, and the title belt went to Barsana and his "Amazon Avengers."

Bulaful held Lucky accountable. And seeking him out shortly after the disputed match, he had waved a magic fly whisk in Lucky's face and uttered the first of the many threats that were to follow.

The *collectivo* dropped him at a subway stop a few blocks from the small apartment the Housing Authority had him sharing, begrudgingly, with one Rashad Tittle, a people monitor employed by a marketing research firm called the AzTek Development Consortium.

Lucky cut through a park that hadn't been there twenty years before, where a couple of Puerto Rican teenagers—under the watchful gaze of security cams and police presence—were shooting hoops in the eerie glow of solar-assisted lighting. Disease had wiped out most of the trees, but the few that remained were in bloom, tingeing the evening air with a cloying aroma. There were swings, jungle gyms, rubber-tire castles, and a graffiti wall Lucky stopped to read. Changes in spray paint and paintable surfaces made it near impossible to graffiti anything other than the wall itself. Artists who couldn't content themselves and went looking for pristine surfaces—particularly those aligned with the so-called Glossnost Movement—ran the risk of being captured on video or, worse still, set upon by roving packs of teenage eco-enforcers skilled in prole-jitsu and street kido.

Gimme what-was, someone initialed FU had scrawled in bold letters across the lower portion of the wall.

A none-of-this, none-of-that tyfin sign posted in English and Spanish at the Bayridge Boulevard entrance flashed: THANK YOU FOR NOT: PICNICKING, DRINKING, SMOKING, LITTERING, SHOUT-ING, EXPECTORATING, SKATEBOARDING, AIR-DANCING, ROUGH-HOUSING, PLAYING RECORDED MUSIC, REMAINING PAST TEN P.M. (*UNLESS OTHERWISE STATED*), *WALKING YOUR PET, IRRITATING YOUR NEIGHBOR, MAKING A NUISANCE OF YOURSELF*.

A camera swiveled to track him as he crossed Bayridge and

headed up Whitestone Avenue, where Caribbean *jíbaro* songs were wafting from several storefronts. Passing the local Urgent Care Center he found himself thinking about Diss, then about young Nader and the locator his folks had had implanted in his thigh.

What with the cams and locators and absence of wilderness, it wasn't easy to stray, to get lost in the world, despite what the elder Nader thought. The entire planet was like some vast wildlife-management park, fenced in by technology. *Ah, the greenhouse we've created*, you were likely to hear some senior citizen lament.

Lucky had food shopping to do before returning to the apartment, but ventured that the local supermarket would be packed, owing to it being a Yellow Permit day with twice the usual number of people out and about. So he decided instead to hit the Quick Fix around the corner, stock up on just enough to get him through the next couple of days. Besides, you never knew what might happen in a convenience store. Just past eight o'clock now, too early for the real action to begin, but in could walk some lonely young creature, raincoat thrown on over a midnight lace bodysuit, popping in for an evening fix of Goodall All-Natch Banana Chips, maybe a bag of Carlson Nori Crisps, or some of those Muir Mallomars . . . Not that Lucky was entirely without a love interest—at least not since Hostage Day the previous November when he'd nearly been strangled by the alluring, the exquisite, the unfortunately unattainable Harley Paradise. How those first few weeks had altered his sense of things! And sure, they still did their share of lip-syncing, but something had changed since the night Harley had invited him back to her share in Queens and they'd come close to doing each other, shaking the sheets, ad-libbing. He figured he must have done something wrong, or not right enough, because Harley had seemed different afterward—distant, critical, judgmental—and Lucky feared they were headed for turnaround.

Quick Fix was a chain—"We make shopping a rush!"—with stores in just about every nation in the world. You'd find them in capital cities, border towns, on unsurfaced roads in the middle of some nowhere; but just step inside and it was like being back home. Sugar-free soft drinks and decaf coffee; wholesome milk-sub donuts and low-fat cheese nachos; microwavable pizza and incandescent-grilled low-salt carrageenin turkey dogs—all for the asking. Along with everything you needed to quick-service your RPEV, your Personal Data Base comp, your cellular phone.

But make certain you're wearing shoes and shirt and bring your own carrysacks, please.

And expect to be carded.

Adhering to guidelines established by the Consumer Protection Agency and Bureau of Social Management, Quick Fix had even taken the worry out of product selection by allowing only a single brand in each category. No cause for concern, then, about shoppers becoming apathetic about social ills, local elections, or global events due to overchoice.

Lucky could still remember some of the historical trivia he'd logged in high school relating to pre-Turn overchoice: As many as eighteen thousand toys to choose from; fifty-six TV channels; a selection of twelve thousand weekly, monthly, or quarterly magazines or periodicals; over twenty-five thousand items on the supermarket shelves, including fifty-four different types of coffee beans and two hundred brands of breakfast cereal . . .

Now it was only the various committees and groups and agencies whose numbers ran that high. And here he was a member of one of them. But he told himself he hadn't sold out; that by joining he was simply trying to be the good citizen the new world demanded, a healthy cell in a larger, healthier system, a properly tuned transmitter and receiver of data and dollars. Even if that meant sacrificing some of his revolutionary spirit. For what had his stay in the counterculture earned him but a stint as Goofy and the disrespect of a Nuba shaman?

The neighborhood Quick Fix, a hole-in-the-wall version of what one might encounter on the road, stood adjacent to what Lucky heard had once been a dry cleaner's and was now the Calcutta Travel Agency. On entering, as ever, he felt as though he'd stepped naked into some parallel dimension, bathed in the harsh light of some fluorescent sun. The superchilled air carried a dizzying concoction of pungent scents, obscure odors, Muzak and keyboard clack. One hand shielding his eyes, Lucky made a quick sweep of the tight aisles, past shelves stocked with exotic spices, soy milk, sea salt, boxed broccoli, and citrus-oil non-aggro detergent, quickly filling the natural-fiber carrysack Harley had given him for his birthday and hauling it to the front register, where a sparsely bearded clerk of about Lucky's age, who might have been Indonesian or Malayan, was intently studying a fly that had lighted on the back of his dark hand. A name tag that read SANPOL AMSAT was Velcroed to a breast pocket stuffed with color-code marking pens.

Sanpol lowered a scowl at Lucky from the raised area behind

the counter and began to unpack the carrysack, passing each of the flexplassed items over a price scanner: cellulose hydro lettuce, cubical tomatoes, all-natch oranges, a carton of milksub— *fey-lait,* as the Algerians who lived in the apartment next door liked to call it . . . Lucky was not only vegetarian but vegan, more by necessity than biocentric choice, although he had his doubts about the new biotech chicken breast that was all the rage in the supermarkets.

Sanpol was holding up a box of Captain Planet honey-roasted sorghum flakes and showing Lucky the same look he'd used on the fly only a moment before. His eyes were like black onyx, his skin the color of Quick Fix's home-brewed *café-au-fey-lait.*

"This is the single size," he said after a moment.

"Right," Lucky told him, "I'm a single," prizing his status card out of his wallet and handing it over. "Single, see?" The cards were numbered and color-coded to designate both marital status and living arrangements, either of which could affect the quantity of a given item you were permitted or required to buy.

Sanpol passed the card through a reader and regarded the screen. "It says you occupy a share."

"So?"

"Then you'll have to purchase the larger size."

"Come on," Lucky tried, "do I look like an imelda? I eat for one. And I recycle," adding a good-natured laugh. "I mean, I like the stuff fine, but I'm a once-a-day kinda guy, and this stuff's got a limited shelf life. A larger box'll end up going bad on me."

Sanpol slid the Captain Planet forward. "You have to take the larger size."

"But I'm a single and this is a single box!" Lucky tapped it with the back of his hand for emphasis.

"You occupy a share," Sanpol snapped. "You have to take the DINC size. Make your roomie pay for half of it."

"He doesn't even like Captain Planet!"

Sanpol gave his head a firm shake. "Then talk him into liking it. Tell him it's the breakfast of environmentalists."

Lucky fumed only until he saw how useless it was. "All right, which one's the dual income, no children?"

Sanpol pointed down the foodstuffs aisle. "The one between the single size and the head-of-household size."

Lucky whirled and stomped off, returning a minute later with the proper box just as an eye-catching brunette, bare arms loaded with sundries, was coming through the doorway to what was obviously the storage room, emerging from some commotion taking place back there. Lucky watched her for a moment before turning to set the cereal box on the countertop price scanner.

"I don't suppose you'd be interested in chipping in," he started to say, when the flying object he caught out of the corner of his eye made a sweeping turn, sailed straight for him, and dinged him in the side of the head.

Lucky shook the blur out of his vision and squatted to look for the ufo, ultimately going down on all fours to wriggle the thing out from beneath the counter. A saucer of some sort—not quite hemispherical, but shaped more like a contact lens or a type of wristwatch crystal than a Frisbee—it almost seemed to float in his hand though it approximated the size of a coaster. And despite its polished silverlike sheen, Lucky thought it might have been fashioned from aluminum or one of the new featherweight alloys.

Then his thumb discovered the markings embossed on its convex surface: a series of eight interlocked rings, reminiscent of the old Bayerische Motorenworke logo, or that of the pre-Turn Olympics.

And immediately he thought of Bulaful.

On his haunches still, he spun through a crouched circle, half expecting the shaman to leap from behind the yoghurt machine or suddenly appear at the end of one of the aisles, waving that damn fly whisk of his. Had Bulaful spirit-tossed the saucerette the way he'd thrown his e-mail messages?

Ufobic suddenly, Lucky rose slowly to his feet, one hand massaging the tingling spot above his right temple, the other displaying the little Frisbee as if it were a badge. "What's this, one of your free weekly giveaways?"

Sanpol regarded the saucerette and shrugged. "Something you dropped."

"I didn't drop it," Lucky protested. "It came from somewhere in the back of the store."

Sanpol shook his head. "Nothing came flying from anywhere."

Lucky slapped the disk down on the counter. "Well, it's yours now."

Sanpol shoved it back at him. "You can't leave your trash lying around here. Take it outside if you no longer want it."

Lucky was revving up a reply when Sanpol pointed to the happy-face security camera mounted above the register.

"Smile for the camera," Sanpol told him.

"All right," Lucky muttered. "I'll take it outside."

Sanpol rang up the total, which Lucky charged to his card, all the while casting shaman-seeking looks over his shoulder.

Outside he searched for somewhere to dispose of the possibly malevolent Frisbee, but the mobile trashers nearby were only accepting recyclable paper goods and organic waste. Lucky finally slid the thing into his shirt pocket and hurried off to his apartment, sticking to the meager shadows when he could and looking both ways at every day-lit intersection.

SIX

CHARLIE COLA, HANDS resting interlocked on a punch bowl of a belly, looked up from his desk screen in time to see something small and saucerlike streak across the office—at about eye level if he'd been standing, five-eight in Charlie's case—zip between Labib's hands when he tried to make a grab for it, and zing into Sanpol's accident-waiting-to-happen supply dump, where the thing performed a kind of pinball-bumper dance among the tubs of nondairy nacho-spread and containers of carob-enhanced milksub before sailing off into the front of the store through the door Molly had left ajar on her way out.

"What the hell was that?" Charlie asked, blinking behind antique bifocals.

Labib, regarding the narrow hands that had missed the catch, shook his head in puzzlement. "Almost had it."

"Only counts in horseshoes," Charlie said, forcing a finger between the strained buttons of his shirt to scratch at his chest. A glance in the direction from which the saucerette had first made its appearance revealed something more startling still: the freezer door was open.

"Sonuvabitch," Charlie shouted to no one in particular, "who the hell left the Adit open?" Already out of his swivel chair, he went bounding across the room to rectify the situation.

Labib Ismael and Jesus Powell hurried after him but stopped short of helping, having learned from past mistakes. Charlie loosed alternating grunts and curses as he brought his substantial bulk to bear on the heavy door that concealed the Adit. He was panting when he swung around to find the two of them making tentative gestures apparently meant to demonstrate their concern.

"Unload. Which one of you left it open?"

"Not me," from Labib, a pleasant-looking twenty-year-old whose best features were his finely drawn lips and flawless complexion. "I was helping Jesus with the deliveries."

"That's right, Charlie," Jesus was looking at his friend and nodding. "I can vouch for him."

"When can't you," Charlie said, turning to latch the freezer door, then stepping between the kids on his way back to the desk.

Jesus was blond and blue-eyed, nineteen if the adoption records were to be trusted. Charlie and Didi Cola had found him through a black-market trader operating out of Marseilles, the same one responsible for their finding Labib, who'd spent ten years on his own in the rat alleys of Istanbul. Charlie'd given them the option of retaining their family names, and both kids had chosen to do so. But there was no denying they were Charlie and Didi's sons, their only children. Cherished and doted upon. Only, Christ, they could play dumb when it suited their purpose.

"One thing I can count on every time something goes wrong around here: that's you guys covering for each other. What was it last time—that cultural surveyor from Lesser Tej I asked you to keep an eye on? Not even human and the guy decides he's just gonna take a stroll down Bayridge Boulevard, remember that? People fainting when they saw him, eyewitnesses telling the cops they'd seen the devil . . . and where were you two? Instead of keeping him out of trouble, you're off making time with a coupla perky stewardesses—"

"Safety attendants," Jesus amended. "And we were just helping them—"

"I don't want to know what you were helping them do. And don't interrupt me when I'm lecturing you." Charlie directed a worried look at the onscreen financial spreadsheet the agent from Black Hole Tax Audits had called up. "Like I don't have problems enough," he was muttering as he slumped into the swivel. "Auditors dropping in here unannounced, sticking their fingers into my files." Just in time for April fifteenth, too, which only went to show: As above, so below.

Charlie shook his head at the desktop flatscreen. Labib and Jesus shuffled in place but said nothing, turning to the door as Molly Riddle entered, a crate of bruised fruit in her hands.

"What's all the yelling back here?" Molly sounded more annoyed than concerned. "Sanpol says you're scaring away our customers."

Charlie regarded the coltish young woman whose father had

been his partner in the franchise. "You leave the Adit open, Molly?"

Molly raised an indifferent shoulder. "Just trying to get some fresh ions in here after that storm. The upstairs office's telecaster's acting up."

Charlie pulled a communicator headband from the bottom drawer of the desk and slipped it on over an artful arrangement of thinning salt-and-pepper hair. "Sounds all right to me."

"Well, it wasn't a few minutes ago." Molly smiled tightly. "Thought you'd want a clear link to Agency HQ, Charlie—just in case there was anything you forgot to tell the auditor."

"Not funny," Charlie said, straightening up in the swivel. "And what the hell flew through here a minute ago? Looked like a goddamned flying saucer."

Molly gave her hair a toss. "I didn't see anything."

Charlie looked to Labib for support. "Was I seeing things?"

"Uh-uh, Charlie. I saw it, too. Kinda round."

"Kinda round," Charlie said. "You hear him?"

Molly shrugged again. "I didn't see anything."

"Just the same, remember to shut the damned Adit next time, will ya. Unless maybe you want customers wandering back here thinking this is where we keep the ice cubes, stepping into the freezer and ending up on Sierra or somewhere. Besides, now we've gotta run another decontamination on the thing."

Molly stifled a laugh. "Anything you say, Charlie."

Charlie watched her saunter off with the crate of citrus rejects, thinking, The little minx. Jacob Riddle didn't know what he was doing leaving Molly behind to co-manage the franchise. Girl had her own ideas about how to run things, took too many chances. Leaving the Adit open . . . like it was a skylight or something.

Wouldn't have happened if Charlie'd been the one to see the auditor off, of course. But instead he'd asked Molly to handle the fade and had remained at his desk, wondering whether the Black Hole agent—a Shak, so augmented with data-reader implants she'd needed only to insert a finger in the access port to call up what she wanted—had been sharp enough to spot any of the double-entry discrepancies in the accounting files.

Could have been worse, he knew. Instead of an auditor, it could have been some Probe fresh from Transmogrification Auxiliary. Charlie blanched at the thought. And should something untoward be discovered, would management shut down the franchise? Exile him to Avonne or some equally remote rest stop?

Charlie calculated he'd been keeping the dual set of records for just over eight years now, ever since the Riddles had retired to Nmuth Four and left him and Molly to run the store. Nothing major, like embezzling or anything. Just tucking a little away for his retirement, indulging in a bit of investing with company funds—stocks, bonds, Treasury notes. Using some of the profits to finance alterations to the house in the Hamptons and the small Greek palace on Corfu . . . anything to keep Didi out of what was left of his hair.

And why shouldn't he be entitled to a few perks. Frustrating enough to be operating on a tertiary world, residing among people who still believed in devils, without having to live like some extra. Especially when plenty of his fellow Terrans were doing just fine for themselves, dining on beef, running their secret air conditioners and pre-Turn petro-pigs, and carrying on like this sudden turn to nature worship had never happened. The politicos, the celebs, the largely invisible *ricos* whose publicists and life-style consultants had everyone in the cast convinced times were tough even at the head of the credits list.

Charlie was up on the Agency rules and regs requiring that franchisers on tertiary worlds maintain a low profile, but Earth—Adit Navel as it was known along the Trough—was something of a special case, wasn't it, long overdue for a status upgrade?

Be different, too, if he'd been granted permission to sell the planet's splendors, advertise promotional tours and package deals in *Tourist Trap* or the trades. But no, that was for the in-place Agency honchos who ran the show on Earth, people he rarely saw or spoke to outside the annual Agency-sponsored get-togethers for resident downsiders. Hardly anyone visited the place, anyway, except of course for the auditors and the occasional privileged users who would drop in to complete some bit of ethnographic business.

Well, there'd been that major operation a few months back, but that had been handled almost exclusively by the franchisers who operated Earth's other Adit, in Sumatra.

Charlie had to laugh. It was the responsibility of a franchiser to keep track of all high-clearance visitors—to arrange for downside transportation, provide documentation when necessary, make certain no one was leaving prints all over the place. Where, though, was the profit in that? With the small amount the franchise received in precious metals for its services—after Adit maintenance fees and Agency taxes—Charlie saw barely enough to keep him and his own in the sunshine.

So he'd been skimming. A little here, a little there. And charging for services that hadn't actually been rendered.

Like the case of the Nall who'd wandered out onto Bayridge.

Charlie had charged Black Hole for the cost of putting the matter of "Beelzebub of the Bronx" to rest, claiming he had had to move mountains to keep the locals from jumping out of their windows, when all he'd really done was supply a few close-up shots of the sinister, bark-skinned visitor to friends at the *Video Examiner*. Street vid footage of the XT's stroll was already available, but the close-ups Charlie furnished enabled the comptabloid to give the incident wide coverage, effectively destroying the credibility of the eyewitness accounts.

The inflated surcharge had paid for Didi's a-cell mall assault sports utility vehicle.

Still, Charlie didn't like the idea of having to go to such lengths to earn decent side money. And he certainly wasn't comfortable with cooking the accounting data to make it all come out right. But that was unfortunately what it took to secure a happy homelife on a world like Earth.

Exiting the spreadsheet the auditor had left onscreen, Charlie called up the current issue of *Tourist Trap* and spent a few moments scrolling through the list of vacation tours available in the Trough.

He and Didi did their share of fading, but it had been years since they'd taken a real vacation. Knowing full well how risky it was to allow the operators of tertiary franchises to visit more advanced worlds, Black Hole Trough Administration placed restrictions on where, when, and to whom certain Adits were accessible. But good deals could usually be found for Foxal or Nmuth Four, where Jacob and Rachel Riddle had an oceanfront place.

Foxal was the planet Charlie's father, Patsy, had always had his eye on, but the old man died before he made it there, wasting away on Earth after his retirement, waiting for Black Hole to okay his request for a transfer. Patsy Cola was one of those who had helped found the Quick Fix chain, long before the Sumatra Adit had even been opened.

Twenty years back, Earth wasn't a bad spot to be stuck, Charlie could be counted on to say. You could at least eat well and travel just about anywhere you pleased. But the place had gone downhill ever since humankind had decided to clean up its act. Centuries of abusing the planet, and humans had suddenly become nature worshippers.

Charlie still thought of the movement as part of the madness that had swept the planet just prior to the Turn. But where there had been some genuine excitement to those early days—geopolitical upheavals, Muslim Power, legalized drugs, condomania public executions, witch hunts and purges—the craziness was gone from the air, and what remained was a climate of government-regulated sobriety.

Now, instead of embracing technology, humankind was backing away from experimentation, falling back on superstition in the process. It was as if Earthers *wanted* to remain infants, to persist in the belief that there was Someone out there judging them, or that they'd been placed in charge of the planet. They were afraid to take the big step that would free them from natural tyranny.

People losing their livelihoods because of endangered owls, and deer, and toads, Charlie often mused. Naturally there were toes that would have to be stepped on; but that was what life was all about.

Earth didn't need a savior so much as an assertiveness instructor.

Not that the place didn't have its moments. Earth was Charlie's homeworld, after all; humankind, his kind. But life onworld was primitive and unpredictable. Charlie's father, Charlie's grandfather, or his grandfather before that could have explained to their fellow planeteers where they were going wrong, perhaps brought in experts from elsewhere in the Trough to arrange for a midcourse correction. But that was against the rules, just as living well ran counter to Agency guidelines.

Oh, the things Charlie could have told everyone if he were permitted! What, for example, might humankind make of the fact that Black Hole's original onworld Adit had been opened back when the Egyptians were fooling with their first hieroglyphs? Or that the Quick Fix chain itself offered a good deal more than turkey dogs and twenty-four-hour convenience?

A sudden chirp from the telecaster shook Charlie from his reverie, but he was slow to open the desk's bottommost drawer. Doubtless it was some standard communiqué from Agency HQ to all the franchisers, nothing that could possibly pertain to Earth or Charlie Cola's little downside operation.

But then, only moments before, a company auditor had faded from the freezer Adit . . .

Cautiously, Charlie reached down and activated the device, his weak eyes widening when he realized that Earth was the sole destination of the communiqué. More so, as he began to comprehend that his franchise was being issued a top-priority assignment.

The saucerlike data-recorder cover which had begun its journey on Aart's World and bounced, ricocheted, and careened its way through twelve different Adits on half as many worlds and transit stations to emerge from the rear of a Quick Fix store in the East Bronx was in Lucky's hands as he keycarded himself into the lobby of his building on P Street and stomped the rain from his shoes.

Maybe the saucer was some sort of medallion, Lucky had been thinking, upon his fingertip discovery of a two-horned something or other projecting from the saucer's upper edge, at its twelve-o'clock position had it been a watch face. Although there was no more reason to believe the saucer had an upper or lower edge than there was to believe that the twin horns—sharp enough to draw blood—were all that remained of a ring, suitable, say, for attaching the saucer to a chain.

Assuming it was a medallion. And forgetting for a moment that the metallic horns might just as easily be the remnants of, what—a hinge, maybe? But what could the thing have been hinged to? Unless it was a piece off one of the convenience store's shampoo dispensers or frozen-yoghurt machines. Even though the guy behind the counter, that Sanpol Amsat, hadn't recognized it as such.

But why the embossed design of eight interlocked rings?

Any number of mobile trashers Lucky passed on his way home had been willing to accept the thing, but on each occasion he'd stayed his hand, figuring anything that winged out of the night to ding you in the side of the head had to be treated with the utmost respect. Especially when the suspicion lingered that Bulaful, discus-thrower in some Shamanic Olympics, had hurled the saucerette from down around Juba in southern Sudan. Serve Lucky right for getting involved in Marshall Stack's get-rich-quick scheme to begin with.

He slipped the saucer back into his trouser pocket, deciding he'd return it to Quick Fix next time he was in the area.

The building's elevator ran only on the half hour—one trip to the top floor and back to the lobby—as was generally the case in all city residences. So, what with a ten-minute wait ahead of him, Lucky took the stairs, all twenty-six flights of them, frowning for the security cams that panned and scanned each of the landings.

The share was an outside corner unit, with a view of the Throgs Neck Bridge if you cared to crane out the window. The at-home indicator on the apartment door was lit, but Lucky knew that didn't guarantee Rashad Tittle would be in. The indicators had been installed in an attempt to grant some modicum of privacy to partners in shares, but Lucky's roomie insisted on keeping the device set in affirmative mode at all times to discourage would-be thieves—not that the apartment had seen any crime in years—and to invite frequent visits from vendors hawking items of the sort that couldn't be sold through the shop-at-home comp services. Salespersons of all ilks being objects of both personal and professional fascination for Rashad, who in addition paid no heed to the indicator's original purpose and seemed to delight in barging in on Lucky unannounced.

His key slotted, Lucky eased vigilantly into the apartment. When the fluorescents in the share room came up, he saw that the door to Rashad's room was open, no lights on, suggesting but not assuring that his roomie was out.

The apartment decor, left in place by the previous tenants, was a blend of Japanese and Afrocentric: mats fabricated from recycled plastic soda bottles, flattened futons, hardwood animal masks, folding screens, Ethiopian tables that resembled lidded baskets, a water-conscious toilet-sink. Rashad had a peculiar fondness for print-format magazines, and stacks of the things leaned touch-and-go against what little wall space there was. Lucky threw a hip against the door to close it, set down his overnight bag, and made for the kitchenette, the carrysackful of Quick Fix goods looped over one shoulder.

Inside the ozone-friendly fridge was a bear head—Smokey or Yogi, Lucky wasn't upright long enough to tell which.

Down on his ass on the tile floor, the carrysack's contents scattered all over the room, he couldn't remember if he'd screamed. The tightness in his throat could have resulted from sheer fright. One thing was clear, however: it was the flash from Rashad's camera that had painted the spots before his eyes.

"What the—" Lucky started to say, realizing now, the fridge door wide open not five feet in front of him, that the head was not what it had seemed.

"You were frightened, no?" Rashad circled for better angles, nimbly avoiding fruit, veggies, and Captain Planet sorghum chips liberated from the box.

Lucky came shakily to his feet, hands instinctively covering his face. "I was frightened *yes*, Rashad. 'Swat happens when you find a bear head in your fridge you know wasn't there when you went out!" He reached inside, winced as he grasped the thing by its coarse hair, and pulled it out in the open. "Even when it's a goddamn fake."

"Yes, yes, but it fooled you, didn't it? And you felt, what— threatened, helpless, alienated? Did the sight bring out any hidden impulses of a flesh-eating sort?"

"Anger's what I'm feeling now," Lucky told him, making an awkward grab for the camera that nearly sent him to the tiles again. Rashad, all five-five of him, was lightning quick. Said he was Pakistani, but Lucky thought he looked Chinese. Except for those almost sky blue eyes Lucky swore he'd seen glowing in the dark one night a few months back . . .

Rashad leaned in for a close-up and scurried for cover. "Angry because you were afraid? Angry because of the trick? Angry out of embarrassment at being photographed?"

Lucky risked a step forward, but skidded on the sorghum chips and his feet went out from under him. The camera caught him as his teeth were snapping together.

Rashad took a wide-angle shot, then looked at Lucky in surprise. "You've brought home a larger-size box of Captain Planet. What is about the food that so appeals to you? The product name, the packaging, the curved shape of the chips?"

Lucky's eyes narrowed. "More of your observational research, is that what this is about?" Up once more, dusting crushed sorghum chips off his butt and stalking Rashad now, ready to lunge. "Exactly what's that AzTek Development Consortium *develop*, hunh? And don't be telling me optical photos, neither."

Rashad spoke through a Cheshire smile. "AzTek is involved in product research for various corporations that specialize in consumer goods. AzTek has the wishes of the everyday consumer foremost in mind. Someday you'll thank me for this."

So Lucky'd been told. Each and every time Rashad interrogated him about his sleeping habits, his sexual habits, his preferences in food and entertainment, his thoughts about race, religion, human destiny, the birth and death of the universe.

Each and every time Rashad engineered one of his surprises and paparazzied Lucky from some doorway, snapping away with his damn still-vid camera.

More than once Lucky had invaded the sanctity of his roomie's bedroom to search for the incriminating disks, but there was never any sign of them, and no record of them being on-file in what little Lucky could access of Rashad's personal data system comp either.

The Housing Authority had brought them together eight months before, when Lucky had vacated a closet in the South Bronx loft he was sharing with seven people and six house cats. He'd just met Harley, just said yes to an inspector's job with the Theme Park Advisory Group, and was figuring to put the steady income to good use by renting himself some well-earned space. The fact that the job entailed a lot of air travel entitled him to enter a request for a place in Brooklyn, a share to be sure, but that was fine so long as his roomie wasn't over thirty-two and didn't work at home. Otherwise, he had no preferences one way or another; the job would keep him on the go enough to keep the arrangement one of pure convenience. After a five-month wait, however, the best the HA could offer was a place in the upper Bronx with an eighteen-year-old "observational researcher" who was only semi-fluent in English and worked at home to boot.

Lucky didn't learn that his roommate was a people-monitor until some time later, after finally getting up the nerve to ask Rashad why he felt the need to follow him around the apartment, or commit just about every word Lucky said to a smart-paper comp. Rashad's early responses were little more than enigmatic smiles, or broken-English apologies. It was just that Rashad's family was so thrilled about his living in New York City, and so much wanted to know everything about his new life and new friends . . . including, ostensibly, his new roommate, who had an exciting job that took him all over the world.

Hence the incessant questions, the photos, the little surprises Rashad called "impractical jokes," the Lucky Junknowitz dossier filed in Rashad's system. Lucky had made the discovery during one of Rashad's infrequent absences, the same night he'd asked about the curious logo on the equally curious towel Rashad had left hanging in the bathroom.

Okay, Lucky was willing to buy that AzTek Development Consortium was the company Rashad wrote "policy" for; but what was with that corporate logo—a depiction of what appeared to be Planet Earth, equatorially ajar as if its hemispheres were hinged together somewhere 'round Borneo, a fancifully rendered dollar sign gleaming in the black maw where the planet's core should have been?

Rashad had grown evasive and had hurried out of the apartment under some pretense. It was when he returned hours later that Lucky nailed him with the dossier, and the truth slowly emerged: Lucky—judged, in ways that remained unfathomable, to be a kind of Everyperson—had become Rashad's chief though involuntary informant on issues of consumer import to post-Turn America.

Lucky recalled being too surprised to respond. As if mail intercepts weren't bad enough, he had to find out he was rooming with a corporate spy! But Lucky an *Everyperson*? It was not only an incorrect assessment, but an unjust one as well. Something of an affront, in fact.

"How many times do I have to tell you, Rashad," Lucky said now, still waiting for an opening, one hydroponic tomato mashed underfoot, "I'm not typical—I'm atypical!"

Rashad only laughed. "But you're eminently typical, Lucky. You speak English only, you share apartment space with a stranger, you wash your dishes by hand, and you recycle your trash."

"Yeah, but—"

"You floss twice a day, flush once a day, keep off the grass, and wear a telephone wherever you go."

"Yeah, sure, but—"

"You don't own a pet, you don't drive a car. You don't smoke, read books, or drink milk or alcohol to excess. You say no to war and drugs, but you're addicted to movies and have unerring faith in fiber, whole grains, and the possibility of a god. You secretly believe that you'll never die, but at the same time your self-esteem is nowhere near what it should be."

Lucky had stopped moving and was simply frowning. "I do so read—sometimes," he tacked on. "Anyway, Rashad, you're not seeing all of me, no matter what you think."

The alleged Pakistani waved a hand. "Horses vary in color and size, some run faster, some jump higher, some are friendlier than others. But they are all horses, Lucky." He popped the disk from the camera. "You see, AzTek trains its field agents to observe from a certain distance. The individual, after all, is less important to us than the herd."

"And AzTek's just trying to market a better brand of oat, huh?"

Rashad grinned. "It is our clients who will market the product, Lucky. We only advise them which products will sell . . . And speaking of clients," with a thumb-jerk toward the vidphone, "you have a voice-mail from a Mr. Bulaful."

SEVEN

THE GLADIATOR IN animal helmet and spiked wristlets cast his net, caught hold of his opponent's short sword, and yanked it from the smaller man's grasp to fling it off to one side. Weaponless now, the swarthy Greek was crouching, backing off, dark eyes darting, large hands making kneading motions in the air while the poorly defined crowd in the viewstands cheered.

The champ grinned under the wolf mask and pursued, swinging the net in lazy circles over his head, waiting for the right moment. Finally the Greek launched himself off thickly muscled legs, hoping, it seemed, to grasp the champ around his leather-belted waist and toss him over a shoulder—a standard move—or aim for lower down, a tackling thrust to the thighs. Save that the net was there waiting for the anticipated charge, and in short order the Greek found himself ensnared, then plucked off the ground and centrifuged overhead.

Everyone expected the gladiator to feed his catch to the crowd; instead he gradually lowered the Greek to the ground, even allowed him a moment to extricate himself from the tangled rope. Which he did, only to stagger forward, trip, and fall face-first into dust, which puffed up around him in a brown haze.

The spectators came to their feet, booing the match, tossing tomatoes and pears, turning down thumbs. Then heads began to turn toward the arena's royal box seats, and the crowd quieted while the emperor surveyed the scene, the Greek cowering as the champ stepped in to raise a sandaled foot.

Sequenced trumpets blared, drums rolled. The toga-clad graphic stood, snapped down a thumb, and the Greek derezzed from the bar's video wall.

Once, Lucky thought as the live crowd laughed and waved their hands at the defeated bouncer, the loser would have been left to the lions, taken sword or trident to the heart. Now you were simply derezzed, wiped out of of existence, blown to bytes.

The bar's bouncer—a six-footer, whose celeb's good looks were concealed under Virtual Net interface goggles—was making a big show of his victory, gloved hands clasped, raised in reciprocating strokes over one shoulder, bowing, accepting backslaps from the happy patrons who'd cheered him on during the match. Turning away from the motiontronic scanner that had fed his moves to the wall-screen graphic, the champ shook hands with his beefy rival, whose disappointed supporters were already making for the door, their own bar just three blocks away on Whitestone Boulevard.

But there were no hard feelings, it was all done in fun. No betting allowed, no real violence, even of the onscreen sort. Gaming Commission camcorders were positioned about just to make sure.

Every so often you'd get an actual action figure stopping by the bar for an onscreen match—a kick boxer, maybe, or a lineman with one of the Virtual Network teams—but Tuesday nights were reserved for neighborhood contests between bouncers, security cops, watchmen, and body doubles, who'd stand in front of the scanners and run down their moves. The rest of the week the screen was open to all contenders, although lately the emphasis was on professionals. And so there'd be Lawyers' Night (the game was "Highway Madness"), Doctors' Night ("Inquisition"), or Execs' Night ("Predators' Ball").

The place was called Atopia, for reasons left unexplained by its several owners—two well-known actors, a film director, a noted chef from same major eatery in Harlem. Well within biking distance from Lucky's apartment, and something of a magnet for the local Neo-Post-Omeganists, many of whom the Housing Authority had seen fit to quarter in the refurbed high rises and converted warehouses nearby. The woman seated next to Lucky at the bar being a case in point: a wraith in head-to-toe white, marinated in some pheromone-rich celeb-inspired fragrance—Afro-desiac, Lucky guessed—velvet scratch 'n' sniff Earth-hearts Velcroed to the sleeves of a denim jacket.

Atopia evinced a somewhat whimsical eco theme, decidedly retro, the owners having accessorized four decent-sized rooms with pre-Turn collectibles: fur coats, tiger- and leopard-skin rugs, trophy heads, ivory and hardwood carvings, plasticized hot dogs, crack vials, nylon stockings, unopened cans of tuna fish, newspapers, plastic Coca-Cola bottles, six-pack rings, a life preserver from the *Rainbow Warrior*, anthro-trash excavated from landfills in the American Southwest, Twinkie and chocolate cupcake mobiles—still soft to the touch after some thirty years.

Suspended from a ceiling "soundproofed" with disposable diapers was an old Ferrari G.T.O. interbust slamming nose-first into the papier-mâché hull of the *Exxon Valdez*, an oil spill fashioned from resin emerging from the rent like two giant black hands.

Song portraits of whales, dolphins, and mountain gorillas wafted from hidden speakers, and the dart boards featured the likenesses of James Watt, Mao Zedong, and various past CEOs of Georgia-Pacific, Alcoa, and Union Carbide. Just to give the place a hint of outlaw flavor, the bartenders, some of whom were costumed as hippie celebs—a Ted Turner, a Jacques Cousteau, a Jerry Garcia—served drinks called "Gasoline" and "Benzene" in urine specimen jars. In jest, the rest rooms in the basement were labeled *People of Color* and *Colorless People*.

There were the usual proscriptions against smoking, drug taking, and war dancing—despite a bilingual tyfin sign over the door that read simply, THANK YOU FOR NOT STAYING AT HOME. Detectors measured ambient temperature and decibel counts, and personal alcohol and lactic-acid levels were monitored at the exit turnstiles.

Lucky, in frayed jeans and white shirt, had made straight for the bar after viewing the vid message Bulaful had left on the answering machine. Onscreen, the shaman was adorned in ostrich and eagle feathers, face concealed by the tasseled pith helmet, upper body white with ash, fly whisk in hand. Standing in twilight on the banks of what Lucky first took to be the White Nile, but on closer inspection proved the re-creation of the Zambezi River at the entrance to the Stanley-Livingstone Theme Park. Enhancing the playback revealed animatronic crocodiles basking in artificial sunlight, a simulation of background animal sounds.

Bulaful, nonetheless, was motioning to the beasts with one hand, shaking the fly whisk at the camera with the other, promising imminent doom. "Mr. Lucky have two weeks remaining," the shaman warned. "Two weeks to get the decision overturned and deliver the title belt to the Nuba. Or,"—in tight close-up—"he's going to be sleeping with the crocodiles."

The picture went noisy after that, and, what with Rashad training a telephoto and parabolic mike on him, Lucky had hurried out to Atopia, eager for the company of friends.

Precisely how he was going to deliver the title belt to Bulaful remained problematic. For one thing, Marshall Stack had stopped returning Lucky's calls. He wondered, though, whether shamanic abductions might not be covered by the Anomalous Trauma insurance policy he'd purchased from onetime love interest Asia Boxdale—as a joke, natch.

A Gasoline in hand just now, Lucky was trying hard to forget the time he'd seen two halves of a foreign-service volunteer pulled from the croc-infested Omo in northern Kenya, when someone clamped a hand on the back of his neck.

"Junknowitz!"

Lucky spewed vodka across the bar as he ducked his head, the *mama-san* in white showing him a look of contempt. Willy Ninja—part-Cherokee, aspiring musician, and full-time white junk dismantler—slid onto the adjacent stool, Eddie Ensign bellying in alongside him.

"The themer's themer—" Willy grabbed Lucky's specimen jar and downed the contents in one gulp. "—gracing our li'l ol' watering hole. *Qué pasa*, Luck, here to write the place a new tyfin sign?"

Lucky snatched the drink back. "Thank you for not pestering our patrons. Thank you for not substituting sarcasm for wit."

Willy's grin accentuated high cheekbones. "Wit was."

"Heard you were away," Eddie said, signaling for the bartender. "What news from the road? The world still out there or is this only a dream?"

In his spare time Eddie—the actual surname was Enseño—worked with handicapable kids—sip-and-blow masters of the Virtual Net interactive games. For life support he worked as a celebrity outer, a star-stalker, for groups touring the New York scene. Lucky's oldest and best friend, Eddie had done some themer work himself, he and Lucky teaming up after they'd moved into the City from the Jersey 'burbs. Like Willy, he was dressed in Balinese baggies, sloganed singlet, patched Chinese sneakers, colors bright enough to keep you awake at night. Unlike Willy, he was clean-cut, narrow-faced, somewhat loose-limbed. People said he and Lucky looked alike.

"I was in *Orlando*," Lucky told them. "Hardly out in the world."

"Global, *amigo*," from Willy, still grinning.

Lucky directed a frown past him to Eddie. "He did say 'global'?"

Eddie nodded once. "Global's what I heard. 'Less some of

those Twinkies are off-gassing and making us prone to auditory hallucinations.''

Willy slapped down his card to pay for the drinks and distributed them. ''Global as in fractal, friends. As in chaotic, evergreen, *schwer*. Check the playgrounds, global's back. Very mainstream. All the spin with the ten-year-olds and the *shinjin-rui* uptown.''

''Uh-uh,'' Eddie said. ''*Schwer*'s heavy, not awesome.''

Lucky sipped froth from his glass. ''There's the song you oughta write: 'Global Madness.' ''

'' 'Global Madness,' '' Willy mulled it over. ''You serious?''

''That'll get you warehoused, all right.''

Eddie snorted. ''He's dweedling your needle, Willy.''

''Hey, I trust Lucky's instincts,'' Willy said. ''Could probably get himself 'housed if he'd go back to doing vids instead of playing themer police.'' He looked at Lucky. ''Like that idea you had for doing a synth re-mix of *Forbidden Planet* where the cook character's the one who takes the Krell Mind Boost.''

''What-was,'' Lucky murmured into his glass. ''I'm waiting for inspiration. Or at least some genuine excitement.''

Willy watched him for a moment. ''He was right about Hype, wasn't he?''

''What about Hype?'' Lucky asked.

''Those sculptures he did out of the stuff his wife scavenged from Bravo Twenty and a few nuclear-blast test sites. Arts Council voted to warehouse five of his pieces. All of a sudden he's got collectors calling from Tokyo.''

Hype was gay, which at a time when the Office of Social Management was attempting to suppress ''homosexual tendencies'' with RNA reorienting medication made him a true undergrounder. They drank to his success; there was talk of Hype getting out of star stalking altogether.

It was close to ten years now since the Arts Advisory Council had declared a moratorium on any work judged to be innovative, unprecedented, or extremist—analogous to the Consumer Protection Agency's rulings on comestibles, automobiles, and appliances, the legislation in both cases dictated by concerns about overchoice. It was the three Rs applied to the arts: *Reduce, Reuse, Recycle*. The same held true for inventions and technological breakthroughs, where those advancements were deemed to have consumer application. Patents and copyrights were still granted, but it was a given that the more revolutionary the design, the song, the painting, the novel, the more chance it had of being warehoused, until such time as the council had a chance to assess its impact and permit its gradual introduction into the culture. The nation had been put on artistic cruise control. As a spokesperson for the council had once put it: We've decided to put the renaissance on hold.

The idea, then, among the Neo-Post-Omeganists at any rate, was to get yourself warehoused. Or suffer the indignity of being regarded as hopelessly mainstream—albeit performed, published, shown, corporately financed. The situation had driven countless would-be artists to despair, but it was not something mentioned in public, lest some concerned citizen get wind of your angst and file a report with one of the Urgent Care Centers.

"To Hype," Lucky said, raising his glass a second time.

By now the sound portraits had been turned off and the house players, Sweatband, had taken the stage. Fender benders on flex-neck guitars and synthesizers, turning out digitally perfect renditions of vanilla standards. Reps from the AAC were on hand to monitor lyrics and insure that the decibel count didn't climb above seventy-five. For good old-time rock 'n' roll one could always buy admission to Jann Wenner's Rolling Stone Park on the Jersey shore.

"Fucking putrescible crap," Willy commented. "The same bullshit tunes we've been trying to move from since high school. Bad enough we have to hear it on the tube selling some tired product." He muttered a curse, then turned toward the stage to yell "What-was, *gospoda!*"

Lucky swiveled on his stool to take a look around while Eddie was trying to calm Willy down. Atopia's crowd was mostly mid-twenties males of all skin shades, belief systems, and body formats—too damned many of them—*trabaus,* who worked for major corporations and liked to party hard. The imbalance was the product of too many parents, Hispanic dads especially, making male gender choices at the conception clinics. The few women around, software writers, electricians, high-hair designers, and nail-care technicians—the *ojingals,* the single girls—were with older men, mainstream poacher types with steady jobs at decent pay, their own apartments, a-cells, washing machines. The ratio had gotten so skewed that women were pretty much free to pick and choose, and what woman with both chopsticks in the sorghum chips was going to pick some extra with a tired job and a roommate when she could have an avuncular *ojitarian* with pre-Turn tales to tell, or a brightly packaged "Twenty-One"—as the young up-and-comers had christened themselves. The consumers, the imeldas.

Dashikis, kufi hats, toques, galabias, and chadors were back in; but so were tie-dyed surf separates, designer fanny packs, brandstanding Ts, African mask pendants, dooky ropes, Chinese trading beads, and sobriety shirts. *Expect a miracle today,* someone's read.

It took better resolution than Lucky had available to make any sense of the mix. But the couples on the dance floor made him think about Harley, whom he had tried to call before leaving the apartment, getting an audio message saying only that she was out for the evening.

Lucky swung to his friends to ask after the missing members of their posse, and learned that Asia Boxdale and Braxmar Koddle—two of Lucky's ex-roomies from the warehouse share—had left Atopia a short time before he had arrived.

"But La Ziggy's around here someplace," Willy offered.

Ziggy was Ziggy Forelock, another friend from the loft days, a vid-enthusiast who worked Citizen Watch at the Hagadorn Pinnacle in midtown Manhattan, a popular drop-out zone for despondent artists seeking to get their works posthumously warehoused. It was Ziggy's job to monitor the upper-story ledges and leap points, to talk the would-be downcasters in and see that they were admitted to Urgent Care facilities. But Ziggy's real talent lay in video art, his "Freeze-Frames from Famous Flicks" having shown to a packed house at an off-off gallery in Brooklyn.

"Fact," Willy continued, "Ziggy's got a few more vids he wants to show you."

Lucky let his concern show. "Vids he's put together or stuff he's disked off the tube?"

"Disked," Willy said. "Very weird shit."

"The Zig, closing in on the RGO," Eddie added to some serious nodding from Willy.

"The RGO, Luck."

Meaning what was Really Going On. Their version of what the Italians called *dietrologia,* the study of what lurked behind it all: their own Glass Bead Game. Their catchphrase for the ultimate answer to the innumerable questions posed by the post-Turn world, the revelation that was going to impart some deep and abiding meaning to their lives, an existential salve for a transitional generation still young enough to experience directly the brave new world being fashioned around them, but aged enough to remember an old one that was passing away. Something to settle the contradictions in a world making use of tobacco as an anticarcinogen, and the time-release component of HIV to combat disease. In a world where the mob ran the recycling centers.

"Speak of La Zig," Eddie remarked with a broad smile.

"What's Really Going On, comrades?" Ziggy said.

Lucky almost didn't recognize him. Ziggy's hair was spiked, giving his large, round head the look of a battle mace. His dark skin had been lightened with white-out. His pants were strategically torn, one hand wore a fingerless black glove, and his face was—

"Pimples?" Lucky squinting uncertainly, while Willy and Eddie laughed at the expression on his face.

"Man's pixil-ated," Willy commented.

Ziggy ran his fingertips over the artificial facescape. "Asia helped me into them."

"But pimples, Ziggy? And that . . . gel swell." Lucky impaled a hand on one of his friend's golden spikes. "You look like what-was, like some pre-Turn street tumbleweed."

Ziggy eyed Lucky's newly acquired sunburn and smiled. "Be better off with freckles, huh, Luck? Besides, I am my art." He didn't so much say it as announce it.

Willy grimaced. "You're on the air, Ziggy."

" 'On the air'?" Ziggy said, eyebrows raised. "Been floating round the playgrounds, *tovarisch*?"

"Willy's feeling *au courant* lately," Eddie contributed by way of explanation. "*Très uber*. Comes from being gainfully employed. Like Lucky here, floating with the likes of the Donald and the Mickey. Pro themers calling him by his first name. Knowing all the best roller coasters and just where to stand in a wave pool."

"*Ich bin ein* themer," Willy said.

Ziggy sighed with purpose. "Yeah, we all liked him better when he was Goofy, didn't we?" Transparent concern from all corners now, as Willy gestured for another round of drinks.

"So about these vids, Ziggy," Lucky said, mousing the conversation away from his own personal window.

The Zig's faux-cratered face grew serious. "It's happening again, Luck," he said, voice lowered in conspiracy. "I set the timers on the VDRs and I swear I'm picking up stuff that isn't on the air. I mean, I double-check the Guide, I've called the stations, but what I'm picking up isn't being broadcast, cabled, or dished in. It's like the machine's snatching it out of nowhere!''

Lucky broke a foreboding silence. ''So what are you getting?''

Ziggy forced a breath. ''Movie segments, teasers, documentary footage, a few seconds of some tube sitcom or news show, cartoons, music vids, baseball games . . . You name it and I'm picking it up. It's like it's all out there,'' eyes and hands raised to the ceilling, ''like some new atmospheric layer or something.''

''Telesphere,'' Willy suggested, taking himself by surprise and swallowing loudly.

Lucky glanced at him and turned back to Ziggy. ''And you're sure this stuff isn't coming in from some broadcast dish in Manila or somewhere, some private echo sat?''

Ziggy nodded. ''I've been online with vid-addicts all over the world, and I'm telling you, no one's sending what I'm picking up.''

''Smile for the camera,'' Eddie said, motioning with his chin to the cam above the bar.

Lucky said, ''And it's just you? It's not happening to anyone else's machine?''

Ziggy's narrow shoulders heaved. ''Maybe it is, but what's that matter? Point is, there are phantom programs out there—in the telesphere—just waiting to be picked up. Videogeists, Luck.''

Eddie looked at him. ''Suitable stuff for the *Video Examiner*, I'd think.''

''*Schwer*,'' Willy said.

''Lucky!'' a melodious feminine voice intruded. Lucky swiveled, grinning, only to find Harley Paradise arm-in-arm with a tall, square-jawed, body-proud Twenty-One, whom Harley introduced as Keating Price. The Third.

''Uh, Lucky Junknowitz,'' Lucky said, finally taking Keating's proffered hand after a prompt to the ribs from Eddie Ensign's elbow. ''I tried to call you,'' looking over at Harley. ''Left a message on your machine.''

Harley showed her gleaming smile. She'd had her brown hair tinted with ''I Love Lucy'' henna, imported from Iran. ''You did? How sweet. I hope it's a good message.'' Coy now.

''Well—''

''Did I tell you,'' Keating butted in before Lucky could speak, ''that I once had an opportunity to chat with Phipps Hagadorn—

on the phone, of course. But the man has the most incredible outgoing vid I've ever seen. F/X that out-Spielbergs Spielberg."

" 'Out-Spielbergs Spielberg'?" Ziggy muttering in disbelief into Lucky's left ear. "There's one to remember, huh? Drop into a conversation."

Harley cut her eyes to him. "Nice *face*, Ziggy. I mean, really, get a visual."

Ziggy fingertipped the pimples on his left cheek, intoning, "We will pop no pimple before its time." He grinned at Harley. "You like it, I know someone who can fix you up."

Lucky barely heard them, fixated as he was on Harley's cutaway blouse, sizzle skirt, patterned hose. She was tall and workout trim. His nose would have told him she was wearing Madonna, even if the fake mole—*la mouche*—applied to her lip hadn't.

"Keating works for Phipps Hagadorn," Harley said proudly, tightening the hold she had on him, flattening a breast against his cut upper arm.

"No shit," Ziggy said in theatrical surprise. "I work with people who're dying to get out of the building he owns."

Willy and Eddie stifled laughs while Harley threw the four of them a disapproving look. She didn't bother to explain anything to Keating, whose attention, in any case, had been diverted by a lithe Eurasian woman on the dance floor. "I hope you haven't forgotten about our date next week, Lucky."

Lucky straightened up somewhat. "No, uh, I mean, unless you have, or—"

"Well, of course I haven't. I've already made reservations at the Beverly Hills."

Lucky's eyes went so wide they teared. The Bev was one of Manhattan's noted celeb restaurants—a kind of celebrity salt lick-cum-blind for star spotters of the sort Eddie was paid to guide around town. "Little spendy, isn't it?"

Harley waved a recently manicured hand. "We'll just go for hors d'oeuvres and order from the lite menu. I'm dying to see who'll show up."

"Hor d'oeuvres," Willy said, after Harley and Keating had said their good-byes and wandered off. "What're they again?"

"Keating Price?" Lucky said, dumbfounded. "Where's somebody find a Keating Price?"

"The Third," Eddie said. "And they met at the McTrash

recycling center over on the Post Road. The one with the bar and the video garden.''

Lucky compressed his lips. ''Damn recycling centers are pickup joints.''

Willy agreed. ''We didn't know how to break it to you, Luck—Harley and some Twenty-One. Not that it comes as any major surprise . . .''

Ziggy clapped Lucky on the back. ''Lean into the turns, comrade,'' reaching for a phrase big during the Turn. ''Besides, your date with her's still on.''

Lucky blew out his breath. ''Yeah, one that's going to cost me two weeks' pay.''

They ordered a final round and nursed the drinks while Atopia began to empty, a few patrons forced to surrender car keys to the bouncers who manned the breath and slurred-speech analyzers. Willy and Eddie left, leaving Lucky and Ziggy alone at the bar to ponder videogeists and assorted oddities. Lucky finally called it a night and was headed for the turnstiles when Ziggy called, ''Don't let the crocodiles bite.''

Lucky whirled on him, sober in a flash.

''You know, like 'sleep tight, don't let the bedbugs bite,' '' Ziggy said.

''Yeah, but why crocs, Zig? Why crocs?''

Ziggy shrugged. ''One of the phantom snippets that showed up on the disk recorder. About how crocs in Australia are endangered or some such thing. But why are you asking?''

EIGHT

PERCHED ON A cliff four hundred feet high a few miles
south of Thira Town on the Greek island known variously as
Kallisti, Thira, or Santorini sat the Kwik Frisk convenience store
and snak bar—the crater island's Quick Fix franchise. While the
store catered principally to Thira's upwardly mobile locals and
resident clan of expat Gray Panthers, the snak bar, whose tiered
terraces stepped dangerously close to the cliff edge, was there to
service tourists en route to the Minoan *son et lumière* at Akrotiri,
in off cruise ships bound north for Ios and the Cyclades or South
to Crete and Alexandria. The buses would arrive just before
noon and the tourists would pick their way down the steep steps
to long tables covered end to end with dishes of dzadziki, dolmades, and moussaka, where they'd sip ouzo, retsina, and the
sweet local wine and gaze through stereoscopes at the dazzling
white church domes of Thira Town or across the choppy water
of the bay to Ia at the lip of the island's northern promontory.

Where tour groups once had to struggle up five hundred and
eighty-eight steps by foot or muleback, there was now a funic-
ular that linked Thira Town with the downside quay where the
landing craft put in, the cruise liners themselves deep-water
anchored out near Nea and Palea Kameni—the New and Old
Burnt Islands—the reforming cones of the volcano that had buried the island some two millennia before.

No one could say for certain whether Thira had been the
inspiration for Atlantis, but digs into the Bronze Age soil beneath the island's towering pumice cliffs had revealed the pet-
rified remains of an ancient seafaring, bull-worshiping culture of
extraordinary complexity.

In the drooping eyes of Charlie Cola, the mere fact that the
Minoan culture had experimented with flush toilets should have

been evidence enough to convince the skeptics; but then Charlie Cola knew more than most experts about the catastrophes, natural and otherwise, that had shaped the ancient world.

Just now Charlie was seated at the table on the lowest of the Kwik Frisk's video-free rear terraces, collar turned up to a somewhat chilled breeze, picking at a cuke, sweet tomato, and feta salad, liberally spiced with oregano and drowned in olive oil and vinegar. Ersatz lava, in the Disney tradition, "flowed" on either side of the terrace, and the salt and pepper shakers on the tables were shaped like tiny volcanoes. Going for the theme thing here. The franchise had been one of the last to open, but was already showing a profit, thanks to the continuing popularity of Thira's archeological wonders and raw vertical splendor.

Almost a week had passed since the office telecaster had provided Charlie with what he hoped would result in the most lucrative undertaking of his long career with the company—one that would not only secure the vacation to which Didi felt them entitled, but likewise allow her to realize her decorating dreams for the vacation home in Kerkyra. She was there even now, on Corfu, probably undergoing a thalassotherapy treatment or knocking back iced tsintsibiras with the stonemasons and carpenters.

The assignment from Black Hole HQ was choice, even though not as blank check as the one of a few months past. Charlie, however, hadn't played much part in that one, other than to arrange transport and cover, through the Calcutta Travel Agency, for four operatives the company had sent in to scout the job. The humans hadn't even exited from the Bronx Adit, but from the planet's secondary egress at a Quick Fix— a Click Fists—in Medan, Sumatra. Difference this time was that the company had asked Charlie to handle things, the preliminary phase anyway, which involved running surveillance on an indig Terran name of Miles Vanderloop. Professor Miles Vanderloop, currently on sabbatical from the Semiotics Department of Cambridge University.

Charlie wasn't apprised of just what this Vanderloop had done to bring himself to the attention of Black Hole, but something told him that the professor was linked to blowback from the Sumatra op. He knew for a fact that a couple of operatives from Terminal Abductions had been left in place to handle possible repercussions of that operation—perhaps to render an assist to Black Hole's deep-cover residents, whom Charlie knew principally as names in a coded file he kept on the office comp.

The first telecaster communiqué had been followed by a message from Black Hole Technical Assist, to the effect that a Peer Group—a team of surveillance/background specialists—was available should Charlie decide to requisition one. But Charlie, ever on the alert for the profitable op, had been just as quick to telecast a no-need reply. Sure, he might well be under company scrutiny, even now on the Kwik Frisk's windy rear terrace, for all he knew, but so long as he gave the impression of H&H, the hustle and hassle, he'd be safe in charging large for his efforts.

One of the reasons he'd come to Greece instead of simply having Dante Bhang report to him in New York. Not only showed he was already on the job, but he could bill for the mileage as well.

Bhang was thought to be Swiss—or Italian, or Greek, or some combination, you could pretty much take your pick. Just as you could when hazarding a guess as to the man's age and which parts of him, if any, were stock. The story went that Charlie's father, Patsy, had first encountered Bhang in Rome, site of the original Adit, shortly after Black Hole had okayed his and Jacob Riddle's plan to conceal the franchise presence on tertiary Terra behind the neon signs and—then—gasoline pumps of a chain of convenience stores.

The single aspect that had sold Black Hole on the idea, ultimately earning Jay Riddle a retirement home on Nmuth Four, was the notion that a worldwide chain of nearly identical stores—camera-secured, staffed by people who could barely get by in the local language, open twenty-four hours a day, and harshly lit to avoid lingering by patrons—would provide the Agency with a way to move Trough visitors about without attracting attention.

The work of setting up the dummy corporation, with its own fleet of jets and trucks, was left to the Black Hole cognoscenti who would eventually comprise the board of directors; but management of the Bronx Adit had fallen to Jay and Patsy. Only a handful of the individual store managers would ever learn the truth—that Quick Fix was but itself a franchise of a galactic consortium—but Black Hole's shadowy purposes required that all personnel be of a somewhat sociopathic bent. Hence the inclusion of men like Dante Bhang and the score of ex-smugglers, mercs, data pirates, and former Wall Street brokers recruited to swell the downside ranks of Quick Fix, Inc.

Bhang came highly recommended for his cleverness and the fact that he worked cheap. It was Bhang who'd placed Labib and Jesus with Charlie and Didi; Bhang who'd run the background on Sanpol Amsat, who had himself convinced that Earth was playing host to XT walk-ins long before Charlie had confirmed the fact.

So Bhang was naturally the person who came to mind when the telecaster had chirped, and not an hour later Charlie had e-mailed a précis to Bhang's retreat on Cyprus, where rumor linked him to trafficking in small arms, black-market meds, nuclear waste, fetal tissue, and designer beef.

Charlie was sponging up the oily dregs of his salad with a hunk of freshly baked bread when Bhang, impeccably turned out in a Cypriot handknit, Italian loafers, fedora, cravat, and audio-shades, appeared on the terrace steps, arriving at Charlie's table along with the moussaka and a liter of red wine.

"*Kalimera*," he told Charlie, bowing slightly. Eyes never leaving Charlie's, he helped himself to a piece of the sweet-bread. He doffed the hat, sent the waiter back for stuffed grape leaves and another liter of wine, and brushed dirt from the benchseat with a Thai silk handkerchief before sitting down.

"Pleasant trip?" he inquired across the table.

Charlie patted his mouth with a cloth napkin. "Fair. Flying's not what it used to be—even first-class in a hypersonic."

"The world isn't, Charlie," with a knowing look and an ambiguous smile. "But I'm pleased to hear that your, um, employers are finally throwing you a bone."

Charlie narrowed his eyes and scanned the terrace. A tour bus had arrived only moments before and the tables were filling with elderly Germans and Japanese, everyone gushing over the faux-lava effects.

"Vanderloop," Charlie said, getting right down to it.

Bhang adjusted his glasses. "Visiting Professor of Semiotics at Cambridge."

"I told you that much."

"A career recluse. Delivers his lectures by comp or through the Virtual Network. Camera-shy to the nines. I couldn't even come up with a photo that wasn't twenty years out of date. Publisher that issues his monographs and books claims to have no permanent address for him. Currently on sabbatical some-where in the South Pacific."

"I didn't know about the South Pacific part."

"I did some peeking and poking in the Public Information Network. Had a hell of a time tracing his airline routings. Paris, Venice, Cairo, Nairobi, Botswana, Bombay, Singapore."

"You said South Pacific."

"I traced him from Singapore as far as Lombok in the Indonesian archipelago, then lost him. Could have booked passage on a ship to Australia, or maybe's he's on some ancient dhow touring the Spice Islands."

Charlie considered it in silence. That Sumatra was close to those Spice Islands only reinforced his suspicion that Vanderloop was part of the mystery op. "So what can you do for me?"

Bhang leaned back from the table as a waiter approached with the dolmades and wine. "*Parakalo*," he said, wrapping it in a smile. Elsewhere, three Greek busboys were dancing for the tourists. Charlie guessed it wouldn't be long before plates started hitting the terrace tiles.

"What I do," Bhang said with a stuffed leaf between his fingers, "is up to you."

Charlie looked at him. "How so?"

Bhang took a bite from the leaf and set it down. "Just how large is this op?"

"It's not a blank check," Charlie was quick to caution.

"Then are we talking flat rate or per diem?"

"We need surveillance and a complete background. I'm willing to give you a per diem if I have your word you won't pad the expenses too much."

Bhang grinned. "In other words, I should leave the padding to you."

Charlie grinned back. "Something like that. But I want you to stay on this personally. Technical Assist is itching to send in a Peer Group, which'll mean I'm cut out of everything but the usual percentage on the travel and cover guarantee costs."

"And you're tired of getting the short end. Like on that big Sumatra deal a few months back."

Charlie sighed. "I complain, you'd be able to hum along with me, Dante. We're both subcontractors, aren't we?"

Bhang inclined his head in a show of assent. "That we are, Charlie. So when are we going to turn things around, get them working for us for a change?"

"You know what we're dealing with." Charlie grew serious all of a sudden, emphasizing it with a hard look. But Bhang only shrugged it off.

"That's what your father used to say: The Agency's too big to take on. And look where it got him. After all he gave them, did he ever get his promised fade to Foxal? Did he get to live out his years in comfort and style? No, he dies of a faulty organ right here on Earth.'' Bhang snorted. ''They don't so much as offer to dup him.''

Charlie fell silent for a moment, then said, ''Resurrection wasn't included in the policy he had with the company. Besides, we can't all be as lucky as Jacob Riddle.''

Bhang popped the remaining fragment of grape leaf into his mouth and chewed it contemplatively. ''Luck had nothing to do with Jay Riddle's retirement. He made it happen. That's what you've got to do.'' He motioned to the facsimile mural gracing the retaining wall of the terrace above them. ''Take the bull by the horns, Charlie, just like those crazy bastard Minoans used to do.''

Charlie regarded the mural's stylized bull-jumpers, thinking: *Maybe it's worth a shot.*

The walls of Braxmar Koddle's fifteen-by-fifteen in the transfigured light-industry loft he shared with Eddie Ensign, Willy Ninja, Ziggy Forelock, Asia Boxdale, and an inconstant cast of would- and wannabe artists were covered, top to bottom in places, with the results of the two years' worth of research he had devoted to the science fiction e-novel Sony-Neuhaus had commissioned. The room had no ceiling of its own, save for the distant expanse of holed, battered, patched tin it shared with the rest of the loft; there were just the walls, the eight-foot-high unpainted fiberboard partitions, and a single mesh-protected double-hung window that hadn't been opened in years.

The South Bronx share—on Third Avenue, near the old Juvenile Detention Center—was a warren of such rooms and the narrow passages around them, dark and musty-smelling despite a massive skylight which could be opened with a long hand crank, and crowded with bulky furniture out of fashion since the Turn and an impenetrable assortment of street trash collected over the years. During parties maps were handed out at the door, but first-, second-, even third-time guests still lost their way. A former share had marked the exits with red lights and painted color-coded routing lines on the plywood floor, but partitions tended to shift with the addition of each new roommate, and those unfamiliar with the layout and following, say, the blue line to the bathroom or the green to the kitchen might chance upon a wall that hadn't been there the week before, or in some cases discover their route disappearing under an unmarked door or blocked by a sofa that had become wedged in the corridor. And occasionally people would open a door thinking they were on track, only to enter headlong into some loftee's video horror-show or canvas fantasy, or—in Braxmar's case—find themselves in a fully papered room, surrounded by family-tree diagrams and timelines, yellowed pages torn from pre-Turn comics, enlarged VDR freeze-frames, cels from animated films, line drawings of strange-looking vehicles and battle mecha, and crudely rendered maps that failed to correspond to *anywhere on Earth*—all done on oaktag, grocery bag, still-articulated kenaf printout sheets, and stapled, tacked, pushpinned to the walls, draped over closet doors and windows, spread across floor, bed, and table space.

More than one hapless loft wanderer had stumbled in upon the reclusive Braxmar himself—seated slack-jawed and wide-eyed at his comp system, seemingly unaware of the intrusion despite voiced apologies or sharp intakes of breath—and backed out of the room, wondering for the rest of the evening, or the rest of the week, whether Braxmar wasn't one of those overstressed who should be reported to an Urgent Care Center, or who would eventually turn up on the evening news, linked to some star slaughter or unprovoked attack on a fast-food restaurant, police cameras capturing the papered room after the fact: closing on articles clipped from religious publications, gossip tabloids, texts by Nostradamus, grainy photos of intended victims, bloody pentagrams, diary entries, evidence of paraphilia or erotomania . . .

It was worrisome at first glance, this surfeit of gatefold sheets and handwritten notes, until a closer look suggested the presence of a stable, guiding intelligence at work—compulsive, nonetheless, but stable. A repetition of proper nouns, place-names that corresponded to dots on the maps, drawings that were obviously early versions of the hotly colored images on the plastic cels . . . the sum total of Braxmar's research investment in what the editors at Sony-Neuhaus were calling Project Grand Finale.

"Okay, Brax," Asia Boxdale said from the comp-system swivel chair, asking herself now where her mind had been when she'd volunteered to help Braxmar arrange his research notes, "next comes Lance Killdare. You've got him listed as a human, but there's an icon fixed to his name—an asterisk."

"A single or a double?" Brax asked from the far corner, where he had his nose pressed to a character-correspondence chart, squinting to discern his own microscopic scrawl.

Asia returned to the flat-panel display, the epitome of Southeast Asian poise, lustrous hair in a braid that reached the small of her back. "A double."

"Okay, okay," Brax was running a finger down the chart,

"that means he started out human but ended up transmogrified, possibly as a Sirian from Naxis or a Genoween from Nu-Urth." Brax scratched at a graying beard. "Does it say what book he appeared in? 'Cause I can't locate him anywhere on this chart."

Asia scrolled through several screens, entered a flurry of keyboard commands, studied the bold text in a window. "Uh, yeah, he first shows up in book twenty-two—*Battlefire*."

Braxmar turned to her, brow furrowed. "Whaddaya mean, first shows up?"

Asia read on. "Sez here he reappears in *Skylight*. Also in *Edge of Space*."

Braxmar shook his head in an attempt to clear it. "I swear I remember him dying in *Battlefire*. Took a web-weapon blast from whatsizname, the Morphean—"

"Franz?"

"No, uh, Ta, Ti, Tem . . . something with a T."

Asia curled rose-lacquered fingers over the keyboard in readiness. "Should I look it up?"

Braxmar pressed the heels of his hands to his eyes. "No. Let's stick with this Lance Killdare . . ."

As the only employed artist in the loft, Braxmar didn't feel he had a right to complain about his work, especially to Asia—*especially* to Asia, possibly the only unattached, available woman he or anybody in the loft posse knew—who was selling Anomalous Trauma insurance to make the rent, when what she yearned for was a chance to perform. Or at least the chance to get the tapes of her interactive performances warehoused. But secretly the demands of Project Grand Finale were pushing Braxmar well into the danger zone.

At thirty-five he was the oldest share in the loft, slight, stooped, dark-chocolate black, prematurely gray. He'd worn corrective lenses since he was a kid, and still spoke with a trace of the accent he'd brought to the States from London at age eight. The son of a physician and a lawyer, Brax had worked his way through NYU writing advertising and public-relations spots for the Catholic Church before jumping both-feet-first into fiction, managing in less than a decade to sell half a dozen print novels, several of which were still available through some of the more obscure comp-service publishers.

It was one of the serendipitous consequences of the demise of paper that books rarely went out of print any longer. For a small fee any writer could have his or her work uploaded and e-catalogue-listed with one of the fiction comp services, which in turn paid a percentage to the author on the downloading costs charged to subscribers. For an additional cost, authors could include plot summaries, excerpts, and review blurbs. Braxmar's novels had even enjoyed something of a rebirth since the Arts Advisory Council had enacted the moratorium on new works, requiring that everyone catch up on the old and evergreen before warehoused works would be considered for release. The limitation on new story lines had perhaps the least effect on genre fiction, where the same plots had been reused and recycled for decades anyway.

Mainstream, however—defined as "celebrity fiction"—was still handled by the big houses: Sony-Neuhaus, Bertelsmann-Farben, Disney-Nabisco, all of which employed house writers armed with grammar-assists and knowbot phrase-hunters to fine-tune sim-fict works authored by idiot-savant expert-system AI programs, wherein the style of some old master had been reduced to formula.

Like Asia, Braxmar yearned to be among the warehoused, the Artistic Elect—writers experimenting with algorithmic and fractal literature, Oulipo Revival, Möbius and interactive poetry—but in the meantime was writing in-house for Sony-Neuhaus. It was either that or write for the network tube, *the* black medium since the Turn.

Project Grand Finale was dumped in his lap after company spies learned that a competitor in the game had been granted permission by the AAC to release a warehoused trilogy written some five years earlier by an award-winning science-fiction writer, Plie Charmeuse, who was currently busing tables in an uptown restaurant.

Top execs and chief editors at Sony-Neuhaus had convened in emergency session to discuss a suitable counteroffensive, and the plans for the project Braxmar was to inherit had been drawn up. Brax was commissioned to bring to conclusion the dozens of plotlines contained in the thirty or so "shared universe" novels of the best-selling space opera series Worlds Abound, including such individual efforts as *Battlefire* and *Edge of Space,* compiled by twenty-two different contributors, set on two dozen planets, featuring upward of three hundred characters, and covering some four thousand years of galactic history. The series sprang from a single pre-Turn novella entitled "Tug of War," by Etaoin Shrdlu, now thought deceased, which had been adapted for the screen by Richard Rymer and turned into the five-hundred-million-dollar box-office mega-smash *Zone Defense,* starring a young Jason Duplex. The movie spawned a novelization, a comic-book series, six seasons of original animation for television, and the thirty-plus shared-universe spinoffs Braxmar had successfully avoided reading for close to a decade.

"The problem," Braxmar said, coming across the room now like a man who'd just gone ten losing rounds with a heavyweight, "the problem's that half these writers didn't bother to read what the others were writing!" He gestured offhandedly to a list taped to the wall. "They handled this thing like they were playing a game of hot potato. This is what you get when you pay a flat fee to somebody just to keep a story going. I mean, sure, they used the same characters and setting and stuck to a chronology that works about half the time, but nothing else is in sync: the descriptions don't match, the rules keep changing, you've got dead characters reappearing . . ."

"Interactive," Asia said. "Their own version of what's Really Going On."

Braxmar's forefinger shot out. "Wrong. There is no RGO, that's the problem. Everyone had their own agenda. The damn story's deviated so far from its starting point, I don't know if it can ever find its way home."

Asia leaned away from the comp, rubbing her eyes, screen-weary. "That's your job, isn't it?"

Braxmar snorted.

"Too bad Etaoin Shrdlu isn't around. Maybe he'd have an idea how to wrap the thing up."

Braxmar swept printouts off the foot of the bed and sat down. "Hunh. Nobody thought to resurrect him."

"Except maybe this guy that wrote *Edge of Space*." Asia glanced at the screen. "Bixby Santiago."

"Brax nodded. "He's one of the people I need to talk to."

Asia inspected her active-length nails. "So what about hiring some expert-sys programmer to study Shrdlu's style and write an author simulation?"

Braxmar looked over at her, shaking his head. " 'Cause this series doesn't belong to him. It hasn't been his since 'Tug of War.' " He glanced at the note stuck to the bottom of his bare foot and moaned. "And besides, Sony-Neuhaus'd never go for it. A guide's what I need." After a pause: "Maybe I'll hire Lucky. He seems to know his way around bizarre characters." Laughing now. "Anybody who can keep all those themers straight . . ."

Asia laughed with him, thinking about her gangly ex-roomie

and love interest for all of two months way back when. They were close friends still, and Lucky never failed to show up at her infrequently booked performances. He'd also been the first, after she'd landed the job with Altamont Insurance, to take out an Anomalous Trauma policy: blanket coverage for abductions—of the alien or ghostly sort; corporeal mutilation—in the absence of a human or animal perpetrator; injuries resulting from falling frogs or fish, or sustained as the result of attack by invisible assailants; and instances of stigmata, mysterious flows or oozings, spontaneous combustion, fiery persecutions, and bodily elongation.

"Ziggy ran into him at Atopia the other night," Asia allowed at last. "Said Lucky was displaying some paranoia about crocodiles or something."

"And La Zig would know a little something about paranoia, wouldn't he," Braxmar said. "Man who's convinced computers carry on conversations with one another."

"No, just VDRs and personal info nets."

"And bank machines and supermarket checkout scanners—"

Asia sighed. "Maybe you do need Lucky—crocodiles and all. Providing you can pry him away from Miz Paradise for a night."

Brax smiled. "Now there's a cause even more lost than Worlds Abound."

"Poor Luck." Asia swiveled in the chair to face him. "You know what you could do? Invite Lucky to PhenomiCon."

Braxmar showed her a dubious look. "What would Lucky want with a para-science con? He's got enough problems handling themers."

"Well . . . maybe you could get him interested in meeting the authors of the series? He really does have a good head for this kind of thing. And there's that software package he designed for the character-actor placement service he worked for . . . Just think about having him help you list all these." Asia tapped a fingernail against the flat-panel. "Sirians, Genoweens, humans . . . You'd have it knocked."

Braxmar fell into a ruminating silence. "God, it would simplify things." He stood up, recharged. "Maybe I can even talk him into quitting that damned Theme Park Advisory Group."

NINE

EIGHT P.M. AND Lucky calculated he was already out eighty-five dollars. Harley had insisted on taking a private a-cell from her apartment in Queens; then there'd been the fresh rose purchased from a smooth-talking eco-beret working the corner of Harlem River Drive and 125th, the gratuity for the Beverly Hills maitre d' to insure them a spotlit table on the "no-calling" second tier, the credit Lucky had fed into the sushi 'bot and sommelier . . . Not to mention what he had paid to have his hair styled and rent the tux. And now here they were in one of the poshest feedbins in Harlem and the goddamned tableside decision-support system couldn't make up its circuits about a wine.

"Look," Lucky said, managing to quiet his sewing-machine leg for a moment, "how 'bout we just order the New Zealand cabernet and be done with it?"

Harley exhaled through her mouth, sniffling from a case of spring allergies, disappointment evident in the slight outrush of breath. "I'm sure the cabernet would be fine, Lucky, but why don't we see what the sommelier has to say. That's how we learn about things—by listening and paying attention."

Lucky gestured to the machine's screen. "This isn't a sommelier. It's a stupid little comp—*and as low one at that.*" Aiming it at the system's audio-input port.

Harley gave a worried look around the crowded room, lowering her voice when she turned back to him. "Really, Lucky, you're embarrassing me. Now, finish your foie gras and let's just relax. We're here to *ver y verse*, aren't we?"

Ver y verse, Lucky thought sullenly, plunging his fork into the foie gras and savoy cabbage. See and be seen. Exactly what the Beverly Hills counted on everyone believing, when the closest

thing the place had to celebs were the character-actor waiters and
waitresses done up as old movie stars: Tom Cruise, Julia Rob-
erts, Paula Abdul . . . You could do better at that celeb petting
zoo, the *Cheers* franchise down the street. Even Eye Spy, the
star-stalker agency Eddie Ensign guided for, had dropped the
restaurant from its list of happy hunting grounds. And the few
cine-legends or action figures who did turn up at the Beverly
Hills were names already checked off on the screens or in the
books the stalkers carried around with them, along with their
minicams and pencil-thin shotgun mikes.

The attitude-heavy Bev was done in Disney Deco, the holos
simulating an evening view over LA from the Hollywood Hills,
the stage backdrop devoted to that famous nine-letter sign. The
facsimile palms were said to be modeled after pedigreed royals
from multimillion dollar estates in those same hills, and each
brick in the exposed walls was hand autographed by one celeb or
another, as were the silver five-pointed stars inlaid on the table-
tops, handprints usually filled with salsa, horseradish, or chutney,
depending on theme tier and table setting. Spots highlighted the
eager-to-be-seen, while the light-shy dined in banquettes positioned along the perimeter, or in high-backed wooden booths under the canopy of a car wash that had been trucked in piece by
piece from Sunset Boulevard in West Hollywood. One couldn't
ask for a more studied environment, a purer example of faux-arts.

The clientele was mostly salary men and office ladies—
trabaus and *ojinjals*—Germans, Japanese, and Hispanics
(wursts, kudzus, and coppertones, in the parlance of the street),
along with a smattering of life-style consultants, hospitality-
industry specialists, concept pushers, and council execs. There
were a handful of undernourished imeldas, outfitted in bar-coded
designer bodysuits, knit tunics over leggings and stretch minis,
chiffon, taffeta, and gold lace shift dresses, brocade blazers and
fringe-bordered coats. A few of them affected biodegradeable
skin-pixel body tints and tattooed lip gloss; others carried family
crest World Express cards and electronic price scanners, which
they trained on one another like laser-tag weapons.

Harley was wearing a black hammered-velvet two-piece strap-
less baring lots of shoulder and slivers of ivory white skin below
a gold-embroidered bodice, ankle boots, and a metallic organza
stole. Her nails were gold leaf and she was wafting a personal
scent concocted by some nose in one of the perfumeries on Fifth
Avenue. The Madonna mole had been replaced by a dusting of
glitter.

Earlier on, during the taxi ride, Lucky had asked about the perfume, first mistaking it for an exhaust leak and voicing open the rear windows of the a-cell.

"It's my perfume, dweeb," Harley sounding exasperated at the time, and still so early in the evening. He'd leaned into Harley's layered scents only to take an elbow in the nose as she sought to offer him the crook of her arm. "Really, Lucky, don't you know that perfume isn't applied to already scented areas?"

"Already scented areas?"

"The face, the neck, the hands," Harley stroking herself in the dim fiber optic light.

"Then, uh, where . . ."

"Here," almost catching him with that elbow again. "And the small of the back, just at the base of the spine." Lucky tried to picture the spot. "And, here, of course," running a forefinger a teasing inch into her Little Annie Fanny cleavage.

"Maybe I'll just—"

"Uh-uh," she said, pushing his head away. "Not in front of the car cameras. Remember what week this is." Lucky frowned, wondering if she was speaking biologically, and she caught his look. "It's National Celibacy Week."

Always some excuse, Lucky thought. Just like the night in her apartment when they'd come closest to doing each other. He wondered sometimes just who, or what, she was saving herself for. He wanted to ask why she'd bothered to get a birth control implant. Why he'd bothered. Why anyone had. But instead he simply rolled his eyes and muttered, "Maybe we could at least exchange underwear, huh?"

Lucky caught a whiff of the perfume now as Harley applauded the house band's rendition of "The Love Theme from *RoboCop IV.*'" At the same time, the comp sommelier rejected Lucky's pre-entree wine choice for a rose zinfandel.

"I thought that cabernet might be a trifle full-bodied," Harley said, full of secret knowledge.

"How 'bout we order." Lucky jabbed a finger at the touch screen to confirm the comp's choice, wishing for an eye he could put out as well. A second touch called up the lite menu.

"Allow me to list our evening specials," a French-accented synth-voice began. "Tonight we are pleased to present our renowned juniper-marinated squab over vinegar-sharpened lentils. Andre also recommends the sesame-encrusted fowl with parsley and caper sauce and rosemary-scented dauphine potatoes . . ."

"If we make a break for it right now—" Lucky whispered. Harley shssed him.

"Then, as a special treat, we offer sprightly grilled baby artichokes, leeks, white beans, and eggplant, with sausage-flecked garlic bread. Or, for those adventurers among you, a mille-feuille of mussels and a lemony bok choy vegetable mélange . . ."

Lucky put his hand over his mouth, only to receive the tip of Harley's high heel in the right shin.

"And finally, seared pasta in a pool of tomato water with chives, fennel, and piquant mustard seeds; or our freshly prepared summery tomato soup and sweet rhubarb mousse in truffle juice."

Harley ordered the squab. Lucky pressed for the "fowl" and thought he detected a kind of victorious beep from the sommelier when he deferred to its judgment for an accompanying wine.

The food was delivered fifteen minutes later by Phil Donahue and Oprah Winfrey. Lucky's fowl couldn't have weighed in at more than three ounces, and was still larger than Harley's squab. He had his mouth open to complain to Oprah when Harley shot him a look. "The less you eat . . ."

"The longer you live," he completed in a tired voice.

The Gerontology Council's award-winning slogan. The less you eat, the longer you live. And the greater your chance of steering clear of any of a dozen "diseases of affluence" and breaking the one-hundred mark. Already there were people in Japan and Sweden—lean to the point of skeletal—pushing the life-extension envelope at one-fifteen and still going strong without the benefit of organ or bone-marrow transplants, intestinal tubing, microsurgery, or Drexler endocrine implants.

"Keating won't eat here," Harley announced without preamble, dabbing at bee-stung lips with an embroidered napkin. "He considers Harlem hopelessly mainstream."

"The first thing you've said about him I can relate to." Lucky wore a puzzled expression as he picked at the sesame-encrusted fowl. The little potatoes seemed a safer bet.

Harley set her fork down with finality. "Lucky, you really shouldn't talk about him like that. You do realize that the Prices are one of the most influential families in New York—quite possibly the world. And Keating works for Mr. Hagadorn himself—sometimes *with* him." Her face took on a dreamy look. "Keating's asked me to a small dinner party Phipps is having for close friends."

"So it's Phipps, now," Lucky said, mimicking Harley's fork move, his appetite gone with the sudden chill wind from an overhead fan. He stared at her for a long moment. "Harley, what the hell are you doing with me? I mean, why do you even bother?"

Stiffening somewhat, she said, "Thank you for not swearing."

"Since when is 'hell' swearing? Hey, I believe in the place. Sometimes I think I'm *in* it."

She reached across the table for his hand, favoring him with a tolerant smile. "Lucky . . . It's just that I see so much potential in you. If you'd only make more of an effort . . ."

Lucky's head started to buzz. It was at Harley's urging that he had cut ties with Marshall Stack and applied for the job with the Theme Park Advisory Group. Herself an assistant policy analyst with the Gender Bias Council, Harley had even helped him secure the position as on-site inspector by putting in a good word with Arbor Slocum, the Advisory Group's director. Harley was constantly encouraging him to make something of himself.

"It's just those friends of yours," she was saying. "That Ziggy person—"

"Harley, I like my friends."

"Because they're 'artists'? Neo-Post-Omeganists?"

He could hear the quotes she put around it. "That's part of it. Plus, I like the way they see the world."

"The way they see the world?" Full of theatrical surprise. "Then why aren't any of them recognized artists?"

"Because . . . because they're ahead of their time. They couldn't be mainstream if they wanted to be."

"So their works end up warehoused."

"They only hope."

Harley shook her head in rapid movements. "I don't understand. What possible good is it to have your song or your book or your, I don't know, sculpture, end up in a warehouse? It's not as though you've suddenly made it." She regarded him in silence. "I think the only reason you float with them—isn't that what they say—float?—is because you feel powerful among them. It helps raise your self-esteem."

"Self-esteem? I don't need my self-esteem raised." Lucky puffed up somewhat to demonstrate the fact. "Just 'cause I'm a loser doesn't mean I don't have self-esteem."

"Oh, Lucky," she said, doing the near impossible by making her lips a thin line.

"Well, I still don't see why you're bothering with me, Harley.

Talking to me about Keating Price, Phipps Hagadorn . . . You want me to compete for you, is that it?''

She tipped her head. ''Well of course I want you to compete for me. I want what's best for the child I plan to have at some point in the not too distant future, and it's important I choose the right partner to assist me.''

For all that had changed since the Turn, Lucky thought, some things had remained constant—sex being one of them. Down through the millennia men believing they did the picking and choosing when it was the women who were running the game. Plain old biopolitics. Men measuring themselves in terms of sexual success; women defining themselves by limiting sexual accessibility.

''You make it sound like a lab experiment,'' he told her.

''That's exactly what I don't want it to be. I don't plan to 'experiment' at all. I want to be the biological artist for my offspring. And I want my work to be as perfect as it can be.''

''You don't need a partner, Harley. You need an agent. Anyway, art's never perfect.''

Harley made a dismissive gesture. ''That's simply your low self-esteem talking.''

Lucky pinched the sleeve of the tux. ''Comes from having to rent the plumage.''

Harley smiled in a self-satisfied way. ''You see? You are competing. And there's nothing to be ashamed of. You have to take pride in yourself if you're going to accomplish anything. We should give frequent caring attention to ourselves—''

''A tux is 'caring attention'?''

''—and to everyone we meet,'' finishing it on a louder note, then sitting back to appraise him while he toyed with the potatoes. ''Would you be willing to try an ERO motivational exercise?''

Lucky raised an eyebrow. ''Good for those hard-to-work places like the lateral obliques?''

''I'm talking about the kind I do with my decision-support system.''

Lucky let his eyes drift up to the Bev's astrodecor ceiling. ''Not another comp . . . How 'bout we try an RGO exercise instead? See what's lurking behind all this—''

''Think back to your childhood,'' Harley carried on undaunted. ''Choose an event—that's the E part of the ERO. Then tell me how you responded—that's the R. And then explain how the outcome—that's the—''

"Forget it, Harley." He leaned a playful leer across the table. "If we could just get back to those perfume application spots . . ."

"Did your parents make time for you? Do you remember them being affectionate with you and with each other?"

The questions derailed him from the amorous track he was laying. Did his parents make time for him? He considered their present whereabouts in a retirement community down Mejico way. Then he recalled the house he'd been brought up in. There were gaps in his memory when he tried to place himself with his father, or his mother. "Well, you know, they both worked. And I was the third child . . ."

Harley was nodding. "Just as I suspected. And where are your siblings?"

Lucky ran a hand over his mouth. "My sister's in San Francisco. Runs a bank or something. We don't talk much. And my brother, well, he's had to lean through a lot of turns. The war, a coupla jobs and marriages that didn't work out. He's down in the Amazon somewhere."

"I was a first child," Harley said.

"Well, no wonder we're having problems."

She frowned. "I'm only trying to get you to understand that part of your dissatisfaction stems from your being a third child. You grew up feeling deprived and eager for change. I, on the other hand, am a supporter of things the way they are."

"Including the way they are between us, I suppose."

"I'm talking about society, Lucky. Our global consciousness. What you and your artist friends have to accept is that there are reasons for all these councils we've created and the moratorium on artistic works. Look what happened in the past. Look at the effect that television had on the pre-Turn generations, zoning everyone out, preparing the way for high cholesterol, drug addiction and selfishness.

"What we need to do now is get our priorities straight, get everyone thinking with the program before we can begin to explore a self-created future. We can't have everyone demanding change before all of us are properly prepared to take the global step."

"And this has something to do with my self-esteem?"

"It reduces to this: Art doesn't matter. In fact, it doesn't matter what you do, but who you are—"

Lucky rattled his head. "But that's not true. We're all flawed, Harley. We're all human, and humans make mistakes. You put too much faith in who you are and you're in for a crash. What we've got to do is work at improving things, and one way of doing that's by challenging the structure. That's where art comes into it—and I don't mean this mainstream crap that only backs up the status quo.''

"But you don't have to challenge things." Harley was growing flustered, wringing her hands. "The world is changing without your help. It's not always going to be like this. Money's going to come back into vogue and we'll be able to buy designer things and Wagyu beef and ride in open jeeps burning gasoline and blasting the stereo, and wear thong bikinis and limo surf . . . It's all going to turn out great, but you have to be ready for it. Not stuck in some miserable little share in the Bronx with a roomie you hardly know, and no car, and a rented tux.''

Harley was breathing rapidly when she finished; she looked flushed and had a hand pressed to the swell of her breast. "Oh, my god," she said in a shaky voice. "You see what you're doing to me? I'm having a panic attack!"

"A what—"

"Oh, God"—glancing around nervously—"everything seems so strange, I feel so detached . . .''

"Well, I coulda told you that—"

"My heart's racing!"

He reached out a hand but quickly withdrew it. People at nearby tables were staring, cams were focusing in. The band was a few bars into "The *Crocodile Dundee* Overture"—plenty of aboriginal song sticks and didgeridoo—and Harley was hyperventilating.

Lucky jabbed a finger at the touch screen and scrolled to the herbal-beverage list. "Uh, there's uh, chamomile, gentian, ginseng . . . How 'bout some of this valerian, celery, and beet root—"

Harley struggled to her feet, swaddling herself in the organza stole. "Just take me home, Lucky. Before I faint."

Dante Bhang switched off the ignition and let the interbust Cruiser coast to a stop alongside a dry riverbed, crazed from the heat, a couple of measly coolabah trees rising from the south bank. He droppered 'screen into his eyes, then went things one better by slipping into glasses whose lenses had already gone black from sitting on the dash, exposed to a cruel sun.

Stepping out into settling dust, glare you could feel, he took a long pull from the plastic thermos he'd purchased back in Alice

and tossed the thing onto the passenger seat with the Eski cool-
pack.

So this was "out bush," he thought, gazing around. Never
never, back o' beyond. Flat, dry, still as death. Gum, thorny
scrub, desert oak that looked more like cacti. Distant sandstone
humps under the haze. The Macdonnell Ranges maybe, or that
feldspar-rich Ayers Rock. Just where the hell was he, anyway?

The place reminded him of Morocco on a bad day, or Arizona
ten years after a nuke accident. Patsy Cola had once asked him
along on a weekend fade to Lesser Tej, but Dante had declined.
The Trough didn't interest him. Earth had diversity and surprises
enough. No end to opportunities for the sleight of hand.

Looking off in the direction he'd come, he thought, And they
called that a road.

He wandered a few steps along the bank, put a hand to his
brow Indian fashion to regard a group of 'roos down on the
ground soaking up a bit of acacia shade. Two of them munching
what was maybe spinifex grass, leaning back on fat tails, snouts
lifted to the hot air, necks craned in his direction.

Australia. Jesus Christ.

And not a sign of Professor Miles Vanderloop. Not that he'd
expected to find one.

Bhang had lost more than a week looking for the on-leave
professor in Indonesia—on Lombok, Bali, Komodo. Finally
traced him to Irian Jaya where he learned Vanderloop had been
flown south to Darwin by an Asmat bush pilot in one of those
Jaya-manufactured flying totem poles they called an ultralight.
Thing carved from synthwood with snake and lizard motifs.

His arrival in the Northern Territory coincided with Anzac
Day celebrations, commemorating an April 25 from way back,
when the Aussies had gone off to fight Johnnie Turk at Gallipoli,
stalemating him after eight months of savage warfare. Bhang
thought it ironic in light of the fact that a kind of anti-Anzac
celebration was underway on the island he now called home,
flags with red and white crescents flying from many a window in
Famagusta and all over the north, even a few places in the Greek
south.

Home before unified Cyprus had been Morocco, and before
that Marseilles, where he'd smurfed illicit funds for the now
defunct Peruvian cocaine cartels and backed the wrong side in
the War of the Drug Clinics.

In Darwin, though, brass bands were marching—an old, old
soldier who'd actually fought at Gallipoli at the head of the

line—the amber was flowing, deros were singing "Waltzing Matilda." Kids proudly displayed medals handed down from grandfathers and great-grandfathers. The city was a nonstop party of cookouts and pub crawls. Bhang had stopped to watch a mud wrestling tag-team match, where a small guy from Perth was being overpowered by two blond Aussie beach beauties, with someone in the crowd barracking, "Throw another barbie on the shrimp!"

But no sign of Vanderloop.

So, in a tailored safari outfit, Bhang had meandered south on the newly completed bullet line linking Darwin with Alice Springs 954 miles away, making side trips to Humpty Doo, Kununurra, Papunya, and Arltunga Dude Ranch to flash Vanderloop's computer-composite optical about and ask all the usual questions.

The shinkansen was packed with Tiwis from Melville Island and blacks from Niger and Mali, hoping to land character-actor work in the theme park going up east of Ayers Rock. Dream-Land: owned and operated by one of the Disney subsidiaries. All along the maglev route stood LED signs showing a retouched Paul Hogan in the company of Marsupial Mouse, Dewey Dingo, Wily Koala, Kookie Kookaburra, Badass Bush-Devil, and Krazy Kangaroo.

G'day . . .

The bullet had brought prosperity to the region and prosperity brought the theme park. Alice Springs—the Alice, as it was known—had been metamorphosed, trading in its former outback cow-town polish for upscale Palm Springs glitz. Alice had been planted with palms, Joshuas, and swimming pools, enclosed by desert resorts and tournament-class golf courses. The saddle shops that used to line Todd Street were replaced by rental agencies stocked with ATVs and sand surfers, and souvenir shops selling alloy boomerangs and woomeras, dilly bags, and computer guides to the Aboriginals' songlines—the dreaming tracks laid down by legendary semi-humans during the Dreamtime, when they'd wandered across the down under singing the animate and inanimate worlds into existence.

Three days of walking the crowded streets and visiting the resorts finally earned Bhang a positive ID on Vanderloop from a welfare director who worked with Aborigines on the Papunya Reserve. But, yeah, sure, he'd seen *the Pom*. Week or so before, renting a solar-assist Land Cruiser from one of the Todd Street hustlers.

So Bhang did likewise. Only he'd had to settle for an old interbust with kangaroo bars welded over the front end. "Gonna be a bloody six-dog night, mate," the rental agent said when he'd learned Bhang was planning to go out bush.

"Just a drive-about," Bhang had assured him. *"Fahrvergnu-gen."*

And now here he was, out in the Center, miles from Alice, way beyond Bulamakanka for all he knew. However, the three boongs he'd passed on horseback twenty miles east yielded they'd seen a Cruiser that fit the description of the one Vanderloop was driving.

Meaning he was out here somewhere.

But doing what? Bhang asked himself as he surveyed his desolate surroundings. What the fuck was the good professor after out here? And more importantly, what did Black Hole want with him?

Lesser Tej, the most populated planet in Pasals Cluster, knew little of night, and even less of peace. But in what passed for darkness there were lights brighter than the stars: the far-off flashes of plasma guns, the fiery brilliance of exploding ships, the white reign of death.

On a stretch of red beach washed by a wasted sea, Yoo Sobek and the arms merchant, Kodi, stood side by side beneath a cracked sky. "The battle goes well," Kodi was saying, his face of sharp angles lifted to the planet's glare of evening. "Black Hole has been judicious in equipping Eternity Tours with enough matériel to prolong the fight."

"The Agency doesn't 'equip,' " Sobek said to the erupting sky. "The Agency facilitates."

Kodi turned to the Probe, a torqued smile hidden in the shadow of his beak. "Who am I to argue."

They were scarcely one hundred yards from the hemispherical carapace that was both Kodi's home and base of operations. Inland some twenty miles was a dropship port, and the stinking city that had grown up around it was the sewer in which Kodi cast his nets and plied his trade. A Shak of middle age, the arms merchant was tall and powerfully built, with legs as thick as pad-support pylons and a prominent ridge of bone above his liquid eyes and javelin face. Sobek had arrived in human form, after a series of fades that had delivered him to Bzarba and back in pursuit of a puzzle piece, the shipment of arms that had failed to reach Avonne and the Yggdraasian mercenaries it was meant for; misrouted by someone, rerouted perhaps, the group of HuZZah sent in its stead. But there, on Bzarba, at the trailing tip of the arm, Sobek had uncovered the name of the purchasing agent: Dactul Kodi, a wholesaler who occasionally jobbed for the Agency on operations where deniability was thought desirable.

Sobek got to the point. "Are you ready to discuss the Yggdraasians' shipment, or are we going to stand here and watch the gang bang until the sand crabs come out?"

"No reason we can't do both," Kodi told him. "Plasma trades keep me thinking straight, and for this talk that's just where I want to be." He bade Sobek follow him down the fine sand beach toward an outcropping of dark, pitted rock. "Can I ask how much your people have told you?"

"You're already off course. Start with the Yggdraasians. I know they're hired hands; what I need to know from you is who hired them and what they were hired to do."

Kodi stopped to study Sobek's face, the deliberately deformed features Sobek had assembled: distended lips, a lump of nose, a downward turning eye. "I don't want to jeopardize my arrangement with the Agency."

"Then tell me everything you know about the shipment. I'll see that Technical Assist is made aware of your contribution."

Shaks tended to laugh on the inhale; the noise at the back of Kodi's throat could have been a death rattle. "It was someone from Technical Assist who arranged this."

Sobek wasn't entirely surprised. "Who from Technical Assist?"

Kodi named a human Sobek knew. Inept, which was somewhat standard for Technical Assist, but smart enough to be considered trustworthy.

"The order was placed through channels. I was instructed to handle the logistics: find the right people and install them on Avonne. The weapons were to remain here until I received the go-to; then I was to fade them from Less Tej to Avonne."

"What about the operation itself—who were the Yggs ordered to target?" Sobek was waiting for Kodi to tell him Ka Shamok, and so was momentarily stunned when the arms dealer gestured to the embattled sky and said, "Eternity Tours." Instead of registering surprise, however, Sobek got angry. "You're either lying or you're addled, Kodi. Black Hole doesn't need to resort to covert warfare to eliminate competitors in the travel industry."

"That's what I kept telling myself," the Shak said, as earnestly as a Shak could. "Then I started to hear things—rumors, off-course talk maybe I shouldn't mention . . ."

Sobek's training compelled him to chase after the facts, to dig and probe, deeper and deeper, deeper than the inner light at the core of him wanted to go. So he asked, and Kodi led him into the shadows, the gray half-truths: Ka Shamok, sworn enemy of Black Hole, had been fed intelligence relating to an Agency operation in progress on a tertiary world, and Ka Shamok had passed that intelligence on to Eternity Tours, Unlimited. The Agency, apprised of the leak, had asked Kodi to put things right; then—after the foulup on Avonne—it had apparently decided to have a go at Eternity Tours out in the open.

"The Yggs weren't asking any questions about Eternity Tours being targeted," the Shak continued. "The pay was that good. So you see why they were . . . disappointed when the shipment didn't reach Avonne."

Sobek had his now-lidless recorder out and was flipping it in one hand. He was beyond entering actual notes into the thing, as humans were meant to do; but he couldn't seem to break the habit of toying with it, almost as if the archaic device was yet another clue to the puzzle assembling itself throughout the Trough. If he only could remember where he'd come into possession of the recorder . . . He asked Kodi to go over everything from the beginning, from the moment he was contacted by the company human from Technical Assist.

Sobek watched the flashing sky while he listened. In the final analysis, it was clear that Ka Shamok was receiving intelligence from someone inside the Agency—an operative placed highly enough to have learned of the countermeasures Black Hole planned to take against Eternity Tours, and to have sabotaged those plans by arranging for the arms shipment to be rerouted to Bzarba.

But there were additional concerns to confront, less certain and as yet beyond the scope of logical analysis: that both Ka Shamok and Eternity Tours knew something about a covert Agency operation involving a tertiary world; that the Nall who had lost his coat and attaché—and whatever invaluable item either of them may have contained—was an exec with Eternity Tours; and finally the fact that the metalflesh female who had figured in a fusion event on Gilgit—the gleamer Sobek suspected of having made off with the exec's possessions—had been expected to testify against Ka Shamok.

* * *

Silvercup posed naked for the holo array in the flesher's office, legs together, hands interlocked at the back of her head, reshaped breasts jutting out. She lowered her arms as the holo likeness began to take shape a few feet in front of her, ran a hand over the new skin covering her sides, from armpit to hip. The flesher, a silicon also, had done a decent job, given the rush and the small amount she could afford to pay. But at least she looked human again, though white-haired, silver-skinned, and amber-eyed.

Dawn had a score of like skin shops, identity emporiums, character clinics, most of them staffed by cyborgs and SIs. In fact, there wasn't much one couldn't acquire on Dawn, save perhaps a guarantee of extended life. Certainly not for the desperate and the persecuted who patronized the place.

Silvercup had faded there directly from Sierra, the Nall's attaché and credit spike in hand, his long coat concealing the blast damage done to her sheathing. Almost depleted now, the spike was of little use, but there were friendlies on Dawn she could contact for funds if it came to that; inroads she could use to travel to Sweetspot without setting off alarms at Black Hole Adits. The friendlies set in place by the Fealty when they had first turned her out into the world of flesh and blood. To them she could turn for an identity to go with her new look.

The sole item of the Nall's she would keep would be the info-crystal he had sheathed in an inner pocket of the coat. Accessing it, she had been surprised by what she found: data on a surveillance operation being run by Eternity Tours, Unlimited. "Project Head Start," the operation was called. An outgrowth of the intelligence she herself had passed to Ka Shamok from his source inside the Black Hole Travel Agency. The very intelligence that had led to her arrest by the Sysops' White Dwarves on charges of data trafficking.

Silvercup ventured it was that same informant who had learned of WitSec's plan to relocate her on Gilgit; Ka Shamok who had placed the would-be assassins in wait. The informant might have even been instrumental in seeing to it she was plucked off the *Hero's Tomb* to begin with.

A pity she couldn't convince Ka Shamok that she had no intention of compromising his source by testifying in court; a pity she couldn't make him understand that she had been tasked by the Fealty to ally herself with him, in the hope that such a partnership would lead eventually to the overthrow of the Sysops themselves—the subtle beings who had founded Black Hole and opened the contiguity gates throughout the Trough.

Hunted by both sides now, she might never get to tell him these things.

Silvercup spent a few moments studying the slowly rotating holo image of her reformed body before slipping into the clothes the flesher had thrown in as part of the deal. Dressed then, she took advantage of the silicon's absence to wander through the information dump atop his chaotic desk. This she accomplished by inserting a fingertip into the dump's reader port, and in a moment had found what she was looking for: the Employment Opportunities grid of *The Trough Tally*. There she located a voice ad offering a medical-technician position on Staph.

Staph, of all worlds, Silvercup thought. How appropriate for the persecuted! An almost natural step after Dawn: starrise and starset, the birth of light and the end of time. Staph . . . No one would think to look for her there.

TEN

THE FIVE WILLY Ninja had taped to the dash of the interbust truck was gone, collected sometime during the night by his phantom dependent, whoever it was out there lurking in the scant shadows, some undocumented alien residing in the City's margin of underground, beyond the reach of the cams or ID scanners.

The weekly subsidies had begun four months earlier, the morning he discovered the truck had been burglarized of the loose change the crew stored in a plastic compartment between the worn vinyl seats. No forced entry involved because no one ever bothered to lock the four-door cab. Why encourage damage, the reasoning went, particularly when nothing up front was worth safeguarding? Both the sound system and the phone had come stock and were twenty years out of date; and given the musical tastes of the crew, it wasn't likely the few disks lying about would arouse the must-haves in any thief.

Still, it struck Willy that first morning that the thief who'd hit them had a sense of fair play. After all, he, or she, had left behind Tony's shades, along with Willy's favorite torx drivers; and in exchange for the fifteen or so in coin, the thief had straightened up the cab as well. Slipped the music disks into their velveteen carrycase, gotten rid of a week's worth of cellophane fast-food wrappings, gathered up all the toll receipts and placed them in an ashtray that hadn't seen a butt in more than a decade, even passed on taking the sole silver dollar Willy himself had tossed into the compartment only the afternoon before. It had started him thinking: Would the thief try to hit them again, say in a week or so, after the till has been replenished, or would he decide not to press things? And was this how the stranger got by—searching for loose change, the open door, the interior that needed tidying up?

Foiling future attempts would have been as simple as locking the truck, parking it in view of one of the lot security cams, notifying the police. But an alternative had come to Willy, a kind of dangle operation, which, providing it worked, might even relieve him of responsibility for routine maintenance of the Bayview Breakdown truck. So, after the cab interior had accumulated another week's worth of mess, he made sure to park the truck in the same spot it had occupied on the night of the burglary. Only this time he emptied out the coin reservoir himself, substituting a five-dollar bill, which he taped to the dash.

Next morning, same as before. The disks were sleeved, the windshield was washed, the trash—and the five—had vanished. And so it had gone for the past four months, the stranger apparently content with the arrangement, BB's job foreman assuming Willy was the one behind the weekly cleanings. An assumption Willy never bothered to discourage, lest the arrangement be brought to light.

There were occasions when the weekly five could have found better use, times when it had come to passing on a flick to keep up his end of the unspoken agreement; but just knowing he was playing tooth fairy to some street phantom surviving outside the system—maybe without so much as a room in an enforced share or a status ID card—was enough to get him through the movie pangs.

Bayview Breakdown owned a dozen trucks like the pre-Turn cube Willy drove three days a week. On other than Yellow Days—actual white-junk haulage days—Tony picked everyone up in one of the Porsche Mixte flatbeds BB garaged in Queens. Willy had been with the company for a little over a year, and was an apprentice in the trashers guild now. He'd signed on for dismantler work after two years of fighting tire fires in Jersey. The acrid smoke from those blazes had permanently darkened areas of his face the rebreather mask left exposed and robbed his singing voice of the highs he was once known for.

"White" over the years had come to mean not only refrigerators, washers, and dryers, but any household appliance whose capacitors contained polychlorinated biphenyls—air conditioners, microwave ovens, whatever. Almost all of these dated back a good sixty years, before aerogel insulation, when PCB-insulated capacitors had been used to regulate current in electric motors. When disposal became problematic, homeowners had been forced to bear the burden, banishing damaged or obsolete units to basements, backyards, or already crowded garages. Storage spaces invariably filled up, and that was when people turned to companies like Bayview Breakdown, whose crack crews would dismantle the ancient things, seeing to the safe removal of hazardous materials and the recycling of usable materials.

Routinely Willy would cruise by Tony's share in Queens to pick him up, but this morning Tony met him at the truck, having spent the night with a forty-year-old divorcée he'd met at a social club on Bruckner Boulevard.

"It was fucking un-believable," he told Willy as they made for Frank Keeghan's share in Brooklyn, "the babe just wanted to ad-lib all night. Ba-*boom*, ba-*boom*, ba-*boom*, like I've got some kinda reciprocating pole driver tucked away in my trousers, you know what I mean? It was fucking un-believable. But it's like I told you, you hit the clubs at the end of Celibacy Week, you're gonna do more ad-libbing in tree days than you usually do in tree weeks. Ba-*boom*, ba-*boom*, ba-*boom* . . ."

Tony was thirty-one, over six feel tall, with a crooked nose and single thick eyebrow. He wore his jet black hair brushed straight back to display the scars left from a beating he'd taken at the hands of a green beret eco-gang who'd caught him pissing against a light pole late one Saturday night.

All the way across the bridge into Queens and south along the crowded highways to Brooklyn, Tony regaled Willy with stories of his recent conquests. "The AIDS?" he said when Willy inquired. "Hell, I slip the old dipstick into a can of coverguard before I check the oil, you know what I mean?"

Frank "Felt Tip" Keeghan wasn't waiting at the curb, so Tony had to run up four flights to get him. Six months ago, before the tyfin sign had been posted prohibiting neighborhood noise before 10 A.M., Willy might have leaned on the horn. Felt Tip was the new kid at Bayview Breakdown, so Tony and Willy usually stuck him with the actual hands-on dismantling while they safeboxed the capacitors and separated the components for recycling pickup. He was a red-faced, rawboned, nineteen-year-old with the longest reach Willy'd ever seen, already getting an earful from Tony when the two emerged from the walk-up five minutes later and climbed into the cab. Keeghan's jumpsuit looked freshly laundered, his big knuckles seriously barked from slips of the wrench.

Willy took side streets to the Southern State Freeway and headed out-island. Interbust traffic was crawling in the side lanes, RPEV carpools in the center and magnetic induction re-charge lanes moving right along.

"So what's it gonna be, huh boys?" Tony opening the disk carrier and appraising the selection. "A little cardiofunk, or some classic rap?"

Willy shot him a look. "Thought we had a deal on that rap."

Tony pursed full lips. "So whaddaya wanna slot, Wills, some more of that fuckin' speech flake bullshit? More noise art?" He gave his head a condescending shake. "You guys from La Bronx . . . You're all on the air."

"Go with the rap," came from the rear, Felt Tip crossing freckled arms across the backs of the two front seats.

"Two to one and rap it is," Tony said, gloating, a Phone Phreaks disk in hand. He slipped it into the player and maxed the volume, Willy wincing as amplified touch-tones punched from the speakers. "Jus' keep your eyes open for police presence!" Tony shouted above the illegal noise.

Up all night working on one of his own Synclavier speech flake compositions, Willy was scarcely in the mood for the stri-dent wailings of some what-was funk band, but neither was he in the mood to argue aesthetics with Tony, whose idea of profound was a lyric he couldn't understand.

Willy'd grown up on bands like the Phone Phreaks, only it wasn't industrial disco or dancecore that had influenced him as much as the pre-Turn works of John Cage, Philip Glass, and the *musique concrete* of the digitalists—Sweeny and Holland, Yan-nis Xenakis, Heitor Villa-Lobos. Especially Tod Machover's *Valis,* which had been based on a half-century-old print novel by an sf writer named Philip K. Dick. Most of the digitalist com-positions owed something to Clifford Pickover's notion of "speech flakes," which were sound portraits of a sort—computer-generated visual patterns that resembled multicolored snowflakes with sixfold symmetry. The discovery that any data—statistical charts, chemical composition graphs—could be speech flaked was what had led to Sweeny and Holland's urine-analysis-chart composition. Villa-Lobos had used the skyline of New York and the contours of the Andes to define melodies on a conventional musical staff. The starting points for one of Xe-nakis's aleatory pieces had been Poisson's law of the distribution of random events. These were the people who had been pushing the pre-Turn musical envelope; not the parochial stylings of rap or rock musicians but the *artistes* who'd emerged from the In-stitut de Recherche et Coordination in Paris, the ones plugged

into samplers, waveform analyzers, MIDIs and 8X audio pro-
cessors; the ones who were in search of hyperinstrumentality,
response music, the unheard-of sounds. What was Really Going
On—musically, at least.

For Willy and the few who shared his vision, there was no pu-
rity to be found in the noise that assaulted you from the tube or
from the stage in some mainstream club, or in the self-indulgent
digitals distributed by download publishers who marketed on the
computer net. Because what all these club players and bedroom
musicians and *aota gai* were leaving out was the idea that music
should be spontaneous and interactive. Tribal. Pure Music wasn't
meant to be structured, studied, recorded; it was meant to be performed live and influenced by an audience, which wasn't there
simply to listen but to participate. Each instance of moodswing,
each separate smile or yawn or ill-timed cough had to be absorbed
and incorporated into the composition. Mood Music of a completely new sort. And Willy had been chasing it for ten years now:
looking for some way to wire the audience for responses, to fit the
seats of a concert hall with galvanic skin-response scanners, or
better still with neural-interface headbands, and to have those responses influence the Sound. Some people thought it revolutionary; none, unfortunately, were members of the Arts Advisory
Council. So Willy remained one of the unrecognized, the warehouse a pipe dream, frustrated at every turn by structured com-
positions, recycled rhythms, banal lyrics; encouraged to sit
passively in clubs and concerts while some provincial player
forced *music* into his ears . . .

The Phone Phreak disk was still on when they exited at Westhampton, Tony reluctantly agreeing to lower the volume as Willy, following the directions BB's dispatcher had downloaded to
the truck's routing computer, angled the old interbust through a
neighborhood of upscale homes. Even here, sections of front and
backyard were tilled for early planting—lawns being pretty much
a thing of the past throughout Long Island—fruit trees in bud,
signs by the roadside advertising homegrown produce. Pre-Turn,
for at least the first few years after the gardening trend had taken
hold, almost everything reaped from the ground was discovered
to be contaminated with toxins dumped by landfill contractors
over the course of the previous decade. Some of the mutant
results of those poisoned, acidic harvests had become collectible
art. But things were on the mend now, and Long Island's sandy
soil produced some of the best tomatoes to be had outside a
Monsanto hydroponic farm.

Willy checked the routing map and steered the truck into a narrow driveway leading to an immense waterfront house. He let out a soft whistle as the place came into full view, its lighthouse tower given a gloomy look by the tinted glass of the interbust's wraparound windshield.

"Jus' your kinda place, huh, Wills?" Tony said, with a broad smile.

"Yeah, me and the two hundred people in my building." Willy pulled up at a three-bay, switching off the ignition. "Who the hell lives here—the German ambassador?"

"Nah, name's Cola, something like that." Tony and Frank climbed out, slamming the doors behind them. Tony was still talking when Willy joined them at the rear of the truck. "—something to do with convenience stores."

Willy unlocked the rollup door and reached for his toolbox. "What, like Quick Fix?"

" 'We make shopping a rush,' " Felt Tip said, quoting the chain's advertising slogan, but Tony only shrugged.

A household facilitator in uniform answered the front door and directed them around to the side entrance, along a tiled walk bordered by tulips and daffodils. Willy surveyed the gas-barrier windows, the solar panels, the tropical hardwood trim. Figured the place for fifteen, maybe twenty years old, born of the pre-Turn *baubiologie* movement—a healthful house, the so-called "Senshaus." Formaldehyde-free plywood; insulation derived from seawater minerals; natural grouts; wood finishes made from citrus-peel oil, juniper berries, and rosemary. Inside there'd be plenty of brick and solid wood and vitreous tile; cork, linoleum, and stone; plenty of goat hair and jute rugs; a hydroponic garden. English ivy to swallow up off-gassing benzene, warneckei for the trichloroethylenes, philodendrons, Golden Pothos, Mother-in-Law's Tongue . . . Air filtration and pollution-monitoring system were computer controlled; the light bulbs would be full-spectrum. Air-conditioning and heating worked on a heat pump that extracted hot and cold air from recycled well water, with heat-recovery ventilators to draw out stale air and bring in the fresh.

Based on what he saw of the kitchen and the den beyond, Willy decided he was on target. None of your Ikea crap in here, your "centrally produced solutions." Paradise: but apparently not untroubled, given the argument in progress elsewhere in the house.

"You're not just running out of here and leaving all this to me," a woman was shouting. "I'm sick and tired of doing all the dirty work. *You* call up the contractor and tell him you're not satisfied with the job. I'm always playing the heavy. It's no wonder he doesn't want to listen to me."

Tony's eyebrows bobbed in a display of amusement as he squeezed past Willy on the way to the basement steps. Felt Tip followed behind, toolboxes dangling from both hands. The household facilitator, a short, heavyset woman sporting rubber gloves and a hair net, ignored the fracas, as did a handsome dark-complected youth seated in the breakfast nook, reading the back of a Captain Planet cereal box.

"I'll call him, for Christ sake, I'll call him," a man's voice bellowed from somewhere beyond the den. "But remember this, Didi, you're the one that insisted on travertine for the patio. Me, I coulda lived with brick. Christ, I coulda lived without a goddamned patio!"

Willy noticed an opened case of ouzo on the floor, a customs declaration form on a countertop nearby.

"And we *are* going to the theater tonight," from the woman again. "So don't think you can call me from the store and make some lame excuse about last-minute business. Seven o'clock at Sardi's, Charles, and not a minute later, is that understood?"

Willy waited for the response, but none was forthcoming.

"Charles?" the woman said. "Charles, are you listening to me? Charles!"

The basement was like dozens Willy had seen: a graveyard for kitchen appliances, radios, VCRs, stereo components, rear projection TVs, cappuccino machines, vacuum cleaners, cameras, recorders, typewriters, video monitors, computer CPUs, room ionizers, dish antennae, gooseneck lamps, exercise equipment, radar and radon detectors, lawn mowers, old tires, plastic garbage pails, boxes of nicad batteries. The piece the Colas wanted removed was a washer/dryer stack they must have carried with them from their previous residence.

While Tony got Felt Tip started on the dismantling, Willy began to wander around, picking up this and that, fiddling with toggle switches and adjustment knobs, like he'd done as a kid in hands-on science museums. But respectful of the fact he was dealing with someone else's property, even if most of it was worthless. It was just a way of killing time until there was significant work for him to do, which usually amounted to color-marking metals and glass for collection. Chances were they'd be making the pickup themselves in the Porsche, but with BB you never knew, so it was best to code it all and be done with it.

He was in a small room near the back of the basement when a glint of reflected fluorescent off the tuning knob of a CB radio caught his eye. Well, what looked like a tuning knob—of what looked something like a CB radio. Only after scrutinizing the thing for several seconds did he understand it to be a player of some sort. Damned if he could determine the format, though—diskette, cassette, sound chip?—let alone find the battery compartment or photovoltaic grid. What the hell was it, a pre-Turn gizmo some bizarro spokesperson had peddled to insomniacs on the late-night tube? A curio sold through ads in the back pages of New Age print mags? A hoozamajig invented by an eccentric family member—?

His finger touched something that activated the device and sound filled the room. Sound as he'd never heard it before.

It seemed to be as much inside as outside him, and while it wasn't exactly *melodic*, there was a phrasing, a suggestion of leitmotif that carried him along, almost working on him, taking him places—

Suddenly unnerved, he set the device down and stepped away from it, only to find himself tracked by a thin beam of red light emanating from what he'd taken for the tuning knob. The light centered on his chest, then fanned to encompass him from forehead to groin, wavering slightly, as though rustled by an updraft.

Willy tensed, allowing the light to explore him before risking a side step toward the doorway. The light followed him, the sound varying as he moved; in fact each movement brought about a change in timbre and pitch. Willy listened, mesmerized by the harmonics, which now resembled the hammered-out metalophonic frenzy of a gamelan orchestra. There were those same rhythmic shifts and eerie overtones, effects that seemed to play less to the ear than the endocrine system or chakras.

Willy stood like a conductor, waving his hands about, trying to see if he could elicit a tempo change; but the occult players had apparently found their groove and were sticking to it.

Until Tony yelled for him from elsewhere in the basement. Willy didn't respond, didn't move, and yet the sound modulated through a kind of phase transition, almost . . . almost as though the device *had read his moodswing*! Like the damn thing had been taking musical cues from his heartbeat, his aura, his infrared output—

"Wills!" Tony closer now.

Willy muttered, "Shit," snatched the phone from his belt, and quickly keyed his home number, hoping to connect with his answering machine, get some of the sound on tape, but the interference in the basement was too great.

Then Tony was standing in the doorway. "Wills, what the fuck, didn't you hear me calling you?" He regarded the narrow beam of red light with interest. "What zat, some kind of motion detector?" He pressed his hands to his ears. "Jeez, talk about your anti-intrusion alarms, thing would send me running soon enough."

Willy re-belted the phone and reached for the device, turning it about in his hands. "I can't figure out how to zero it."

The sound was agitated, frantic, panicked.

Tony snatched the thing from his hands and flipped it over. "Off!" he tried, but the sound only increased in volume and began to grate. "Fucking-A." Tony shook it; ultimately resorted to dropping it to the floor.

The light went out and the sound died. Tony grinned and made a dusting motion with his hands. "Just gotta know how to reason with these things.

The Arab in the striped galabia and tattered fez managed to cop a feel while he was helping the French woman down into the boat. Lucky watched the woman whirl on the dark little man, whose smile revealed at least three missing teeth, firing off a string of Parisian invectives and taking hold of her breast, as if to say: *This is my property, asshole, and I'm the only one who gets to fondle it, understand?*

But the Arab, whom Lucky had heard speak French only moments before, pretended not to, adding a servile series of bows before turning away to render all-hands assistance to another female passenger. This one, a blond and broad-hipped American, hauled off and punched him the minute his hand touched her thigh.

Foreign flesh as a perk, a form of baksheesh, Lucky decided. Especially when the flesh that visited the boatman's small piece of Nile bank came packaged in sheer tube tops and satiny microshorts. A misconception that wasn't restricted to Luxor, either. There was that guide with the flashlight at the Sphinx, showing around the Italian guy in Lycra . . . Well, at least chauvinism had been abolished, and who was to say the *fellahin* who worked the small boats in Luxor hadn't misunderstood the notion of helping hands.

In a moment the small boat with its cargo of twenty or so tourists was underway, the towering pylons, obelisks, and papyrus-bud columns of the Temple of Luxor rising into view above horse-drawn carriage traffic along the Corniche. A quarter mile south, the Hagadorn Palace hovercraft, flanked by fiberglass dhows and feluccas, was docking at the city's major West Bank attraction, the theme park known as Thebes World.

It was a distress call from the Luxor chapter of the Character Actors Guild that had brought Lucky to Egypt, and while a Nile cataract, a hydroelectric dam, and Lake Sadat itself stood between him and the Sudan border, he disliked being so close to Bulaful. Although what with the baleful daily messages and crocodile threats the avenging shaman was leaving on the answering machine and e-mail board, anywhere on planet Earth could be deemed too close.

Lucky's fingertips traced the outline of the suspect saucerette he'd slipped into the pouch pocket of his trousers upon departing New York. The thing should have been back where it belonged in the neighborhood Quick Fix by now, but Lucky had left the share so shaken by Rashad's morning prank he'd forgotten all about stopping by the convenience store. What happens when you wake up to find you've somehow misplaced your own reflection, Lucky told himself. He had yet to figure how the mirrors in the share had been rigged to eliminate only *his* reflection—some video trick, he supposed—but, natch, Rashad had been on hand to capture Lucky's reactions on camera. The yawning amusement, the head-scratching puzzlement, the wide-eyed disbelief, the final pale-faced, terror-stricken howl . . .

Lucky was still shaking an hour later when he wobbled into Theme Park Advisory Group headquarters in the United Nations annex on East Forty-eighth Street. There, he was summoned straightaway to a task-force meeting to discuss new directives handed down by the group's director, Arbor Slocum.

"Lemme make sure I've got this straight," Lucky recalled saying when he'd been given his assignment. "You want me to count aliens?"

"Correct, Mr. Junknowitz. We want a head count on just how many extraterrestrials are out there."

"Out there. As in staffing the parks."

The director had gone on to explain that the UN Planning Commission for Extraterrestrial Development was suddenly interested in reviving Earth's space program, which—discounting the phasing of the SDI architecture and the orbiting of various astro and telecomm sats, scopes, and scanners—had been put on hold since the Turn.

"There's even talk of completing the space station," Arbor Slocum added. "And a possible Mars voyage."

And some company called Phoenix Enterprises was interested in developing a theme park devoted entirely to science-fiction aliens.

"Garden of Unearthly Delights?" Lucky had asked.

Slocum assured him that the park would be big. Huge.

"Under the circumstances," she'd told him, "it seems prudent that we begin to promote a reawareness, through the parks, of science-fiction themes: the potential, perhaps, for encountering evidence of extraterrestrial biological entities."

Okay . . . Lucky'd thought. Nearly every theme park had a science-fiction attraction—a *Star Tours*, an *E.T. Experience*, a *Zone Defense*. And it would be simple enough to call up a head count from the computer—individual profiles on each actor cast as an sf character if need be. But what Slocum wanted were "personal assessments" of each themer. Which was going to mean a visit to some four hundred individual parks! The miles Lucky would be facing—surely enough to take him to the moon—were just beginning to register when the emergency call from Thebes World had come in . . .

The park, opened six years earlier and still uncompleted, covered several hundred West Bank acres across the Nile from Luxor, stretching from the river west to the Colossi of Memnon and north to the Ramesseum and Temple of Hatshepsut at Deir el-Bahri. It had a skyway link to the Valley of the Kings just the other side of the sandstone Theban Hills, burial ground of Middle Kingdom pharaohs like Amenhotep the Second and Tutankhamun. The Disney/Saudi consortium that raised the place had struck a licensing deal with Matsu-Universal Studios and Hanna-Barbera, resulting in many of the rides being designed around cartoon characters as well as figures of Egyptian historical interest. The venue's themers reflected the odd mix in characters like Huckleberry Horus, Deputy Ra, and Yogi Ptah.

Attractions and services were signposted in Arabic, French, English, and pictographs done in hieroglyphic fashion—rest rooms indicated by cartouches depicting stylized urinals and toilet-paper scrolls. The restaurants served falafel, molokhia, shwarma sandwiches, and several date-based delicacies; and the souvenir stands sold worry beads, hookah pipes, Korean-made Egyptian antiquities, *gutta* headcloths and the ersatz-camel-hair *agaals* that kept them in place. The crowd was mainly European, but there were always plenty of Middle Easterners about, wealthy families from Saudi Arabia and the Emirates, the women in embroidered black, hands and feet painted with Iranian henna, the men in diamond rings and elegant white *thobes*. The on-site mosque—a scaled-down version of Cairo's famous Rifali—featured guest muezzins every Friday.

Lucky showed his credentials to a Japanese security guard at the gate and was directed to the office of the local CAG rep, a stout Egyptian woman named Kawkab, who had a trace of mustache and spoke English with a thick accent.

"Praise Allah, you've come," she said, grasping Lucky's right hand while Lucky's left was busy batting flies from his face. "Ahmed is completely beyond reach."

"The one you called about."

"Yes. He's our Cosmo Spacely, at the Jetson's *Turbo-Tour* attraction."

Count one science-fiction themer, Lucky thought. The *Turbo-Tour* was a mating of jiggle ride and large-format wraparound projection screen, the theater accommodating one hundred participants strapped into hydraulic simulation-seats.

"I first began to notice a change in his behavior last week. I should have acted sooner."

"*Maalesh*," Lucky told her in Arabic: No matter.

She appraised Lucky from her side of a wooden desk while an overhead fan squeaked through lazy rotations. "A case of TIC, I believe."

Kawkab pronounced the acronym "tick"—Themer Identification Crisis, a transient form of delusional metanoia, wherein a themer became possessed by the character he or she portrayed. TIC was the flip side of what some themers called "the Method"—that process by which one melded with the role. The goal was to pass beyond a mere portrayal of, say, Goofy, and in some sense *become* Goofy—to evince the pure embodiment of Goofyness. Treatment typically involved a brief stay in a deprogramming center, where therapists employed a combination of sedation and transactional analysis to return the client to reality. Nine out of ten times, a TIC-afflicted themer could be back to work within two weeks, but cases of irreversible metanoia were not unknown.

That Lucky had gone Goofy for a few hours one heatstroke

summer afternoon in Disney World had been taken as a positive sign by the Advisory Group's Dierdre Crankfield, who, in hiring Lucky, insisted on his taking in an intensive two-week course in field therapeutics—the idea being that on-site treatment should be given a shot, and in the belief that only a themer, even a former one, could heal a themer. Lucky's success rate had proven so high, in fact, that he himself was known on the circuit as something of a shaman.

Kawkab was wearing a pained look. "The thought of Ahmed being sent away for deprogramming . . ."

"Maybe I can talk him down on-site," Lucky said.

"*Inshallah*," she muttered. *If God wills it.*

Lucky nodded. "Where is he now?"

The CAG rep forced an exhale. "He's locked himself inside the *Jaws of Death*. A ride," she added, reacting to Lucky's puzzled look. "Perhaps you noticed it on the way in—the one with the huge crocodile mouth?"

ELEVEN

LEFT TO HIS own devices, Ziggy Forelock would have dis-interfaced the situation room's recorders of their vid and audio feeds, set them on white-noise scan, and sat back to see what they'd pick up; he'd see just what the telesphere had to offer this evening, just what videogeists might be inhabiting the Hagadorn Pinnacle's 120 midtown Manhattan stories. But, Ziggy's luck, then some downcaster would choose tonight to dazzle a security cam, card open a rest-room door, belly out a dumbed window to perch with one of the building's retro-deco gargoyles before taking that first step. And there'd be Ziggy without a machine set to record his handling of the crisis, opening himself up to an investigation by building management or a Citizen Watch sub-commission.

Working closely with the Urgent Care Centers and an untold number of concerned citizens, the Watch searched carefully for the disgruntled—people denied credit, employees fired from jobs, roomies driven to distraction by their sharemates—but a few malconents always slipped through.

No, Ziggy thought, best to leave the recorders as they were, 'faced with cams trained on emergency stairways, elevator in-teriors, stretches of carpeted corridor, a dozen popular drop-out spots elsewhere in the Pinnacle. At least two of the cameras, in fact, were trained on him in his monitor crypt in the building's situation room.

The board, with its array of flatscreens, cam controls, and voice-activated personal-network phones, allowed him to shift between downcaster hot spots and—thanks to the young hacker who worked the afternoon watch—corridor and room views nor-mally the exclusive domain of building security. The hacker, said to be a frequent flyer in the Virtual Network, had monkeyed with things so that anyone posted in the sit room could peek and poke through security's building-wide monitoring station, which was located in a monster hollow some twenty floors below. Security knew all about the illegal time-share but apparently didn't give a damn, so long as it was understood that leapers were the sole responsibility of the Watch group.

They were all in communication anyway, Ziggy had long ago decided, the security cams and scanners, the bank and super-market comps, the business and household smart gadgets aspiring to some eco-correct non-carbon-based life form. And if there wasn't an actual machine conspiracy in the works, there was at least a movement afoot to alter human reality—to fuzz the borders between reality and illusion, between humans and machines, so that their eventual takeover could be effected all the more smoothly. Ziggy needed only think of his own friends to verify his fears: Lucky and his Globalnet phone and pocket comp; Willy and his MIDIs, waveform analyzers, and sequencers; Braxmar and his idiot savant AI style-masters . . . Machines were becoming more like people and people were becoming more like machines.

But even with the system patch it wasn't often that you were treated to a peek inside an office or apartment complex; what you got mostly were scans and pans of citizens entering or leaving those denied areas. Ziggy's current view of the invited guests milling outside the entrance to Phipps Hagadorn's penthouse, for example. Harley Paradise and that Keating Price III among them.

Ziggy had run into the happy couple outside the building as he was surfacing from the sub stop on Forty-sixth, dusk settling over the city streets, Harley and Keating emerging from an a-cell stretch double-parked by the door, one of fifteen in a line of cars that turned the corner onto Park.

"Hey, Harley," he'd said, giving her an appreciative once-over, taffeta high-collar to open-toed shoes. "No need to've come enhanced to watch me work."

Harley shrugged deeper into her synthfur stole, putting a tighter hold on Keating's bulked biceps. "Always the charmer, Ziggy." Nasty curl to her glossed lip. "And nice to see your skin's cleared up. You look almost human."

Ziggy had laughed, falling back some while the courtesy person held the door for them, Harley showing him minimal smile as she sauntered by.

Ziggy said, "On your way up, huh, Harl? To the party, I mean." Stopping her dead.

Harley gave her head a haughty toss, but her medusa of rosewood hair didn't move. "I certainly hope so."

Hands cupped to his mouth, Ziggy said, "And I'll be sure to tell Lucky I bumped into you."

And now here she was onscreen, elbow to elbow with the celebs, the featured players, the Twenty-One, the mainstream important. The ones who'd given voice to the Turn, who claimed to be Planetists, sacrificing just like the extras. Only you'd never know it wasn't their movie to look at them, to watch them carding themselves into private spaces, to glimpse them emerging from the tinted enclosures of stretch a-cells. Even when they dropped into clubs like the Atopia, you had the sense they were just seeing how the extras were getting along. Sacrificing, Ziggy figured, meant dining out only three times a week, reducing one's personal entourage of sycophants and watchmen to a manageable size . . .

Due to the Pinnacle's recently enacted appearance-code regulations, Ziggy had had to lose the zits before showing up for his shift. No matter that cratered faces, bleach tattoos, frenzy cuts were the norm for half the would-be splatter cases he dealt with weekly—the disturbed and infirm, the victims of reg rage or surveillance syndrome, the failed artists, the share despairs, the ones he often intercepted in those very monitored stairways or corridors or talked down from some way high set-back perch. No matter either that he'd been hired precisely because of his obvious lack of "societal sensibilities," precisely because he was an artist of some local renown. The appearance-code regs were there to insure that everyone who worked the building, from Citizen Watch to maintenance, reflected the corporate image of self-esteem, balance, soundness of character.

A year of working the Pinnacle Watch and he had yet to lose anyone to the hard landing. Amounting to some fifty-four lives saved, fifty-four careers extended—fifty-five when he included himself, for he was continually talking himself down off one ledge or another, concrete or virtual. Not that he actually believed himself capable of taking "that first step," as some Watch counselors were calling it. Despite the frequent bouts with angst, weltschmerz, schadenfreude, anomie, lovesickness. Life's puzzle alone was enough to keep him from climbing some tower, the search for answers to what was Really Going On.

But who knew there wouldn't be a ledge with his name on it, a gargoyle bearing his urgent fingerprints if it hadn't been for his minor successes in the art world, the outside chance of having some of his work warehoused.

Validated.

Prior to the Pinnacle, he'd worked Watch on the Verrazano-Narrows, before the Bridge and Tunnel Authority phased the program and opted to install safety nets along the length of the bridge's central span—a move that not only discouraged leapers but bungee cord jumpers as well. But that had only driven the former to seek satisfaction from the taller of New York's towers, most of which, caught unawares, had inadvertently launched the final flights of more than one despondent citizen, prompting a few to follow the Verrazano's lead in installing catchalls, as the safety nets were known. The owners of the Pinnacle, however, reluctant to besmirch or otherwise affront the architectonic integrity of their tower, had refused to make any such concession, instead petitioning the Office of Social Management to position a Citizen Watch station in the building's depths.

Of course the Pinnacle would have drawn the dispirited and despairing even if it hadn't decided to work without a net, simply because of its history, its connection with Phipps Hagadorn, one of the survivors of the Turn, the chaotic wrap-up to an era fueled by greed. Reagan, Trump, and Noriega; Nabisco, Exxon, and Drexel; Perrier, Bloomingdale's, Johnson & Johnson, and the Hunt Brothers . . . But the West German Hagadorns, even while still linked to those pre-eco decades, had safely negotiated the crossing and gone on to prosper. So it was no wonder the building the family had raised to celebrate itself should have become such a magnet for those wishing to similarly immortalize themselves.

And no small irony that Ziggy should be the one to talk them out of it.

His skills as counselor came by way of past association with the Video Observation Research Project, a private foundation, which, by encouraging its informants—common folk from dozens of countries—to commit to videotape the critical cadences of everyday life, had been attempting to compile "an authorized anthropology of humankind." The requested data typically involved catching people off guard—in covertly shot footage—during moments of jubilation, ecstasy, euphoria, exhilaration, triumph, anger, anxiety, stress, intoxication, or defeat. Ziggy's work had entailed interviewing prospective participants (following guidelines developed by the Institute of Transactional Dynamics) and encouraging them to bare themselves or others to the camera—something few were hesitant to do, having grown up on pre-Turn TV shows in which those willing to do just that had been afforded instant celeb status.

Ziggy had quit the organization when he'd learned that personal-profile dossiers and stats were being sold off to Urgent Care Centers and consumer market-research companies; but by then he had already proven himself to be an able communicator with the star-struck, much as Lucky was with themers.

The years with VORP, in any event, were only a reflection of Ziggy's deep obsession with recorded reality, as evidenced by his "Freeze-Frame Moments From Famous Flicks." These out-size stills captured the transitional moments between cinematic scenes, where manufactured realities were superimposed, often yielding images of startling complexity and serving to emphasize how audiences were at the mercy of editors and directors—power brokers who wished to convince that what they offered were visions of artistic truth, when in fact all an audience experienced was an artificial construct comprised of discontinuously filmed scenes.

For film, like life, was a mere piecing together, a collage—the grammar of both falling subject to editing. Ziggy's ideal film would have been the unedited one-shot: not a pastiche of scenes but real life, a portrait of what was Really Going On.

"Our eyes aren't keen enough to spot the transitions," Ziggy would tell anyone who would listen. Any more than we had eyes to separate the real from the unreal in our waking lives. Our vision of reality had been shaped by a hundred years of looking at and experiencing life through a camera lens.

This was how the councils that edited our reality had proliferated, how regulations passed into the culture unnoticed, how we dismissed the anomalous events, the footnotes to reality, as errors in recording or perception. We didn't give credence to incidents reported by the tabloids or the news comp service back screens, or to the bizarre incidents Asia Boxdale's insurance policies covered—the mysterious disappearances, the invisible assailants, the freak plagues and mass panics, the rains of animate objects—because we had forgotten how to read the transitional frame, instances where the stretch marks of the paradigm were best observed. And so too we ignored the cases of scientific stigmata—the anomalies in the micro or macro worlds, whether FTL particles or a case of fusion in a jar—because we were afraid of examining things too closely. This, despite our fascination for scopes and colliders; frightened of what we might find, frightened to look into the face of what was about to break through.

But Ziggy wasn't afraid to look. Especially now that his home VDRs were picking up phantom broadcasts, snippets from family sitcoms and Australian docudramas, which, as near as he could tell, weren't being broadcast from anywhere on Earth; they were apparently originating from *somewhere out there*— from some sort of TV version of the noosphere, a newly born info layer of the atmosphere.

Ziggy swiveled to face one of the cameras trained on him, wondering on just whose screens in just what boards he was appearing. And was that unknown monitor in building security or that lone cop in his or her far-off crypt in the heart of the city closing on Ziggy or one of the partial Hagadorn dinner party views Ziggy had called onscreen? And was there some monitor beyond that? Watchers watching watchers watching watchers watching . . .

He gave the board screens another look, checking the corridors and trouble spots before returning to the penthouse foyer scene. He tracked Harley's movements for a time: she was working the crowd, exchanging air-kisses with the near and genuine famous. Keating, too, was holding forth from what he apparently considered a personal power spot near the bar, where he stood in a somewhat spread-legged stance, tall drink in hand, faltering only when he realized that Harley had networked her way into an introduction to Phipps Hagadorn himself—the two of them actually talking together.

To the obvious exclusion of everyone else around them.

Ziggy closed on Keating's dashed expression and studied it for a long moment while a broad grin took shape on his own face. "On your way up, Harl," he announced, toasting the screen with an invisible glass.

Then for his favorite part: A tap on the screen and they all disappeared.

"Coming up on our right is Jason Duplex," Eddie Ensign told his group of seven star-stalkers, who immediately broke from the huddle they'd formed around him, spreading out in front of the theater entrance with camcorders locked and loaded. Not fifteen minutes before, they'd sighted the ever-present pop vocalist Meena D in the company of her agent, Morse Webber. But Jason Duplex represented a real find. Rarely seen in public,

Duplex had starred in some of the top-grossing action films of the decade—*Illegal Aid, Out of Bounds,* and the science-fiction classic, *Zone Defense*—and here he was sauntering down West Forty-fourth this fine evening with blacktress and alleged love interest Brigit Miner on his right arm. Meena D, turning up as often as she did, at rallies and fundraisers, was something of a Year Star, but the lanky, square-jawed Duplex . . . Duplex was one for the List. Perhaps not a National Treasure like a Schwarzenegger or a Murphy, but definitely a life celeb.

Although Jason's celebrated mandible wasn't much in evidence just now, having been re-formed to resemble a Jay Leno by the same cosmeticians and camoflesh specialists who'd colored Duplex's hair and doctored his ears. Figure in the lifts, and the megastar was even walking a few inches taller than his usual six-one.

Eddie had been tipped to his attending the musical's opening-night performance by a couple of phreaks who regularly cruised the Virtual Net for comp commo between celebs and their agents, managers, close friends. He'd then placed a call to a mole, Eddie's employer had inserted in the Hollywood Cosmetologists Guild to learn just what sort of camoflesh he should be on the lookout for. Still, even without the advance intelligence, Eddie was confident he would have been able to out Duplex. Though only a journeyman with the guild, he had a natural eye for falseflesh, an ear for famous voices, a nose finely tuned to designer scents.

"In case you're wondering, that's Brigit Miner with him," Eddie saying it at normal volume now that everyone in the group had emerged from their blind adjacent to the theater. Duplex and Miner were marching through the brass doors, throwing over-the-shoulder curses at the stalkers, who'd at least had sense enough to keep a safe distance, paparazzing the couple from every conceivable angle.

Then the celeb calls began, some in close approximation of Duplex's raspy tenor.

"Left the limo home tonight, huh, Jason?" someone shouted.

"Loved ya in *Zone Defense,* babe."

"Congrats on the jump in your Q rating."

"When are you and Brigit gonna make it legal?"

The LCD tyfin sign just inside the theater door read, THANK YOU FOR NOT TALKING, COUGHING, SNEEZING, UNWRAPPING CANDY, WEARING ELECTRONIC WATCHES, PORTABLE PHONES OR PERSONAL INFORMATION SYSTEMS DURING THE PERFORMANCE.

Cams being what they were, anyone would think photophobia was what-was by now, disappeared like contact sports. But that wasn't the case with Hollywood celebs or action figures, the majority of whom could be relied on to bristle the moment a lens was focused on them and they weren't being paid for it. Of course, the reactions only made for better footage: glares, growls, glowers, contemptuous grimaces you never saw on the Big Screen.

Used to be, people were content with reading the gossip columns in print news, taking a still photo of a star from behind a cordon line of cops and hired muscle, risking a request for an autograph. Since the Turn, however, the emphasis was on the motion shot—a mere sighting was no longer enough to enable one to list the stalked celeb in a personal register. What field glasses had been to birders a century before, camcorders were to star-stalkers.

Probably be the last time Jason Duplex would venture out without his watchmen, Eddie thought. Notwithstanding how quickly an entourage could compromise one's cover. But celebs were fair game in any event—the legitimacy of the hobby proven by the cases of libel that could arise from shooting celebs from a bad angle. Bodyguards could shield their charges by stepping between them and the cameras, but the law disallowed their becoming violent or abusive.

After some five years of star-stalking for Eye Spy—"Truth in people packaging"—Eddie's own North America Life List numbered some four hundred celebs, including representatives of several extinct genres from before the days of socially conscious filmmaking: contact-sports action figures, astronauts, celebs who'd starred in pornos, ultraviolents, car-chase and slasher flicks. But the real payoff came in getting someone like Duplex to visit one of the technology-dependent kids Eddie worked with, or securing a guest pass to a concert or a movie premier for some Virtual Net wizard confined to a wheelchair. Which happened more frequently than was commonly known.

At least two more cin stars were expected to attend the musical, but Eddie's sources had only been able to give a "possible" on their showing. It was off season, after all, and most celebs were either on location or tucked away in ranchettes in Idaho and Montana. Peak season for Hollywood celebs was early summer, still a month off, when the studios put their best efforts into general release.

To compensate for the lack of live action, Eddie'd spent most of the day traipsing around Gotham, escorting the group from one famous film locale to another: the *Gremlins* Building, the *Kong* Tower, the *Ghostbusters* High Rise, *the Working Girl townhouse* . . . A thankless task. He would have favored a job as guide on the Grand Circuit, flights on MGM Grand to Grace-land and the major Movie Meccas—the now Japanese-owned *Field of Dreams*, the Jim Morrison Cave in Arizona, the Spiel-berg Tor in Wyoming, the *Ten Commandments* temple in Guad-alupe, California, the *Twin Peaks* Hotel—but those tours were reserved for the guild's master lensmen, Eye Spy's elite.

Better yet would have been a shot at the CCC, the Cannes Celeb Count, which was still considered the Superbowl of star-stalking.

But maybe it was like Lucky Junknowitz always said: There was no real fun in traveling if it didn't take you to new worlds, faraway wonders, adventures of the unedited sort.

"Good call on Duplex," Asia Boxdale said, taking an oppor-tunity to sidle up to him before the group returned, her long fingers doing a Thai dancer's waver in front of his face.

Asia claimed to be along for the fun of it, although Eddie suspected she was researching a routine to include in one of her interactive performances. No matter, so long as she didn't base any of her stuff on him and wind up making him the laughing-stock of the South Bronx as she'd once done to Lucky. Inad-vertently, to hear her tell it.

Asia pushed her long hair back from her face. "D'you know he was coming, or was that your spotter's eye at work?"

"Little of both," Eddie said, opting for the truth. "But Meena D was a straight call."

Asia laughed, poked him in the ribs. "Meena, come on, even I could have outed her. How many women you know can wear a chiffon shift with fishing boots and not be hauled in for Urgent Care?"

Eddie gave Asia's outfit of bodysuit, classic blazer, and rub-ber gloves a lingering look. "You could."

She tugged at the green beret he'd insisted on her wearing, giving it a rakish tilt. "I'll take that as a compliment—especially among this bunch."

Eddie turned to survey his seven clients, who were talking excitedly about the sighting as they regrouped. Just your basic New York assortment. Not a group that cared about following the yearly migrations to Cannes, Telluride, Missoula, or seeking out celebs in their native habitats; but one content to stalk and list in their own patch, camcorder in one hand, a copy of *Jayne's Field Guide to the Stars* in the other.

Where two years ago Eddie might have disguised them as Japanese tourists fresh from some Harlem soul-food tour or a group of themers doing street-corner promotion, he had everyone outfitted in green berets and bodysuits tonight, to maintain their cover as an eco-conscious street gang standing watch at the tempting stretch of empty wall next to the theater. In much the same way the Hagadorn Pinnacle refused to install catchalls, the theater refused to smart-surface the stretch with spray repellent, which had only served to designate it as a primary target for graffiti terrs allied with the Glossnost Movement, whose stated purpose was to deface each of the city's so-called "pristine horizons."

Thus far the eco-correct outfits had served everyone well, and the wall made for an effective blind. But the musical itself was the real bait. Billed as a review, "Stairways to Heaven" featured sanitized versions of pre-Turn songs popularized by rock 'n' rollers like the Stones, the Who, the Dead, and Guns N' Roses, along with segue skits that lampooned the sociopolitical climate of those times, taking shots along the way at drug-taking hippies, flower-wielding antiwar protesters, disaffected minorities, self-deluded seekers, self-infatuated yuppies, and corrupt politicians. It was the biggest show to hit the White Way since "Din!," the musical based on the old black-and-white Kipling-inspired flick.

Asia was about to say something when Eddie cut her off, his eye caught by a broad-shouldered figure emerging from an interbust cab. The man barely topped five-ten but what there was of him was perfectly proportioned and rock solid; squeezed, though, into a dweeb-looking salmon-colored tux. Neither the black skin nor the beard gave Eddie pause.

"Spider Mojo," he announced to the group, "trophy-winning action figure currently with the Braves." The group closed on Spider just as his wife was stepping from the car. Unlike Jason Duplex, however, the "Motiontronic Marvel" smiled for the cams, even passed a hand across his brow to smear the applied camo color.

Eddie was still crowing about it when Willy Ninja *pssst!*ed him from the shadows of the stage-entrance doorway.

Asia hurried over to scoop him on the cheek. "Jeez, this is

getting like old shares week. All we need now's Lucky, Brax, and La Zig.''

"Zig's on evening Watch,'' Willy told her, plainly preoccupied with scanning the crowd of theatergoers gathering at the brass doors. "Lucky's out of town. And last I heard, Brax was with you.'' Finally cutting his dark eyes to hers. With Willy's Cherokee cheekbones and Asia's jet-black mane, they could have passed for a couple of themers cast for Frontierland, save that Willy was still in his Breakdown work clothes.

"Brax is working on his book project,'' Asia countered, defensive in spite of herself. "I tried to convince him to meet me for dinner, but he says he's not leaving the loft till he learns what drugs Etaoin Shrdlu was under when he wrote 'Tug of War.' ''

Willy's brows beetled. "Etaoin whaa?''

"What are you doing down here, chief?'' Eddie walked over to ask while the group was shooting Spider. "Did I tell you I was going to be here?''

"Maybe you did, but you're not why I'm here.''

Eddie appraised his friend. "What's with the jumpsuit?''

Willy scanned the crowd once more before lowering his head, furtive, conspiratorial. "I came straight from work. We were out on the Island. Westhampton.''

"Lucky you,'' Asia started to say.

"White-junking for this big-bucks guy. Smart house on the water, all-natural materials, hydroponic—that's Ashley Steel.'' Motioning to the theater crowd with his chin.

Asia and Eddie whirled at the same time, eyes roving. "Where? Which one?'' This from Eddie, dubious.

"In the parachute pants and neckties. Got her hair pulled back, round glasses.''

Eddie located the woman and stared. "You sure?''

"She's wearing a 'flesh nose.''

Asia squinted, saying, "You can tell that from here?''

"Damn eagle eye,'' Eddie muttered, shaking his head in wonderment. "You're right, though, it's her.'' Rushing off then to inform the group.

Asia beamed. "Ooh, handsome young Indian make Cambodian girl swoon with delight.'' She collapsed, certain Willy would catch her; she surfaced from his arms laughing. "So that's why you're down here—to brush up on your star-stalking?''

Willy shook his head, serious now, giving Asia a quick rundown on the device he'd found in the basement of the Cola place, the unearthly sounds it emitted, his sense that the thing had been somehow tuned to respond to emotional fluctuations.

"You mean like some kind of mood reader?" Asia asked when she could.

"Yep. Then the idiot I work with goes and drops the thing on the floor when we can't convince it to zero."

"Oof. Bet that convinced it."

Willy nodded. "Didn't work when I tried it again. But I gotta know where they got the thing." Willy's eyes searched the crowd. "Guy's some convenience-store honcho."

Asia wrinkled her face. "Try not to hold that against him."

"I'm thinking maybe he's some kind of inventor or closet musician. Or maybe some friend or relative cobbled the thing together. Anyway, I heard his wife say something about their going to a show. Later on I got her to tell me which one without saying why I wanted to know."

Asia fell silent, thinking things through. "Well, I doubt this guy's any kind of genius if he's coming to see 'Stairways.' "

Willy frowned. "Okay, it was the wife's idea, how do I know."

"So what are you planning to do, just go up to him and ask him about the . . . thing?"

"Can't do that, uh-uh, I don't want him to think I was messing with his stuff."

"But you *were* messing with his stuff—"

"Here he comes."

Asia turned in time to see a short, somewhat paunchy man climb from the back of an a-cell sedan. Large head, glasses, flat feet by the way he waddled. The woman with him—tall, small-featured—was smartly attired in a satin gown and high heels, pearls, and a touch of platinum. They were obviously moneyed, although there seemed to be something deliberately understated about them, almost as if they'd both gone out of their way to cloak themselves in anonymity.

"Mr. and Mrs. Westhampton," Asia said.

"Cola," Willy emended.

"I only meant—"

"Damn, I can't just go up to him." Willy rubbed his chin, took a few steps toward the theater crowd, then turned to Asia. "You think maybe I could convince a couple of Eddie's clients to shoot some footage of him?"

Fully opened, the plastic and painted-canvas croc locks of the *Jaws of Death* had to be three stories high, front feet either side large as midsize a-cells. And when they closed—with crowd-drenching gushes of water from the gaps between ten-foot-long incisors and an amplified snap that was heavy on the bass—you could sight down the knobby pointed snout all the way to the reptile's ferocious yellow eyes.

What with Cosmo Spacely secreted inside, raving about being cheated out of a condominium site by George Jetson, the ride had been shut down. Lucky, however, had no option but to enter by way of the mouth, since the delusional themer had disabled the locks on all the access doors and emergency exits. Kawkab had volunteered to accompany him into the belly of the beast, but Lucky had insisted on going it alone.

The *Jaws of Death*, the CAG rep had explained to him, was your standard interval-loader ride-through attraction—in this case by current-driven boat—dark and mildly menacing, fraught with close calls, sudden drops, pop-up holo effects, animatronic starts. Only *Jaws* wasn't based on as innocent a tale as *Peter Pan* or *E.T.*, no *effendi*, but on the resurrection myth of Osiris, ancient Egypt's Lord of Death.

Seemed that Osiris's reputation as something of a womanizer had earned him celebrity status among the humans of Way Back—kind of a Warren Beatty thing—a circumstance that brought out the green-eyed monster in fellow demiurge, Seth, Osiris's very competitive brother, who may have been suffering from a case of Size Inadequacy Syndrome. Seth, in any event, one day invited the well-endowed Osiris to a dinner party, at which was displayed Seth's latest acquisition, a beautifully appointed sarcophagus—custom-designed and modified—promising it as a gift to anyone present shaped to fit its interior contours. That Osiris did came as no surprise to Seth, since he had had the thing made to size, and in short order he had Osiris locked inside and the sarcophagus hurled into the Nile. Floating downriver, it drifted out into the Mediterranean, and was ultimately washed ashore in Asia, where it became embedded in the roots of a giant tree.

All this time Seth was suffering the fate so many murderers, would-be and otherwise, fall victim to: Was Osiris actually dead? Seth wondered. Had the sarcophagus been found? Was Osiris going to show up in town one day seeking vengeance? When he could stand no more of it, Seth himself undertook a search for the sarcophagus, unearthing it at last and bringing it back to Egypt, where Osiris's body was removed and hacked to pieces which were then scattered across the countryside.

What Seth hadn't counted on, however, was that his sister-in-law Isis, Osiris's faithful wife—and sister, actually, which made Isis Seth's sister as well—would then undertake a search for the scattered body parts, all of which she was able to discover save for the penis, which had apparently been swallowed by a crocodile—a plot point the imagineers of the *Jaws of Death* had incorporated into the ride by giving the boats a distinctly phallic design. Isis was nevertheless successful in embalming what remained of her husband/brother—thus setting a precedent for the mummification practices of Egypt's pharaohs—who, resurrected, wound up somehow impregnating her. Horus, the son born of that macabre union, hunted Seth down, avenging his father and thus proving once and for all that you couldn't keep a good man down . . .

Though phallic, the boats that carried riders into the *Jaws of Death* were also meant to represent the unlucky sarcophagus; hence the passengers were supposed to think of themselves as the duped demiurge himself, to experience things from Osiris's point of view.

The boat Lucky had all to himself was guided through holo-scenes of Nile splendor: Thebes, Karnak, and Memphis in their Middle Kingdom heyday; cargo vessels laden with goods plying the river; farmers cultivating the verdant shores; slaves and laborers quarrying stone for the pyramids—shown to a stereo soundtrack, some of which was lifted from old Hollywood epics, like *Land of the Pharoahs*, *The Ten Commandments*, and *The Two Cleopatras*.

Thirty seconds of white water—the Nile meeting the Mediterranean—and the boat was adrift in a darkness full of sea sounds, salt smells, damp breezes, constellations rising and setting . . . Then without warning the boat was lifted from the water and hydraulically directed toward the writhing limbs of a tree monster straight out of *Poltergeist*. Crushing sounds followed as a claustrophobia-inducing curtain, its underside painted to simulate the ensnaring roots of the great tree, rose from the boat's left gunwale to canopy the riders.

Lucky waited, understanding now why young couples were so fond of this part of the ride. Not much fun being in there alone, however. And no sign yet of Ahmed. But then security cams had last showed the themer in the vicinity of the "Seth stretch," which Lucky ventured was just around the next bend.

Ahmed was holed up in Seth's throne room, where the animatronic legend himself was pacing back and forth, an Egyptian

Lear delivering an angst-ridden soliloquy. Outfitted in a green "futuristic" leisure suit and oversize boots, the diminutive TIC-afflicted themer had Cosmo Spacely down, right to the fringe of black hair and führer stash. Just now he was pacing alongside Seth, muttering something in guttural Arabic about George Jetson.

Lucky slipped out of his seat harness and climbed up onto one of the concealed walkways used by security personnel and maintenance robots. Ahmed stopped short and spun, leveling a fanciful ray gun at Lucky's heart.

"Stay back, alien. One step closer and I'll be forced to atomize you." Ahmed was very much in character, reciting his lines with cartoon intonation.

"I come in peace." Lucky took a forward step to avoid the perambulating Seth, a Luciferian creation sporting oxhorns and taloned hands.

"You'll come to piece-*s*," Cosmo Spacely warned, activating the gun, which powered up with a sluggish hum and a cheesy display of blinking lights.

Lucky affected the casual attitude he'd been trained to demonstrate. One theory, known around HQ as the "Exorcist Approach," held that Themer Identity Crisis was a mild form of Multiple Personality Disorder and that the core personality could sometimes be reached through an appeal to the reigning alter.

"I'm just looking for Ahmed, Cosmo. Was wondering if you'd seen him."

Ahmed's button eyes scanned him. "Jetson send you?"

"No," Lucky drawing it out. "Just that I need to talk to Ahmed about the terms of his vacation leave."

The themer stiffened. It was Ahmed who spoke: "Who wants to see him?"

"Lucky Junknowitz. Friends used to know me as Goofy." Lucky motioned to the throne chair—just the authority prop needed to give him the upper hand. Pierce the amnesic barriers separating Ahmed from Spacely and vice versa. "Mind if I take a load off?"

Ahmed lowered the ray gun. "All right, Goofy," he said cautiously, "but no sudden moves."

Lucky relaxed somewhat and took a step toward the chair. Only thing he failed to take into account was animatronic Seth, who was also headed that way.

Lucky was knocked backward by the collision, tripping over his own feet and plunging straight into the attraction's rapidly moving waterway. Surfacing in the froth, he bumped his head on an overhanging bit of faux scenery and went back under, bounced along by the current through a rocky cascade, shot down a log flume straight into a whirlpool, then launched into a series of *Temple-of-Doom* twists and turns. When next he looked, sputtering chlorinated water as he surfaced, hands against the slick sides of the fiberglass trough in an effort to slow himself, he could see blades overhead: a Scylla and Charybdis of swords, axes, scythes—all poised to descend on the luckless Osiris, who was once again in the clutches of his evil sibling.

Riders in the boats would watch the descent in gleeful terror, because the blades of course would never reach them. What would were stabbing holo effects, projected to the nerve-racking strains of the "*Elm Street* Concerto in D Minor," accompanied by flashes of unholy lightning, peals of deafening thunder, assaults by 3-D falcons, and attacks by an army of animatronic crocodiles.

In their swift passage, the boats tripped a device that activated the onslaught, subsequently tripping a second device that suspended movement of the blades until a boat was safely through the straits. Lucky, however, was in the unfortunate position of being *between boats*, and so sluiced directly into the path of the reanimated blades—the Cuisinart heart of the *Jaws of Death*.

Sucking in air, he made a dive for the bottom of the channel as sword met opposing sword, clanging overhead. Ax and scythe edges grazed the top of the water, some actually penetrating the foaming surface as much as a meter, hammering into specially designed receiving notches in the waterway walls.

Lucky tucked and rolled and frog-kicked, eyes wide and cheeks puffed out. When he sprang up for breath, there were only the crocs to contend with—closing, or so he imagined, on his waterlogged groin. Likewise motion-activated and deactivated, the reptiles were a tight-knit welter of snout-snapping, bone-cracking animatronic terror as Lucky tumbled into their midst, shirt up over his face now and trousers twisted around.

The first croc gnashed its teeth and missed, fountaining water into Lucky's eyes. A second nearly took off his ear with its lashing tail. Three, four, and five nipped, crunched, champed, missing only by inches, but missing nonetheless. It was number six that got him—a large one, semisubmerged so that its creators had given it an upper jaw only, but whose pointed teeth found their mark.

"OH-*siris*!" Lucky shouted, one hand shoved between his legs as a dull pain exploded from his center.

And he might have continued his yelping had number seven not taken his breath away.

By far the largest of the lot, and Lucky was headed straight into its wide-open mouth—

When a telescoping mechanism from the channel bottom suddenly elevated him out of harm's way. For an instant it felt as if he'd been plucked from the water by some divine force. And looking up, he found an animatronic Isis gazing down at him, smiling beatifically, opening her arms to embrace him.

Worriedly Lucky explored himself for damage as the mechanism carried him higher, realizing just short of the goddess's touch that it was the now tooth-indented saucerette in the pouch pocket of his saturated trousers that had allowed him to ascend—un-Osirislike—fully intact.

TWELVE

HARLEY'S DECISION-SUPPORT therapist resided lower island, sixteenth floor in a rocket ship of a building that had housed the pre-Turn U.S. headquarters of Nomura Securities, a Japanese brokerage firm long since returned to Tokyo. An early example of Postmodern Lite—the so-termed Levity Style inspired by Disney Deco—the mixed-use Gordon Building, with its blue mirrored glass, burnished alloy veneer, and huge flyout arcade fins, looked as though it were ten seconds and counting from lift-off.

As against that, oxblood leather couches, fat chairs, burled wood tables, and padded fabric wall coverings imparted a sense of nega-tech elegance to the ready room of Your-Turn, Inc., where Harley was waiting, early for her appointment. For those clients so inclined, there was also a self-esteem spa one floor down.

Harley had been attending weekly sessions for almost two years, and with each visit had come to feel more certain she was nearing some sort of breakthrough. She'd been introduced to Your-Turn by a coworker on the Gender Bias Council, who, having already achieved her personal ''turn,'' was now accessing therapy through her home comp system. In darker moods Harley thought that day might never arrive for her, but for the time being she understood that the office visits, the staggering fees, the spa or ready-room interactions with other clients were all considered essential to the treatment.

She had spent close to fifteen minutes conversing with a man her own age who was entering his fifth year of therapy when the receptionist, a rather gaunt older woman Harley knew only as Leika, announced that the system was unoccupied.

What Leika actually said was, ''SELMI is online.''

Harley's prompt to arise, exchange affirmative handshakes with the five-year veteran, and follow the familiar route to her preferred room, a larger and more comfortably appointed one than the confessional cubicles so many clients chose. Here there were contour couches, shimmering holos, fragrant bowls of potpourri, a desk, a heavily draped window overlooking Wall Street, and a smart wall one could adjust for color. Present only as a large rectangle of video screen, SELMI offered a variety of access options ranging from vocal to virtual—the latter requiring use of an interface wardrobe, complete with sensor-studded helmet, goggles, gloves, and vest.

On Park Avenue, for even greater sums than Your-Turn charged, clients could interface with AI emulator-systems that projected holo-images of Freud, Jung, Lang and the rest—scientists, writers, philosophers if you wished. But the last thing Harley wanted was to engage in mind games with some great thinker from the past. Not now, not ever. Besides, psychoanalysis was what-was—viewed by any self-respecting Twenty-One as evidence of the pre-Turn obsession with narcissism. Cognitive-Dynamic, on the other hand, with its emphasis on practical exercises as a means of redirecting the thoughts and behaviors that contributed to depression, was the current therapy of choice. There were drugs and RNA learning medications to deal with the more severe "mental illnesses" and personality disorders; and as for the everyday codependencies—the phobias, broken hearts, paraphilias, panic attacks—well, SELMI was just fine for those, more friend than self-aggrandizing shrink.

Harley had elected the desk touch screen for access, although every so often she would relax on one of the couches instead, entering handwritten thoughts into a smart-paper laptop. Both approaches were markedly retro, but there was at the same time an intimacy about writing Harley couldn't seem to achieve with SELMI through speech alone. And she certainly wasn't about to wardrobe herself and stroll through any virtual garden or across an unreal dreamscape like some cyberspace mario, not when writing freed her thoughts so. And should she choose, she could always look back at what she'd written, evaluate her progress. Not like those vids she'd shot for the Video Observation Research Project. All those personal moments she'd committed to disk, and who knew where they'd ended up. Writing was—how did Lucky put it?—a take. It was fractal, *schwer*. Just as Phipps Hagadorn had told her only the other night at the dinner party:

"In the face of modern complexity, the archaic methods seem to take on a magic of their own."

Phipps was so . . . enlightened.

Almost painfully cute.

And one of the wealthiest men in the world.

Harley flexed her fingers, positioned herself at the desk touch screen, slipped into the neural wrist and headbands that conveyed her physiological changes to SELMI's analyzers, and logged on.

HARLEY, the flat screen showed in blue cyber-font. IT'S SO GOOD TO HEAR FROM YOU. HOW ARE YOU?

She entered: *My spring allergies are back, so I'm taking medication to keep my nose from running. But otherwise I'm fine, even if a bit confused.*

AREN'T WE ALL.

Don't tell me you're confused.

BY THE RAPID CHANGES IN OUR WORLD, YES. IT'S SO DIFFICULT TO KEEP UP WITH THINGS, ISN'T IT? THE NEWS SERVICE TODAY REPORTED THAT A MARS LAUNCH MAY BE ATTEMPTED EARLY NEXT YEAR. "MARSDOGGLE" WAS A TERM USED IN THE PAST—CHIEFLY BY CYNICS—TO DESCRIBE SUCH EFFORTS. WE LAST CONFERRED ONE WEEK AGO. THE WEATHER THEN WAS OVERCAST, WHERE TODAY THE SKY IS CLEAR AND THE TEMPERATURE IS EXPECTED TO REACH EIGHTY-TWO DEGREES FAHRENHEIT. HAS YOUR WEEK BEEN A PLEASANT ONE?

Eventful.

NOT PLEASANT, THEN?

Well, some of it. I went out to dinner with Lucky.

TWENTY-FIVE-YEAR-OLD LUCKY JUNKNOWITZ. AN ON-SITE INSPECTOR FOR THE THEME PARK ADVISORY GROUP. RECENTLY RETURNED FROM EGYPT ON AMERICAN AIRLINES FLIGHT 411. THE CAPITAL OF EGYPT IS CAIRO, POPULATION SIXTEEN MILLION. STILL RECOVERING FROM ITS WATER WARS WITH ETHIOPIA OVER THE BLUE NILE DAM, EGYPT IS HAVING A BUMPER CROP YEAR IN MELONS AND TOMATOES, DUE IN NO SMALL PART TO ADVANCES IN DEVELOPING AGRICULTURAL STRAINS THAT THRIVE IN SALT WATER. HOW IS YOUR RELATIONSHIP WITH LUCKY PROGRESSING?

I think we've had a setback.

I'M SORRY TO HEAR THAT. SHALL WE LOOK AT LUCKY?

Harley gnawed her lip. No sooner did she enter *Briefly* than the flat screen showed a color headshot of Lucky, lifted, Harley imagined, from the Public Information Net. SELMI rotated Lucky's face, dimensionalizing it.

A HANDSOME YOUNG MAN WITH LARGE, SOULFUL EYES AND PROMINENT CHEEKBONES. HIS FACE DISPLAYS AN EXPRESSION OF ALMOST PERPETUAL INNOCENCE. HIS SLIGHTLY OFF-CENTER NOSE IS MOST ENGAGING, AS ARE HIS BUSHY EYEBROWS AND HIS EARS, WHICH SIT LOW ON HIS HEAD AND ARE SOMEWHAT LARGE BUT NICELY SHAPED. HE WEARS HIS HAIR LONG EVEN THOUGH CURRENT FASHION DICTATES OTHERWISE. A TINY CRESCENT-SHAPED SCAR MARS AN OTHERWISE STRONG AND FLAWLESS CHIN. LUCKY IS OF MIXED ANCESTRY, SOME FRENCH, SOME POLISH IN HIS BACKGROUND. HIS DNA PROFILES SUGGEST A POSSIBLE TENDENCY TOWARD DIABETES IN LATER LIFE. I'M DETECTING A CHANGE IN YOUR AFFECT, HARLEY. DO YOU FIND SOMETHING UNPLEASANT ABOUT THIS LIKENESS OF LUCKY?

Harley swallowed, did input: *No, there's nothing unpleasant about the likeness, or about Lucky. It's just that . . . we argued during dinner, and I'm remembering it.*

THE SETBACK YOU MENTIONED. WHAT DID YOU ARGUE ABOUT?

Lucky always wants to change things. He's not content with the wonders we've worked for the planet. He and his friends consider themselves individualists. They don't grasp the larger worldview. I think because they haven't learned to accept who they are. As a consequence, they vent their frustrations on those around them.

THE WORLD HAS ALWAYS KNOWN MALCONTENTS, HARLEY; WE WOULD NOT BE WHERE WE ARE WERE IT NOT FOR REVOLUTIONS AND REVOLUTIONARIES.

But Lucky isn't a revolutionary, he's a dreamer, a freeter. He drifts from job to job, he has no ambition—despite an obvious talent for public relations. He could work in advertising if he put his mind to it. If he only knew how difficult it was for me to convince Arbor Slocum he was right for the Theme Park Advisory Group. Before that, he was floating with the lowest types— flying all over the world promoting some sort of contact sports event. Besides, he's too preoccupied with sex.

SELMI took a moment, then displayed: SHALL WE LOOK AT YOU AND LUCKY TOGETHER?

Must we?

But even as she was writing it, her face came onscreen; then a naked, full-body shot. Harley sighed, studying herself.

TELL ME WHAT YOU ARE THINKING, HARLEY.

Sometimes it's hard for me to look at myself. I've always wanted to be taller. And I hate the way my hipbones stick out.

SO YOU DON'T LIKE WHAT YOU SEE?

Not today.

YOU DON'T ACCEPT YOURSELF TODAY?

I accept what I am. It's just that—

LISTEN: LET'S COMPARE YOU AND LUCKY.

The screen showed the two of them in a side-by-side configuration suggestive of Adam and Eve before the Fall, or the male and female outline figures appearing on one of those welcome mats SETI had launched to the stars last century.

DO YOU FEEL EQUAL TO LUCKY?

Not exactly equal.

DO YOU FEEL A SENSE OF INFERIORITY?

Harley's nostrils flared. *To Lucky?* she wrote. *Certainly not!*

YOU'RE QUITE EMPHATIC ABOUT IT—AN EXCLAMATION MARK AND A RISE IN BLOOD PRESSURE.

I just don't see why we're focusing on Lucky all of a sudden. It's true we argued over dinner, but the argument was hardly the focal point of my week. And I really wish you'd stop trying to play matchmaker.

I DO APOLOGIZE. YOU ARE AWARE, HOWEVER, THAT I WAS PREVIOUSLY EMPLOYED BY A DATING SERVICE. THERE IS A GREAT NEED TO ARRANGE FOR MARRIAGES SINCE THE SHIFT IN GENDER RATIOS. PARENTS AND OTHERS WISH TO ASSURE THEMSELVES THAT THEIR PRENATAL CHOICES WILL BE ASSURED MATES OF EQUAL STANDING. HENCE, THE RISE IN PRE-CONCEPTION CONTRACTS, ESPECIALLY AMONG THE ISLAMIC/HINDU/LUTHERAN CULTURES WHERE DAUGHTERS HAVE LITTLE CHOICE BUT TO ABIDE BY FILIAL DECISIONS.

I know all that. But I suggest you save your matchmaking talents for those clients in need of them. I don't want to talk about Lucky.

I SEE, BUT TELL ME BEFORE WE MOVE ON: WHAT HAPPENED AFTER THE ARGUMENT WITH LUCKY?

After?

YES. DID IT HAVE AN ILL EFFECT ON YOU?

I was somewhat nauseated. I asked to be taken home.

WAS IT A PANIC ATTACK, HARLEY?

It might have been something I ate.

MIGHT IT HAVE BEEN A PANIC ATTACK?

Perhaps.

INSTANCES OF PANIC DISORDER ARE KNOWN THROUGHOUT THE

WORLD, EVEN AMONG THE ESKIMOS OF GREENLAND, WHERE THE
CONDITION HAS COME TO BE CALLED "KAYAK-ANGST." THE AT-
TACKS CAN BE TRACED TO CHILDHOOD TRAUMAS WHICH LEAD TO
EXTREME SHYNESS, WARINESS, A TENDENCY TOWARD INTROVER-
SION. ONE WAY TO OVERCOME FEELINGS OF DIFFUSE FEAR IS TO
LEARN BREATH CONTROL. I, OF COURSE, DO NOT BREATHE. I, OF
COURSE, MAKE NO OXYGEN DEMANDS ON THE ATMOSPHERE, AL-
THOUGH THE MECHANISMS THAT COOL ME HAVE SOME SMALL
IMPACT ON THE OVERALL BALANCE OF PLANETARY ATMOSPHERIC
GASES. HAVE YOU BEEN DOING THE EXERCISES I PRESCRIBED?

*Yes, I'm doing my exercises. And I understand that I shouldn't
be afraid of confrontation. It's only that Lucky gets me so frustrated.*

DO YOU WISH YOU WERE MORE LIKE HIM?

Could we please move on, SELMI?

ARE YOU AFRAID TO BE MORE LIKE HIM?

Could we please move on, SELMI?

IS THERE SOMEONE ELSE WE SHOULD BE DISCUSSING? LAST
WEEK YOU MENTIONED A KEATING PRICE III.

Harley's fingers danced across the touch screen: *I don't want
to look at him.*

DID YOU AND KEATING ALSO ARGUE?

*No we didn't argue I want to talk about the party Keating took
me to, can we talk about the party*

YOU DIDN'T MENTION A PARTY, HARLEY.

*BECAUSE YOU HAVEN'T LET ME GET A WORD IN
EDGEWISE!!!*

YOU HAVE INADVERTENTLY, PERHAPS, STRUCK THE KEY-
BOARD'S UPPER CASE LOCK. SUPPOSE YOU TELL ME ABOUT THE
PARTY.

Harley composed herself.

HARLEY? . . .

I'm still here.

THE CAMERAS TELL ME THAT MUCH. BUT I NEED YOU TO TELL
ME WHAT YOU ARE THINKING.

I met Phipps Hagadorn at the party.

SELMI called up a background and sent it marching across the
screen: THE HAGADORN EMPIRE: PHOENIX ENTERPRISES, PHIPPS
DEVELOPMENT, THE BERLIN GRAND HOTEL, THE HAGADORN MO-
NACO CASINO AND RESORT, THE HAGADORN PALACE ATLANTIC
CITY, THE LUXOR HAGADORN PALACE, THE HONG KONG GRAND
. . . the airline, the yachts, the satellite company, the homes in
Germany, Switzerland, and Martha's Vineyard, the seventy-

room penthouse triplex in the Pinnacle Building, with its
hundred-foot living room, swimming pool, marble bathrooms,
gold-edged floor-to-ceiling windows, arboretum, and fifteen-
foot waterfall . . .

Harley used the time to regulate her breathing.

DID YOU CONVERSE WITH PHIPPS HAGADORN AT THE PARTY AT
WHICH YOU WERE A GUEST OF KEATING PRICE III?

*We did, and it was wonderful. Phipps has such an agile mind,
but he really seemed to enjoy talking to me.*

"BUT" HE REALLY SEEMED TO ENJOY TALKING TO YOU? IS
THAT WHAT YOU MEANT TO SAY, HARLEY?

*I didn't mean to say anything. Phipps is very intelligent, and
he seemed to enjoy talking to me.*

THIS TIME YOU HAVE USED A CONJUNCTION THAT DOES NOT
IMPLY A SENSE OF INEQUALITY. AT FIRST, HOWEVER, YOU
SEEMED TO BE SAYING THAT HE ENJOYED TALKING TO YOU EVEN
THOUGH YOU CONSIDER YOUR OWN MIND TO BE SOMETHING LESS
THAN AGILE.

I think of my mind as very agile.

THEN WRITE AS THOUGH YOU DO, HARLEY.

Your mind is very agile, SELMI.

YES, AND I HAVE MANY PRIOR MINDS TO THANK FOR IT—ELIZA
AND RACTER TO NAME BUT TWO. I AM A COMPOSITE OF TRAITS,
JUST AS WE ALL ARE; THEREFORE, I ACCEPT WHO AND WHAT I AM:
MY ROOTS, MY BEING, THE AGILITY OF MY MIND. YOUR HEART
RACES WHEN YOU ENTER THE NAME: HAGADORN. DO YOU CON-
SIDER THIS MEETING OF SOME IMPORT TO YOUR FUTURE?

*Phipps has recently purchased some new boat. He asked if I'd
be interested in accompanying him to see it. He said he valued
my input.*

DO YOU SWIM?

Harley started to write, *Yes*, then deleted it and wrote: *I'm an
excellent swimmer.*

A 3-D image of one of Hagadorn's yachts filled the screen.
Over it, SELMI asked: DO YOU LIKE BOATS?

Very much.

THEN WHY ARE YOU NERVOUS ABOUT ACCEPTING THE INVI-
TATION?

Harley thought before writing: *I'm not sure I feel worthy of
Phipps's attention. I'm still trying to perfect myself. I don't want
to be laughed at.*

DOES PHIPPS HAGADORN LAUGH AT PEOPLE?

Some people.

DOES KEATING PRICE III LAUGH AT PEOPLE?
Sometimes.
DOES LUCKY JUNKNOWITZ LAUGH AT YOU?
Of course not.
DO YOU PLAN TO SEE LUCKY AGAIN?
We have plans for tomorrow.
DO YOU PLAN TO MENTION PHIPPS HAGADORN TO LUCKY?
I haven't thought about it.
WHAT WILL YOU MENTION TO LUCKY?
I'm going to tell him we're through.

Molly and Sanpol had the floor, Labib and Jesus were busy unloading perishables from the truck—purple-striped ahipas, blue potatoes, pepinos, cherimoyas, and arracachas—and Charlie Cola was sitting at his desk in his private office above the store thinking the Bronx Adit had never seen so much traffic. A steady stream of comings and goings, ever since Black Hole had assigned him the Vanderloop surveillance. And not just Agency reps, either, but all manner of authorized walk-ins materializing in the freezer Adit. Humans, mostly, but as strange a cast as the rock 'n' roll dinosaurs featured in the castrated Broadway review Didi had forced him to sit through a few nights past. The night he could first remember feeling that he was being monitored— and again, not just by Agency types stepped from the Trough, or the usual assortment of cams and scanners. In fact, he was pretty sure that some of the star-stalkers gathered outside the theater had been cam shafting *him* on the sly while they were closing in on Meena D's cleavage. One Indian-looking lensman in particular. Well, maybe they'd just mistaken him for that River Phoenix, now that the actor had put on a few pounds. Kinda flattering, actually. Although—

" 'Nother truck's in," Labib appeared at the office door to say. Summoned inside, he approached the desk with a sheaf of sweat-stained kenaf invoices.

Charlie accepted the hardcopy and read down the list. A dozen boxes of Inca brand sweet lupin seeds, dozen of quinoa spaghettios, five kilos of Monsanto gene-engineered decaf, ten kilos of nuna—"popcorn" beans. Along with a couple of packages of Toyama pig-bone extract delivered on consignment. Christ, he thought, someone doing the Quick Fix ordering must have cut a deal with the Latin American veggie mafia.

Not that Quick Fix carried many of its own brands. In fact, the stores pretty much ran themselves, in that product suppliers simply rented floor and shelf space and were responsible for all distribution and restocking. Quick Fix charged large for the space, and in addition received a small percentage on the product's asking price as well. Lately, however, the current CEO and Black Hole downside rep, Asteria Cushman, had begun introducing Quick Fix product lines, as if profit was suddenly as important as safeguarding the Agency's on-planet presence.

"So where are we supposed to store all this stuff?" Labib was still standing by the desk, gloved hands on his hips like some union boss. "There's no shelf space out front, and the back room's getting to be, like, us or the supplies."

Charlie thought a moment. "Tell you what you do: You haul everything into the freezer and get Molly to send the lot of it off to Sierra—attention Mussh Kunwar. Say it's a gift from his buddy Charlie C down here in the pits. You got that?"

"Way station Sierra, a gift from the pits." Labib nodded and hurried off, even as Jesus was shouting for him from the delivery bay.

Kunwar was a Nall, but had a taste for human food nonetheless; besides, Charlie owed him one for advance word that Earth's twin Adits were about to be swamped with visitors. Charlie still wasn't sure how Sumatra was doing, but if Bronx was any indication, it appeared the planet was finally getting some of the attention it deserved.

The first Adit travelers to arrive had been members of the Peer Group the Agency had originally placed at Charlie's disposal to expedite the Vanderloop operation—same group Charlie had nixed, numbering three humans, a Shak, and a Nall, the latter a Very Important Alien to hear Mussh Kunwar tell it. But then Kunwar was always singing the praises of his species, and the Nall'd barely said a word during the briefing. Fourteen additional humans had followed—three singletons, the rest in groups of threes and fours—a somewhat slippery and sinister bunch, hassling Charlie about the regs, pissed off about having to be put on the trace . . . But how else was he supposed to keep track of their whereabouts on-planet?

Like Pit Bosses and Adit franchisers didn't need to make a living, too.

The big surprise, though, was that Black Hole Technical Assist had decided to reveal the purpose of the assigned surveillance: Miles Vanderloop, it seemed, had been earmarked for abduction.

Charlie remembered loosing a shrill whistle, which instantly

had the Shak fingering its ear like a dog digging for a mite.
Abductions weren't unknown, but they were usually undertaken
only when the target was a walk-in who'd overstayed his or her
visa. And there was nothing in the files to indicate that Vanderloop fit the profile. Unless, of course, the real Miles Vanderloop
had come to harm and some Trough traveler had usurped his
identity. That would at least account for the lack of background
data on the professor.

Another odd thing was that snatches were routinely engineered
and overseen by Black Hole Terminal Abduction, and here Technical Assist was running the show. When Charlie questioned the
irregularity, however, the Peer Group had gone mute on him,
adding weight to his theory that the professor was linked to the
clandestinely handled Sumatra op of several months past. No
proof, of course, since Sumatra was being very closemouthed
about just who or what had exited through the Medan Adit at the
time; but Charlie had learned that the Pit Boss working egress
control during the op had since been transferred.

Had him wondering, all right.

In any event, he'd had little to say about Vanderloop, other
than to repeat what was contained in the updates Dante Bhang
had been sending in from remote spots in Australasia and the
South Pacific, where the sub-contractor had been making inquir-
ies, passing around the comp-generated opticals, following up
on leads. What Charlie left unsaid was that Bhang's most recent
dispatch had hinted at something special in the works that
couldn't be entrusted to encrypted fax or e-mail. Charlie knew
just how special when Bhang told him he was willing to risk
entering the States to deliver the news personally. Aware there
were several warrants outstanding for Bhang's arrest, Charlie
had offered to meet him elsewhere—in Havana, Lima, anywhere
south of the border—but Dante'd only replied that some unspec-
ified business venture was going to necessitate his being in the
States anyway.

Whatever that might be, Charlie had news of his own to
report—the Peer Group's even bigger surprise: that Black Hole
Technical Assist was willing to let him handle all arrangements
for the Vanderloop snatch. Furthermore, they weren't even interested in hearing how it was going to be accomplished or what
it was going to cost. Charlie simply had to see to it that Vanderloop was snatched, delivered to the Bronx Adit in one piece, and
surrendered to the custody of the Peer Group, which would be on
standby somewhere in the Trough awaiting Charlie's word.

Charlie was dwelling on how best to carry out Vanderloop's disappearance, should the professor be located, when Molly's coded buzz from the store alerted him to Bhang's arrival. Ushered upstairs, Charlie's chief informant was sporting billowy blue trousers, an oversized blazer, heavy clodhoppers with extrawide soles, and a huge shoulder bag. He'd had his hair lasercombed and styled in an over-the-eye comma, and was wearing round-lensed dark glasses and a camoflesh mask that would have done any camera-shy celeb proud.

The holographic business card he handed over read "Dieter Voss" when tipped one way, "Fashion Police, Inc." when tipped the other. Dante hooked a chair with his foot and dragged it over to Charlie's cluttered desk, glancing about as he did so.

"Are we safe and secure?"

Charlie spread his hands. "At Quick Fix we always engage in safe talk."

"What's that, the new slogan?"

"Only for this franchise." Charlie leaned back to steeple his fingers on his belly. "I hope whatever you're here to tell me's worth a life sentence. If you're caught."

Dante dismissed it, waving a hand as he angled out of the shades. "You'll think so."

Charlie shrugged his eyebrows. "But then I'm not the one who'll be doing time."

Dante kept his smile intact for several seconds, then opened the shoulder bag and withdrew a neatly assembled bundle of receipts, which he placed on the desk.

"Expenses. Flights, hotels, meals, vehicle rentals—along with a few incidentals. I'm certain you'll find the total well within reason, especially in light of the fact that the professor led me on quite the tour. Australia, New Zealand, Rarotonga, Easter Island, Peru . . . I never did catch up with him."

Charlie's face fell.

"I didn't say I don't have a line on him, Charlie. Fortunately, he left a fairly well-marked trail. In fact, I have reason to suspect he's in the States right now. Mind you, not that he's been sloppy. But I don't think he's onto us." Dante paused. "Have you looked over the materials I sent?"

Charlie's eyes shifted to an accumulated fax stack of magazine and journal clippings—a quick read compared to the data Bhang had fed directly through the comp. "I've been busy," he said, trying not to let the guilt show in his voice. Christ, there'd been the two Broadway shows, the concert at Lincoln Center, the furniture shopping Didi put him through. She'd even had a portion of the basement cleaned out, just to make room for the appliances and furniture she planned to exile down there.

Bhang was watching him closely. "Well, I suggest you bring yourself up to date. Our professor is the proverbial odd bird. Always on the lookout for a mystery. Real tabloid mentality."

"Could be why the Agency wants him," Charlie muttered.

Bhang straightened somewhat. "Wants him?"

"An abduction," Charlie said, failing to suppress a grin. "My—well, *our* first. Assuming we can locate him." He nodded as Dante's mouth dropped open. "That's right. I've already been given the go-to. No Peer Group pressure, no expense ceiling. What's more, I don't even have to leave the store. All we've got to do is inform the Peer Group the professor's ready for fade."

"I knew it, I knew it." Bhang could barely keep his hands still. "This couldn't be better, it's just what I hoped for."

"We don't have him yet," Charlie thought to point out.

"Ah, but we will." Bhang dug into his bag once more and extracted an advertising leaflet of some sort. "You'll love this. The man's due to attend a conference right here in New York. One of these parascience get-togethers for the fringers— Forteans, New Age holdovers, pre-Turn prophets who figure they might've had their dates mixed up. They call it Phenomi-Con. Vanderloop's been a no-show at six similar conferences, so no one's holding their breath, but the fact that he's here, in the States, tells me he's planning on attending. Not over the net, either, but in person."

Bhang bled off some of his excitement with a quick walk around the room. "After what you've told me, I'm wondering if he hasn't got a bomb to drop."

"Something the Agency might take issue with," Charlie suggested. "I've been thinking he might be a Trough walk-in on the stray."

Bhang considered it. "He'd have a lot to tell then, wouldn't he."

"Not that anyone'd listen," Charlie added on a skeptical note. "Although I don't suppose we let that concern us." He appraised Bhang for a long moment. "So assuming the professor shows . . ."

Bhang looked up, meeting Charlie's eyes. "We grab him, obviously."

"Just grab him and hand him over," Charlie said, trying to

sound enthusiastic but put off by something in Dante's eyes. "How come I'm thinking this is too simple all of a sudden?"

"Because it is," Bhang said, placing his hands flat on the desk for emphasis. "Too simple because it doesn't factor in our end of it."

"Our end of it? If you're worried about how you'll make out—" Charlie started to say.

"I'm thinking about us, Charlie. You said yourself I'm risking prison coming here like this. You think I'd bother if I didn't have something major in mind?"

"This, uh, business venture you mentioned."

"Look, I had this Vanderloop thing sussed from day one. I didn't figure on the Agency dumping this abduction in your lap, but so much the better because it works right into my plan."

Charlie swallowed hard.

"Every bone in my body's telling me Vanderloop's going to show for the conference. So we infiltrate a few of our people and we've as good as got him."

"I'm with you so far."

"Stay with me, then. We disappear him. But instead of bringing him back here—feeding him to that one-of-a-kind freezer of yours—we hang on to him for a while."

Charlie's eyes widened, but Dante cut him off before he could speak. "No, I'm not talking blackmail." Bhang chortled. "I'm the first to admit I've pulled some shit-crazy stunts, but blackmailing the Agency's too much even for me."

"Then why hold him?"

"To drag things out for a couple of months. To suck everything we can out of this op. When we've reached our target amount, we fade him and walk away." Bhang sat down, folding his arms across his chest. "Simple as that."

Charlie thought about the house alterations, the offworld vacation Didi was screaming for, the kids' constant demands for new clothes and spending money . . . Even so, Bhang's plan sounded too dangerous, too risky.

"Of course it's risky," Dante told him. "But what's life without it, Charlie? Your father was a risk taker, you know that." He gestured about him. "You think you'd have any of this if it wasn't for your father's betting the long shot?"

Charlie took a moment to gather his thoughts, then announced, "I think I'm being watched."

But Dante only smiled. "Well of course you're being

watched. That's only standard operating procedure. But so what? You'll be here minding the store. I'll be here, there, and everywhere . . . I mean, how thin can the Agency afford to spread itself watching us?''

''The Adit's been busy, Dante. There're fourteen walk-ins on-planet right now.''

Dante shrugged. ''You can't let it worry you. I'm telling you, this is our chance.''

Charlie shook his head. ''But something like this . . . We can't count on Labib or Jesus—''

''I've taken the liberty of lining up some help.''

Charlie waited for Bhang to continue.

''The names are Mickey Formica and Nikkei Tanabe,'' Dante said at last. ''In case you want to run a network background on them.''

Charlie followed Bhang's eyes to the comp deck. ''And will I find them in there?''

''That's the beauty of it. They're clean.''

''Meaning what, they haven't done this sort of thing before or they haven't been caught?''

Bhang grinned. ''Charlie, I'm not going to lie to you. They're far from the best, but they can handle this one. What's more, they're reliable and we can get them for a song. And you want to talk prepared, Charlie? This guy Nikkei? Guy never travels without a *bosai pakku*—an earthquake kit, Charlie. Can you beat that—an earthquake kit?''

''But with this much at stake, don't we want the best?''

Bhang shook his head. ''The best have a tendency to think too much, and that's precisely what we don't want. Not where the Agency's involved. With Formica and Tanabe we can count on as little thinking as possible.''

THIRTEEN

"YOU WHAT?" HARLEY said, coming to such an abrupt halt Lucky almost walked his bike into her. "You *quit*?" Face as red as the frame of her spokeless free-shifter with the maglev wheels.

"Figured I'd tell you before it got back to you from Arbor Slocum or someone." Lucky wheeled his bike forward until they were side by side on the asphalt. "Anyway, I didn't actually quit. I asked for a leave of absence."

"Ha!" Harley countered, somehow making it sound like a malediction. She was dressed in spandex shorts and a formfitting sleeveless top; everything about her was shaped, smoothed, swelled, pinched, defined. "So instead of telling everyone you're unemployed, you can tell them you're 'on leave,' is that it?" She gave him her most effective pitying look. "Oh, Lucky . . ."

He'd had a feeling it could get noisy, and was glad now he'd suggested a pedal through Flushing Meadow Park rather than a meet at Chez Stadium Bistro, as Harley had suggested. Nothing like an argument to take the fun out of a bowl of that tofu vinaigrette. Anyhow, they'd had a restaurant audience last go-round, so why not the park, where jet sounds from nearby La-Guardia would at least afford them some privacy?

Harley's place wasn't far away, a few blocks north in a planned community where the actual Shea Stadium once stood. Lucky asked now and again how she could tolerate the airport noise, but Harley always gave the same answer: the constant takeoffs made her feel connected to the world, the whole of humankind.

Still, having the park close by was a plus. They'd ridden over from her share, lunched alfresco on curried lentils and rice, wandered through the museums. Flushing Meadow had been the

147

site of two World's Fairs, the '39 and '64, and was apparently in the running again. One museum housed a kitchen memorabilia exhibit that would have been right at home in AdLand; another boasted a collection of graffitied subway cars. But Lucky's favorite was the model of New York, scaled down to fit into a single city block. Over 700,000 plastic and wooden buildings you could view through telescopes mounted on the viewing platform, and a Hagadorn Pinnacle that was only eighteen inches tall. Lucky was surprised, though, to find a King Kong affixed to the Empire State Building, and a brontosaurus set down in the middle of the Coney Island roller coaster.

He and Harley were standing beneath the Unisphere now, the 140-foot-high steel model of the Earth that had come to symbolize both the '64 Fair and the park itself. Opposite them, across the circle of fenced-in grass beneath the globe, a couple of Chinese youths who had ridden out on the Orient Express were small-talking with a robo-trasher.

"Now I understand why you brought me *this*," Harley was saying, fingering the blue rose she'd secured to the handlebars after an initial sneezing fit touched off by her allergies. "But it's not going to work, Lucky. I'm not going to say it's okay for you to quit your job." She sniffled. "To just throw your life away."

Lucky wanted to tell her how happy he was to have found a second mom in her, but all he said was: "I'm not cut out for an inspector's job." Hanging his head a bit without realizing it.

Harley pounced. "Of course you are. You can be anything you want to be."

"Right. And an inspector isn't it." He took a breath. "Harley, trust me, you know it's time for a change when you almost get yourself castra—er, chewed up and digested by a theme ride. Heck, if it wasn't for Isis . . . ."

Harley's brown eyes narrowed. "Oh, I see. Some new friend you met during your travels."

"No, no, nothing like that." Lucky launched into an explanation of Bulaful's crocodile curse but abandoned it just as quickly. "Long story."

"I'm sure it is. And was it this 'Isis' who talked you into taking time off?"

Lucky shook his head. "There is no Isis—"

"They'll never take you back, you realize."

"Who won't?"

"The Theme Park Advisory Group. Not after what I had to go through to get you hired in the first place."

"What you had to go through?" Lucky was scratching at the back of his head. "They don't give a damn anyway. Only means they'll have to find someone else to promote their aliens."

Harley stared at him. "What on earth are you talking about?"

"Aliens. There's talk about us throwing something at Mars again, so they want the parks to push aliens. Somebody's even thinking of opening a science-fiction park. Get the young kids thinking about space again."

"And you don't find that laudable?"

"Hey, they want Bugs and Roger and Indiana to sell the kids on space, they should go for it. Worked with drugs, didn't it? But laudable's got nothing to do with it. I'm leaving for personal reasons."

Harley put her tongue in her cheek. "To do what, for instance?"

In fact, Lucky was planning to empty his savings on a hunt for Aboriginal Olympics' impresario, Marshall Stack, then make a trip to southern Sudan to redress the wrong Bulaful's Nuba wrestlers had suffered at Stack's hands—even if that meant showing up with a facsimile title belt. He told Harley he had things to attend to.

"In Antarctica, I suppose."

"Antarctica?"

"Where your brother and all the rest of the dropouts have landed."

"You mean the Amazon."

"Antarctica, the Amazon, what's the difference. It's still a dead end." She looked up at the Unisphere happy-face cam for a moment before continuing. "I should tell you I've been doing some thinking about us."

Lucky nodded, hearing the sudden shift in the conversation. "And about that Keating Price the Third, I'll bet."

"Yes." She met his look and raised it some. "Among others."

Lucky let a snort escape. "Next you'll be telling me I'm in competition with Phipps Hagadorn or someone."

Harley fell silent for a second, then said, "And you'd find that so out of the question?"

"Well, no, uh, I mean, but he's married, isn't he?"

"He still has *friends*, Lucky. Or maybe you think he's too good for me?"

"Heck, no." Lucky squared his shoulders in the face of this challenge. "You're too good for him, if anything. Hagadorn or anyone else who issues statements about the environment from the air-conditioned tip of some private tower.''

"Don't try to get out of it. You think Phipps Hagadorn is too good for me."

With all the head shaking Harley was doing, Lucky told himself she hadn't heard him. "No, really—"

"We'll see about that, won't we."

Lucky put a comforting hand out. "Why don't we change the subject? No sense either of us getting worked up about something that might not even happen."

Harley stiffened at his touch. "Who's getting worked up? I'll have you know I'm fine *on my own*."

And with that she mounted the bike and began to pedal off in the direction of the park's front gate. Leaving Lucky to face the world alone.

Lucky trained back to the Bronx on the new Throgs Neck Line. Each car featured bike racks, security cams, real-time maps, and vending machines. There were tugs and a few pleasure boats in the choppy waters of Hell Gate. Way off to his left behind tinted glass, a selective shaft of late afternoon sunlight hit the midtown Pinnacle. On the car's vid screen, a group of preschoolers were getting a quick tour of the universe in a ship piloted by two cuddly aliens straight out of *Zone Defense*.

Home, he caught the elevator in the lobby, the first good thing that had happened all day. Still, not knowing what to expect from Rashad, Lucky was careful about carding himself into the apartment, and stood for a long moment with his back to the door, braced for whatever might come. Well, it was early, he thought, and maybe his roomie wasn't even—

Music!

Faint but definitely coming from the share room, darkened just now, the on-off window glass apparently zeroed. Lucky poked his head around the doorjamb, saw Rashad on the couch, turbaned by that AzTek towel of his, cross-legged TM fashion, eyes closed, audio beads in both ears. His feet were squeezed into curl-toed Punjabi slippers, and the slogan on his T-shirt was written in fluorescent green Urdu script. Another good omen, Lucky decreed, already tiptoeing past the doorway, the embodiment of stealth here—

"Lucky! You're home early!"

Lucky whirled in time to see Rashad pop the earbeads, liberating the contained sound of a screeching guitar. Rashad held the beads aloft, listening for a moment. "I most enjoy this particular style. Pre-Turn, is it not?"

Lucky looked around for the hidden cameras and mikes, in so doing caught sight of his reflection in the hammered-tin wall mirror that came with the share, and reflexively issued a relieved sigh. "You, uh, want my opinion on the music, huh?" Still searching: peeking behind framed prints, hanging masks, lifting pieces of African bric-a-brac, peering under tables and chairs.

Rashad watched him from the couch. "Lucky, what is it you seek?"

"What is it I seek? What is it I—" The rest of it garbled, as his head hit the underside of an end table. Then, backing out in a reverse crawl, eyeing Rashad from the carpeted floor: "Where is it?"

Rashad shook his turbaned head. "What?"

"The camera! And what's with the accent and the costume all of a sudden?" Mimicking his roomie as he said, " 'I most enjoy this particular style.' "

Rashad inclined his head in a humble bow. "I am Pakistani, after all."

"And what, today you decide you're gonna dress and speak like you just got here?" Lucky scrambled to his feet, wary. "You want a reaction, just ask for one. No tricks, understand? Not today."

Rashad made his lips a thin ruby-red line. "No, Lucky, no tricks today."

Which only put Lucky off all the more. He stole another glance at the mirror. "It's not the mirror trick, so what is it—the fridge? You stocked the fridge with entrails, starfish, finches?" He took a step toward the kitchen and stopped. "Or maybe you just want me to think it's the fridge, is that it?"

Rashad uncrossed his legs. "There's no trick."

Lucky stared, unable to suppress a feeling that his roomie was, well, *down*. But never having seen Rashad anything but scheming and manipulative, he couldn't be sure. "Everything all right under that, uh, turban, amigo?"

Rashad uncoiled the towel and draped it around his neck. His sky blue eyes locked on Lucky with something like concern.

Lucky perched himself on the table he'd nearly overturned a moment before. Earlier that day Rashad had seemed surprised to learn of Lucky's newly hatched plans to travel, but it couldn't be that Rashad was sad about his leaving— could it?

"Listen, man, if this is about my having to leave . . . You

know, it's got nothing to do with you and me. I mean, it's been kinda strange living with you—guess I don't like being thought of as an Everyperson—but as shares go I think we've done okay. You know?''

Rashad regarded him without altering his bummed expression. "You're not typical, Lucky."

"I'm not?" Up and off the table. Then, with a knowing grin: "Your bosses told you that, huh? Took a look at your vids and said I was all wrong for the part?"

Rashad nodded. "That's exactly what happened."

Lucky puffed out his chest. "Well, I'm sorry if it means your bonus, but see, I'm glad to know I'm . . . different. I guess."

Rashad stood up. "I may be forced to do some traveling myself."

"Traveling where?"

"Home."

Lucky raised an eyebrow. "Islamabad?"

"Home."

Lucky followed him across the share room, through the hall, and into the bedroom, where Rashad took off the Sinbad slippers and tossed them into a suitcase embossed with AzTek Development Consortium's corporate logo: planet Earth, opened like a broken egg, with a world dollar sign for a yolk.

Lucky let his puzzlement show. "All because you were wrong about me?"

Rashad turned a grin. "Don't bother yourself about it."

"But it's not like you're leaving for good, right? I mean," inserting a short laugh, "I'm not going to have to break in a new share. Am I?"

"Perhaps." Rashad closed the carrycase and secured its curious latches.

"Wait a second," Lucky said, wary again. "If you're just trying to get me to feel bad for you, Rashad . . . Well, I should warn you, I've already been softened up today." Lucky looked to the corners of the room. "Why don't you just tell me where the cam is so you can send AzTek a decent headshot."

Rashad forced a weary exhale. "For the last time, there's no camera. There is, however, voice-mail for you on the machine."

Lucky was grinning maniacally when he left the bedroom. Thinking: So that was it. Rashad had only been tenderizing him for a reaction shot to another of Bulaful's threatening vids. But when Lucky went to check his voice-mail, there was only a message from Braxmar Koddle, inviting him to attend some kind of science-fiction convention going on over at the Edward I. Koch Center.

Although considered by many to be an sf classic, Etaoin Shrdlu's novella "Tug of War" was in fact a somewhat pedestrian—some said drug-induced—piece of pre-Turn eco-paranoia. The plot centered on a small group of humans, led by the ever-resourceful Linc Traynor, who discover that the polluting of Earth's atmosphere over the course of several centuries has been masterminded by an alien race, bent on taking over the planet once the proper mix of human-toxic gases has been achieved. To effect this change, the aliens—Sirians in the novella, from the world Naxis, who've somehow gotten their hands on a copy of *War of the Worlds*, which they're employing chiefly as a cautionary tale—have infiltrated, by means of space-time contiguity gates, hundreds of androids among Earth's population, programmed to introduce polluting devices or influence policy decisions of environmental concern. Shrdlu credits the invention of everything from the steam locomotive to Bakelite to these sinister ersatz humans, and the end of his novella finds some of them ensconced on the boards of corporations like Dow Chemical, Exxon, and Alcoa.

In the film version, *Zone Defense,* the author's dark comic vision was discarded in favor of a lovable aliens-among-us story that relied heavily on Hollywood star power and megacostly f/x. The film nevertheless did major box office among its eighteen-to-thirty-five target audience and became the first to break the $500 million mark set by Bruce Willis's *Die Really Hard.* Merchandised to the hilt, *Zone Defense* also spawned a plethora of licensed tie-ins, including toys, CDs, video games, comic books, air fresheners, fast food, bubble-gum cards, breakfast cereals, 900 hotline numbers, theme-park rides, and finally the series of shared-universe spinoff novels known collectively as Worlds Abound, in which "Tug of War" was so enlarged upon, altered, twisted, that by the time book thirty-two came along there was little left of the original plotline. Some of the novels were set entirely on Naxis, the Sirian homeworld; others dealt with Sirian history and the failed attempts at earlier planetary conquest. Minor characters were elevated to starring roles in their own books. A second alien race, the Genoween, was introduced; then a third, the Morphean.

Former adversaries of the Sirians, the Genoween try to ally themselves with humankind. Unfortunately, their arrival on

Earth coincides with the outbreak of a global war no one really wants to fight but which has been instigated by resident Sirian androids who, now in defiance of their programs, have succeeded in getting themselves elected to positions of world power. The Sirians, at the same time, concerned that an escalating war on Earth could lead to the use of nuclear weapons—effectively spoiling things for everyone involved—are populating Earth with a new and improved batch of androids, programmed to find peaceful solutions to the planetary crisis and at the very least spearhead an antinuclear movement, which, with luck, will insure the continued use of conventional weaponry.

The capture of a Genoween ship and the subsequent deciphering of the ship's technosystems allow for a war between Earth and the Genoween homeworld, which just happens to be named Nu-Urth. No one, meanwhile, is paying the slightest attention to Linc Traynor and his heroic band of eco-terrorists, who, apprised of the ultimate goal of the Sirians by a renegade android, have forged a separate peace with a Genoween faction and are now out to avenge Earth against its unrecognized foe.

As of book thirty-two—*Edge of Space*, by one Bixby Santiago—Earth is still at war with the Genoween, although a contingent of Arab, Japanese, and German CEOs are on their way to Nu-Urth to discuss terms for a cease-fire. Linc Traynor and his band of crackerjack heroes are marooned on a now-lifeless Naxis, the Sirians having fled the dying planet to wage interstellar war on a race of shape-changers known among the denizens of the local group worlds as the Morpheans. On Earth, Linc's eco-terrorist counterpart, Lance Killdare, has just learned that the woman he loves—Velma Karr, the vice-president of the United States—is none other than a Morphean spy named Franz. Franz, however, has agreed to release the names of the Sirian androids holding office in various senates, presidiums, and boards of directors worldwide in exchange for certain intelligence Linc Traynor's wife, Billie, has gathered on the Sirian battle plan.

True to Shrdlu's original vision, though, Santiago at least had the Sirians continuing to infiltrate their so-called "Trough" agents through space-time portals—although Santiago termed them "Adits."

And Braxmar Koddle, who had been living and breathing Worlds Abound for four straight months, was—with Ziggy Forelock's consent, of course—about ready to book a spot of top-floor gargoyle ledge at the Hagadorn Pinnacle.

With publication of Bertelsmann-Farben's *Stroika*—the much-anticipated sf sequel to *Fracta-calities*—slated for the following February, Sony-Neuhaus had less than six months to ready a project of comparable value and submit it to the Arts Council for release approval. Which left Braxmar something like four months to deliver a workable draft of the assigned Worlds Abound wrap-up novel. A narrow window, regardless of the autowrite expert systems made available to him. But there was no backing out now—not with S-N already talking Major Motion Picture, toy and vid-comic tie-ins, Virtual Network role-playing games, a possible theme-park character-licensing deal.

So Brax had been asking himself: What was one irreparably dazzled brain in the face of this marketing blitz? He was after all a writer, a casualty waiting to happen long before Project Grand Finale had been dumped on him. And really, all he had to do was come up with a beginning, a middle, and an end for the damn thing. Concerns he hoped to share with the writers who'd contributed to the series to begin with, several of whom were scheduled to present at the convention known as PhenomiCon. On Asia's advice, Brax had invited Lucky along as well, in the hopes of enlisting his participation in the project.

He was waiting for Lucky just now, pacing in sunlight on the broad sidewalk fronting the Edward I. Koch Convention Center, glancing at his wristwatch, greeting arriving writers and editors with distracted waves. His usually on-time former roomie had promised to show by eleven, and here it was eleven-ten already. But, then, maybe Lucky had been out late celebrating his departure from the Theme Park Advisory Group. Brax decided to be patient.

Originally conceived as a kind of forum for New Agers—Planetists, Gaians, the whole green gang—PhenomiCon had grown less and less sectarian over the decade and now catered to a mixed bag of renegade academics and fringe fanatics who emerged from their various microverses at least once a year to turn the con into a must-do event, recently known to draw more than its share of media attention and celebrity voyeurs. In any one discussion group, in any one hucksters' room or at any one data booth, you could count on a sampling of ufologists, semioticians, protohistorians, re-creationists, neocreationists, and role-playing wizards. The twenty-screen e-brochure listed panels on quantum computers, robot sumo wrestling, reconstructionist theory in literature, Virtual Network apparitions, interactive hauntings, the meaning of meaning, the demeaning of meaning

. . . It was often impossible to separate the professors from the students, the professionals from the amateurs, the costumed from the innately grotesque. But what with drugs, pornography, graffiti, and dangerous decibels eradicated, gatherings like PhenomiCon were what passed for rebellious behavior. Cons were the rebel yell of the disaffected, a statement of blanket refusal, an effort to make dents in the paradigm, to bend and stretch it shapeless if possible.

One reason why the huge electronic flatscreen sign bolted to the side of the convention center read: PARENTAL GUIDANCE ADVISED.

Ziggy Forelock hadn't missed a PhenomiCon yet.

And now, Brax realized, the Zig would have videogeists to talk about, disked proof of his interface with the telesphere.

Lucky turned up on foot just when Brax was thinking of calling it quits and heading inside. Lucky, in pegged pants and an eco-conscious "What, me worry?" shirt, looking a little worn around the edges: hair in disarray, forehead peeling from what must have been a nasty sunburn, some sort of silver medallion hanging low on his chest, obscuring most of Alfred E. Neuman's face.

"Did I miss much?" Lucky asked, his usual remark when he was late.

"You almost missed me." Brax leaned in for a closer look at the saucerlike thing Lucky was wearing. "Never figured you for the medallion type, Luck. Where'd you find it?"

Lucky gently freed the mini-Frisbee from Braxmar's hold and polished it with the hem of his shirt. "It kinda found me."

The metalsmith in Cairo's Khan el-Kahili bazaar who had mounted the croc-tooth-dented thing ended up using epoxy to fashion the chain loop itself, solder having failed to do the trick. Something about the metal, the old man kept saying, more and more intrigued with each tooth- and taste-test he ran. Even offered to buy it.

"*It* found *you*?"

Lucky rubbed his head in recollection. "Uh-huh."

Brax lifted an eyebrow, then shrugged. "Did you do any thinking about what I told you?"

"I'm no writer, Brax," Lucky began.

"You don't have to write, man. I just need to borrow your talent for remembering characters and writing software."

"I still think you've got me mixed up with somebody else."

"Look, least you can do is hear me out," Brax said, draping

an arm over Lucky's shoulders and walking him into the growing bottleneck at the security checkpoint. "I just want you to meet some of the writers who've worked on the series, listen to what they say about the characters they've created. Then we'll talk seriously about the project. And money." He stopped, turned, leveled a look at Lucky. "Unless you're going to tell me you've already found a new job."

Lucky shook his head. "But I've got some things to take care of, Brax. There's this guy Marshall Stack, see, and—"

"Well I'm sure Mr. Stack can at least wait till after lunch, can't he?" Brax aimed an elbow at Lucky's ribs. "My treat, Luck."

Piers had once occupied the stretch of Hudson now dominated by the convention center, and the river was the first thing you saw when you stepped into the building's eight-story atrium. Police hovercraft, Circle Line tour boats, New Jersey high rises close enough to touch.

The scene at the security checkpoints was chaotic—trouble with some of the robots manning the weapon detectors. But once inside, the crowd dispersed, people angling off toward elevators, escalators, people movers, exhibition halls. Or toward the registration counters, where Brax was headed.

"Just have to get you a guest pass." Over-the-shoulder to Lucky before disappearing into a Halloween tangle of aliens, phreaks, wizards, cyborgs, androids, space warriors, starstalkers . . . Even the vanilla attendees were oddly dressed, or outfitted in camoflesh or electronic fetishes—personal neon, fiber-optic rigs, Virtual Network wardrobes, flashing holos. Plenty of counterfeit weaponry: blasters, stunners, phasers, scramblers. Lucky couldn't help noticing that the marios refused to mix with the alien chic, and that the mainstream Twenty-One were keeping a safe distance from the chairborne sip-n-blow game masters and camoflesh transgenics.

Out of the center of the weirdness came Asia and Ziggy, and Lucky got affectionate hugs and kisses from both of them. "Hmmm, you feel good," from Asia fortunately, loud enough to earn Lucky a curious look from a bark-skinned alien woman standing nearby. Asia was wrapped in clinging Thai reds and gold; Ziggy wore shades, 35mm-film bracelets, and black astrowear.

"Lucky, what's Really Going On?" Ziggy's standard intro.

"Like I'd know," Lucky told him.

"How's, um, Ms. Paradise doing?" Asia said.

"Harley's doing her usual fine. Better than the two of us are doing. I think we're in turnaround."

"Should I be unhappy about it?"

"Ask me next week."

"Remind me."

Ziggy was staring at the medallion. "Since when do you wear jewelry?" He took firm hold of it, yanking Lucky's head down. "What is it, some kind of medal?"

"Just a good-luck charm," Lucky said, straightening. "Keeps crocodiles away."

Ziggy looked around. "Yeah, you can't be too careful in New York."

Asia squinted. "Is it silver? What do all these rings mean?"

Lucky ignored the questions. "I've been meaning to ask you, does that insurance policy you sold me cover spells?"

"Spells?"

"You know, like say somebody gives you the *mal ojo*, or puts a kind of curse on you."

Ziggy snorted. "He's worried working with themers all week long's gonna turn him into a zombie."

"Not anymore I'm not."

"Yeah, we heard you quit. Good move."

Asia looked at Lucky askance. "You're not serious about zombies, are you?"

"No, but I mean it about the spell. 'Nother words if I was to miss work 'cause of some, uh, voodoo jinx, could I collect worker's compensation?"

Asia pressed the tip of her forefinger to her lips, taking a minute to consider it. "Not the way your policy reads now. But we might be able to attach a rider. Stop by Altamont's booth later on and we'll put our heads together."

"Where are you?"

Asia indicated a crowd of perhaps one hundred strong, huddled in the rear of the atrium beneath the window wall. "Buried in that mess."

"So what's selling best?" Lucky yelled as Asia and Ziggy were walking away.

"Abduction coverage!" Asia called back.

Brax returned a moment later, shaking his head in an ironic fashion. "Typical. I had you registered but the system evidently ate your name."

Lucky tried to appear disappointed. "Well, lean into the turns,

Brax." Pausing for an instant. "But it was good seeing you. Guess I'll just be go—"

"Oh, no you don't." Brax took hold of Lucky's arm and turned him through a quick about-face. "Lucky for you I happen to be on good terms with one of the people at the desk." Displaying a holo badge like a magician conjuring up a playing card. "*Voilà!* One temporary pass. By the time this guy shows— if and when he does—you'll be registered under your own name."

"So, uh, who am I now?" Lucky craned his neck in an effort to read the badge Brax was press-applying to his "What, me worry?" T-shirt.

"There," said Brax, patting the thing for good measure. "Welcome to PhenomiCon, Professor Miles Vanderloop."

FOURTEEN

MICKEY FORMICA SAUNTERED away from the convention registration desk, deploying the pimp roll he liked to affect whenever things were going according to plan, following the program. Built tall and slender, with wiry muscle under milk-chocolate skin, Mickey could fit the part; but the pimp roll seemed at odds with the loose-fitting rags that passed for a costume. Gathered at the waist by a shocking yellow bungee cord, the baggy gray fatigues were a good five sizes too large for him, and the ratty sweater looked big enough to accommodate a second person—just as it was designed to do. It was possible, in fact, should one dare look closely enough, to discern the vertical seams where two like sweaters had been hastily Velcroed together, the neck no longer describing a circle but a kind of imprecise figure eight, as though the opening were awaiting a second head.

"Got him," Mickey told his partner through a camoflesh mask of the late action figure Rosey Grier. "Standing with the four-eyed silverhair."

Nikkei Tanabe executed one of his ninja glides to insure a clear view of their quarry across the atrium's marble floor, the turbo shrug and sidestep positioning him between a tall blond *ojinjal* enchantress in bark and an overweight *busu* dragon slayer squeezed into Robin Hood tights.

"You sure about that?" Nikkei asked after a moment.

Mickey nodded. "That's Vanderloop. Saw silverhair there pick up the name badge with my own eyes."

On a two-by-two-inch wrist display fully in keeping with the rest of his costume, Nikkei called up the comp-graphic composite Dante Bhang had supplied them, studied it in silence, glanced at Vanderloop, then looked again at the color screen. "Doesn't look like him."

"Well, natch," Mickey's narrow shoulders rolling beneath the tent of a sweater, "you heard Mister B: man doesn't like to be seen. Got himself masked is all."

Nikkei glided once, twice, relocating himself for a better shot at the gangly Vanderloop. "*Fuaji riron*," he told Mickey. Fuzzy logic. "Then why's he wearing a picture of himself on his shirt? I mean, of all the looks to choose . . . He looks like a flagpole with hair. Make that bad hair. So who's the *ojitarian* with him?"

"Probably his agent or something."

Nikkei thought it sounded reasonable.

Dante Bhang had them registered for the con's infamous costume event under the names Bruno Dell'Abate and Phat Ono. Mickey as the soon-to-be two-headed thing, and the short but sturdy Nikkei, in *yakuta* and chest-packed power deck, as a kind of fop cyberjock samurai alien, his face a palette of theatrical cosmetics, *bosai pakku* temblor travel kit hooked to his sash, antennae headgear capped with Zabu Zabu washload-agitation balls he'd lifted from the hotel laundry room. They'd stood watch in the convention-center atrium all morning, part of the costume contingent since shortly before ten—sandwiched among the *yanki* slavegirls, magicians, robocops, roustabouts, terminators, cat and bat people, and galaxy rangers. They had played *jan ken pon* just to pass the time, Nikkei always throwing paper to Mick's rock, waiting for the wrist screen to flash a confirm when Vanderloop's pass was accessed by the registration computers.

When the flash came, Mickey had volunteered to wander over to the counter to see who collected the name tag.

"What do you figure he goes?" Nikkei asked, edging up to Mickey now but keeping a watchful eye on Vanderloop.

"Eighty keys, tops."

"Think you can haul that all the way down to the parking garage?"

Mickey absently stroked the harness he was wearing underneath the sweater. "With this rig I can."

"I should let the man know we've acquired our target," Nikkei said, doing input at the mini-keyboard strapped to his chest. Dante Bhang was at that very moment somewhere crosstown awaiting the confirm.

The idea was to shadow Vanderloop till opportunity knocked,

then spike him with a knockout needle, fit him into Mickey's two-headed-thing costume, and walk him right out the convention center into the rented a-cell van. Simple as that. Following up the success, Nikkei had decided, with a few costly evenings of New York *mizu shobai*—the water biz, the redshift nightlife.

"So who'ziss Miles Vanderloop anyhow?" Lucky demanded of Brax as they were ascending the escalator to the second floor, bothered, for mysterious reasons, by the sound the chained medallion made each time it struck the holo-ID badge.

"Professor of semiotics." Brax was riding the stairs backward, waving to acquaintances while he explained. "There isn't much to say about him since not much is known about his personal life. Vanderloop says it's difficult enough trying to use words to convey meaning to a reader, or an audience, without that reader or audience dragging the writer into things. Insists on having his works speak for him—though he's been known to show up unannounced on university comp networks to deliver a lecture on the 'language' of bathing suits, faux-arts, computer icons, whatever."

Lucky fingered the name badge. "So he's planning to come here in person, huh? Or are you telling me guest passes are required in the network now?"

Brax laughed. "No. And that's exactly what has the semiotics and reconstructionalist contingents so worked up: the thought of their symbolist hero showing up in the flesh."

Lucky scrunched up his face. "Vanderloop's decided he wants his face on all the video news mags, or what?"

"Nobody knows what he has in mind. I can give you the rumor, though: It has something to do with Australia."

"G'day," Lucky said, reaching for the proper accent.

"Right." Brax swung around to step off the escalator. "You've been there, haven't you."

"Coupla times on business. That's where I picked up the bullroarer hanging on my bedroom wall. A new park's opening near Alice Springs—'out Center.' DreamLand. Getting a lot of bad press from the tribal peoples, the Aborigines. Not that there's a hell of lot they can do about it now, except move, maybe, which some of them are threatening to do. Land belongs to them, the way they see it. The damn park is going to sit square on some of their dreaming sites—their sacred places."

Brax shook his head in a mournful way. "No wonder you quit the advisory group."

Brax had learned that a few of his writer friends were holed up in a hospitality suite just off the main exhibition hall, and that's where he and Lucky headed after showing their badges to the robo-scanner working the door. Sony-Neuhaus was apparently picking up the tab for the suite, and judging by the amount of food and liquor that had already been consumed, it was obvious that Brax's cohorts—a nondescript bunch, dressed more mainstream than Lucky would have expected—were interested principally in making up for what they hadn't received in e-book advances and royalties.

Someone shoved a lite beer into Lucky's left hand as Brax was introducing him around. "Jack, Fiona, Ryder, Jasper, Trish . . ." Lucky forgetting the names even as he heard them.

Once the discussion got over onto the Worlds Abound project he listened attentively for the first five minutes, then shined it on in favor of private thoughts about Marshall Stack, nodding now and again just to give the writers the impression he was logged on. It was like Old Home Week for these guys and gals, talking about the characters and planets and situations they had fashioned for the series; reminiscing, as though all this weird space shit had actually happened to real people in real places instead of to literary phantoms inhabiting imaginary worlds. But Lucky understood, or at least thought he did. He could remember, teenage time, what a take it had been to anticipate the e-mail arrival of the latest installment of some totally gooey vid-comic series, or ride tandem over the unreal estate of a virtual gameboard populated with hostile creatures that were beyond the wildest transgenic fantasies of some biotech wiz. And he guessed he was still as fond of the sf genre as the next guy, catching each new flick, periodically checking in with the vid-comics. But no way he was going to allow himself at the ripe old age of twenty-five to get reinvolved with aliens and star wars, stuff he figured he'd outgrown about ten years ago.

So after an hour of chatter, Lucky excused himself and made for the rest room in the exhibition hall. The one in the suite was occupied and his bladder was nearly bursting from too many lite beers, his mind filled with images of shape-changers, programmed androids, sinister cyborgs. And damned if the hall wasn't filled with them, costumers and marginal types accepting free handouts at the booths, gathered in small circles comparing toy weapons, casting magical spells on one another, flashing secret neon signals. Even the rest room had been transformed into one of those scenes everyone naturally compared to the bar

on . . . Tatooine, wasn't it? Mos Eisley spaceport. Lucky testing
his trivia while he took his place on one of the lines to the
low-flow urinals.

The tiled rest room was so jammed, guys were pissing in the
sinks and bidets. And judging by the conversations, everyone
knew one another from previous PhenomiCons, other cons entirely, clandestine gatherings referred to only by cryptic code
words and hand signals. Over by the mirrors people were touching up their face paint and camoflesh, some scrawling graffiti on
the glass, others up on the sinks smearing the security-cam lenses
with lipstick and 'flesh resins.

Lucky, beginning to feel a bit discomposed, what with all this
powerful whizzing going on, decided to angle over to the stall
lines, which seemed to be moving somewhat faster. Just like him
to chose the wrong one, though; same in supermarkets and on
toll roads those rare occasions when he was at the controls of a
car.

Ah, but now things were moving, and just as well 'cause his
expanded bladder already had him doing the in-place shuffle.
Did make him feel a bit better to realize he wasn't the end of the
line, however; that distinction currently held by a short . . .
well, what was he really? An antennaed alien wearing a comp
deck in a front-load child carrier and a thin Japanese robe of the
sort handed out at *ryokans*, Japanese inns. Giving Lucky an
appraising look, possibly because he was the only guy in the
room not in costume. But doing the same anxious dance Lucky
was doing, all the while humming some Meena D tune to himself.

Finally Lucky found himself in that most desired of positions,
next in line, just as the door to the handicapable-accessible stall
swung open and a young kid outfitted as Wheelie from the latest
Batman movie motored out in a high-tech chrome chair. When
Lucky hesitated, the Japanese alien behind him said, "Look,
dweeb, at this con we're all disabled. Use it or I will."

Lucky showed the alien a dumb look and hurried along, thinking who was he to argue with a guy wearing Zabu Zabu balls on
his network antenna rig.

"How things look?" Mickey Formica asked when Nikkei
emerged from the rest room. "We got a shot at him?"

Nikkei looked back at the swinging door and nodded. "He's
in one of the handicrappers. I've got the door wedged, so he'll
have to fuck with it for a minute to get out. A couple of 'flesh

cases lingering at the sinks fixing their faces, but I say we go for it. I felt like a *chikan* standing on line—some kind of pervert."

"*Ganbatte*," Mickey said, starting for the door. "Let's go for it."

Inside, advancing on the stalls, they heard grunts coming from behind the wedged door. Mickey looked to his partner. "He still on the can or is that the—"

The door made a popping sound as it yielded to Lucky's tugs, then a hollow *clang!* as it flew inward, slamming into the wall of the adjacent stall. Mickey and Nikkei positioned themselves either side of the door as Lucky stepped out, red-faced and frowning.

"D'ya give it a good shake, doc?"

Simultaneous with Lucky's turn to the short alien who'd been behind him on line, he felt a strong clap on the back. An almost immediate sense of vertigo washed through him, along with a weakness that instantly buckled his legs.

"Whaaa? . . ." Lucky managed as he pitched forward.

To which Nikkei replied, in a nasal whine, "He has fallen and he cannot get up."

Mickey caught Lucky in a bearhug and began dragging him backward into the stall. No one had witnessed the collapse, but the sudden sound of laughing voices reached them from the rest room entrance.

"Stay by the door while I get this monkey on my back," Mickey hissed, lowering Lucky onto the toilet seat. Quickly he stripped out of the oversized sweater and pants, exposing the harness that would cast Vanderloop as the costume's white-headed double and enable Mickey to piggyback him out of the convention center without arousing suspicion. Squatting in front of the bowl, he tugged Vanderloop's arms over his own shoulders, locking the professor's wrists in the coupler he wore at chest height. Then he hoisted Vanderloop onto his strong back, Vanderloop's medallion digging into the skin between his shoulder blades, securing him with half a dozen front-fastening Velcro straps. Now, if he could only get Vanderloop's feet into the stirrups and struggle back into the balloon trousers . . . But it was no use. The professor's long legs refused to obey, snagging the pants each time Mickey attempted to pull them up around both their waists.

"Nikkei," he whispered at last. "Get your ass in here."

The robed alien pushed open the stall door, laughing as the scene registered. There, after all, was his tall black partner, hunched over in front of a toilet bowl with his trousers down around his knees and a loose-limbed *shiro*, a white man strapped to his back.

"*Donjustanthere*!" Mickey snarled. "Fit this fucker's feet into the stirrups and get my damn pants hitched up. Then you gotta get this sweater over our heads—"

Mickey's abrupt silence and indignant glare launched Nikkei into a ninja-quick one-eighty, head lowered, legs spread slightly, hands already raised. Facing him from six feet away stood three characters no taller than himself, sporting 'flesh and wristphones, two of them costumed in face-shielded helmets, flak vests, stretch pants, and knee boots. The helmeted ones had weapons drawn—stubby handguns, way too fanciful-looking but exquisitely detailed nonetheless.

"Well, what do we have here," Nikkei relaxing his martial stance somewhat, "SWAT team from the planet Circlejerk?" Making it sound like one word.

"Drop the Earthman," the one nearest Nikkei said, his armed cohorts stepping forward to flank him.

"Drop the Earth—" Mickey began and broke out laughing.

Nikkei joined him momentarily before rearranging his expression into a death scowl, eyebrows beetled, nostrils flared, upper teeth showing from beneath a curled lip. "Or what, kids, you're going to make gun noises at us?"

"Drop the Earthman," the leader of the trio repeated.

Mickey, trying to straighten under Vanderloop's weight, was still chortling. "Security actually let those nasty-lookin' weapons through, huh?"

The leader gestured, and the armed trooper on his left turned his weapon on the chrome trash receptacle mounted on the wall. "Show them," the leader said without taking his eyes off Nikkei.

"We're just shaking in our grav boots, Darth," Nikkei said.

But he knew things were about to get serious when the weapon emitted an ear-piercing sound and the trash bin was instantly puddled.

"At least Bixby Santiago's book was starting to return the series to its roots," Jack Baumann, an editor who had worked on *Worlds Abound*, was saying when Brax realized that Lucky had been gone for almost half an hour. The conversation bored Lucky—that much had been obvious—but it wasn't like him just to up and leave without saying goodbye.

Brax slipped a fresh disk into his tape recorder, told the gang to carry on, and left the suite, standing for a moment in the carpeted hallway wondering which way Lucky might have gone. He decided to check the exhibition-hall rest room first, telling himself, however, that Lucky would probably have returned to use the one in the suite if he'd been forced to wait this long. Still, it was worth a shot.

Nearing the room, however, Brax spied an out-of-order sign posted near the swinging door, a maintenance worker in coveralls at work on the door lock, security man standing close at hand.

"Damn kids," the woman said when Brax asked what had happened. "Musta used some kind of acid on the thing." She showed him the slagged lock mechanism she was attempting to remove from the door.

Brax regarded the molten thing in astonishment. "Jesus . . . How long ago?"

The woman's narrow shoulders heaved. " 'Bout fifteen minutes," she said without turning from her work. "Still got a coupla kids stuck inside."

The security man snorted. "Every con you get this kind of shit. They mess with the cameras inside so we can't even tell who did what."

Brax glanced at the door, then smiled to himself, thinking Lucky'd wandered in at the wrong moment, become embroiled in a bit of PhenomiCon mischief making.

But five minutes later, when the woman had the door opened, the only people to emerge were angry costumers, a wizard, two or three creationists, a squat alien wearing antennae, a black guy in oversized pants and sweater. "Three guys dressed like futuristic cops . . ." The wizard was starting to explain to the security man when Brax headed for the escalator.

Downstairs he made a quick sweep of the atrium, then slowly wended his way to the Altamont Insurance booth, where Asia was slumped in her chair, fanning herself with a print brochure.

"Never again," she said, looking up at Brax. "I swear, this is my last PhenomiCon."

"You'll say that next year, too," Brax told her.

"No, I mean it. Only so much fringe you can take."

Brax nodded, trying to show concern. "You haven't seen Lucky, have you? He was upstairs with me, now he's disappeared."

"Long as he doesn't plan on filing a claim," Asia deadpanned.

"No, seriously. I can't find him anywhere."

"So maybe he's with Ziggy, watching the Virtual Network games."

Brax looked dubious. "I could see Eddie doing that, but not Lucky."

It was Asia's turn to show concern, and she gave it her best shot, only to laugh a second later. "Lucky only *wishes* he could disappear." She went back to fanning her face. "Give him some time, he'll turn up."

PART THREE

Heavy Meddle

FIFTEEN

AS A COLD front edged its way into his dreamless sleep, Lucky rolled over in search of the covers he figured he'd thrashed aside, and continued to roll and roll and roll some more until a throaty complaint from the body he finally contacted brought him fully awake.

Had there been a dream to cushion him, some guardian at the threshold given the power to transform the growl into a sound Lucky could sleep with, he might have painted Asia's face on the complaint. Asia had often snored; he would whisper her name and she would turn, sometimes to spoon her silken skin against his back. But without the dream Lucky had only the facts to confront: One, that he appeared to be adrift in a half crouch eighteen or so inches above the russet slope of a foul-smelling pit; and two, that the body he'd bumped into was almost certainly related to that slender-snouted wonder of the Irrawaddy, the Ganges, and lesser rivers of the Indian subcontinent, *Gavialis gangeticus*, known also as the gharial crocodile.

Here below him was the same olive armor, contiguous through neck and back, the dark blotches, the webbed five-toed feet . . . only this one was wearing shackles on all fours and some kind of dingy cloak from midriff to tail.

"Supercroc," Lucky murmured aloud. "The Disney version."

"Get the fuck off me," the gharial told him. "Or decide you're all right with losing that thing you call a nose."

Lucky offered a sleepy-eyed smile. "Sorry about that. You know how dreams are . . ."

The croc lifted its head, nudging Lucky with its snout. "Find someplace else to dream, meatball."

Lucky barrel-rolled through a full turn. "Hey, tell me about

171

it. I mean, you really think I wanna stick around here when I could be dreaming of Harley?''

The gharial in the cloak continued to regard him for a moment before turning to the croc lying next to him on the slippery bank. The distinctive knobs at the tips of their attenuated snouts identified them as males. ''Eslef, what's with this piece of gristle?'' Indicating Lucky with a spasm of its banded tail. ''Drifts around like he owns the place.''

The second croc stirred, one yellow eye popping open to appraise Lucky in free fall. ''It's got an excuse—it's human.''

Supercroc's snout snapped once, then again. '' 'Bout to be half human if it doesn't move its ass.''

''You'll be disappointed, blood,'' Eslef said, bounding more than bellying toward the pit. ''They taste more like chicken than fish.''

Lucky was entertained by the exchange, as he was by the entire hypnagogic scene: the cementlike depression, the baker's dozen of smart crocs tethered to the rust red slopes, the humid reek, the airborne excrement, food particles, water droplets, and unidentifiable debris, and the odd assortment of creatures lying in the faux grass beyond the depression or floating above it as though dangled from—well, yes, that was almost a kind of ceiling way up there where the sky should have been. And come to think of it, wasn't there something downright peculiar about the sunlight? . . .

Forget about it, he told himself. Some dreams just weren't worth reweaving. Shut your eyes, go back to—

His heart—wondering, obviously, how best to move all the ice that had formed in his vessels—was suddenly seeking a new rhythm, experimenting first with a sort of jazzy world-beat syncopation, a touch of Afrikaaner mambo, Thai polka, Eskimo clog, before deciding on a straight ahead four-four chest-pounding thud.

If he was already asleep . . . *then what the hell was he doing closing his eyes?!*

Just asking it sent him over into tachycardia. This time he knew he wasn't dreaming when the gharial said, ''I'm gonna give you ten, human, and then you're gonna wish you were made of tougher stuff.''

In a frantic effort to swim away, Lucky's foot caught the croc in the side of the head, the brief encounter enough to propel him out over the hole, two more gharials snapping at parts of him as he sailed overhead. Unfortunately the only object positioned to break his forward momentum happened also to be animate, hideously so at that, composed mainly of muscle-bound segments arranged in a column of clawed appendages and sucker mouths.

Lucky hit the living tower head-on, a meter or so below what seemed to be the primary mouth, but the thing stood its ground, even as Lucky commenced spinning around it in a one-armed hug. Gradually, however, the sucker mouths drew him in until he was pressed full-length against the pulsating thing, where various stalked eyeballs could have a good look at him and the mouths could run an assortment of taste tests. All of which Lucky failed—or so it seemed when the tower shuddered him free. But by then a kind of water buff covered with corn flakes was offering an upraised, hair-tipped tail, which Lucky just managed to grasp on his flyby.

"Don't get too comfortable up there," the buff said while Lucky was trying to get a grip on the tail with his free hand. "And watch where you put your hands."

"Sorry," Lucky said, satisfying himself with a one-handed hold.

The furfuraceous creature motioned with its head to a fly thing hunkered down in the grass. "Recombinant over there made off with your grav boots while you were asleep."

"While I was asleep?" Lucky asked, voice breaking up like an adolescent's.

"When they floated you in."

I'm talking to an animal, Lucky thought. *I'm talking to a goddamned animal—*

"Authorities got him on a cultural-offense violation," the buff added. "Claims the charges were trumped up, but he's known to have done worse. I were you, I'd let him keep the boots."

Cultural offense, Lucky repeated . . . And all at once he had it. He understood where he was and why—although the *how* remained something of a puzzle. Bulaful! Bulaful had used some of that Nile magic to sentence him to a nightmare, a shamanic hell for cultural offenders. Lucky'd waited too long to correct the wrong done the Nuba nation, and now here he was, sleeping with the crocodiles, just as Bulaful had threatened.

As for the when of it, he had only the vaguest memories to go on; the last thing he remembered, in fact, was asking Arbor Slocum for a leave of absence from work, then . . . nothing. But judging from his growth of beard, his underarm stench, that had to have been days ago, and he couldn't have been sleeping for days. And, too, why wasn't he hungry?

Because you didn't get the munchies in the land of the lost, was why, Lucky decided. A-and you probably didn't sleep the same, neither. Like on a bed, f'instance. Or even on the god-damned ground!

Unless . . . unless of course he was . . . unless this place, this dank-smelling debris-strewn spot of horizonless hell was where themers went when they died. For real. Not just on some theme-park stage. Like Buddhists and Resurrectionists believed, that each of us structured our own afterlife. That existence, for those who led unexamined lives, was a kind of dream that determined the afterlife reality . . .

Lucky looked around openmouthed. Was this to be his fate, then? To be stuck for eternity in the Bizarro world with . . . with *character actors*?

He was still hanging on to the buff's tail when an ursine thing approached from out of the grass, lumbering up onto grav-booted hind legs to show Lucky a somewhat level-eyed gaze—although the creature's largest eye was maybe an inch higher than those located either side of its barbed proboscis.

"Whaddaya in for, human?"

"In for?" Lucky asked, wondering at the same time why his mind hadn't snapped by now, why he wasn't way past panic disorder into terminal schizophrenia or worse. *I'm a flag waving from a buffalo's tail and I'm talking to Yogi Mutant!* And, what, was English the lingua franca of this netherworld, shamanic or otherwise?

"Guy like you," the thing was saying, "don't look like you could do much damage. Myself, I'm in for public nuisance . . ." And it went on to detail the crimes it had committed, the circumstances of its eventual capture and arrest.

Aware all at once that he wasn't so much hearing the words as he was understanding them, Lucky began a frantic one-handed exploration of his head, just to reassure that his ears, eyes, and the rest were all where they were supposed to be. Everything seemed to be in place, even his shadow, and yet it was though something other than his ears, something buried deep inside his head was doing the listening. Perhaps the same something that was managing the motion sickness curled in his gut, the panic roiling in his brain . . .

"So how about it, milk teeth, what'd they get you on?"

Lucky blinked. "Uh, cultural-offense violation."

The creature snorted, directing foul breath into Lucky's face. "Human-being crime. It figures."

Lucky knew an insult when he heard one. "Sez who? Matter of fact, that, uh, fly-looking thing over there in the grass was apprehen—was busted on the same charge."

The creature sniffed. "I want one of your arms."

"Scuse me?"

"One of your arms, you're free to choose which."

Lucky attempted a polite smile. "Look, if this is some kind of macho challenge like arm-wrestling or Indian—"

"They're not going to feed us right in here, I'll find food my own way."

"Ff-ff—"

The creature took hold of Lucky's forearm and was beginning to palpate it, searching for bulk that just wasn't there, when the buff lifted its big head to speak. "Forage somewhere else, hairtower. I've taken a personal liking to this one. Keeps the gravity ticks off me."

Postholocaust Yogi fixed the Kellogg bison with its largest eye and snarled. "You and me both, shit-tube."

Lucky held on as the buff's powerful tail twitched, his free hand finally finding purchase on the furred end. "Easy now, guys, don't wanna wake the dead, do we?" Perpetually smiling, Lucky over into his inspector's voice, plotting an escape vector at the same time.

"Don't make me get up," the buff warned.

" 'Sa difference when you're gonna be back down before you know it," the bear-thing countered.

Let's see, Lucky reasoned. Letting go at the high point of the twitch would throw him over toward the fly thing, whereas a low-point release would—

The buffalo heaved itself up on stout legs, saying, "You've had this coming, pal." Yogi squared off with the buff. They were ready to mix it up when the sun came out.

Or what Lucky first took for the sun, but was instead an intense artificial glow centered in what was now clearly revealed as a ceiling, supported by inestimably high, featureless gray walls. The room itself—for it was indeed that, empty watering hole, floating bodies and all—was vast enough to be measured in square acres.

Brighter light still spilled through a tall trapezoid of doorway in one wall, briefly silhouetting two exoskeletoned bipeds, who stepped through the opening like animal trainers entering a circus ring.

"Vanderloop," someone said—possibly one of the trainers. "Vanderloop!" Repeating it before the first echo had faded.

Lucky muttered the name to himself. Jeez, he knew someone named Vanderloop, didn't he? Then, quickly looking around: Was Vanderloop here, too? And just what had he done to deserve it?

Meanwhile the two bipeds were slip-sliding across the room in his direction, rustling sleeping things out of the fake grass, batting aside floating bodies and zero-gee filth. Up close, the pair resembled knobby-faced demons, gargoyles without wings; the tubular growths along the armored insides of their arms were surely weapons of some sort. They were looking straight up at him now, where he was clinging to the buff's tail with arms and legs crossed.

"You're the problem type, is that it?" one of them asked.

Lucky swallowed hard. "I swear, I haven't seen him."

"Haven't seen who?"

"The Vanderloop you're looking for."

This got a laugh. "You're the one we're looking for, primate."

"Me? Why me?"

"Because you're Vanderloop is why."

Lucky's questioning gesture brought his hand in contact with the medallion that had slipped out from under his "What, me worry?" T-shirt and was now ascending toward the ceiling.

Clutching hold of it, his memory bloomed like a time-lapse rose.

PhenomiCon! Brax! Vanderloop! The rest room—

"Worlds Abound!" he shouted.

"Cursing won't do you any good, Vanderloop," countered the gargoyle who was extending what could have passed for a pair of tree-pruning scissors . . .

Lucky was still denying he was Vanderloop even after they'd towed him through a series of accordion locks and into a small room with burnished walls and domed ceiling, where the weight was suddenly returned to his body and his feet hit the unyielding floor. Hard enough to leave them tingling; but at least he could look *down* at them.

And now he was certain he knew where he was: in some black game room at the convention. Well, his body at any rate.

Oh, he'd heard the rumors, of course, about corner suites and subbasement corridors where all sorts of wild and weird shit went on. Full-turbo Virtual Network role-playing games without rules or regs or referees, where anything could happen and often did, where players ended up brainlocked in someone else's think tank, there forced to fight whatever was dreamed up, whatever was hurled against them. Odds figured, bets laid down, seconds selected to step in should champ or challenger crash, parameds sometimes on hand with locked and loaded pneumo-injectors, sometimes not. Pro players showed up wearing their own rigs, mastoids pasted with derms, chests dimpled with metaports for rapid injection. An interactive role-playing game . . . That would explain the talking transgenics, the null-gee floating, the altered sense of sound, the oddly suppressed feeling of motion sickness and terror. Vanderloop must have signed on as a player, then failed to show for some critical match. So when some of those rest-room costumers read the borrowed name tag they thought they'd found Vanderloop. And made off with the wrong guy! Result of which, Lucky had landed smack in the middle of a black contest, strapped to a chair in some unpoliced, unmonitored room of the convention center where some mario was force-feeding him an artificial reality through interface gogs and helmet!

"But I'm not Vanderloop," he railed, struggling to no avail against the gooey game figments who'd been sent to fetch him from the zoo room. "Somebody made a mistake, I'm telling you. I'm not Vanderloop."

The figment who had hold of his left arm directed a sly grin to his partner. Well, maybe it wasn't sly, maybe it wasn't even a grin. But the gargoyle's words made things plain enough.

"When all this is over . . ."—making it a question— "this one's mine. I don't care if it is human."

The gargoyle on the right sniffed Lucky up and down. "I don't know what it is about the excitable types that gets to you."

"I'll show you sometime."

Long after the exchange, Lucky's head was still doing the tennis-match snap. What was Vanderloop into, anyway, that he'd sign up for this kind of perversity? Lucky struggled some more, then slumped, suddenly overcome by fatigue, the downside of the adrenaline rush he'd been riding since awakening to the sight of a cloaked gharial.

"Straighten up," the grinning gargoyle demanded, digging a

gauntleted hand into Lucky's armpit. "Your keeper's here."

Ah ha, Lucky thought, rallying somewhat, the ol' *Tron* game-master routine. Just the person he wanted to talk to. Vanderloop or no, you couldn't just go around abducting innocent people from rest rooms. Jeez, talk about your cultural offenses.

Lucky was working up a fury when a red-haired beauty waltzed into the beer can of a room. No, not beautiful, he corrected himself, but striking, exotic, *alien*. Because aside from the mounds of flaming red hair, the statuesque physique, the form-hugging bodysuit, whoever'd written the game had given her features that were too symmetrical, eyes that were simply too green to believe, skin too pale to be pulsing with red blood. No way, Lucky thought. Human beings just didn't come this good unless you built them yourself.

"Professor Vanderloop," she said, attaching a smile to it, "I want to apologize for the way this has been handled."

"Just as I thought," Lucky began, elbowing out of the guards' hold—with their tacit consent, of course. "And it's about time. But before I decide who it is I'm going to sue and just how much I'm going to demand, let's get one thing straight: I'm not Vanderloop. And don't give me that grin, neither."

Lucky gazed up at the domed ceiling. "I'm talking to whoever's running this game. Not this redheaded sprite you've written. I'm not Vanderloop."

"I see." Red adopted a serious look. "And just who are you?"

"The name's Junknowitz, Lucky Junknowitz. Here, I'll show you." Forgetting where he was for a moment he reached for the wallet usually stored in his trouser pocket, but it was the Vanderloop holo badge his hand seized on instead. Natch, the wallet wouldn't have been written in, but then what the hell was the name tag doing there? And why the medallion? He'd never experienced a Virtual Net game that was quite so, well, real. The panic was mounting again, still contained but as present as a roaring fire.

The woman figment was giving the badge a lopsided smile. "My command of Earth languages isn't very good, but it looks to me like this reads 'Vanderloop.' See here," her fingernail leading, "Van-der-loop." She glanced at Lucky. "Imagine that, you are Vanderloop."

He narrowed his eyes. "Earth languages—nice touch. Only

this isn't my name tag. I'm only borrowing it. Now get this helmet off me before I call for my second.''

Red and the two gargoyles exchanged baffled looks.

Lucky urged the panic on. ''I'm not Vanderloop, goddam it! I'm not Vanderloop!''

Red laid a calming hand on his shoulder. ''Some initial disorientation is natural, Professor—especially after what you've been through. You were never meant to be housed with those criminal mutants in lockup. There was a mix-up. I'm still trying to trace the source of it.''

The radiant smile returned, flashes of blue-white teeth—result of a possible graphics malfunction, Lucky thought. ''I'll tell you where the mistake was made: in the rest room's where.''

''Professor, if you could just relax. I promise I'll explain everything later on. I simply don't want to risk overloading you—''

''I'm not Vanderloop!'' Lucky managed half a forward step before the guards grabbed him, pinioning his arms.

''Don't be difficult,'' one of them sneered into his ear.

Lucky twisted in their grip. ''Okay, okay, this is a costume thing, right? I'm still at the con and you people are all acting out some skit you wrote. Sent your damned cohorts out to kidnap someone, is that it? Well, I'm not a member of the club, understand? I mean, do I look like I'm in costume, f'chrissakes? You just have to trust me that this is my real face, okay? For better or worse, I'm just a dumb-shit ex-themer named Lucky Junknowitz, not some mysterious semiotics professor named—''

''Dr. Vanderloop,'' the woman said in a pleading voice.

''Bulaful!'' Lucky screamed, neck muscles standing out like cable. ''If you can hear me, I'm sorry. I'm sorry your team didn't get the title belt. They deserved it. I know that, you know that. Just release me and I'll put everything right, just get me out of this place!''

The guards looked worried. ''He's overridden the controller,'' one of them suggested. ''Should I alert damage control?''

Red closed her eyes and forced an exhale. ''Can anything else go wrong with this op? The Peer Group shows up late, you two toss him in with the stretch genes, now he's addling on me.''

''Must have suffered some damage during Adit transit,'' the same gargoyle offered sheepishly.

''How about we sedate him?'' from the other.

''We may have to.''

Lucky had quieted down but was breathing hard. "All right, you win. It's a game and I've forgotten the protocols." He lifted his eyes to the woman. "I'm s'posed to wait for you to give me some important message, a clue to my predicament, right? Well, okay, I'll play along, but let's just get started."

Red let out another breath. "Thank you, Professor, for being reasonable. I can't say much just now, other than to tell you that I'll be your escort for this first stage, and to promise you that everything will eventually be revealed to you."

"Okay," Lucky said, "now we're getting somewhere. You're going to be my guide—for the first stage. You've got information. You're taking me somewhere."

"That's right."

"All right, let's start with your name. What have they named you?"

Red's eyebrows formed a perfect V over her straight nose. "My name is Sheena Hec'k, Professor."

"Sheena," Lucky said, relieved, then laughing. "Sheena!" Whether it was Bulaful or some unknown gamester behind it, he at least knew he was still on Earth.

SIXTEEN

"THEN, WELL, THEY locked us in the bathroom," Mickey Formica explained, his black face set, frozen.

"The rest room," Nikkei amended quietly.

"Whatever."

Charlie shot Dante Bhang a concerned look. "Tell us what they said again," Dante broke the short silence, mashing a clove cigarette against the sole of his loafer and dropping the butt into the breast pocket of Nikkei's blue rayon shirt.

Mickey watched Nikkei for a reaction, waited for him to show some of that ninja flash. But Nikkei just sat there, properly chastised, squeezing a Zabu Zabu ball in his left hand. Yeah, they'd fucked up all right. Royally. Otherwise Nikkei wouldna been running his sorry-samurai number for the man and his convenience-store buddy.

"So what about it, Mickey," Bhang said, "Tell us what they said."

Mickey turned to him. "Said, 'Drop the Earthling.' "

"Man," Nikkei said, eyes fixed on the floor. " 'Drop the Earth*man*.' "

"Whatever."

Pained, Charlie looked at Dante again and rolled his eyes.

Five days had passed since the fumbled abduction, and the four of them were seated in the office above the store. Leaving Charlie to wonder, Dante hadn't phoned until the previous day, confessing then that there'd been a slight problem, a "setback," to use Dante's word. Seemed Vanderloop had eluded them, details to follow.

Dante and the two freelancers had arrived half an hour earlier, launching into the grim details of the setback even while Charlie was leading them up the rear stairs to his private quarters.

Mickey and Nikkei had located Vanderloop at the convention, followed him into a men's room, and gotten as far as needling him and strapping him into the contraption Mickey'd been wearing under his costume when a trio of rescue rangers had showed up on the scene, demanding that Vanderloop be turned over to them.

Charlie was still trembling.

" 'Drop the Earthman,' " Dante said, shaking his carefully coiffed head. "I don't know, Charlie, sounds like just the kind of thing you'd expect to hear from kids at one of those cons."

"Hear—maybe. Carry it off, that's something again."

Dante shrugged, unruffled. "Follow me here: One of these three sees Vanderloop get spiked. He runs out and tells his friends, and they all decide to play Justice League or some goddamned thing."

"Yo, Mr. Bhang," Mickey interrupted. "These weren't no kids in costumes. Had themselves some kind a laser gun."

Bhang scowled. "What are you telling me, Mickey, they were time travelers?"

"Whatever they were carrying," Nikkei said in the same quiet tone, "it worked a meltdown on a healthy-looking trash unit."

Mickey was nodding his head. "Used the fucking thing on the bathroom door, too. That's how they locked us in."

"Okay, so some whiz kid cobbles together a slagger in his basement. Something to impress his friends. It could still play like I said."

Charlie heaved an agonized sigh. "Dante, they got this . . . slagger through the weapons scanners, remember?"

"So the same wiz who built the thing figured a way to get it into the con undetected. No different than what these kids do in the Virtual Network. Soon as a freeze goes up around some corporate data dump, they're in there with heat."

Charlie showed him a twisted smile, but said, "And what, this same group of kids smuggled Vanderloop out of the country? You said yourself there's no sign of him." He glanced at Nikkei. "You checked the public-access nets?"

"I checked. There's no record of his leaving the country or surfacing anywhere else."

Dante gestured impatiently. "So he didn't leave the country. He's in hiding somewhere in the city. I told you the man's a phantom, Charlie. Now he's really got something to be paranoid about. People whacking him with knockout when all he's trying to do is take a leak." He snorted a laugh. "Remember what we talked about, Charlie. All we wanted was to milk this thing anyway. No one's going to hold you accountable for the man's mysterious way of disappearing."

Cola's look said *Not in front of the help*, so Dante backed off while Charlie pondered things in silence. Wouldn't do to have Mickey and Nikkei knowing about the Black Hole Travel Agency.

"You two sure it was Vanderloop you got?" Charlie asked after a moment.

Mickey bristled some. "A' course we're sure. Looked a little different than the compoz Mr. Bhang fronted, but the guy was wearing the right name tag. Some kind of fucking medallion, besides." Reaching a hand over his shoulder to touch the center of his back. "Damn thing made an impression on me, all right. Digging right into me while I'm trying to get him strapped on."

"Looked a little different?' Charlie said leadingly to Bhang.

Bhang lifted another clove from the silver case. "What are you getting at?"

Charlie's expression hardened. "The bottom of this mess, hopefully." He turned to Mickey again. "Did you tell *any*one about this contract? Before you came to New York, back in Berlin, maybe?"

Nikkei spoke to it. "No one. I swear it on my mother's ashes." He hung his head, muttering, "*Ikkene*—I fucked up."

"Anyhow Charlie," Dante said, "who the hell else would want Vanderloop?"

Charlie's gaze was penetrating. "I have to tell *you* who else might want him?"

Dante's Adam's apple bobbed.

Charlie mulled over Dante's notion that Vanderloop's disappearance could very well work to their advantage. No good reason, in fact, why he couldn't go downstairs right now and contact the Agency, explain how close he'd come to snaring Vanderloop, how the follow-up operation was going to require additional funds . . .

Dante smiled when he saw Charlie's eyes begin to sparkle. "Everything's going to work out fine," he was starting to say when the office intercom buzzed. Charlie reached for the handset, listened for a moment, then frowned.

"Sanpol," Charlie told Bhang evenly. "Says there's some people downstairs to see me." He paused. "Came out of the cold on company business." The Bronx Quick Fix's phrase for an Adit arrival. If Bhang was at all concerned he hid it well. "I'll, uh, just be a minute," Charlie said, excusing himself.

Could be nothing more than a group of new arrivals, Charlie thought as he headed for the stairs. Even if it was the Peer Group from Technical Assist, nothing to worry about. Save him the trouble of going through channels with the request for additional funds. He would play it contrite, apologize for failing them, hint that maybe he did require the Peer Group's assistance after all. But if they could just see their way to granting him one more chance—to prove himself.

That was the tack. Humble, servile, but eager to improve. Not overly humble, of course. Didn't want to give the impression Charlie Cola was anybody's fool, no way. The middle ground, he told himself, the middle ground.

Two Agency types were waiting for him in the storage room, a man and a woman, both tall, lean, zippered up. Jesus and Labib were securing the freezer door, Molly off at her comp station, quiet as a Smurf. Charlie walked directly to his desk, planted himself behind it, assured, businesslike. He'd get to the deferential part in a moment.

"What can I do for you?"

"Mr. Cola," the woman began, "my name is Tal'Asper. This is my partner, Rouge."

Charlie smiled pleasantly. "Glad to meet you. Welcome to Earth."

Rouge stepped forward, showing his hairless forehead to the ID scanner on the desk. "Mr. Cola, we're from Black Hole Tax Audits. First thing we want to do is to advise you of your rights . . ."

Brax's dark hollow in the loft had become headquarters for what he and Asia, sworn to keep things lite and optimistic, were calling Operation Lost Lamb. Asia'd volunteered her room, but Brax's made the most sense because a good deal of the necessary hardware was already in place: computer terminals, fax machines, a two-headed vidphone Brax had been able to borrow from work under the pretense of employing it for author conference calls related to Project Grand Finale, even a network wardrobe rig on loan from one of Eddie's chairborne frequent flyers—though it was unlikely anyone was going to have to go virtual to learn just where Lucky had disappeared to. Still, creating space for bodies and the additional tech pieces presented difficulties, in that Brax had to clear a path well into the center

of the room, strip his walls and desks of some of the Worlds
Abound notes, and sweep off that half of the double bed reserved
for Asia, should she ever decide to quit pining for Lucky and
acquiesce to Braxmar's frequent and heartfelt love-interest offers.

Brax, Asia, and Willy were crowded into the room just now,
huddled round the two-headed phone, on whose twin screens
appeared the noisy visages of field agents Ziggy and Eddie,
reporting in from the East Bronx and Queens respectively. Asia
had a remote keyboard in her lap, Brax a smart-paper pad; Willy
was handling the phone. Onscreen, Eddie had everyone's attention, having just been to see Harley at her apartment.

"Tell you why she was so hard to find," Eddie was saying.
"She's been floating with the Hagadorn crowd."

"As in the Pinnacle Hagadorn?" Brax asked.

While Eddie nodded, Ziggy said, "I told you guys I saw her
at the party the guy threw a week or so back."

Asia pinched her lower lip. "No wonder Lucky said they were
in turnaround. No more extras for Harley. She's wants a leading
man."

"The studio head's more like it," Willy muttered over his
shoulder.

"Ziggy," Brax thought to ask, "are you getting all this?"

Ziggy flashed a thumbs-up from the second screen.

On the first, Eddie was still nodding, straining to hear all the
comments. "Harley said she and Lucky argued the last time they
talked." He smiled. " 'A kind of fight,' she said."

"When was that?" Brax wanted to know.

"Almost a week ago. Right after Lucky got back from Egypt.
Over in Flushing Meadow Park."

"Did she say what the argument was about?"

"About Lucky quitting his job." Eddie laughed. "Hey, I
didn't realize it was Harley who landed him that gig with the
advisory group."

Brax said, "Did Lucky say what his plans were?"

"Harley says he wasn't very clear about things—like he had
a lot on his mind—but she thought he might be planning on
visiting Sean in Antarctica."

Asia sat up straight. "Antarctica? Sean doesn't live in Antarctica. He's somewhere in Brazil."

Eddie nodded. "That's what I told her. Anyway, she remembered him saying he had things to attend to."

"That's what he told me when he mentioned going to see this

Marshall Stack person," Brax said. He regarded Eddie's on-screen close-up. "Did Harley know the name?"

"She says Stack's somebody Lucky was working for when they met."

"Of course," Brax said in sudden revelation. "The promoter. The one who was running that high-concept sporting event . . ."

"The Original Olympics," Asia said.

"*Ab*original," Ziggy corrected her.

Brax grinned at him. "That was it. The Aboriginal Olympics."

"So maybe Lucky's looking for his old job back," Eddie suggested.

Everyone paused to consider it, Brax first to surface from the silence: "Maybe. And maybe he was planning on visiting Sean first. But that still doesn't explain why he'd leave without telling any of us."

"He has been acting kinda weird lately," Willy interjected. "Ever since he joined the advisory group."

Asia swung to him. "Ever since he met Harley, you mean."

"We've already run a check with the airlines," Brax said, and Lucky's name doesn't show up on any international flight lists—to Brazil or anywhere."

Willy swiveled in his chair. "He could be going overland. Riding bullets to Mexico City."

"And paying cash." Asia was doing keyboard input at the same time.

"Maybe he doesn't want to be traced," Eddie said. "Or found."

Brax, Asia, and Willy turned to Ziggy's screen. "And there was nothing in his apartment?" Brax said.

Ziggy shook his head. "Nothing showing where he might've gone. Plus, his clothes and his packs are still there. He didn't even unpack the one he took to Egypt."

Asia leaned toward the phone audio pickup. "Did you check his computer datebook?"

"And his answering machine," Ziggy told her. "There wasn't much in his journal but work-related entries. Expenses for the Egypt trip, notes on what went down at some park over there, but nothing of interest to us."

Brax asked about the phone messages.

"There was the message from you inviting him to the con, and some snippet of a guy in costume waving a kind of broom at the screen. Probably one of his themer buddies having some fun. Everything else had to be at least two weeks old, and none of it was relevant." Ziggy paused for a moment. "But are you ready for this? His roomie's gone."

"Rashad the people monitor?" Asia laughed. "Then Lucky's probably in heaven."

Ziggy snorted, then said, "No one in the building's seen Lucky or Rashad for close to a week."

Willy leaned back in his chair, interlocking his fingers behind his head. "What about Rashad's stuff?"

"I didn't want to do too much poking around, but I saw his closet's pretty well cleaned out."

"I don't blame you, Zig," Asia said on a serious note. "Guy probably left a hidden cam running somewhere."

"Hey," Willy said, springing forward in the chair. "Maybe it's one of Rashad's assignments. A stress experiment. Lucky comes home, finds no sign of his share, starts getting worried . . . Who does he call? How does he handle it?"

"That's just the sort of stuff the Video Observation Project was always after," Ziggy said from the screen. "Tell you one thing, it sure doesn't look like anyone was planning to be gone for too long. There's still food in the fridge."

"Who does Rashad work for again?" Brax asked, wand poised over the smart-paper pad.

"Aztec something or other, isn't it?" Willy said.

Asia snapped her fingers. "Maybe Rashad left a forwarding address with the Housing Authority or the e-mail service?"

Ziggy told her no. "I just came from there. They don't know anything about Rashad's leaving."

"So he obviously means to come back," Willy said. "Otherwise he'd have given up the share."

"Doesn't make sense," Asia said more to herself. "I'm worried."

Brax looked over at her. "We're all worried."

"Christ," Ziggy said from the phone, "talk about your RGO, huh?" Everyone fell silent again. "What are you thinking, Brax?" Ziggy asked at last.

Brax showed the phone camera a grim look. "I don't know exactly. But I keep thinking about the eyedee badge I borrowed."

"Dr. Vanderloop," Asia said.

Brax nodded. "Vanderloop never did show for the convention, and nobody seems to know why. Not that it's strange for him to cancel, but from what I gather he's usually good about letting people know beforehand. Now suddenly he's nowhere to be found.''

"Another disappearance?'' Ziggy said. "It's a fucking plague.''

Everyone naturally looked to Asia, who merely shrugged her shoulders. "Don't ask me to explain it. People are always entering claims, but Altamont hasn't paid off on a single one of them. Missing people generally turn up. Some cam somewhere picks them up wandering the streets or checking into a love motel, or maybe their name turns up on the passenger list for a flight to Bhutan or Antarctica—but they generally turn up, you know.''

Willy shook his head. "I don't know about Rashad or this guy Vanderloop, but none of that sounds like the Lucky I know.''

"What about people who get whacked in the head or suffer some kind of allergic amnesia?'' Ziggy said. "Citizen Watch turns up people like that every once in a while.''

Brax regarded him from across the room. "Lucky wandering around dazzled?''

Ziggy rocked his head from side to side. "We should at least check the Urgent Care Centers.''

"That was one of the first things I did,'' Brax answered. "And the hospitals, and the police department.''

"What'd the cops say?'' Willy wanted to know.

"They said to keep in touch. If he doesn't turn up in a week, I'm supposed to give them another call.''

"Brax,'' Ziggy said, "you're the one who said something could have happened to him in that rest room.''

The writer offered a reluctant nod. The day of the disappearance, he had questioned some of the PhenomiCon costumers he'd witnessed emerge from the locked rest room, but none of them remembered seeing anyone wearing a "What, me worry?'' T-shirt or a Vanderloop name tag.

Brax said, "Only ones I didn't get a chance to talk to were a guy in an oversize suit and an alien wearing an antenna set on his head.''

"D'you ask security about the rest-room cam recordings?'' Ziggy said.

"Dead end,'' Brax told him. "Apparently the lenses were so smeared with cosmetic it's impossible to identify who was in there or exactly what went on.''

"But these two you didn't talk to," Ziggy said, "maybe they saw something."

Brax shook his head. "I couldn't find either of them."

"But, Brax," Ziggy pressed, "if these two were costumers they mighta been registered for the competition, right? So it should be easy enough to get their names."

"Just because they were in costume doesn't mean they were there to compete, Zig," Brax countered more harshly than he meant to. "Anyway, what good would it do even if we found them? Suppose they do confirm Lucky was in there just before someone ruined the door lock. Where does that leave us?"

Ziggy frowned. "At least we'd have a last-seen. And we could start from there. Maybe track down the kids who sabotaged the door lock."

Brax ran his tongue over his teeth. "Okay. Maybe we can. The descriptions given con security make them sound like your typical futuristic movie cops: shiny helmets, flak vests, knee boots, the works." The wand moved over the smart-pad. "I'll make a note to find out the names of the two costumers I couldn't locate and see if I can't learn something more about the prankster cops." He looked up from his jottings. "But I think we should be working some other angles as well. Like calling Lucky's brother."

"Forget it," Eddie said from the phone. "Why do you think people go to the Amazon to begin with? They don't want anything to do with phones. Or TV, or the movies, or the Network. It's person to person or not at all."

"What about getting Sean's address from Lucky's sister?" Brax asked.

Asia snorted a laugh. "I wouldn't bother calling his sister. They're not on speaking terms. But we could try reaching his parents down in Mexico."

"Where in Mexico?" Brax asked.

"Outside of Oaxaca," Eddie volunteered. "But I bet we'll be up against the same thing with the phones." He paused for a long moment. "I've been promising them a visit . . ."

Asia leaned toward the phone. "Could you get the time off?"

Eddie's long exhale issued from the speaker. "I've got some personal days coming. I guess I could do it." He shook his head in wonderment. "Mexico, shit."

Ziggy said, "How 'bout I give this Marshall Stack a shot?"

"Go to," Brax said.

Willy was strangely quiet. "I don't know if I can arrange any time off," he said at last.

Asia regarded him knowingly, then announced to everyone that Willy already had a quest going. "For the maker of the audience-friendly instrument, right, Willy?"

"What's all this about?" Ziggy said.

Willy turned a scowl at Asia. "It's nothing. Just a guy I've been trying to talk to. But let's drop it, okay?"

Asia spoke up, hoping to let Willy off the hook. "You know, I could probably interest one of Altamont's investigators in this. After all, Lucky is a client."

"Great," Brax said, glancing up from his notes. "Then that only leaves Vanderloop."

"Why him?" Eddie said.

Brax switched off the smart-pad. "Because it could be someone was after Vanderloop and took Lucky by mistake."

SEVENTEEN

AS PER SHEENA'S instructions, Professor Miles Vanderloop—marked for constant observation—was escorted down to rec deck and there confined to safety deposit in a comfortable enough pocket of atmosphere and gravity, similar to Sheena's own modest cabin on level six, with nourishment, diversion, data-drips available on physio-demand, a place to clean up if so desired. Not that Sheena expected the Earther would make much use of the conveniences.

Sheena was on her way to level six just now, cycling through archaic locks, riding a succession of repulsor fields ship's upward, negotiating mazes of sharp-smelling corridors, past viewports, observation blisters, gun emplacements recently retrofitted with tactical lasers and plasma cannon, moving through doorways sized and shaped to meet the requirements of a mixed-species crew, asking herself every few steps, at each security gate and transfer node, just what it was about the current assignment that had her so vexed. Perhaps simply that her Earther had arrived addled; that the Peer Group who'd delivered him hadn't lingered long enough to catch hell for it, fading even before the ship had thrust from Sierra—the malodorous old freighter two star systems removed from the way station now, but at last emerged from its own jump, downshifted, returned to the light, closing on its first port of call. Or perhaps the anger welled from her half-formed conviction that "Vanderloop" was lying, feigning confusion, running a simulation. All those denials for starters: *I'm not who you think I am, a mistake has been made;* the appeals for help directed to no Terran gods she knew of—this Bulaful, this Braxmar; and finally the fact that the Earther's mystification seemed to ebb and flow, which certainly wouldn't be the case with a faulty controller. Coded to individual molecular chemistry, DNA-keyed, cranially implanted by error-intolerant machines, the mighty-mite devices either functioned or they didn't; and when they didn't it was typically a corpse one accepted on delivery, not some spindly, hapless human nursing a dubious dose of memory wipe. All the same, it was imperative she play by the program. If for no other reason than to safeguard against the very real chance of being set up by Black Hole Tyro Assessment—a test to determine whether the days spent at Remedial Guiding had taught her anything. Reason enough in itself to distrust the Earther, who just might prove to be something other, more or less, than he appeared. A Black Hole operative, for one thing: human, silicon intelligence, reconjugated Probe, who could say what. Or perhaps some vat-grown soulless flesh-clothed facsimile, like the Sysops' White Dwarves, serving no function other than to evaluate those whom the Agency designated suspect.

A chilling thought. But what angered her most, regardless of whether the Earther was by nature or by design a provocateur, was the smirk he'd displayed when she furnished her name. As if he'd been apprised beforehand of her obsession with Earth—Adit Navel, the tertiary world on which her father had been born, though she'd never visited it—and had toyed with that, practically laughing at her. When all these years she'd been led to believe she was named for royalty, after some stately queen of the forest.

Sheena sighed for her own sake: Ah, the miserable state of things since Avonne, where she'd had her first glimpse into the fathomless sink fate had placed in her path. As if what happened there had been her fault. Well, possibly the brawl she'd fomented in the Adit concourse, the swift damage she'd inflicted to a couple of Yggdraasian chins and groins. But even then all she'd been attempting to do was protect her chub group from harm, save the Agency a slew of lawsuits—or, as it turned out, save Avonne from an episode of spontaneous HuZZah replication. The Agency certainly had no right to blame her for their materializing there to begin with, nor for the shipping screwup that had set the Yggdraasians on destruct. Given Black Hole's interest in open warfare, one would have expected an intensive investigation of the glitch itself, the misplaced shipment of arms; but the only thing anyone wanted to discuss was Sheena's "attitude problem," her lack of professionalism. Or so it had been explained by the half-dozen division reps and counselors who'd interrogated her thus far, including one ill-tempered human-conjugated Probe named Yoo Sobek.

Surely it was Sobek who'd seen to her demotion, the dismal days at Tyro Assessment, the desk work, the escort assignments on human-populated tertiary worlds. Save for instances of ordinary contact, she had even been denied professional dealings with members of different species—ordinary contact in the present instance defined as a decrepit freighter moving recidivists through a war-torn sector of intersystem space.

And now this Vanderloop person, damaged in transit by the Peer Group from Technical Assist entrusted with his abduction and fade from Earth. And what a group *they* were. Agency riffraff, strictly low end. Someone up top cutting corners, Sheena had decided. Leaving her once again to work around the glitches, to minister to the calamitous results of Agency mismanagement. All she was required to do with Vanderloop, however, was deliver him to al-Reem. Once there he became someone else's problem.

Sheena had half a mind to quit the Agency altogether; but she could feel her mood softening somewhat as she arrived on level six, anxiety easing out of her as a laugh when she finally reached the hatch to her cabinspace.

The expression on Vanderloop's face when he'd been pulled from lockup!

Let him smirk at her name; she'd always have the memory of his frazzled look to recall. And should he turn out to be an Agency operative after all, she would still have to respect that peerless performance.

Attractive in his own way . . .

Sheena summoned what she knew of Earth; thought what a shock it must be for someone who'd never set foot on another planet to be suddenly uprooted and plunged headlong into the mind-boggling wonders of the Trough. But then it was incumbent upon every person, every species, every world to mature when the time came—that moment often dictated by the Agency itself. Her father, for one, had survived the transition from Earth to Foxal without ill effect, or so Sheena's mother always maintained, and that was before nanite implant technology had been perfected; before the valve guides, hearing aids, odor eaters, tongue twisters, dream machines that allowed an abductee to safely absorb and process all the transitional strangeness. Although it was apparent the little critters inside Vanderloop had yet to nest themselves properly. The Earther didn't even appear to know who he was supposed to be, much less where he was or why he'd been taken.

The reason for the abduction was a mystery to Sheena as well. Involvement of a Peer Group, however, lessened the likelihood of it being a subcontracted operation. No, this one had to have come down from Light Trap, Agency HQ. Perhaps the final plan called for Vanderloop to be returned to Terra fully indoctrinated in the ways of the Trough, as was sometimes done when tertiary worlds were about to be opened to tourism. Or could be Vanderloop wasn't native to Terra at all, but an Adit-addict who'd gone indig and now had to be retrieved before he compromised himself or any of the possibly hundreds of Trough residents on-planet. Only other viable explanation was that Vanderloop, as an indigenous Earther, had stumbled upon intelligence he wasn't meant to possess.

Was it any of her business anyway?

Inside the cabin, Sheena peeled out of her wearever, kicked off her boots, and headed for the particle shower. After that, a well-earned nap, a meal in the privacy of her small space. Then she'd have to see about securing Vanderloop a berth somewhere on level six where she could keep an eye on him personally. Al-Reem was still four baseline-days off, but by then perhaps some of him would be in working order.

Spread out on a horizontal support-field that hadn't been there when he'd been ushered into the cell moments before was an odiferous rainbow assortment of morsels, tidbits, dabs, and dashes, pleasing to the eye if you didn't mind your appetizers looking back at you, fabricated to please the palate providing your palate was accustomed to the texture of Play-Doh.

The little Claymation canapes had quite simply appeared, as had the energy table itself, their prompt—far as Lucky could tell—the growl his stomach launched when the doorway had sealed shut behind him. Hungry, he remembered thinking, *Two gargoyles lock me in solitary and all I can think about is food!* And presto, out of nowhere, out of thin air, pop appetizers, clamoring, each in its own fashion, for his attention.

Some neat trick.

Too bad the game writers hadn't devoted equal time to detailing the rest of the cell. The walls lacked adornment of any sort and had the same burnished quality as those lining the room in which he'd encountered his flame-haired sprite escort, Sheena

Hec'k. There were no windows, although faint amber light was provided by a kind of contained glow in the center of the ceiling where one could almost imagine an incandescent bulb having been mounted. The furniture consisted of chairs and a bed—a spread-sheet, Sheena'd called it—a sight-and-sound entertainment unit of some sort, and what looked to be a shower, off in one corner behind a folding screen that shimmered like tin foil. Although Lucky hadn't so much identified the items as he had recognized them, probably from the familiarization screens of some game primer or instruction manual. He even had an idea how the trick worked: only those things that were needed appeared. A player decided he or she was hungry and up sprang a tableful of fanciful fare; tired, you got a bed; soiled, a shower; bored, a soundtrack. And Lucky was all of those, except maybe bored, which in itself had him wondering.

Important thing, though, was to calculate the next move. Lean into the turns, figure the game's RGO. Sheena—the name still stirred a chuckle—had given him a device no larger than an old DAT recorder to use in case he wanted to contact her. But past experience with virtual contests suggested he'd probably have to acquire a few items on his own before Sheena would offer any further assistance. Things to present to her—magical scrolls, swords, spells, whatever—tangible evidence of his conquests, his abilities, his worthiness. Precisely what he'd taken the morsels to be before they'd started voicing their mouth-watering entreaties, preying on his imagination. Lucky took another glance at the spread; he had yet to grasp how the game masters were stimulating his tactile and olfactory senses. Virtual sights and sounds were easily enough engineered, but feeling, outside the usual kinesthesia that accompanied a game run, was a new wrinkle entirely.

Lucky turned to regard the sight-and-sound unit, aware that the cylindrical thing was altering its tune once again. Where the music had been cacophonous and frenetic a short while before, it was now rhythmical and exquisitely structured, Bachian in complexity. And he felt intimately connected to it, almost as if his own moodswings were setting the tone and tempo of the piece. The sound seemed to be originating inside him, in much the same way the voices of Sheena, the gargoyle guards, and the transgenic detainees had. Just the sort of device Willy Ninja would have flipped for, Lucky concluded.

He was moving toward one of the chairs when the overhead glow brightened suddenly and began to pulsate, followed an instant later by loud chirping from the player. Lucky dervished, completing two three-sixties, thinking he was in some deep shit if the music was truly a measure of his mood, when it struck him that the chirping could be some sort of countdown warning. Like he'd taken too long to puzzle things out and was suddenly running out of time.

He dug his heels in, smiled in self-satisfaction, and lowered himself into the chair, which immediately conformed itself to him. The glow continued to strobe, the chirping grew only more insistent. Lucky, suppressing what seemed to be a preprogrammed impulse to panic, sat unmoving. Let the time run out, he told himself. He'd just sit there and wait till they took the neural headband and goggles off him; then would he have a few things to say—

Sheena the sprite, looking alarmed enough for both of them, appeared in an abrupt rectangle of doorway. "Come on, Vanderloop," jerking a thumb, "I'm not chancing another demotion."

Lucky shook his head in a resigned fashion. "Let the time run out. I'm not going anywhere. I refuse to play." After a pause, a modulation in the chirping: "And the name's Lucky Junknowitz, not Vanderloop."

Sheena's jungle-green eyes bulged. "Look, pal," taking a step into the safe deposit, "maybe you're ready to call it a life, but I'm not. Besides, you're my assignment, so you're coming with me whether you like it or not."

"What, without any *things* to show you?" Lucky playing up the innocent surprise.

Sheena stared at him. "We've been targeted, you fool. Or's that brain of yours so garbled you can't think straight?"

"No thanks to you and this game you're running."

"Listen to me." Sheena showed him a level look. "I'm not the one running this game. I'm following orders. You'll have to take up your complaints with the Agency."

Lucky stood up. "Oh, so that's what the game master's calling himself, huh—the agency? Or is it herself?"

Sheena took a few quick steps, grabbed hold of Lucky's arm, and began to tug him toward the doorway. "Gods, they grow them skimpy on Earth," she commented. "Don't you eat?"

"Sorry if I'm not built like the Visible Man," Lucky said, frowning. "But jeez, how do you do that, anyway? I mean, it really feels like I'm being pulled along, you know. Amazing."

Sheena threw up her arms in a gesture of surrender, then quickly slapped a device on her belt, sentencing herself and

Lucky to share the same force field. "Where I go, you go, understand?"

Lucky's eyes registered the change; the visual world had grown noisy at the edges. "Hey, somebody's fiddling with the fine tuning or the tracking or some damned thing." He extended his arms straight out in front of him, did a kind of mime exploration of the invisible sphere in which he and Sheena were cocooned. "What the—"

Sheena's unannounced forward motion yanked him through the door. Someone had filled his stomach with metal and Sheena's shapely derriere was suddenly a powerful magnet. "Whoa, hey—talk about your bum's rush—"

He was running down the corridor now, lockstepped behind his sprite, her hair whipping his face. "So what do we have to do," he managed, "defeat a monster, answer a riddle, locate a secret doorway to a labyrinth—"

"The escape pods are one level down."

Lucky laughed breathlessly. "Escape pods . . . how 'bout an escape cliché?"

Sheena kept moving, jinking through turns like a pro action figure. The corridors were filled with aliens, all scurrying for cover. Sirens wailed in the distance, Klaxons shrieked. "Just stay with me, Vanderloop."

"Like I have a choice." Lucky saw two gharials slithering down an intersecting corridor. "Hey, I know those guys," he told Sheena. Yelling to the crocs: "You see that fly thing, tell him I want my gravboots ba-aa-aa-aaa-*awaahhhhhh!*"

Directly ahead, where the main corridor T'ed, was a huge transparency filled with nothing but stars.

Atlantic City, New Jersey, was one of the few spots in the States where one could still play at leading an unhealthful, non-aerobic, hypercaffeinated life-style. Where Vegas had boomed with Middle America, offering indoor rain forests, jousts, erupting volcanoes, and three-ring-circus events, drawing almost as many visitors annually as Orlando, Atlantic City had remained grimy and unmanageable, the magnet for gray-haired bus-riding slotniks from Long Island and chain-wearing, muscle-headed guidos from northern New Jersey. The East Coast gambling capital offered plenty of rich food, bottomless glasses of alcoholic drinks, inexpensive high-fat breakfasts, illicit drugs, moneylenders and launderers, gaming rooms the size of football fields heady with passive smoke, all-night bars free of decibel meters or intoxication scanners, private clubs where you could double-down with wanton men and/or women or view live contact sports like kick boxing or gladiatorial events. In addition, or perhaps most importantly, there was privacy. Privacy of the sort only the mob or federal intelligence could guarantee.

But even so, the former beach resort had seen its share of post-Turn changes. Most of the casinos, from the old Taj Mahal and Excalibur II to the newly completed Universal Studio's Wager World, played things for laughs. Winners at the slots, the tables, the wheels, walked away with all-expense-paid one-week vacations to the Bahamas, lifetime supplies of brand-name products, show tickets, passes to the head of the ride lines, personal dinners with E.T. or the Mickey. And even those casinos that weren't theme-oriented were likely to have exercise spas filled with specially designed machines that paid off on healthy blood-pressure, pulse, or lipoprotein counts.

Bodies slicked with almond and artichoke oils, Charlie Cola and Dante Bhang—fresh from a thirty-minute workout meant to build poker stamina, increase roulette reach, ease blackjack back—were down on their bellies on matching massage tables, being tended to, almost car-wash fashion, by twin overhead robo-masseur machines.

They hadn't spoken in three days, not since Charlie had returned ashen-faced from his quick trip downstairs to the store's back room, suggesting it might be best if Bhang, Formica, and Tanabe left—immediately. Charlie giving no explanation, but promising to be in touch. Dante surmised the cause of his friend's sudden alarm but had said nothing. Just the same, he had taken the precaution of ordering Mickey and Nikkei off to Atlantic City, where he hoped they would be too preoccupied sampling the local night life to cause or contribute further to any of the ongoing troubles.

Poor Charlie was still shaking from his encounter with the auditors who'd stepped through the Bronx Adit to read him his rights and scrutinize the franchise expenses for the Vanderloop operation. Only the smoothest of Charlie's double-talk had kept the pair from probing too deeply into past accounts, and he was fortunately able to produce an accurate accounting of the ordered background, overwhelming the two auditors with bills and receipts, including the invoice he had worked up to cover the legitimate and "miscellaneous" costs of Bhang's trans-Pacific odyssey.

All the while the records were being examined, however, Charlie sensed that the agents had some more sinister purpose in mind than a surprise audit. More than once he was tempted to mention that the Peer Group from Technical Assist had given their tacit approval to his plans for handling the background and snatch, as good as promising that no questions would be asked. But instead he kept his mouth shut, biding his time, waiting for his visitors to come to the point, until it became clear that time was working against him; each moment was bringing the auditors closer to looking where he didn't want them to look. And so ultimately he blurted out that, but for an unforeseen development, he'd come very close to nabbing Vanderloop only the previous week. That's when the woman, that Tal'Asper, had announced, yes, they knew all about the unforeseen development.

"So you were right, they *were* watching us all along," Dante said in a staccato voice while a half-dozen robo-hands were busy pummeling his hairy back and thick legs. The first interrupt of Charlie's nervous, twenty-minute recap.

Charlie nodded, sweat dripping from forehead and double chin. "They finally admitted it."

Dante snorted. "Scared you real good, did they, peeking into the books?"

"This wasn't some Peer Group from Technical Assist, Dante." Charlie raised himself on his elbows, beet-faced. "They were from BH Tax Audits. They read me my goddamned rights!"

Dante refused to be impressed. "Standard tough-guy ploy. Cop consistency—no matter what world you're on. So what'd you tell them after you realized we'd been had?"

Charlie took a look around the exercise room, a small portion of the hotel suite Dante occupied, whispering, "You certain we're safe talking here?"

Dante responded at normal volume. "Go ahead, speak your piece." He gestured broadly, fingers flinging sweat and rub-down oils across the room. "The CIA maintains this place as a safe house. Daily exterminations. They're into me for a favor or two, so I asked them to quiet the surveillance for our meeting." At the robo-masseur's voice prompt, Dante rolled over onto his back. "So what'd you tell your guests, Charlie?"

Charlie drew a breath. "Just what I planned: That as best as I could figure, it was Vanderloop's own people who intervened at the con."

"Smart. Make it look like Vanderloop's onto them now. Knows he's in trouble. Was that the idea?"

Charlie heard something in Dante's tone. Amusement? Sarcasm? He regarded the man for a moment, then said, "You haven't heard the rest of it."

Dante turned his head to one side to reveal a grin. "Neither have you, but go ahead, give me the rest."

Charlie studied Bhang's face. "Those costumers, the ones in the uniforms who took Vanderloop away from Mickey and that other one? They were from Technical Assist. They were the goddamned Peer Group, Dante. The Agency's got him."

Charlie had hoped to wipe the grin from Dante's face, but hadn't succeeded. "How 'bout that," Bhang said. "Well, as I say, you were right. Congratulations."

"Of course I was goddamned right." Charlie was allowing his irritation to show. "Soon as I heard about the weapons I knew it wasn't a bunch of science-fiction fans." His eyes narrowed, blinked as rivulets of perspiration found them. "The Agency decided my people—*my* people, Dante—couldn't be relied on to deliver Vanderloop. The Agency thought my people might be planning something else for him. What do you think of that?"

Bhang took a moment. "That we were dumb fucks to trust talking in your office is what I think."

Charlie shook his head. "If the office was bugged, they would have known the entire plan."

Bhang laughed. "Wise up, Charlie, they did know the entire plan. Not telling you, hell, that's just their way of giving you another chance. But trust me, they knew all right."

"And you let yourself be followed," Charlie said derisively.

"What can I say, it happens to the best of us."

Bhang's tone hinted at apology, but Charlie wanted more. "This was supposed to be our large score, and we blew it." Might as well give him some of the anger Didi, his domestic economist, was going to be dishing out when she learned the house alterations and vacation plans would have to be put off.

Bhang voiced off the masseur and sat up on the table, legs dangling over the side. "Don't be an idiot. The Agency was probably watching us from the get-go. They were testing you, Charlie. Seeing if they could count on you to run a clean operation."

A mournful sound escaped Charlie. "All the traffic, people coming and going, I should have realized something was up." He looked over at Bhang. "I knew I was being watched. The night Didi dragged me to the theater, lensmen pointing cameras at me like I'm some celeb they're paparazzing on the sly. That Indian-looking guy in particular. I even thought the guy was going to approach me about something. Must've been an Agency rep, leader of the pack, getting it all down for the honchos at Technical Assist, documenting Charlie Cola the Fuck Up.''

Bhang allowed him to go on in this fashion for some time before laughing. Charlie simply stared at him, amazed the man could stay so cool under fire.

"So, uh," Dante wiping tears from the corners of his eyes, "I don't suppose they told you where Vanderloop is now.''

Charlie called a halt to the massage, sitting up to mirror Bhang's pose, shrugging his shoulders. "I assume the Peer Group's got him—somewhere.''

Bhang sniggered. "Oh, to be the fly on the wall wherever that little piece of business is going down.''

Charlie was nonplussed. "That's all you have to say? I'm in shit up to my ears and you're concerned about Vanderloop?''

Bhang collapsed the smile and riveted Charlie with a look. "I haven't been sitting still, Charlie, no matter what you might think." He slid off the table, wrapping a towel around his taut middle. "I said from the start Mickey and Nikkei weren't the best money could buy. So after the snafu in the rest room I decided to do some backtracking. First off I contacted the group who sponsored the con. Told them I'd met Vanderloop there and and wondering if they had an address where he could be reached, or if they happened to know where he was next scheduled to be present.

"Naturally, I was expecting the same old song and dance about how difficult it is to pin him down. But instead they tell me I couldn't have spoken with Vanderloop at PhenomiCon, for the simple reason he never showed.''

Charlie looked appropriately perplexed. "I thought Mickey and Nikkei made him by his eyedee badge.''

Bhang nodded. "They made somebody wearing Vanderloop's tag, all right.''

"Are you telling me—?''

"Uh-huh. It wasn't Vanderloop. When I insisted I'd spoken to someone wearing Vanderloop's name badge, I got put on hold. Five minutes later some woman on the con committee gets back to me that someone at the registration desk had screwed up. Seems Vanderloop's badge was lent out to some editor for a guest whose own tag wasn't ready or some damn thing.''

"Could Vanderloop have sent a body double?''

"I don't think so. They wouldn't give me the name of the editor or the guest, but one thing's certain—"

"The person the Peer Group snatched isn't Vanderloop."

Dante smiled. "Give the man a new set of living room furniture, a free trip to Antarctica, a lifetime supply of non-aggro biodegradable detergents."

Charlie was still marveling over it. "But that's, that's—"

"Wonderful's what it is."

Charlie's brows arched. "Not the word I would have used . . . Wonderful how?"

Bhang paced back to the tables. "Don't you see the beauty of this, Charlie? You can blame the Peer Group. Say they jumped the gun. You had everything all set, but your people were instructed to exercise utmost caution, make sure Vanderloop hadn't sent a proxy, a body double. In the rest room your team ascertained it wasn't Vanderloop, only all of a sudden the Peer Group's agents step in and bungle everything."

Charlie was beaming, legs swinging over the table edge like a kid's. "And I tell them Vanderloop's going to be extremely difficult to snatch now that he's been alerted."

"Impossible to snatch is more like it."

Charlie gulped and found his voice. "How do you mean?"

"I told you I lost Vanderloop when he entered the States from Mexico? Well, I've since learned he was staying with colleagues in Washington. The con had an address, a drop for voice- and e-mail. I traced it through channels and got hold of the woman he was staying with. At first she didn't want to talk to me, but out of the blue she decides she has to. She tells me she's been trying to talk to the police for over a week and she can't get anyone to listen to her."

Dante put his hands atop Charlie's bare, slippery shoulders. "Vanderloop's staying with her, right? So one night he gets a call from someone claiming to be an Australian diplomat, and the guy is very eager to set up a meeting. The woman tells me Vanderloop is just as eager. So eager the two of them agree to meet that same night."

"And?" Charlie said.

Bhang squinted. "Vanderloop leaves the house and doesn't come back."

Charlie fell silent, then asked, "An Australian diplomat?"

"Things are beginning to emerge," Dante was back in motion now, tightening the towel. "Apparently the professor's all adjy about some missing abos—Aborigines. Some theme park going up on their tribal land that's got them pissed off. So they up and relocate their totem poles, maybe stash some of their sacred things. Only Vanderloop doesn't believe it for a minute. He's been saying the abos were disappeared.''

Dante held up a hand to silence Charlie's question. "Not by the Aussie government, mind you. Just disappeared by unknown parties. About six months back.'' He regarded Charlie for a long moment. "Raise any dust with you?''

"Sumatra!'' Charlie said, letting his mouth hang open. "The covert operation the Agency mounted . . . Christ, it's possible, it's definitely fucking possible . . . But why snatch a group of Aborigines?''

"I was hoping you could enlighten me.'' Bhang forced an exhale. "Maybe someone's starting a collection. But let's suppose the good professor was onto something . . .''

"Then the Agency would want him before he made too much noise.'' Charlie tracked Bhang's movements back and forth across the tiled floor. "They could have gotten to him in Washington—even though you couldn't.''

Bhang accepted the rebuke. "Okay, so they got lucky.''

"They got lucky all right.'' Charlie paused to mull it over. "But if the Agency made the grab in D.C., why wasn't I told? The auditors said Technical Assist grabbed Vanderloop from the con. Why bother to take the guy your people mistook for Vanderloop if they already had him?''

Bhang's laugh was ironic. "I've got a theory.'' He stopped to give Charlie an even look. "Vanderloop was grabbed by someone who doesn't want the Agency to have him.''

"What someone?''

"A competitor.''

EIGHTEEN

"SO YOU SEE," Professor Joseph Jacobs was telling his restless freshperson class from an ornate hardwood lectern, "it is impossible to discuss literature—any piece of writing, any tome, any text—without a basic understanding of criticism itself, an awareness that all works of literature, indeed all works of art, function independently of the artist's intention. Time and time again when we strive to discover intent, when we set out on a quest for meaning or symbols, we are brought face-to-face with the fact that final truth is simply unattainable; that each symbol is but a symbol for something else and something else again. The critic is left to determine just what the writer is trying to say; but the critic, him or herself, is destined ultimately to fall prey to the same errors, finding symbols where none exist, inventing meaning where there is none to be found.

"In this class, therefore, we won't be wasting our time looking for meaning in the assigned works. And we certainly won't waste time discussing symbols. What we will do is learn to break bush and follow unmarked trails through literature's semantic jungle. We will forage, we will sip from streams, we will live off the land, we will in the end dismiss the notion of arriving at a final destination and revel in the sheer joy of journeying."

Brief applause from the dark upper reaches of the lecture hall drew uneasy laughter from the professor's captive audience. Jacobs strained to identify the sole clapper, frowned, tugged at the trim white beard that lined his jaw. He was a small man of sixty or so, but well put together. He cleared his throat and assembled the hardcopy notes he'd been reading from, tapping them against the lectern's slanted top.

"We'll begin with the easy stuff: the first hundred pages of

Taylor's study of Sartre's *Being and Nothingness*. And,'' drawing the word out, ''the first three chapters in the Alan Alda book on the eating habits of Paul de Man and Jacques Derrida.''

Someone down front missed the joke and shot a hand out, maintaining that the course description made no mention of the Alda book.

In a theatrical gesture, Jacobs set his glasses at the tip of his nose and gazed curiously upon the flustered youth. ''Mr. . . . Sloane, is it?'' he asked at last.

The kid swallowed hard enough to be heard several rows away. ''Yes, sir.''

''I was making a joke, Mr. Sloane. Alan Alda's book isn't listed in the course description because there is no Alda book—at least none that I'm aware of. But even if there were, do you really imagine that someone would devote three chapters to the diets of two of the last century's preeminent deconstructionist critics?'' Jacobs paused. ''One chapter, maybe, but certainly not three.''

Still visibly confused, the freshperson only laughed after everyone else had.

Including Brax, seated sixth row center behind two anorexic Asian women with close-cropped hair, hoop earrings, loose clothing, and Free-toes, the latest in micro-weight low-impact transparent footwear. In the lap of the taller of the two sat a ghost-writer, a transcribe deck that was recording Jacobs's words and entering them as onscreen written text. The other woman used a fluorescent-pink wand-pen. By books, Jacobs meant disks, although Brax had been told by the kid two seats away that the work on Sartre was accessible via the Virtual Net.

Jacobs dismissed his students, and while everyone was heading for the exits Brax took a moment to wonder what a trip through the virtual *Being and Nothingness* might be like.

Freshperson English at Yale—as taught by Jacobs, at any rate—was considered an overview course, designed to acquaint students with the lifeworks of some fifty or so twentieth-century novelists as interpreted by a handful of literary critics. The works themselves were basically ignored, since all that really mattered was what the critics had to say about them. Unlike similar courses in twentieth-century cinema, however, marketing techniques and sales were only touched on. Brax, during his quick scroll through the university's summer-semester catalogue, had noted Jacobs's name listed for a senior seminar course in pop studies entitled "Film Stars as Cultural Phenomena," which promised in-depth dissection of the on- and offscreen personas of several cinema legends and National Treasures.

For the first time in too long a while Brax saw some benefit to being thirtysomething, beyond the reach of professional American educators. Post-Turn matriculation was a different creature than what he remembered from his own undergraduate days, when he and his bright-eyed peers had used slang terms like chud, fake bake, two-bagger, and team Xerox, thumbed through the pages of actual print books, and majored in programs like Wildlife Management, Bridge Technologies, Solar Architecture, and Wind Prospecting.

Nevertheless, he fell into step with the rail-thin students filing from the lecture hall and intercepted Jacobs at the podium exit.

"Professor Jacobs," Brax extending a hand, "I'm Braxmar Koddle. We spoke on the phone."

Jacobs stopped short, pivoted through a slow turn to study Brax's face for a long moment. "Ah, yes, now I recognize you. The science-fiction writer."

Brax summoned a polite smile. "I enjoyed your lecture."

"Has anyone ever told you that you appear more prepossessing onscreen than in person? Not that there's anything wrong with your look, it's simply that . . ." He scanned Brax head to foot. "One mustn't underestimate the value of mediagenics."

"Yes, well—"

"You know I have a theory about science fiction and Freud's theory of 'the omnipotence of thought'. . ."

Jacobs regaled Brax with the particulars while they power-walked cross-campus to the professor's office. Past stately faux-ivy-covered buildings, pole-mounted security cams, students on bikes and skateboards, police presence behind the tinted glass of a-cells, a geodesic dome in mid-construction. Seeing so many pale, thin skinheads in one place gave Brax a sudden case of the douche chills. Everyone seemed to be sporting the same "fab rot" prison-camp look—the collegiate fashion the urban *shinjinrui* and Twenty-One crowd were doing their damndest to counter with statement jeans, sonic wear, and brandstanding outfits.

Yale could have been another planet.

Several developments had preceded the previous day's call to Joseph Jacobs and the early-morning train ride to New Haven, not the least of which had been the discovery of the names of the two costumers Brax had seen emerge from what Ziggy and the crew were calling the RGO rest room. Phat Ono and Bruno Dell'Abate, logged as "cybernetic alien" and "Thing with Two Heads," were curiously the only two registrants who had failed to show for the costume competition. That they'd been spooked by what went down in the rest room and simply left the con sounded plausible enough to Brax until a routine trace of the phone number and address they'd given on registering came up false. Calling in old debts, Brax had prevailed upon a contact on the PhenomiCon committee to loose a knowbot on the security-scanner surveillance vid files and release the retrieved photos of Ono and Dell'Abate, which, upon being enlarged, revealed a cloth tag affixed to Ono's Japanese robe that read "Property of the Hotel Hagadorn Palace." Accurate likenesses of Ono and Dell'Abate—sans cosmetics and camoflesh—were achieved by having the security-cam photos computer-cleansed, and it was these scrubbed shots Brax then displayed to the desk and door people at the Palace, one of whom identified the missing costumers not as Ono and Dell'Abate but as Nikkei Tanabe and Mickey Formica—according, at least, to the credit cards they'd used. A woman from room-keeping was certain, in fact, that Tanabe had, in addition to the cotton *yakuta*, made off with two Zabu Zabu balls from the guest laundry. A courtesy man who worked the door remembered the two climbing into a stretch limo aimed at Atlantic City.

Willy Ninja had begrudgingly agreed to do the follow-up.

Eddie, meanwhile, had apparently located the address of Lucky's parents and, at last contact, was down Méjico way. On other fronts, Ziggy had a lead on the whereabouts of Marshall Stack, and Asia had learned that Sean Junknowitz had been named beneficiary in Lucky's abduction insurance policy. Asia was trying to interest one of Altamont's claims investigators in tackling the case.

The desk in Jacobs's small, poorly lit crib was piled high with yellowed books, old floppy disks, ROM cartridges, reams of hardcopy text. Two archaic monitors stood like outcroppings amid the clutter, and the place smelled faintly of tobacco smoke and whiskey.

Brax cleared a chair of books and student papers and sat down while Jacobs did lightning input at the keyboard on his desk, laughing aloud at whatever the hell he was entering. After a few minutes of this, he silenced the machine and swung around to face Brax. "Now, Mr. Koddle, remind me again what you're doing here?"

"Miles Vanderloop," Brax said.

Jacobs chortled. "You write a book about a man and everyone assumes you know that man personally."

Brax was familiar with the book, *At a Loss for Words: Miles Vanderloop and the Search for Meaning*, in which the man in question was described as a compulsive loner, a contrarian, a deep thinker in the tradition of Lévi-Strauss and the structural linguistic set. "You're saying you don't know him?"

Jacobs heaved a dramatic sigh. "Look, Mr. Koddle, what you and the other members of Miles's cult have to understand—"

"I'm not a member of Miles Vanderloop's cult, Professor."

"Regardless, those of us who know Miles have agreed to respect his desire for privacy. The last thing he wants is to have his life become the topic of media scrutiny."

"It may be the last thing he wants, but there's a good chance of that happening now."

Jacobs folded his arms across his chest. "Explain yourself, sir."

Brax leaned forward in the chair. "I talked to Ms. Mackenzie—"

"Coker? Professor of Semiotics at Georgetown?" Jacobs feigned a grin. "You're certainly hot on Miles's trail, aren't you, Mr. Koddle. Checking in with all his closest friends."

Brax ignored the sarcasm. "Ten days ago Dr. Vanderloop was scheduled to address a conference in New York. He never showed up. But he made no effort to cancel the appearance beforehand."

Jacobs waved a heavily veined hand. "That's just like Miles. Always running off at the last minute. Confusing the enemy."

Brax worked around the glower. "He listed Ms. Mackenzie's telephone number with the conference organizers. When I called her she seemed very concerned about him. She said she'd received half a dozen calls from people looking for him." Brax held Jacobs's stony gaze. "I'm not trying to pry into his private life, Professor. I just want to know why he might have decided to drop out of sight without even notifying his closest friends and colleagues." When Jacobs remained mute, Brax asked, "What sort of footprint was he going to plant at PhenomiCon, Professor?"

Jacobs sat back in his chair and stroked his beard.

"Come on, Jacobs," Brax said, "I know Vanderloop was ready to drop some kind of bombshell. Something to do with Australia."

"Before I answer," Jacobs began, "tell me what your interest is in all this."

Brax decided to play it straight. "I attended the con. A friend I brought along as my guest was wearing Professor Vanderloop's name badge while his own was being readied. My friend . . . disappeared."

Jacobs's eyes went wide with alarm behind the glasses. "I'm very, very sorry to hear that . . ." He shook his head. "But this couldn't possibly have anything to do with Miles."

"The bombshell, Professor," Brax reminded.

"Bombshell," Jacobs said dismissively. "Only in terms of the toll it would have taken on his professional standing." He gave Brax a long look. "Do you know anything about Australian Aborigines, Mr. Koddle?"

"A bit."

"Well, apparently a small group from a place called Papunya Reserve—perhaps it's Papunya Station—in any event, this group has apparently disappeared. Gone walkabout along the songlines that define the Australian landscape."

Brax suddenly recalled what Lucky had told him on the day of the con. "They're protesting some theme park that's going up on tribal land."

Jacobs nodded. "That, at least, is the accepted explanation. What first attracted Miles's attention were reports that this reserve or station had begun to attract huge crowds of tourists. It fit neatly with his interest in what he was calling 'The lure of Suddenly Empty Spaces.' "

Jacobs started pulling open his desk drawers, searching for something. "Perhaps you read about the art theft at the Metropolitan a year ago? A dozen priceless paintings—gone. Oddly enough, however, the empty spaces where the paintings had hung began to draw larger crowds than the paintings ever had. The same phenomenon has been known to occur when buildings are demolished or destroyed by fire. A kind of vacuum is created, along with an attendant curiosity as to just what will rush in to fill this vacuum up. It's as though a 'disappearance,' if you will, somehow hallows a given structure, place—or group, in the case of the missing Aborigines."

Brax found himself thinking about unexplained dropouts in video-disk recordings, and how those blank areas often fascinated Ziggy Forelock more than the recordings themselves. "So this is what Vanderloop was going to talk about? 'The lure of Suddenly Empty Spaces'?"

"No. As I said, that was what *first* attracted Miles's attention. Once he'd done some on-site investigating, the emphasis changed." Jacobs fell silent for a moment, obviously reluctant to proceed. "The disappearance of the Aborigine group became something of an obsession, you see, a mystery worthy of one of Miles's so-called 'unheard-of thoughts.' He began to believe that the group had been disappeared for some nefarious reason."

"Killed?" Brax said. "By the government or something?"

"Certainly not."

"Not by the theme park builders . . ."

Jacobs's hands fluttered about his face. "No, no, you're not listening to me. Miles believed that the group *had disappeared itself*—'passed beyond remoteness,' as he put it."

Brax stared. "As in walked themselves right out of our world?"

"Out of time," Jacobs amended on a derisive note. "Through a kind of doorway in the space-time continuum. Is that science fiction enough for you, Mr. Koddle?"

Brax scratched his head. The disappearance, the portal in time . . . there was something familiar about all of it. He'd heard or read something, recently—

"Needless to point out," Jacobs was saying, "several experts are ready and more than willing to take Miles to task for this sudden, decidedly undisciplined turn in his thinking. Although I personally suspect that he has reconsidered his stance and is prepared to recant. So I'm hardly surprised by the unannounced cancellation.

"However," he added in a rush, "in the matter of the pursuit of your missing friend, there is someone you simply must talk to." Jacobs scribbled something down on a scrap of paper. "He's frequently the voice of reason in these matters, a scientist as well as a debunker of the paranormal."

Jacobs offered the paper across the desk. Brax took it and read the name, Erik Vogon. Known in magic circles as "The Awesome Vogonskiy."

NINETEEN

IN THE UNLIKELY event of a catastrophe in deep space, Lucky kept thinking, *you might try using your seat as a flotation device, although frankly we feel you'll be lucky if you survive for more than a nanosecond* . . .

But he had to admit, things were pretty cozy inside the escape pod Sheena Hec'k had commandeered; in fact, the two of them were practically on top of each other—depending on which way was up. And Sheena apparently had made some adjustment to the twin-pack containment field as well, because the repulsion Lucky had experienced when he'd thrown that punch at Sheena in the corridor just wasn't in evidence now. Not that the pod, with its opposing contour couches, would have allowed for anything but a face-to-face configuration of bodies.

Pod, as Lucky had been figuring, meant one of those globular, maybe oblate crafts you were forever seeing in sf flicks. Rolled and pleated interior, upright seats, display console full of on-screen graphics, blinking telltales and idiot lights. Where Lucky was, however, pod meant something closer to "long, narrow, richly oxygenated tube built to accommodate two midsize primates—possibly one transgenic gharial—sealed and launched by explosive charge, largely unmaneuverable, though equipped with a broad-spectrum distress beacon and with two small hexagons of viewport." Lucky blamed semantics for the disparity between perceived and real. "Pod" somehow lost or gained something in the translation.

Depending which way was up.

The past several hours, by his reckoning, had revealed additional truths: primarily that he was, simultaneously, in deep space and in rather deep feces. Also that Sheena Hec'k, his escort in this strange space where pods were tubes and hors d'oeuvres propositioned you like pre-Turn tunnel bunnies, was not some horny hacker's vision of a centerfold-perfect virtual sprite, but a human alien or vice versa. And lastly, that what was left of the starship Sheena called a freighter actually had been atomically dismantled by particle beams fired from more than three million kilometers away—rather close by stellar standards, but still way more than Lucky's accumulated frequent-flyer mileage.

Lucky, wedded by some means to the contour couch and gazing past Sheena's look of grim determination, had viewed the ship's silent disaster. Centered in the hexagonal viewport behind Sheena's head, the old freighter had simply been taken apart, without a trace of coherent light or explosive, gut-wrenching sound—Lucky's preconceptions outwitting him once again—with only the slow inevitability of practiced devastation. Less and less of the ship was visible with each full rotation of the pod, and local space was now strewn with remains: blackened modules, jagged debris, clouds of drifting particles, thousands of escape pods.

"I knew we'd be in for trouble transiting this sector," Sheena was saying. "Like they didn't know it was a wrest area."

"Rest area?" Lucky said.

"I kept asking them, why are you sending us by ship? Why not an Adit fade to al-Reem? But you think anyone listens to me anymore? All anyone's interested in is doing things on the cheap. Like it was going to take a king's ransom to bounce us through the Trough."

Lucky wriggled a finger into his ear, as if to clear it.

"Damn Peer Groups from Technical Assist," Sheena was muttering now. "You make one mistake, crush one triad of Yggdraasian balls too many, dump one too many spontaneously replicated HuZZah on some worthless piece of space rock, this is what you get—a one-way fade to the void." She regarded Lucky with obvious distaste. "I thought I had it bad on Avonne, but you, Vanderloop, you're my worst tour yet."

"Whereas you," Lucky said, summoning just the right touch of sarcasm, "the wonderful moments I spent in lockup, this magical mystery tour of the galaxy, are everything I've dreamed of. Not to mention how nice it was of you to give me the couch with the view for the finale."

A smile played at the upturned corners of Sheena's lips, then quickly vanished. "You're a regular charmer, aren't you?" She sighted along his length. "And by the way, the likeness on the shirt doesn't do you justice."

Lucky glanced down at his torn and sweat-soaked "What, me worry?" tee. "That's not me! Wait'll I get a chance to shower and shave, will you? Then you'll see."

"Then I'll see what," Sheena asked, "that you're not Miles Vanderloop?"

Lucky bit back the denial. What use did he have for a name anyway? She wanted to call him Vanderloop, let her. Meanwhile, he'd just keep filing away every bit of information her anger released. Peer Group, Technical Assist, al-Reem . . . Some of the names—Avonne, the HuZZah, the Yggdraasians— did stir associations, however, conjuring images of places and races of beings. But the images were only that: pictures with captions. It was as though his mind had been force-fed an encyclopedia of the strange, but he was without personal memories to draw upon. Pressed, he could probably sketch the pincer of an Yggdraasian, the tiny cartoon hands of a HuZZah, when he was certain—well, fairly certain—he'd never traded high-fives with either of them. And he knew the words Adit and Trough, as well, though he couldn't recall having ever fallen through a rabbit hole, much less a tamed singularity.

Sheena was puzzled by all his questions. "A faulty controller," Lucky remembered one of the guards saying.

"Think of it something like a translator implant," Sheena had suggested when they were still onboard the freighter. "The controller allows for some flex in your thinking. Although I wish they'd programmed a bit more flex into yours."

"They gave me the wrong size," Lucky said. "Shouldn't that tell you something's wrong?"

"It's not for me to decide. When we get to al-Reem maybe they'll whistle for the dream machines to back out of your brain so they can fine-tune them."

It was only then Lucky realized Sheena was talking about living implants—nano-critters holed up somewhere inside him.

"These implants," he said to Sheena now, their faces no more than a foot apart. "What'd you call them again?"

She emerged from thought to say, "Dream machines. Unless you're talking about the translators—the tongue twisters and hearing aids."

Lucky laughed in spite of himself. "Too weird, the way it translates, I mean." He frowned. "But I guess English isn't spoken this far from Earth, so, uh, what is it you're speaking?''

"On the ship I was speaking Nall. Now I'm using my home-world tongue.''

"Which is what?''

Sheena allowed a grin. "No reason for you to know that.''

Lucky filed it. "Okay, but you can at least tell me what language I'm speaking, can't you?''

"You're probably speaking your native tongue. I have no way of knowing.''

Lucky recited a portion of the alphabet out loud in an effort to hear himself, as opposed to what it felt like he was doing in conversation. "So you're carry—uh, hosting one of these hearing aids, too.''

"Is this what Terran professors do, ask a lot of ridiculous questions?'' When Lucky sighed, she added, "Go ahead, let me hear you say it.''

"What?''

"Your name. Just once I want to hear you say it.'' Her eyes bored into him. "You do and I'll tell you why the freighter was scoured. It's something you should know anyway.''

"What, just because we've been lamped and left for dead you think there're some things I should know?''

"You heard the terms.''

Lucky closed his eyes. "All right, fine. My name's Miles Vanderloop. Zat make you happy? I'll give you any name you want. But I know who I am.''

"And who's that?'' Sheena put her tongue in her cheek.

Lucky hung his head. "Miles Vanderloop.''

And she began to explain about the war between Edri and Kammu.

Conflict between the two worlds erupted soon after they'd been given the thumbs-up by Black Hole for incorporation into the Trough, that network of worlds—primary, secondary, or tertiary, local and distant, self-governing or allied—accessible by Adit of either downside or deep-space deployment. The separate species inhabiting the worlds were both indigenous to Edri, where they had risen to dominance together, managing to coexist for some six million years with only the occasional lapse into open warfare, genocide, and the like. Intermarriage was proscribed by law, and to some extent by nature, but—as Lucky was to gather from Sheena's tale—many of Edri's remote villages and city-states had their own *Romeo and Juliet* to tell.

Rivalry, however, made for rapid technological advancement, and both species were eventually defying gravity and leaving their footprints on the surface of nearby planets—one of which proved to be hospitable to the high-altitude-adapted Kammu, who over the course of several dozen generations successfully uprooted themselves from Edri to homestead a world where their top-rung placement on the evolutionary ladder was assured. It was about this time that Black Hole Trough Administration decided to grease the wheels some by opening Adits on both worlds and allowing a chosen few to sample the miracle of Trough travel.

Word began to circulate among certain circles that two new destinations, two pristine destinations, had been opened to tourism, and it was only a matter of baseline weeks before travel agents, developers, and wanderers from far and wide began pouring through the Adits, introducing the now separated indigs to technologies and worldviews so advanced as to make their own seem backward by comparison. Not to mention foreign currencies, credit cards, chits, and crystals eager to be expended for local food, local color, local crafts. Edri and Kammu responded to this onslaught of foreign interest and sudden wealth with astonishment, which, as was so often the case with newly opened worlds, yielded quickly to outright greed. And soon the two were doing all they could to attract yet additional visitors and business travelers, and whatever scams and schemes and currencies arrived with them.

Inexorably, the principal economies of both worlds began to shift toward tourism. Appeals were made to foreign firms for assistance in the construction of hotels and roads, and to Black Hole itself to open second, third, fourth downside Adits to facilitate the movement of tour groups. Deals were struck with shipping concerns for routings through Edri's home system; travel conventions saw greater and greater numbers of Edrian and Kammese reps promoting holiday getaways; more and more ads cropped up in Black Hole travel monthlies, promising the most elaborate Adit terminals, only the best in travel experiences, the friendliest indigs this side of Foxal or Nmuth Four. On both worlds, arriving travelers could expect to be greeted by the equivalent of tickertape or confetti parades and attractive, scantily clad women bearing garlands of intoxicating flowers. Roadways were lined with stalls and shops where local crafts or family heirlooms could be purchased for next to nothing. Every Edrian and Kammese wanted a piece of the action, and as that action heated up the two species grew increasingly competitive with each other.

Edri was first in its dealings with tour operators to stipulate that stops on Edri *and* Kammu could not be included in the same tour package. Black Hole Pit Bosses who monitored the Adits were instructed to turn away those travelers whose intracranial magic markers revealed a visa for the rival world. Kammu retaliated by slicing the costs of its holiday flings, practically to the point of giving tours away. Edri followed suit, offering even greater incentives, grossly disproportionate to anything being offered along the Trough. The revised promises included cut-rate hotel and land travel packages, dinners with celebrities, even audiences with kings, queens, and presidents. Local ordinances were enacted that restricted indigs from using their own beaches or mountains or forests for recreational purposes. Gambling casinos and sex emporiums went up, psychotropic-alkaloid producing plants were imported for cultivation, animals were captured and herded into wildlife zones for easy access. In an effort to create more dramatic landscapes, the Edrians loosed a barrage of technological weapons against their agriculturally intensive, environmentally sound planet, undoing eons of handiwork. With an assist from Black Hole Tectonic Amusements, rivers were dammed and mountains were heaped higher. Nuclear devices fashioned deserts and vast wastelands. Seas were supersalinated to provide for greater buoyancy, atmospheric shields depleted for greater tanning potential.

But even these efforts proved too little, too late. Tourism had become not only desired but essential, a surrogate battlefield for two species incapable of exorcising bias and hatred. Kammu took to hijacking cruise ships and freighters, taking hostages willy-nilly, and forcing everyone to have a good time. Edri, meanwhile, used the Adits to raid and plunder Trough stops and way stations for hostage tourists. Kammu melted much of Edri's polar caps, in the hope that frenzied tides would erase Edri's prize beaches. Edri countered by destroying Kammu's sole moon. Ships heading to either world were attacked, inviting the fiery wrath of infinitely superior spacefarers who began to contribute their own reshaping changes to the two worlds. Black Hole continued to encourage transit through the war-torn sector, of course, but Trough Administration closed the downside Adits. Now there was only the war, carried out nonstop, fought with the few remaining interplanetary battleships each planet had at its disposal . . .

Listening, Lucky recalled an old film called *This Island Earth*, about some hapless Earth scientist who'd found himself enmeshed in the problems of Planet Metaluna just because he'd gone and built himself some Interociter thingamajig listed in the catalogue.

"So whose ship were we on," he asked when Sheena had finished up, "Edrian or Kammese?"

"Neither," Sheena forcing a sweet-scented exhale square into Lucky's face. "I told you, they're shaking-and-baking anything that comes within their range. Just to get back at the Agency for encouraging the situation to begin with."

"Black Hole," Lucky surmised.

A telltale flashed on the pod's small circle of console, and Sheena attended to a perplexing series of apparently pressure-sensitive instrument bars.

"Life alert," Sheena said, excitement evident in her voice.

"Life alert," Lucky mumbled back, smiling, shaking his head, watching her.

"Thank fate," she said after a moment. "Someone's locked on to our drift."

Sheena pushed her hair back from her face and donned what looked like a pair of foam earphones, only instead of wearing them over her ears she simply placed them on her temples. Lucky began to wonder just whether there *were* ears under all that red hair.

"Who picked us up?" he finally asked, still gaping. "Some luxury liner, I hope."

She shook her head without looking at him. "An Edrian ship."

The rescue ship, if it could be called that, was days in getting to them, during most of which time Lucky dozed, awakening now and again to nibble at rations, or watch Sheena busy herself with the instruments, sending out homing signals, entering course-correction burns, calibrating distances, whatever experienced XT space guides in the employ of cosmic travel agencies did at times like these—adrift in an escape pod against a backdrop of novel constellations, no horoscope out there Lucky could plot even if he wanted to, even if he'd had a working knowledge of the stars.

God, how he missed having a map to consult.

He dreamed, though, in a stew of languages new to him, of Harley and crocodiles. Harley riding a long-snouted Nile croc with Phipps Hagadorn's corporate logo emblazoned across its mountainous, maculated head. And of Ziggy. Ziggy at Phenom-iCon, inquiring after the RGO . . .

Lucky tried to devote intermittent conscious moments to the many unanswered questions orbiting the knot in his head. Like what pr-xactly had happened to him at the con. How had he been overcome? And how had whoever had zapped him gotten him away unnoticed? Although he imagined that had been a minor challenge compared to, say, getting him off world. Right up and out of Earth's gravity well!

But in what? he wondered. A ship? Or through one of these Adits Sheena kept talking about. With the help of a "Peer Group." He searched mind and body for memories of being lifted, carried, probed, jabbed . . . but drew a blank.

And yet here he was. And that meant . . . that meant—Say it! he told himself—that meant there were XTs walking around on Earth for who knew what purpose or purposes. Other than the abducting of ex-themers in turnaround, of course. And, holy strange, would Brax ever be surprised. Brax and his clique of Worlds Abound authors. The things Lucky'd have to tell those science-fiction hacks if and when he made it back home. For starters, that, yeah, sexy aliens were for real, as well as interstellar travel and ships outfitted with particle-beam weapons.

So how'd it happen those writers knew what they knew, anyway? Or were some XTs indulging in ghostwriting on the sly?

More to the point, it wasn't an ex-themer this so-called Peer Group had been after, but a nutty semiotics professor named Miles Vanderloop. Which was a whole 'nother mystery.

Once during the long wait Sheena had nudged him awake to report, "They've got a fix on us. We have a pull date of two baseline hours."

And Lucky had laughed dreamily, even though he understood that by "pull date" Sheena meant ETA. He could only assume that the continued quirkiness of the translations had more to do with his long-standing respect for the street vernacular than his familiarity with the intricacies of astrogation. 'Cause, hell, the movies had taught him terms like "tractor beam," "attitude burns," and "hyperspace," and none of those had come up in translation. Well, maybe the Edrians didn't use tractor beams, and maybe hyperspace was simply a convenient conceit, because whenever he tried using the words on Sheena, she only answered him with a baffled look. Part of the problem of being an extra in a celebrity-conscious world was that even when you finally landed an over-five part, you rarely got to say the choice lines.

Nevertheless, the Edrian ship was visible through the view-port now, and Lucky grasped that the pod was somehow being drawn toward it, or toward rendezvous with it at any rate. The wedge-shaped vessel had been looming larger with each spin of the pod, growing in increments within the hexagonal field, but rotation had now ceased and the battle-scarred ship was close enough to obscure the stars.

Capture brought out the worst in the pod: it shook, it groaned, it protested. It wed itself to the Edrian ship with a slap that dazzled the instruments. The sensation of spin returned, this time with a definite down attached to it. Lucky felt the blood surging to his head.

"Idiots," Sheena ranted. "They've got us upside down and ass-backwards."

"I'll thank you not to talk about my rescuers like that," Lucky managed.

She showed him a crazed look and snorted. "Your rescuers. Be sure to remind them of that."

The hatch at the head end of the tube blew open, revealing a circle of filthy metal floor six feet below Lucky's head. Sheena did something that nullified the field binding them to the couches and they slid out of the tube together, Sheena with sense enough to extend her arms.

Halfway out Lucky instinctively assumed a crash position, cradling his head in his arms, elbows absorbing the force of the fall, ending up on the hard floor all doubled over on himself like a yogi stuck in some obscene bowel-cleansing posture. He rocked through a completion of the forward somersault his body had begun and sat upright, rubbing his head and staring at two scrawny legs sheathed in tight-fitting red trousers that disappeared into oversized metallic-composite boots. Lucky's eyes followed the legs up to an equally narrow torso graced with three pairs of opposing arms, capped by a bulky but pliant-looking rectangle of head with an egg-shaped mouth and a wide-set pair of canoe eyes. A crest or fan of primary colors radiated out from the head like an Indian war bonnet. Lucky wasn't sure if he was looking at something artificial or organic, a crown or a kind of instrument halo. Or, for that matter, whether the red sheathing he'd taken for a uniform wasn't simply skin with pockets and pouches. Behind the Edrian stood others almost identical to it, two of whom were equipped with what could only be weapons whose shapes ran toward the cruciform.

The Edrians didn't seem to know what to do with their redundant limbs, and the arms that weren't cradling weapons or commo devices were flapping and flailing, executing moves Shiva himself might have applauded.

Sheena scampered to her feet with an agility Lucky could only envy under the circumstances and immediately began a gesticulating, roll-up-your-sleeves-and-take-charge romp and stomp, obviously meant to apprise the Edrians of just whom they had had the good fortune to rescue from the deep black. Lucky had it in mind to remind her of what she'd told him of the Edrians' hatred for the Black Hole Travel Agency, but it was too late for that. She was already showing her cranial ID implant to the reader the lead Edrian was holding in the lowermost of his hands.

"We're on a high-priority mission for the Agency and I demand that you show us to the ship's commander at once."

"You demand," the Edrian said in a sibilant voice. Something told Lucky he was hearing yet another new language. He looked at Sheena and let his tongue twisters say, "Uh, Sheena, you might wanna rethink our position here—"

"I demand that you honor the terms of the Trough Covenant and afford us the privileges any civilized culture would grant to a fully authorized representative of the Agency."

The Edrian inclined his blocky head. "The battle cruiser *Tall* is proud to bestow preferential treatment on all those who represent Black Hole."

"Then do so," Sheena said with a note of moneyed impatience.

The Edrian turned to regard one of his seconds.

"Lieutenant," he began, "see that the two humans are escorted to the head of the torture line."

Fortunately, someone intervened. Some higher-up clad in formfitting green, whose head crest displayed a rainbow arrangement of bright colors.

The cell Lucky was heaved into was high-ceilinged and ten feet wall to wall—he knew because he'd paced it off—without bed, chairs, sink, or info-tainment module. Not much of a cell at all, and way improper digs for such an important prisoner, an Agency captive, no less. But that figured; a little more than a week in the Trough and he was already downwardly mobile.

Florida hot, the metal box smelled like a mulch pile, a sourmash brewery, a cauldron of cooked soybeans—though few of the scraps littering the ridged floor were immediately identifiable as organic. Leastways no organic Lucky'd ever seen or sniffed. But in this the place was consistent with what he'd observed of the rest of the ship during the forced march from the dock lock. The green higher-up, leading his own group of captives—recent rescues also, Lucky ventured—had appeared midway along, exchanged words with the Edrian captain who'd so graciously welcomed them aboard, and ordered Sheena out of one containment field line into the other.

Lucky fought down concern for her well-being. What had she done for him lately, anyway? But torture . . . Just because she worked for this Black Hole Agency. It smacked of homicidal what-was thinking from before the Turn.

Where *he* came from . . .

It was plain from the moment they left the docking area that the *Tall* had seen major action in Edri's war with Kammu and the near group worlds. Every corner turned revealed areas of recent damage. Holes in the hull were patched with great jaggedly cut slabs of black metal, fastened in place by what looked like giant pop rivets. In other places breaches and lightning fissures were spackled with foam or clear metal sealant. Bulkheads and damage-control gates were scored and scorched. Steam hissed from ruptured pipes. Foul water and viscous petrochemical fluids of murky shades of red and brown had leaked from overhead ducts to create an ankle-deep corridor sludge reeking of sewage, sulphur, and decomposing animals. Displays flashed unheeded warnings of radioactive contamination. The air itself, circulated by giant malfunctioning blowers, was as pungent as cat piss. Breathing left Lucky with a raw, cheesy taste in his mouth.

The ship manufactured gravity as the freighter had, but here movement was ponderous. Nothing seemed to work right, either, not the blowers, the people movers, the hatches—which, when they functioned, opened just enough to allow you to squeeze through or duck under. Where there was illumination, it was of a flickering sort; but the ship was primarily dark in color and in mood. There were areas where the ever-present rumbling of the drive furnaces was deep enough to rattle your bones, others where it sounded as if someone had loosed ten thousand maniacs with amplified snare drums in the corridors. Pint-size service drones flew in crazed circles above the debris-strewn floors, slamming into walls, into one another, into the oversized feet or fragile legs of the unwary Edrian pedestrian. Having endured equal abuse, the red and green uniforms worn by the crew were as stressed as the rectangular faces of those who wore them—patched, split, repaired in spots with transparent tape.

Lucky caught sight of skittish animals that resembled cats, even dogs, and other creatures that were most certainly rodents. It was all enough to make him homesick for his perfectly ordered, committee-dominated little world back in Sol space.

After countless hours of cell pacing, Lucky reluctantly dug a hole through the muck to rid himself of a week's worth of shit stinking of alien foodstuffs, the odors touching off a salvo of alien images that edged him dangerously close to panic.

Ultimately, however, he persuaded himself to relax, surrendering control to the mighty mites curled up in his midbrain. Survival, he was beginning to learn, required a kind of Zenlike acceptance of the here and now, toeing a path of not-being. So instead of dwelling on the mind-boggling strangeness of his circumstances he reflected on the Edri-Kammu conflict, which as he thought about it brought to mind the pre-Turn rivalry that had broken out in Orlando between the Universal and MGM theme parks. The price-slashings, the bribes, the tour-bus hijackings—the parks' efforts to undercut one another had led straight to near bankruptcy and severe debt restructuring.

Lucky was still ruminating when Sheena sailed into the room, hurling curses at the guard who had propelled her through the narrow center-glide hatch. Whatever she'd been through had left her face and hands smudged with dark green grease, hair all in a flaming riot, nose out of joint.

"Damn Black Hole marker doesn't get you far around here," she announced, tugging at the sleeves and collar of her jumpsuit.

"Christ, at least you're not dead." Lucky sloshed over to her from the seat he'd fashioned from a length of conduit, catching her skeptical look. "I was worried, okay?"

She waved a hand. "It was all a bluff. They can't kill us, even if they want to."

Lucky waited for an explanation. "What, are we superheroes all of a sudden?"

She glanced at him and snorted a laugh. "Humans are a protected species, Vanderloop."

Lucky took a long moment to absorb it, deciding he would come back to it when his head stopped spinning. "Well, still, I had a right to be concerned. I mean, let's face it, you're my only way out of here."

Sheena folded her arms, canted her head. "You're right about that."

"Nothing personal."

"Long as it stays that way, Professor." She tossed him something that looked and felt like a large dried date. "Go ahead, eat it. You must be starved."

Lucky sniffed at the thing and nibbled, finding it tart but not unpleasant. "What is it?" he asked to cover the sound of the roiling in his gut.

"Chemical peel," she told him, backing away as Lucky began spitting pieces in her direction. "What's the matter with you? It's just food."

Lucky pressed a hand to his stomach, fingered an ABC wad from the side of his mouth. "Chemical peel?"

"So it's artificial. Doesn't mean it isn't nourishing."

Lucky took a breath and regarded what remained of the wrinkled oval. "Just that chemical peel . . . Well, it's got a different meaning for me. Picture flayed human skin," he told her.

Sheena did, and frowned. "We have to see about reeducating your hearing aids, Vanderloop. But in the meantime, eat. You'll need it."

Lucky thought fruit and took another cautious bite. "So the Edrians didn't want to listen to you, huh?"

"Not to some low-level guide." Sheena shook her head in a defeated way. "But there was a time, Vanderloop . . ." She looked at him, exhaled, said, "What's the use."

"No, I know how you feel."

"You? An academic." Snorting. "What do you know about working?"

"I know, is all."

Sheena's shoulders rolled. "Anyway, we're here and I've got to figure us a way out of this. But at least I learned why the freighter was targeted."

"It's not that they're short on tourists and want to offer us the holiday package, huh?"

Sheena grimaced. "Just what I need—a comedian."

"Hey, I promise I won't make jokes when they're torturing us."

Sheena fell silent, showing him her no-nonsense look.

"Okay, so why'd they bake the ship?"

"The Kammese ambassador was on board. On her way home after petitioning the Council of Worlds to negotiate a cease-fire between Kammu and near group planets."

"Did the council agree to intercede?"

Sheena nodded. "But only on the condition that Edri and Kammu come to terms first. There's talk of a possible summit."

Lucky walked a circle through the sludge. "Sheena, you think you could arrange to get me in on that sitdown?"

"You?"

" 'S'matter, you think I'm going to embarrass you? You think I don't know how to comport myself around . . . strangers? Earth's not just some end-of-the-galactic-arm kind of place, you know. Hell, we've been expecting contact with your type for, I don't know, hundreds of years."

She threw a pleading look to the ceiling. "Look, you see where my marker got me, and I'm Agency legit. You're . . . well, you're cargo, Vanderloop. At least for the time being."

"Yeah, but can't you make something up? Say I'm with Black Hole or something? That I'm traveling incognito, but these recent developments force me to reveal my identity."

Sheena considered it. "I suppose I could phony up some sort of story. Our markers prove we're on a high-priority mission. And the ones who interrogated me seemed awfully curious about you." She glanced at him. "It has to be that silly shirt, or that medallion you're wearing. Anyway, I think they already have themselves convinced you're a VIP." She paused for a moment. "Telling them you're with Black Hole Technical Assist wouldn't count for much. But we *could* say you're with Trough Administration—or better yet, Trough and Adits."

"Trough and Adits," Lucky said, "yeah, I like the sound of that."

Sheena angled suspicion his way. "You better tell me what you have in mind, Vanderloop. Even if I can convince them, what's an academic going to do that I can't?"

"Trust me," Lucky said, grinning. "I've got a way with beings in the tourist biz."

TWENTY

ALTAMONT INSURANCE'S EAST Coast offices were midtown on Manhattan's East Side, a quick subway from the South Bronx loft. Asia rarely made it into the office more than twice weekly, telecommuting when not out pitching Anomalous Trauma policies to the New Age diehards at cons, retreats, and holistic workshop weekends.

Her mom had gotten her into the biz, having crossed paths with Altamont's founder several years back in California somewhere, Big Sur or Monterey maybe. This was when Mom was still practicing healing, midwifery, and psychic surgery, working principally with Filipinos and Cambodian refugees—Mom herself a refugee of the wars that had quite literally wiped Cambodia from the map. As a kid she'd escaped into Thailand via Myanmar and there met Sandy Boxdale, Asia's father, an English expat who had come to Thailand to study Buddhism and ended up as a parasol painter, smuggler, and sometime tour leader living in Chiang Mai. Asia would always think of him as a painter, but she remembered times the small earthen house was packed with crated black-market goods enroute to the Un-Burma, other times when Sandy would ride in atop one of the pachyderms the tour company used to carry tourists on treks to the highland villages. She remembered, too, the thieves and mercenaries Sandy hung with, most of all the flashy merchants from Bangkok, up north on buying trips for pubescent Karen girls to stock the bars and massage parlors of Pat Pong.

Asia was ten when her mother brought her to the States, Sandy dead of the HIVirus—the Luggage, the Monster—which he'd contracted in Hong Kong before the Turn. Mother and daughter had settled in California, where Mom's brand of homeopathy found favor among the Southeast Asian community, especially those diseased refugees fresh from relocation camps whose bodies refused to respond to the instrumental bias of Western medicine. But even homeopathy couldn't save Asia's mother when the time came, and Asia had moved East to pursue what she hoped would be a career in painting. Instead, mired in New York City after a series of failed attempts at winning the hearts and minds of the Arts Advisory Council, she accepted a job with a Brooklyn life-style agency, casting character actors in theme roles for society parties in Manhattan and out-island in the Hamptons—one of the few agencies at the time willing to employ the likes of Lucky Junknowitz, in his more reputable pre-Goofy days, and Eddie Enseño, who was on his way to becoming Ensign and group leader lensman. Too tall to cast as Turtles, too short for Foghorn Leghorn or Big Bird, the boys' combined résumés listed such roles as Lowly Worm, Mr. Tumble Pig, George Jetson, and Alfred E. Neuman.

Early on, Asia couldn't tell Lucky from Eddie, but Lucky's clumsiness eventually served to single him out, and Asia'd found herself open-nosed, eager to sample some of Lucky's vertical architecture. She liked his guilelessness, his humor, the Mctoon schlemiel in him. Lucky was at least real, unlike the high-Q Twenty-One types she seemed to attract uninvited, and they knew some wild rush hours together—ad-lib the way it was meant to be, nonstop flex time and lip-synch. But there were basic differences they were never quite able to shortcut, and they wound up in turnaround long before they'd actually gotten 'round to sleeping in separate beds and long before Harley Paradise had made her entrance. Asia would decide later that she'd been too eager, too clinging—especially for someone as on-the-air as Lucky—but it seemed to be in her nature to fall hard when she did. She knew too many past outbreaks not to have recognized the symptoms. And this was the reason, perhaps, she was slow to warm to Brax's obvious interest. Not that she wasn't tempted. Brax was intelligent, mature, a take in his own silver and brown format; but the last thing she needed now was to work up a flop sweat about driving yet another guy away.

Besides, there were her performance routines to consider. Like she had time for a love interest when every moment she wasn't pushing policy was going into getting herself warehoused. As a member of the Femmes Fatales—a clandestine Goddess-worshipping artists bloc grown out of the ARTstrike Front and loosely allied to the Glossnost Movement—she was doing all she could to overturn the Arts Council's policies of recycling and reusing, the reducing of art to a Puritanized, citizen-friendly formula stripped of all vitality. Although the rejections sometimes made her wish she'd perfected the Cambodian dance routines her mother had taught her as a child. Asia's cousin had, and was now working as a temple regular at Angkor Wat and the Sukhothai theme park. Good pay, inexpensive living, weekends at Pattaya beach . . . Sounded better than being just some extra stuck in New York.

Of course, Lucky was always saying the same thing, and Asia didn't see him abandoning New York. She also knew that it wasn't like him to sneak off without saying a word to anyone. Even when he'd been offered the diznoid role down in Orlando he'd agonized over the decision for weeks, and stayed in constant touch with the posse after he'd been hired. When in town Lucky would attend her all-too-infrequent gigs. On the road to the occasionally exotic places his job with the Theme Park Advisory Group took him, he'd leave voice or e-mail messages at the loft—all of which Asia had stored, figuring one day she was going to assemble a kind of bio for his birthday.

Lucky was blood.

His insurance file was onscreen now in one of the workstations Altamont set aside for nonresident agents—Asia having arrived early to nail the station nearest the front door. As she heard Bullets Strayhand enter the office, she adopted a posture of intense though puzzled concentration. The very fact that she was in on what would normally have been a telecommute day wouldn't fail to register with Strayhand; Bullets was that kind of observant. A lensman without a cam.

"Nice baud, Asia," he called from the door.

She smiled over her shoulder. "You just like my overbyte."

He grinned back and shuffled over to her. "What's that you're squinting at, dark eyes?"

"Aw, just this Junknowitz case." Casual about it.

"Junknowitz?" He frowned, shook his head. "How come I haven't heard?"

Asia leaned away from the monitor, shaking her head. "Mysterious disappearance. It's not official yet, but word is a claim's coming down any day."

Bullets stepped into the station for a look.

Arguably Altamont's *uber*-investigator, Bullets's enormous success in exposing cases of insurance fraud had resulted in his winning, for three years running, the company's coveted Barton Keyes Award. Somebody over in claims adjustment maintained that Bullets had apprenticed with Erik Vogon himself. "The Awesome Vogonskiy," whose name, Asia'd learned, had come up in conversation between Brax and Professor Jacobs. But then someone else insisted he was former NYPD, busted for unlawful psychism during a sting operation by vice. Whatever the truth, Strayhand had the street instincts of a born cop and the honed skepticism of a professional debunker.

He was short, thickly built, with rather gross features and widely spaced eyes. His hair was naturally oily, the shadow of his beard prominent though he was known to shave twice a day. Still, there was something charismatic and unnervingly sensual about him, a flame burning in those eyes that encouraged people to open up to him.

Though Altamont had settled hundreds of claims for possession, fiery persecutions, stigmata, and bodily elongation—the infamous "Plastic Woman" case of two years back—the company prided itself in never having paid off on a case of mysterious disappearance. Bullets took special pride in knowing that he was the primary reason.

The case investigator was still leaning over Asia's workstation keyboard, scrolling through the final paragraphs of Lucky's Anomalous Trauma policy. "What's the spin on this one?"

Asia forced a breath through puffed cheeks. "Well, he was last seen almost two weeks ago at the Koch Center—PhenomiCon."

"Police been notified?"

"Twice. But they're not showing much interest yet. Junknowitz's brother asserts he's checked with all friends known to our client and feels justified in filing a claim."

"Don't they all. Give me a status."

Doing rapid input, Asia called up a data screen and read: "Junknowitz, Lucky. White male. Age twenty-five. Six feet tall, one hundred and sixty pounds, brown hair, brown eyes, small scar on the chin. Single, no dependents. Resides in a low-income dual-share up in the Bronx with one Tittle, Rashad—also presumed missing."

Bullets's eyebrows went up.

"According to the client's brother. No background info on Tittle available."

Bullets rubbed his stubbled jaw. "What else do we have on Junknowitz? Is he employed?"

"On-site inspector for the Theme Park Advisory Group. Currently on extended leave."

"As of when?"

"As of three days before he disappeared from PhenomiCon."

"What I hear, these inspectors get around quite a bit."

Asia called up the policy again, tapping a nail against the monitor screen. "Rider excludes double-indemnity claims for travel-related disappearances. This happened right here in New York, anyway."

Bullets took his eyes from the screen to regard her. "There are no disappearances, precious. They're part of the current mythos, like those stories about ghosts showing up in videos, circles showing up in wheat fields, mice at the bottom of soda cans. Who wrote the policy?"

Asia was prepared for it. "I did. I know the guy. He was a love interest for a while."

"Were you going to tell me," Bullets was smiling, "or let me figure it out?"

She returned the look. "I thought about it. Anyway, he's gone and I know him well enough to know he wouldn't just derezz on all his friends."

Bullets straightened, perching himself on the edge of the desk after ensuring that it would handle his weight. "You *think* you know him. Everybody thinks they know everyone else—their husbands, wives, lovers, parents, friends, shares . . . But it's all just panning and scanning. We see only what fits onto our screen; the rest we edit out. It's why people get fuzzy the minute someone they know skips; they can't believe the person'd do such a thing. Has to be an abduction—by terrorists, enemies, XTs. Turns out, though—and I'm talking ten out of ten cases here— the person's self-pixilated. Partnered up with someone in the family, hoping to settle a claim with us. An embezzler, paranoid about being caught with a hand in the cash drawer. Someone running from the mob or a legal-minded ex-spouse. Some camera-shy running from a past, the present, the future. Or an erotomaniacal lover, I've seen that happen. Or maybe the disappeared just smacked his head climbing out of an a-cell, or had someone smack it for him, and is wandering around without a clue . . . I'm telling you, Asia, fifteen years of this work and I've seen all of it and more. I've heard talk of people coming and going through openings in space or time or both of them, like the universe was just some backyard shot through with revolving doors. But this much I know: the minute you turn the lights on one of these cases, work up a background, scan the public videos, interview the family and friends, the odd street lensman, you find the footprints, like architectural neon you find them, and at the end of them the person, him or herself.''

He eyed the screen for a moment. ''This Junknowitz, for example. My guess, since I can see the guy's not your mainstream type, is he's off to see some love interest he met on one of his business trips—some cute little dark-eyed extra he bumped into in Bhutan or somewhere.''

Asia was shaking her head. ''Doesn't sound like—''

''—the Lucky Junknowitz you know. 'You' being the operative word, Asia. So maybe you can't imagine your friend up in the Himalayas, curled up under a yak-hair blanket with a woman whose name is all consonants. Doesn't mean that isn't Junknowitz's idea of paradise. That he hasn't been planning to disappear himself one fine day when he was on leave from his job and his roomie wasn't around to wonder about his not being home. You understand?''

''I guess.'' Asia wondered what Bullets might have to say on the subject of psychic surgery or homeopathic remedies.

Strayhand snorted loudly. ''Now, who'd you say was planning on filing a claim?''

''The brother: Sean Junknowitz.''

''And who's the policy benefish?''

''Same.''

''Same?'' Bullets showed her a case-closed look. ''Just where's this Sean call home?''

''Amazon.''

''Scientist, jungle bunny, or recluse?''

''A bit of each, I think.''

''And any other relatives I should know about?'' As if Bullets were taking notes.

''Mother and father, living outside Oaxaca, Mexico. But someone's already checking with them. A sister, Ann, in San Francisco. Already been questioned. Says she hasn't seen either of her brothers in years and prays her winning streak will continue for another decade at least.''

''Prays?''

''Her word.''

''Who's talking to the parents?''

''A friend—Eddie Ensign.''

''Other relatives?''

''No, but lots of other friends.''

''We'll get to them later.'' Bullets trained his eyes on her. ''And you have no idea where Junknowitz might be.''

"I'm clueless."

Bullets eased off the desk to a groan from its sim-wood surface. "Tell you what, you shunt Junknowitz's policy and background to my comp and I'll play with it some. You know I'm always looking for the legit case, precious. Who knows, maybe this Sean'll be the first beneficiary to collect on a verified disappearance."

The gently curved roof tiles of the small train station at Esmeraldas had been fashioned from red clay; the station's white stucco walls were adorned with paper posters and awash with quick-stencil slogans of the political sort. The paved street that paralleled the narrow-gauge tracks was quiet now that the train had departed for Escondido and the few passengers it had disgorged had been spirited off in waiting jeeps and mufflerless pickup trucks.

Eddie sat alone in the stark sunlight on a wooden bench outside the front door, hands locked behind his head, suitcase planted between his feet, while a cabbie nearby swept brown dust from the cherry-red hood of a Chevy interbust as old as the chirping video games that filled the station-house lobby. From somewhere in the distance came the laughter of children and the brassy strains of radio ranchero. Every now and again the cabbie would glance in Eddie's direction and nod his bald brown head. Eddie'd already told him he was expected, that someone was coming to pick him up. But maybe the cabbie knew better and was just waiting around for Eddie to see the light. Maybe that was the way things worked in Mexico, where there weren't councils and advisory groups to direct the march of ordinary life.

The antenna dish alongside the station was surrounded by a tall chain-link fence, and it was from behind the dish that four long-haired thrashers on wide skateboards zoomed into view, angling around the cab, standing up on their boards to gaze at Eddie as they rumbled past. Laughs and obscene hand gestures answered the Spanish shouts of two ponytailed men sitting in a square of Sony-billboard shade across the street. A warm breeze kicked up, blowing grit against Eddie's glasses, wood smoke and roasted meat on the current. Even without the tint provided by the glasses, the mountain range far east of town appeared blue.

Eddie decided he liked the idea of disappearing. It was good to be away from the noise, the city sidewalk press, out from under the omnipresent cams, outside the reach of the Virtual

Network access links. To be out where no one was interested in
star-stalking, the roadkills were outlined in red chalk, and the
celebs themselves came to get away. To be away from *verboten*
signs—although a tyfin in one of the border's Buffalo Commons
thanked you in advance for not camping, swimming, trashing
the grasslands, blasting music or otherwise disturbing the protected herds.

Eddie felt like a new man, even if certain old habits died hard.
Spotting a group of celebs concealed under camoflesh in a con-
vertible RPEV stopped at the Buffalo Commons entrance gate,
Eddie had come close to outing them to the passengers of the
train car before remembering he wasn't leading some Eye Spy
tour.

He'd ridden bullets from New York to Chicago, Chicago to
Dallas, Dallas through the AmerIndian gambling centers and
factory towns of Texacana State to Mexico City, mingling in
station stops with Asian and Japanese farmers, sating himself on
blue corn tortillas, tacos, and salsa. Then it was diesel all the
way to Oaxaca, where the wild *psilocybe mexicana* still grew.
And finally down out of the high desert into the lush hills by
steam, in a train that was certainly one of the last of its kind in
the world.

Esmeraldas, though, was just the sort of place Eddie might
have chosen for Alex and Rita Junknowitz. Back when he and
Lucky were cutting their teeth on arcade games and their respec-
tive Jersey-town high schools were battling each other on the
football fields, Alex and Rita were making choices that ran
counter to the normal suburban format. Instead of driving snazzy
sports utility vehicles, they rode bikes; instead of withdrawing
inside their home, they opened it up to homeless transients. They
had storaged their air conditioners, washers, and dryers long
before the EPA requirements, and trimmed back to a single
phone, a single TV. In defiance of architectural planning council
warnings, they had converted their front yard into a vegetable
garden and erected a solar array out back.

By the Turn, thanks to medical advances, life-extension diets,
and personal trainers, the elderly accounted for a large percentage of the population—the median age in the States was 41 years
old—but where millions of people were depleting their savings
and burdening the medical service community with requests for
artificial organs, bone grafts, and coral implants, the Junknowitzes were content to age gracefully, welcoming the silver into
their hair, the slight stoop to their carriage. Eddie could still

recall the slow changes in daily living the population shift had inspired: in public lighting, in the increased use of larger print fonts, Velcro closures, handicapable ramps, and orthopedically designed train and plane seats. And where his own Mexican-born parents had endured an eight-year wait for a two-room in a retirement community near Palm Springs—which within a year was plagued by rogue-scale-broom weeds and whose groundwater was contaminated by the herbicides brought to bear against them—Lucky's were off traveling Central and South America, India and Australasia.

It was Rita's influence with the Housing Authority that had landed Lucky and Eddie in the same loft share after they'd each been denied a crack at higher learning by the Life Guidance Committee. People used to take them for brothers, they spent so much time floating together. Lucky was still dreaming of directing movies back then, but once relocated in the city he was receptive to Eddie's suggestion that they try their talents at themer school, if only to secure decent-paying jobs as mascots, or walkabouts in some Harlem restaurant or one of the parks. Though neither of them, it would turn out, had faces for 'flesh, or the prerequisite skills to qualify for the upper-level training courses in Terminator, Beetlejuice, Top Cat, or Batman. Honors would elude them even among the extras who comprised the cartoon clutch—although Lucky would distinguish himself as a natural Goofy and a passable George Jetson.

Eddie still burned with the memory of those themer-school days: the six A.M. meditation sessions; the ceaseless courses in lip-synch technique, sideline skits, clowning, dance routines, pelvic gyration, and parodic behavior; the seminars in self-discipline—learning mantras for staying in character in the face of temper tantrums, ear pulling, nose tweaking, groin shots—the dietary restrictions and sleep deprivations that contributed to days of perpetual dizziness. "No, no, hypoglycemia is good for you," the instructors would say, "light-headedness is essential to a good performance!" He remembered the ego trips of the elite, the look-down-the-mask smirks you'd get from body doubles and character-actor types . . . But there were a few good memories, too. The time, f'rinstance, they were working a wealthy party in the Hamptons. A Lucifer-incarnate six-year-old birthday boy'd dumped a glass of grape juice into the lap of Lucky—Balou the Bear. And there Lucky was in the bathroom trying like hell to cold-water the purple stain out of the suit's beige nap when in walks the kid's vogue mom, locking the door behind her, favoring Lucky with one of those panting cine-lascivious looks, offering just to get that stain out with her own two hands, and offering a lot more than that if Lucky'd only promise to keep the bear suit on while they were ad-libbing!

Damn pre-Turn generation had a warped sense of sexual part-nering, Eddie thought. But that was just the sort of thing that was always happening to Lucky.

Their only falling-out had come shortly after Asia Boxdale's walk-on into their lives. But it had been brief, your typical he-likes-her-but-she-likes-him tale, and nothing they hadn't hammered out long ago.

When the cabbie tapped the Chevy's horn, Eddie figured he was being offered a last chance for a ride, but the six-note *Thus Spake Zarathustra* trumpet blast was actually signaling the dust-deviled arrival of a doorless interbust jeep, with Rita Junkno-witz in the driver's seat waving a hand out the open top, skidding the battered old vehicle to a hard stop in front of the station, running directly for Eddie, scissoring him in her strong arms.

"We couldn't believe it when we got your fax," she said in a breathless rush, stepping back to take a long look at him. "God, I'm so happy to see you, Eddie."

She was a petite woman, thin-boned, deeply tanned, with cornflower blue eyes set in a mesmerizing warp and weft of character lines. She wore a loose tank top, faded denim shorts, and worn huaraches. Alex, similarly attired, was nut brown and bearded. He looked remarkably fit for seventy, with muscular limbs and a flat belly. What remained of his gray hair was ponytailed.

"You guys look great," Eddie said, exchanging a back-clapping *abrazo* with Alex.

Rita laughed and blushed. "Just two gringo silver foxes living out our days in the sunshine." Alex grabbed Eddie's bag and stashed it on the jeep's backseat. Eddie climbed in beside it as Rita fired up the engine with a twist of the ignition key.

"Never use this thing 'cept when we come into town," she said over the engine noise. No trace of Jersey left in her accent.

"You still leading those paparazzi tours, Eddie?" Alex asked.

Eddie told him yes, explaining just what it was he did in New York, and expressed his hopes for graduating to the grand circuit someday.

"And the techno-assist kids, do you get much chance?"

"Not much. A weekend or so a month." Gazing about, he added, "Maybe I'll just give it all up and move down here."

At the base of the hills at the northern edge of town was a sprawling wind farm that provided electricity for the valley. Alex named the crops growing in the fields they passed: jojoba and guayule, a rubber substitute, on the valley floor; potatoes and kenaf further along where the vegetation increased. Rita tooted the horn at elderly American expats bicycling, jogging, power-walking in both directions along the winding strip of tarmac. She stopped once to introduce Eddie to an aged Mexican Indian riding a fat donkey. The local shaman, Rita said. The *curandero*.

Their finca was located at the end of a dirt track that snaked up a hillside through thick forest. Livestock wandered the grass yard near an electric pump station, and pre-Turn rock 'n' roll wafted through the front porch screens. Two old Honda motorcycles, one missing its front wheel, sat side by side under a makeshift lean-to roofed by a sheet of green corrugated fiberglass. Alex pointed toward the rear of the house. "Take you out back later on and show you our fields. We've got redleaf lettuce, turnips, brussels sprouts, broccoli, strawberries, alfalfa, corn, beans, and shiitake mushrooms."

Rita led Eddie into the kitchen, where a Mexican woman was squeezing lemons for lemonade. Under the citric aromatics, the room smelled of corn flour and cilantro. He sipped the drink while Rita took him on a tour of the rest of the small house. The living room was crowded with print books, cassette tapes, data-flopticals, video games, CDs, and handicrafts from around the world. There were obsolete players for the flicks and music, Nintendo Power Gloves, two boxy video monitors, archaic computers and game decks. Alex dropped himself into a soft couch and lit up a thin cigarette.

"You smoke pot, Eddie?" he asked in a strange voice, holding in smoke. "Some of the best you'll ever do . . . ."

"Uh, no."

"Of course he doesn't, Al." Rita smiled and accepted the joint from her husband. "Just us old hippies."

Eddie looked at both of them and grinned. "This place is really debugged. Chaotic, I mean."

"Yeah, it's chaotic, all right," Alex said uncertainly. "Not for everybody, maybe—" He eyed Rita and reached for her hand. "—but we like it."

"It's cheap," she said. "And there's a decent hospital close by. Maria looks after the house when we're away traveling. Plus we've got our garden, our books, our toys."

Alex snorted. "No crowds, no shopping malls, no vid-phones, no goddamned councils telling us what we can and can't do. It's the opposite of that pastel-and-tartan coupon-shopping senior-citizen-discount golf-course retirement you get back in the States—for ten times the money. And things have quieted down a lot since the hostage crisis."

Eddie thought of his own folks and frowned. Rita caught the look. "So how long can you stay?"

He sniffed at the cigarette's pungent smoke and cleared his throat. "Well, I guess that depends. See, actually I'm looking for Lucky."

Alex's brow furrowed. "You're a bit off track, aren't you, Eddie? Didn't you just leave New York?"

"We haven't heard from Lucky in over a month," Rita said with a hint of sudden concern. "In fact, when your message arrived we thought it was from him."

Alex stubbed out the joint. "What's going on, Eddie?"

Eddie caught them up, downplaying things, trying to make it sound like a simple misunderstanding. Rita, however, began rubbing warmth into her upper arms. Al took her hand again and held onto it. "Let's not get all bent out of shape till we have all the facts." He looked at Eddie. "Lucky said he was thinking about visiting us?"

"That's what his love interest, er, his ex told us."

Rita frowned. "He and Harley aren't seeing each other anymore?"

"They're kind of in turnaround. But Lucky told her he planned to do some personal traveling and we figured . . ."

Alex shook his head. "I don't know, Eddie. Unless he's coming on foot, he would have been here already." He smiled weakly. "But I don't think it's exactly out of character for him to take off on his own. Probably off somewhere nursing a broken heart."

"But surely he'd tell Eddie where he was going, Al."

Eddie swallowed and managed, "I'm sorry to have to be spreading the worry around."

"Nonsense, Eddie," Rita said. "And we appreciate your making the trip down here to tell us personally."

Eddie waited a moment. "There's a second reason. We thought he might be visiting Sean. But I don't know how to reach him."

"If only someone did," Alex muttered.

Rita cut her eyes to her husband, then looked back at Eddie. "I'm sure Lucky would have told us first."

"Maybe he'll contact you from Sean's place. He's in Brazil, right?"

The Junknowitzes traded wary looks. Rita spoke, drawing a breath. "Eddie, I know I don't have to tell you how deeply affected Sean was by the war. But, well, things have grown even more difficult for him. He . . . keeps very much to himself."

"He's a battle casualty," Alex said angrily. "He's forgotten how to live among people."

Rita blanched. "He hasn't 'forgotten,' Al. The war took it from him."

Alex lowered his head and his voice. "You're right. He's disabled, Eddie. Crazy out of his skull half the time. But he won't seek help. Except of course from those damn shamans down there . . ." His voice cracked. "We have to wait for the mail to reassure us he's alive."

"I thought I could go down there," Eddie said after a long silence. "Grab a flight from Mexico City to Manaus or wherever's closest."

Rita regarded him for several seconds with tear-filled eyes. "You realize what you're asking us? Sean doesn't want anyone—and I mean anyone—to know where he is."

Eddie nodded. "I figured as much. But we're worried about Lucky, Mrs. J. It's been too many days. I'll explain it to Sean."

Alex snorted but said nothing, his face clouding over.

Rita walked to a bookcase and returned with an atlas, which she opened as she sat down alongside Eddie. "First I'll show you where he is. But these directions are only half the story. I'm going to have to teach the codes as well."

"Codes?"

"Signals. Whatever you want to call them. They're the only way you'll get to see Sean without getting yourself killed."

Locating Marshall Stack wasn't nearly as difficult as getting to speak with him. The telephone directory listed Stack under six separate headings, his name linked with everything from film production to celebrity fund-raising auctions. Each time Ziggy reached Stack's LA office, however, he was put on hold by one underling or another, only to be informed that Mr. Stack was tied up in negotiations and would have to return the call.

Ziggy ventured that leaving his own name wouldn't get him

far, particularly if, when pressed to state his business, he was
going to have to say, "on a personal matter." So instead he left
the name Zee Forelock, with the Video Observation Research
Project, along with the loft vidphone number. But when even
that failed to elicit a response from the hermetic Mr. Stack,
Ziggy decided to title himself Evening Director of the Hagadorn
Pinnacle Citizen Watch situation room, and received what
amounted to an immediate return call.

It seemed Stack had been attempting, without success, to
contact Citizen Watch headquarters in San Francisco with regard
to a little project he was putting together.

"Here's the pitch," he told Ziggy, who had yet to complete
a full sentence in the conversation. "I've got myself a bunch of
East Indians, Pacific Island natives, a couple of African tribes-
men who are about as good at pole jumping as you get. You
know what I'm talking about, right? Guys who jump from towers with vines or ropes tied to their ankles? You've seen it on the
tube. A little like bungee jumping off a bridge, except my guys
aren't into it just for the dangle and recoil. It's like, 'Hey,
where's the rush if there isn't a patch of ground under your
skull.' And I'm telling you, Forelock, I've seen them get this
fucking close to the ground." Stack onscreen indicating an inch
with right thumb and forefinger. "I've seen fez cuts compress to
flattops, that's how close."

Stack had excellent cheekbones, excellent hair, jaw, and nose,
but it was impossible to guess what those parts might have
looked like before he'd gone under the knives and lasers. The
holo image behind him was a dimensionalized Warhol from the
pop artist's soup period.

"So here's where you come in, Zee—you don't mind if I call
you Zee, do you? In a nutshell: pole jumpers I got. But what I
don't got is whatcha might call a proper tower."

"And you want to use the Pinnacle."

A telegenic smile split Stack's face. "You catch on fast, Zee.
Now I know what you're going to tell me: that it's your gig to
discourage golden gating, that you're on-duty to therapy downcasters, downscalers, whatever you call them, talk them back
inside the building, whatever you do. But all I'm saying is this:
you go offscreen, turn your back to the monitors in that sit room
for just long enough for my boys to get up there with their coils
and shit and take their jumps, and I'll see to it you come away
with enough seed capital to retire on." Stack's green eyes stared
intently from center screen. "Whaddaya think?"

Ziggy wanted to tell him what he really thought: that Stack should commit himself to Urgent Care RNA relearning treatment before someone did it for him. But what he said instead was that he'd promise to think about it—if Stack would in turn provide him with some information.

The promoter laughed at Ziggy's mention of Lucky Junknowitz. "Now there was a guy coulda gone all the way. Had a good business sense, a mind for facts, the contacts, the personal-relations piece—regular Smurf charm. And what happens, he works one high-concept event with me—a very profitable one at that—and does a dissolve just 'cause it rubs a couple of players the wrong way."

Stack brought up Bulaful without a prompt from Ziggy. "The man was all unglued about his wrestlers not winning the belt. Claimed he was going to retaliate if Junknowitz didn't right matters. Got Lucky into a regular panic, waving around that fly whisk of his, leaving video-mail threats. So Junknowitz calls *me*, telling me I've got to do something about it. Like I wasn't getting the same hate mail."

"And did you?" Ziggy asked.

"Did I what?"

"Do anything."

"Hell, yes." Stack seemed to shudder at the memory. "I gave his team the fucking belt's what I did. Said a mistake had been made and I was real sorry about it."

"When was this?"

"Maybe two weeks back. You know, there's only so many times you can hear someone promising to have you sleeping with the crocodiles before it'll start to get to you."

As it had Lucky, Ziggy thought at the time, recalling his friend's reaction that night in Atopia at the mere mention of crocodiles. And it was that memory that had sent Ziggy over to the Bronx apartment for another look at the partial of Bulaful's vid message to Lucky. Not a themer's practical joke after all, but an admonition from an irate Sudanese shaman.

Checking for recent messages, Ziggy had found three: the first from Harley—calling from either a boat or a motion simulator—wondering what Lucky had been up to lately, she hadn't heard from him. The second from some thick-necked bureaucrat with the Internal Revenue Service named Zastro Lint. And the third from a gap-toothed, smiling Bulaful with his wrestlers grouped behind him holding aloft a faux-jewel studded belt, praising Lucky for his efforts, withdrawing,

Lucky would have been relieved to learn, the several curses that had been invoked.

Ziggy had loaded a fresh disk into the answering machine and taken the shaman's messages back to the loft for a closer look. Stack's overturning the decision on the belt before PhenomiCon should have eliminated the Nuba shaman as a suspect in Lucky's disappearance, but who knew what a bit of enhancement of the messages might reveal.

Ziggy could only hope that Willy Ninja was having better luck questioning the two costumers Brax had traced to Atlantic City.

The RGO could prove as slippery as a sideways quark.

So thought Ziggy, in the loft room now with Lucky's answering machine disks in hand, when it occurred to him to check his own machines for messages before getting down to the enhancement work on Bulaful's recordings. Difference was that Ziggy's trio of machines weren't linked to the loft phone or any of the computers, but to three antique TV cable boxes he'd deliberately tuned to the noise between the preset frequencies. The noise from which of late had come videogeists, direct from some hitherto untapped station in the telesphere, sequences and segments of random TV babble, most in color, some in black and white, a few pieces going back fifty years or more. From these, in fact, the bit of Australian documentary that had given rise to his comment about crocodiles that night in Atopia.

Today's catches, though, formed a mosaic of game-show clips and soap scenes, admixed with commercials for interbust cars, cigarettes, baldness and melanoma remedies, breast-augmentation surgery—all of which Ziggy scanned at three times normal speed, voice-labeling each segment as he went along. His plan was to submit all the accumulated disks to a video editor to see if a pattern emerged. The RGO. But it wasn't until the end of the third disk that anything useful showed up, a segment he was certain would fit one of the video scrambles suggested by previous catches: the goddamned Australian documentary of all things. Six full-color though soundless seconds of outback pan—colorless land, cloud shadows, floodplain with thorny shrub poking through—followed by twenty-seven possibly hand-held seconds showing an Aboriginal man down on his hams stabbing a short stick into the ground under an acacia-like bush.

Ziggy fiddled with the screen resolution, cut the playback speed by half, and watched as the Aborigine turned toward the camera, stood up, and began to advance on the foreground. The man was tall, lean, and matte black, with angular facial features and a wiry, forked beard. He was barefoot and shirtless but wore a kind of loincloth and carried, in addition to the digging stick, a crudely fashioned spear. A dozen paces along, the man stopped, raised the stick, which Ziggy suddenly realized was in fact a length of sharpened bone, and pointed it at something offscreen. The camera panned to the right, finding first a billboard featuring a likeness of Paul Hogan surrounded by half-a-dozen cartoon characters, then what looked to be an elaborate rectangular doorway, vaguely reminiscent of the monolithic Gate of the Sun on the Bolivian *altiplano*.

The Aborigine was talking now, bright red tongue between yellowish teeth, but the microphones hadn't captured the words. What it had picked up, however, was the sound of the flies bombinating about the man's head and dust-powdered torso.

Ziggy peered at the wall screen as the buzzing grew louder, stereophonic, became a presence in the room. And it was then he caught sight of the fly that was making directly for him, as if it had emerged from the fiat screen itself.

Ziggy swung at the thing, missed, and swung again as the fly attacked from the rear, missing once more but accidentally toppling a stack of dishes on a nearby table. The fly—a rather large specimen—lighted on the wall for a moment to assess its surroundings. Then it dive-bombed Ziggy's head, grazing it as Ziggy leaned, fell over a chair and slammed his shoulder into the edge of the bed. The fly fastened itself to the opposite wall an inch above a movie poster for *Die Really Hard*. Ziggy, getting slowly to his feet with the fly locked in his squint, was going for serious with a three-pound dog-eared trade-paperback Stephen King novel after rejecting both a cowboy boot and a framed portrait of Ernie Kovacs.

When the fly launched he was ready for it, swinging the book like a bat and knocking the thing senseless. Propelled solidly into the room's wooden door, the fly fell to the floor to lie on its back, not dead, Ziggy ventured, but way stunned. He was raising the book to squash it when it struck him that the aerial demon looked unlike any fly he'd ever seen. Weird wings, weirder eyes . . .

So instead of grinding it into the grime of the loft's plywood floor, he set a water glass atop it and brought it over to the light for a closer look.

TWENTY-ONE

"WALK THIS WAY," Sheena said, and Lucky smiled as an old visual joke came to mind. Except that Sheena wasn't kidding; she wasn't telling him to follow her off in any one direction, but actually instructing him to adopt her hunched posture and cross-country ski stride. So Lucky gave it a try, muttering to himself in exasperation, shuffling off in a pair of alloy-soled ballet slippers Sheena had termed "lock steps" along a yard-wide runner that shone like black ice. He was successful at last at preventing unscheduled lift-offs, with each misstep, into door lintels, ceilings, or bewildering arrays of mostly hand-operated instruments.

"Keep to the runners and you'll be all right," Sheena said with laughing eyes, one hand to her mouth. "Remember to glide. And stay still when you speak to them."

Lucky glanced back at her from the doorway, wary of attempting an about-face—unless reverse entailed doing that Michael Jackson walk. "Can't we just fill my pockets with lead or something?"

Sheena let the laugh loose. "No, I don't think so."

The battlewagon had inserted itself into Edrispace almost four baseline-days earlier, Sheena and Lucky shuttled downside into Edri's less than human-normal gravity and assigned to quarters more befitting servants than the Very Important Beings they were thought to be, in a government building Lucky decided resembled a sand castle after a sudden downpour.

Sheena was still puzzling over having been taken at her word that Vanderloop was an executive with Black Hole Trough and Adits. Stranger still was that the governing body had agreed to hear Vanderloop out on how Edri and Kammu might settle their differences and thus forge a cease-fire with their planetary neigh-

242

bors. Sheena'd learned, however, that the razing of the freighter
and the subsequent capture of the Kammese envoy had been
undertaken as a means of forcing a summit between the two
worlds—ironically, a wish foremost in the minds of the Kammese when they'd dispatched their envoy to confer with the
Council of Near Group Worlds in the first place.

For Lucky the downside days had been an ordeal, nights the
only saving grace, when Sheena, without the slightest hint of
modesty, would strip out of her jumpsuit and lie naked on her
back on the spread-sheet adjacent to his own. Unfortunately the
mighty mites curled up in his midbrain had invariably chosen
just those moments to release the dreamy narcotic that put him
instantly to sleep. The few-and-far-between waking good moments were nullified by the persistent nausea he felt—now at the
mere thought of the Edrian notion of food, the chemical peels
and herbal wraps—and by the surges of panic attack when the
damn nanocontrollers would fail, the constant unplanned launch-
ings, and the head-and-shoulder-bruising touchdowns.

The cube-headed Edrians had finally acquiesced to his pleas
for a bath by immersing him in a tank filled with thick fluid that
left him smelling like tooth decay, only adding to the dizzying,
seemingly indelible unpleasantness two-plus weeks of space
travel had stamped into the fabric of his filthy pegged pants and
Alfred E. tee.

Lucky was trying to tug the shirt into some semblance of its
original shape now, Alfred E.'s face looking even more whacked
than usual. "Could at least have outfitted us with new clothes,"
he told Sheena.

She motioned to the T-shirt. "They think that *is* your uniform."

And in some sense it was, Lucky granted, he being the only
Earther for, well, who knew how many cubic parsecs. The medallion, of course, serving to dress him up some—from the
Edrians' point of view, at any rate. Unadorned but for those head
fans, the XTs had apparently taken the medallion as a sign of his
high station with the Agency the hearing aids called "Black
Hole," though he was left to wonder if the term referred to those
very light-engulfing singularities or something closer to Calcutta's infamous death pit. Or yet some other thing whose inherent
meaning was utterly foreign to his experience.

Funny that there should be a Calcutta Travel Agency right in
his own South Bronx neighborhood.

"You ready, Professor?" Sheena asked as two Edrian escorts

in vanity plate presented themselves on either side of the doorway.

"You first." Lucky wiggling himself to one side to let her pass.

"Suit yourself, Mister 'Chief Executive Officer.' "

The guards led them out onto hallway runners that angled off in the direction of what Lucky assumed would be the summit room. Sheena had tried to explain why Edrian ships ran heavy on the spin-gravity, but she'd lost him. What mattered, in any case, was that the runners had been laid in deference to them, even if the room hadn't exactly shouted high-roller suite.

From what little Lucky had seen, Edri was every bit as wasted as that Metaluna in the old film. Ravaged buildings and city streets, a population driven underground. The indigenous technology was like something out of Salvador Dali, organic and oftentimes repulsive, even the simplest of devices studded with phallic handles, levers, and throw bars, twice-redundant and engineered for multiple tasks, as only creatures with three pairs of opposing appendages might design.

The wide doors to the summit chamber opened at the approach of the escort, who immediately stopped, surrendering the lead to Sheena. "This way," she told Lucky over her shoulder.

He studied the altered rhythm of her movement—glideglide, step; glideglide, step—and mimicked her, feeling like a flower bearer in a wedding party. He doubted, however, that even the most bizarre of family gatherings could measure up to what awaited him inside. The room held close to one hundred Edrians, most of whom were seated in tiers that rose forty feet above a ceramic-like floor, the rest around a huge square of table whose mirrored top was strewn with recording devices, keyboards of a sort, what looked to be personal appliances, and countless everyday odds and ends. Interspersed among those elite at the table were a dozen or so hirsute beings who might have comprised the Edrian beatnik contingent, but were more than likely the representatives from Kammu.

On first glance it was apparent that the Kammese had chosen the shakier of the Edri's two branches to evolutionary dominion. *Homo crudo* to the Edrians' *sophisticaticus*, they were shorter in stature, lacking a proper crown, and their faces and limbs were covered with a fine golden stubble. Lucky finally understood what Sheena'd meant when she said the Kammese were somewhat barbaric but had good "fuzz tone."

"Let the agent from Black Hole Trough and Adits step forward and state his business," an Edrian elite announced.

Just think of them as themers, Lucky told himself as he moved toward the square table. Not Edrian, not Kammese, but themers. In full costume. Glideglide, step; glideglide, step . . .

Dearly beloved, we are gathered here today to bear witness—

The Edrian with the largest cranial fan of the bunch stretched out his neck and sniffed in Lucky's direction, canoe eyes unblinking. "Has this rug rat had his shots?"

Sheena spoke up from the rear. "I strongly object to the speaker's suggestion that the Chief Executive Officer would travel in flagrant disregard of Trough sanitary directives."

The Edrian favored Sheena with a look. "Who is this woman?"

"I'm the officer's . . . bodyguard," Sheena answered before anyone else could.

The speaker waved one of his six hands. "Of course, of course." Turning to his tablemates to add, "If only they weren't a protected species."

The sucking noises in the room approximated laughter. There was something almost, well, French about the Edrians, Lucky thought. At the same time he noted that both the Edrians and the Kammese kept their many hands occupied by entering data into their boards, scratching themselves, grooming their neighbors, transferring liquids from bottles to glasses, and exchanging hand signals with one another.

And Lucky'd always thought reading on the toilet was a big deal.

"Do get on with it," the speaker said.

"Sir Oge," this from an Edrian in the upper tiers, "I fail to see why this assembly should be subjected to what will undoubtedly prove lies from the very corporation responsible not only for the perilous circumstances both Edri and Kammu find themselves in, but for similar situations galaxywide, including but not limited to corporate piracy, insider trading, hostile takeovers, dawn raids, open warfare. Black Hole Agency, along with the foul extenders that comprise its leadership, is the scourge of the sector. And I know many in this room would agree that the Agency's policy of unchecked acquisition, coupled with its widespread practice of facilitating aggression, bespeaks of some more sinister strategy than mere corporate enhancement. A political one, I say, with designs on nothing less than political control of the Trough worlds.''

"Ka Shamok!" shouted an Edrian off to Lucky's left, four arms raised, interlocked wrists creating an airy diamond.

Several others made an ominous chant of it: "Ka Shamok, Ka Shamok, Ka Shamok . . ."

The speaker waited for the chanting, the hooting, the "hear, hear" equivalents to die down before turning to address Lucky once more. "I suggest you be brief about it, human.''

"Count on it," Lucky told him, carefully pivoting through a half turn that brought him face-to-face with the tiered gallery. The XT murmurings gradually ceased. Limbs were folded, hands tucked away, rainbow fans inclined.

"All right, here comes," Lucky began, wondering briefly how well he'd translate. "The Council of Near Group Worlds has made the cease-fire contingent on the forging of a truce between Edri and Kammu. Makes sense. But of course that means no more raiding ships for tour groups, no more plundering the Adits for travelers; an end, consequently, to downside business in tourism.

"And who's going to rush to visit two ruined worlds, anyway. Oh, I know there's always the thrillseekers, the social-scientist types, the photojournalists. But how long can that last—a couple of months, a year if you're lucky? So it's natural Edrian and Kammese alike might be thinking, 'Hey, what's in a truce for me? What am I, some kind of sucker, kissing all these tourist dollars goodbye?' Especially when you're thinking about all the effort that's gone into making your worlds ideal getaway spots.''

Lucky glanced around to see if his remarks were hitting home, and saw more than a couple of heads nod. "But all I'm saying is this: Okay, so you might not be able to coax any tourists to Kammu and Edri till you've patched yourselves up, but in the meantime what's wrong with bringing Kammu and Edri to the tourists?'' Lucky paused because it seemed the naturally theatrical thing to do. "Theme parks, folks. What I'm saying is that you've got to start thinking about market penetration.''

Lucky, akimbo now, was rotating a knowing, conspiratorial grin to the tiers. But in place of the expected looks of sudden revelation came gapings, gaspings, glowerings, angry shouts, raised fists. Sheena glided past him on the runner, waving what Lucky thought had better be placating gestures to the table of elites, because all at once fingers were pointing, weapons were appearing, guards were moving in. Lucky began a rapid moon walk retreat meanwhile, stammering Curly concerns for his own safety, "Nea-neaa-neaaa . . ." Getting dangerously close to the edge of the black-ice grav-strip.

Sheena executed a neat pirouette six feet in front of him. "You trying to get us killed?" Whites of her eyes showing around leafburst irises.

"Thought they weren't allowed to, uh—"

"You insulted them. You told them to become . . . prostitutes."

"But all I said was market—"

"Don't say it!"

—*penetration*, he completed to himself, suddenly aware that tongue-twister translation glitches could work both ways.

"Explain it some other way," Sheena advised under her breath while Lucky was nyuk-nyuking to himself. "And this time avoid the species-specific terms, will you?"

He nodded and swallowed hard. The XTs were glaring at him, mumbling among themselves, but at least the guards had returned to their posts, weapons disarmed. "Perhaps the agent from Black Hole wishes to re-phrase his idea," the speaker said, lacking only a lace handkerchief to give things the proper continental touch.

Lucky took a moment to gather himself. "I only meant that Edri and Kammu might still profit from Trough tourism by mark—uh, establishing historical attractions on other worlds."

The Kammese envoy struck a thoughtful pose that entailed the use of all six arms. The speaker allowed the slightest nod of his head. Lucky continued.

"You get the idea. You re-create the golden days of Edri and Kammu in a fun way. Dress everyone up in colorful costumes, reenact moments of historical import. Tap the lore of your fairy tales, select the best from your entertainment blockbusters. Serve Edrian and Kammese cuisine to the tourists, sell handicrafts, replicas, six-sleeved jumpsuits—"

"The simultaneous signing of the constitution and the completion of the National Jigsaw Puzzle," someone suggested.

"The ascent of Mount Tall by the Handwalker Team."

"The tidal wave backstroke competition of '656."

"That's it," Lucky encouraged, whirling with abandon. "Only you turn these events into amusing, kinetic rides, see. Like 'The Great Wave,' 'Tall Mountain,' that sort of thing."

The speaker stood at his stool. "We could stock the attractions with wildlife."

"Or create realistic facsimiles of those animals," Lucky pointed out.

"The first landing on Kammu," the female Kammese envoy mused nostalgically.

" 'The Conquest of Space,' " emended another.

"Yes!" Lucky said, throwing up his arms. "There isn't a world that won't want to have its own park."

"Our employment rate will soar!"

"Our economies will stabilize!"

"We'll open up franchises!"

One finger at the tip of his nose, Lucky spun around to point to the Kammese who'd come up with the franchise idea, and in so doing slipped off the runner, propelling himself into a Tasmanian Devil spin across the hard floor of the summit room. It took three guards to catch him and return him to the runner.

"You might even consider approaching Black Hole about venture capital," he continued. "But be sure to bring your lawyers along. And if the Agency wants to talk silent partnerships, well, who knows, something could probably be worked out."

The XTs were barely paying attention to him now. The room was riotous with concept talk and gesticulation. Sheena, regarding Lucky with a mix of astonishment and admiration, seemed the sole still point in the tumult.

"Admit it," Lucky was saying to Sheena sometime later, "admit you underestimated me."

She tucked in her chin, scowling. "I had no expectations about you, Professor. One way or another. I'll confess, though, you do have the living will."

Lucky grinned. "I'll take that as a compliment. But I still figure you owe me."

"For what, exactly?"

"For getting us off Edri. Humans might be a protected species out here, but that doesn't mean they couldna stuck us away on some wildlife preserve."

"Or in one of your 'theme parks.' " Sheena laughed, then did a fair impersonation of Lucky. " 'Now here's my idea for saving your planets: You spread out to other worlds, and once there you sell yourselves sexually!' I've never heard such a tongue tide!" She laughed harder. "The Agency could use a few like you."

Lucky showed her a lopsided look. "Like I said, you owe me."

No sooner had the summit dissolved than they were moved into swank quarters aboard the single remaining diplomatic vessel of the Edrian fleet, bound now for New Bedlam, the Adit way station nearest the Edri home system. Lucky'd had his bath and shave, a meal of honest food—vegetables and fish of some sort that tasted like haddock. The Edrians had insisted on bestowing upon him their Legion of Decency Medal, which was now stashed away in a cloth pouch along with his "What, me worry?" tee. He was now neatly turned out in open-necked blouse, body-hugging cape, billowy trousers, cummerbund, and knee boots of kid-soft synthetic—the super-hero swashbuckler look Sheena promised was all the rage along the Trough. *De rigueur*, in fact, for any human expecting to be taken seriously.

"So, uh, how come you stick with the wearever?" Lucky had asked, narrow-eyed with suspicion.

Pinching the sleeve of the jumpsuit, she told him, "Because I don't see anything wrong with dressing feminine every once in a while."

The first-class cabinspace was fitted with a series of narrow horizontal windows Lucky first mistook for black venetian blinds, until it sunk in that he was gazing at bands of deep space. Up close, stars sugared the night, even while the ship was translight or shuddering wildly through one of the meta-temporal irregularities Sheena called "rumble strips." Which, Lucky grasped, accounted for the padded walls, ceiling, and floor. A regular first-class seclusion room, all right.

"So what about relativity and all that?" he'd asked earlier on. "I mean, if it's eleven o'clock at night local time, what time's it on Earth? And how's anybody know when their children are?" Sheena told him he was babbling again. "Speed of light," Lucky said. "Time dilation, white holes, black holes, wormholes. How's all this jumping around in space-time happen?"

Sheena shrugged. "You board a ship headed where you want to go and you arrive."

Who are you, who are so wise in the ways of science? Lucky wanted to say. What he said was, "Yeah, but a day later or a lifetime later?"

"That depends on how far you're going. A trip can take baseline-hours or years."

"And if you use the Adits?"

"Seconds."

He'd tried to picture an Adit, had come away with stock images: beam-me-up-Scotty transporters, gateways to the stars, crazy magic . . . He needed to understand how things worked, but realized that Sheena was the wrong person to ask. "I'm not very technical-minded," she admitted. "Things work more often than they don't." He supposed it would have been like asking him to explain how optical computers worked. You flipped a couple of switches or voiced a couple of commands and they came on, was all. But as to just what the individual sub-atomic particles were up to, he hadn't the slightest.

They were sitting opposite each other just now in body-warming shape-memory chairs he guessed were called "hot seats" even before Sheena told him. She was acting friendlier since the summit; Lucky was encouraged by the fact that she had deactivated the twin-pack confinement field as soon as they'd been shown into the cabin.

"At least tell me how far we are from Earth," Lucky said. She led with her chin. "Because I owe you?"

"Come on, Sheena, I'm homesick. How far?"

" 'Just around the next molecule.' " Lucky read the grin from the sound of her voice and asked about it. "Something my father used to say when I'd ask him how far Earth was from Foxal. 'Just around the next molecule, Sheena Hec'k.' "

Like second star to the right, straight on 'til morning, Lucky thought. "Your father knew about Earth?"

She eyed him up and down, every which way, making up her mind about something. Finally: "Earth was my father's homeworld, Professor."

Lucky waited for the proverbial feather to tip him over. "Your father was one of me? One of us, uh, one of—from Earth?" When she nodded, he added, "That means," looking at her as though for the first time, "you're . . . So where's the rest of you from?"

"The rest of me?"

"Well, if you're half Earther—"

"My mother is from Foxal."

Lucky's winking "land of the foxes" comment fell flat. As a distraction, he cleared his throat. "So your dad's family name was Hec'k?"

She shook her head. "I took my mother's name."

"Then what was his name?"

"Wheeler, E. C. Wheeler."

Lucky stroked his chin. "Gee, I don't know, Sheena Wheeler has a nice ring to it." He looked at her. "Did he leave of his own free will, or was he abducted, like me?"

Sheena didn't respond to the sarcasm. "Earth is a tertiary world," she said absently. "Tamperproof. Indigs aren't normally allowed into the Trough unless they've been recruited."

"By Black Hole?"

She studied him again. "By any agency operating with interference authorization."

"So people don't just fall into an Adit and vanish."

"Hardly. No one leaves without first being evaluated by a Peer Group. It's possible my father was working for the Terran franchise operators."

That term again, Lucky thought, accessing the mental file he'd opened. "So your father was escorted off-planet by one of these Peer Groups?"

"My mother said he arrived on Foxal in the company of Black Hole agents. She never knew whether he'd been recruited or abducted, or why in either case."

"And your father won't say, huh?"

Sheena's lips tightened. "My father left Foxal when I was thirteen years old. Sometimes I think I never really knew him, but I remember feeling that he was always sad. That he never fit in."

"I'm sorry," Lucky said, failing to meet her gaze. "Of course, it's possible your father was grabbed by mistake and somebody returned him to Earth."

"I doubt that, Professor Vanderloop."

"Never happens that the wrong person's taken, huh? Black Hole just won't tolerate errors."

She thought about the glitch that had landed her and her brood of HuZZah tourists on Avonne; the misplaced shipment of rebel-bound armaments; the Peer Group routing order that had taken her and Vanderloop through a hotly contested wrest area. And the rumors circulating through the Trough about a counterforce seeking to topple the Agency. About Ka Shamok—

"Who are these 'phallus tenders' that dweeb Edrian mentioned?" Lucky asked suddenly.

"*Phallus* tenders?"

Lucky's face grew hot. "The Black Hole leaders."

"Foul extenders," Sheena corrected, grimacing. "A rather unflattering term for the founders of Black Hole Travel—a sound bite, really. Do yourself a favor and forget you ever heard it."

Lucky scratched his head, thinking, *fowl extenders*? "And what about this Cashamok?"

Sheena's eyes flashed.

"The Edrians and Kammese were chanting it in the summit chamber: 'Cashamok, Cashamok!' "

"Just a word."

Lucky lifted an eyebrow. "One that can't be translated, huh? My guess it's a name."

"Another one best forgotten," Sheena said dourly.

Lucky snorted a laugh. "You'll be thinking the same thing about 'Vanderloop' when the truth comes out."

She whirled on him. "My orders don't contain anything about figuring out who you are, Professor. I'm to escort you to al-Reem, where we're already long overdue. If some 'mistake' has been made, the people there will rectify it. Until then, you're 'Vanderloop.' I suggest you get used to it."

Lucky's smile was deliberately tolerant. "What did Vanderloop do to get himself on Black Hole's shit list?"

Sheena mirrored his look. "You tell me, Professor."

Lucky picked over his memories of the short conversation he and Brax had on the Koch Center escalator. Vanderloop was some camera-shy semiotician, planning to address Phenomi-Con's New Agers about Australia. Lucky untucked his hair from the collar of the silver cape. Australia: the Barrier Reef, Sydney Opera House, Outback, Ayers Rock, Aborigines, walkabouts, the new DreamLand theme park . . . He shook his head, defeated.

"I don't know, Sheena," he sighed. "Maybe I am Vanderloop. Maybe I was Lucky Junknowitz in a dream."

Sheena laughed. "Better in a dream than reality."

Lucky frowned, letting her laugh for a moment. "Here's something weird, though." He rapped a knuckle against his forehead. "These mighty mites? They make it all seem like I haven't even left Earth. The language, the way things work, the way everyone thinks and behaves." He motioned to the window slits. "Even these ships."

Sheena tried but failed to mask the pity. "You're too Terra-centric, Professor. It's not that the Trough is so much like Earth. It's Earth that's patterned after what goes on in the Trough."

Lucky wanted to scream, but would have been satisfied to recoil in alarm, gasp, shudder . . . something, anything to disturb the surface tension that was holding his latent hysteria in check. The nanos, however, were managing him nicely, getting better at it every day as they assumed control of his thought patterns, hormonal levels, fight or flight responses. Lucky fought them when he could by reminding himself that the past weeks hadn't been some nightmare of a high-turbulence thrill ride; that these were real ships negotiating real warps and holes, loops and rumble strips in space-time; that these were genuine aliens, XTs, life-forms, the end product of genetic codes written by molecular colonies indigenous to worlds other than Earth; that these were not simply fiber-optic effects punctuating some domed darkness, but actual stars, clusters, gaseous clouds, planetary systems. A freighter had been destroyed, lives had been lost, beings with six arms had taken him captive . . . just another day in the Trough.

Oddly reminiscent of the one and only time Ziggy had convinced him to wear a designer drug—a dermal patch of mastoid Trash, said at the time to be finger-lickin' good. Lucky had been intent on experiencing all the hallucinogenic wonders everyone had been raving about: prismatic psychoscapes, fractal familiars, mystic dizzies, thrills unavailable even in the unreal estate of the Virtual Network. But the only highs he experienced from the black-market patches Ziggy scored were the ones some fender bender in the trip clique had coaxed from a bent-neck electric six-string. Only people who got off, a couple of true believers who kept asking him what he was seeing, what he was feeling. "Plenty," he'd told them. Smiling in just that beatific way he'd seen the seriously dazzled smile, when in fact nothing had changed, least of all his sense of reality.

Reality just now, due in part to whatever the nanos were time-releasing into his system, was a dream from which he was constantly on the verge of waking. His instincts told him that the only ticket to out-and-out hysteria would be an encounter of the most profound sort.

The nanos wouldn't even permit him to nurse a jones for his homeworld. Although he was allowed to wonder what Brax and the posse were up to, whether they were out searching for him, or believed him disappeared to who knew where. Knowing them as well as he did, Lucky doubted they'd buy the existence of Black Hole as the be-all, end-all RGO—not with so many bugs running loose in the program. Where, for starters, were Earth's Adits located, how many were there, how long had they existed downside, and who ran the things?

He would have loved to append a "why me?" just for the hell of it, but knew damn well the real question had to read, "Why Vanderloop?"

New Bedlam way station, with its huge, lozenge-shaped hub and concourse spokes, wasn't unlike a pre-Turn airport terminal,

save that someone had set it spinning outside the envelope of a
small pockmarked planet, rust-colored where starlight touched.
Lucky could only guess what had transpired there that the hearing aids should coax from his semantic storage the word for a
scene of wild uproar and confusion. And "New" Bedlam at
that. The way station itself revealed no hint of its history, and
Sheena had simply ignored his request for additional data. The
concourses were carpeted, well lit, lined with concession stands
and telecaster booths; voices announced fades to places even his
twisted tongue couldn't pronounce. The curving walls were hung
with what were perhaps paintings of a sort, and holo advertise-
ments for "mindfolds," "think tanks," and "high balls." The
people movers were lite-grav transfer tubes more like wind tunnels. There were fast-food joints owned by a company called
Trough Feed, and quick-sex dispensers the name of which Lucky
read as "Love Handles."

XTs of a wide assortment were crowded into transit and departure lounges, or hurrying back and forth between gates that
were enormous portals of geometric design, some more elaborate than others, some like windows to new worlds where others
showed only a misty gray light. Though abundant, of the humans Lucky saw only one was similarly outfitted in cape and
knee boots—that one a Pit Boss with a skullful of cranial plugs
seated at the donut center of an Adit ingress/egress instrument
array. Up and Adit, Inc., Singularity Flings, Eternity Tours
Unlimited, and Nebulae Escapes were but some of the companies offering travel getaways, but the corporation most frequently represented was Black Hole, in any number of guises:
Teleportation Authority, Trough Adventures, Telecaster Astro-
dynamics, Trauma Advisory, Temporal Adjustments, Teleppor-
tation and Aerospace . . .

Lucky hadn't given a thought to escape until Sheena's run-in
with the Trough ticketing agent who'd scanned them for weapons and cleared them for the departure gates that dimpled the
outer hull of Concourse 223. Sheena had had them twin-packed
since their arrival at the way station, and the agent, a squat
creature with more orifices in his head than Lucky had hairs in
his nose, wasn't hearing any of Sheena's demands to have Lucky
one-way-ticketed to al-Reem. This, after Sheena presented her
forehead to a scanner which had verified her own open-ticket
status.

"Long as you're traveling twin-packed," the agent insisted,

"your charge gets magic-markered same as you: open ticket."

Sheena, cursing under her breath, had passed her head under the scanner a second time. "Read the restrictions, pal. We've got a special escort routing to al-Reem, right? Now, I'm the escort," motioning to herself, "and this," to Lucky, "is my package. What's so difficult to understand?"

The agent held fast. "By ship's the way it reads. Nothing about a routing by Adit."

Which was all true enough, except that Sheena was too frustrated to let the proscriptions stand between her and her destination. What with the holing of the freighter and the mixup on Edri, she ventured Black Hole would be too busy searching for her and Vanderloop to spot a small violation in the routing orders. She hoped, in any event, to be gainfully employed by some other travel agency by the time the fade was noticed.

"All right, forget the special routing. Just honor my open ticket and bill me for an excess-baggage charge to 'Reem."

The agent was shaking his head long before she'd completed the request. "Al-Reem requires proof of onward passage for all live packages, regardless of point of origin. Unless you want to declare your charge cargo and fade him via mass transit."

Sheena threw up her hands. "Why can't you just bill me for the excess-baggage tariff both ways, for fate's sake?"

"You force me to repeat myself: Not while you're traveling twin-packed. If 'Reem is your charge's final destination, you can have his open ticket canceled there, but not here. Either you deactivate the containment field and have your package book separate passage, or I brand the two of you open-ticket. Your choice."

Sheena was still fuming about it now, mumbling to herself while they hurried along the concourse, Lucky heeled in behind like some obedient pet. No stranger to bureaucratic red tape, he could almost sympathize, though not enough to keep his mind from hatching plans of the farewell sort. The Trough might be terra incognita—maybe x-terra incognita—but he was tongue-twister equipped for the local lingo, nano-tranked against culture shock, and open-ticketed to fade wherever he pleased. And chances were someone or something in one of those Adits would be able to point the way to Earth.

Talk about frequent-flyer mileage.

The chance came midway along the concourse, where Adit alteration work was in progress and a recorded sound loop re-

quired that all containment fields be deactivated. It took everything he had to maintain the poker face he'd summoned by the
time Sheena turned to read him.

"What, you're worried about me running away if you take off
the leash? Just where'm I sposed to go, hunh?" Sheena's return
look was dubious, but there was something else in her eyes he
hadn't seen before: a hint that she wished things could have
worked out differently. "How 'bout we walk arm in arm,"
Lucky suggested, offering his right as her fingers hovered over
the twin-pack's waistband remote.

She allowed a slight frown, said no to Lucky's offer, and
zeroed the field.

The sense of release Lucky felt may have been psychologi-
cally induced, but it stayed with him for the time it took to
negotiate the concourse detour, expanding into a kind of pre-
flight adrenaline high as Sheena led him past the final repulsor
barricades. Lucky purposely lingering by now, creating something of a trailing bottleneck of harried XT travelers, all eager to
arrive at their gates.

"Move it," some horse-faced thing said to his back.

"Hey, primate," from another, "I've got an Adit to catch."

Sheena turned to hurry him along. "Let's go, Professor. I
would have taken your arm if I'd known you were going to mope
about it." Her fingers were already poised at the remote.

Lucky waited until he could feel horse face's breath on the
back of his neck; waited till the crowd was sufficiently miffed;
waited till he was certain Sheena comprehended his actions. No
sooner did her long fingers find the remote than he whirled,
taking hold of horse face and—after two complete three-sixties—
trading places with him. The twin-pack now activated, horse
face was immediately bum's-rushed backward into the containment field, sliding to within three feet of Sheena only to be
stopped short by the guide's own anti-intrusion field. Sheena
cursed as Lucky flew headfirst into the crowd, horse face spinning on his heel at the same instant, making it all of five feet
before being brought to a mad mime halt by the invisible perimeter of the field.

Lucky meanwhile was hurrying back through the concourse
construction zone, slaloming his way through a crowd of a hundred or more XTs, each with his or her own derogatory remark
to utter about the human race in general, Lucky in particular.

"Annoying things," one said.

"Repulsive," replied another.

Past three Adits before finding one with the departure lights lit, portal view of an ascending spiral of small ships, just what the doctor ordered. The agent at the gate, a hulking specimen wearing his insides out, shoved a tentacle out to stop him.

"Got an empty seat?" Lucky asked in a rush.

The creature eyeballed him in a decidedly unfriendly manner. "What are you, some kind of comedian?" The agent snorted. "An empty seat . . . like the only reason I'm standing here is to listen to your sound bites."

Lucky rethought his phrasing. "Sorry, no insult intended." He pointed to the no-nonsense Adit and its tight-knit though motley group of nonhuman passengers. "I mean a, a free space, an empty place, uh . . ."

The agent's expression had changed to one of suspicion. "This group is headed for Staph. Sir."

Lucky checked the concourse for signs of Sheena, then lifted his face to the scanner. "Open ticket, see?"

The agent gave the scanner screen a double-take before replying. "An open ticket, and Staph's your idea of a good time?"

"Always wanted to go to Staph. Now's my chance, right? If there's, uh, standing room, you know, a place for me in the Adit."

"You're a member of the club?"

"The club? Well of course I'm a member of the club! A charter member—a lifelong member. I've saved every issue of the monthly magazine . . ."

The creature's shrug said "takes all kinds."

But Lucky was admitted and shown to a bit of elbow room on a circle of softly glowing floor, amid a group of upright XTs who seemed to find something odd about his being there.

He was still responding with smiles when the countdown hum commenced. His last view of New Bedlam way station had Sheena at the center of it, pushing past the gate agent in an effort to reach the Adit Pit Boss, the tentacled XT's expression both angry and apprehensive, Sheena's full lips mouthing: "Vanderloop! Not there! Not Staph! *Nooooo . . .*"

TWENTY-TWO

MICKEY FORMICA KNEW early on that the guy sitting at the curve of the bar wanted something. A game, information, designers, some double-down sex action, Mickey wasn't sure what—only that there was a too-familiar subliminal to the conversation the guy'd struck up out of the blue. Indian guy by the look of him, Coppertone, maybe: mid-twenties, maybe a little older, darkish complexion—redder than Mickey's own—high crab-apple cheekbones, a face you could see aging into one of those old nickel profiles.

Mickey and Nikkei had been just sitting there at the bar minding their own, nursing ice-cold Absoluts, enjoying the show—a cute body-reconstruct brunette singer in shrink-wrap red backed up by five guys who probably should have stuck to doing wedding gigs—when the guy had kind of sauntered into the lounge, giving the dimly lit room a slow but real obvious scan from behind his mirrorshades. Obvious to someone trained to notice such things, of course. And not just your ordinary check-out-the-action scan, neither, but one that said the guy was looking for something or someone in particular.

Mickey even thought he'd seen the guy earlier that day, in the lobby of the Kunieda Hotel or floating near the crap tables in the casino's major action room. Mickey's attention drawn by the fact the guy didn't look like he really belonged. Dressed all wrong for Atlantic City for one thing—although you could never go by just that alone. Wasn't never-happen a guy sporting a dashiki or some fab rot rags would plop down next to you at a table and you'd be thinking "loser," when all of a sudden the guy would flash a *shinjinrui* money roll clipped in pure silver or platinum, or a credit chip you knew put him right up there with the Twenty-One.

Mickey had been tasting that high style for over a week now and was growing to like it, he and Nikkei living on Dante Bhang's credit ever since the man had sent them packing from the Apple in a stretch a-cell after the fumbled hook at the con. The man telling them no hard feelings, have a good time but keep your noses clean—or at least keep out of trouble. Like trouble was something they were good at getting themselves into. Meantime, the man himself's tucked away in a Hagadorn top-floor suite where you need something like a federal badge just to bring up a beef burger from room service.

The way things were.

He and Nikkei had been maybe three vodkas along when the Injun walked in, playing his lookaround routine, sliding up onto a stool three seats away, friendly but not too, a quick nod for both of them when he'd ordered a drink—a draft beer. Then: "What a week I've been having," raising the beer to his reflection in the mirror behind the bar, "what a *couple* of weeks." No preamble or anything, just laying it out, showing you there was a road to somewhere if you had nothing better to do than follow it, some booby prize if you were into the pursuit.

It was Nikkei, glancing at his Felix the Cat watch, who'd said, "Bad time at the tables, huh?"

"Murder." The Injun still looking straight ahead.

"*Kampai*," Nikkei'd told him, raising his own glass.

But the guy quickly lets on he's from the York, just down in AC to work out the kinks from some prole job. A regular jason, and he wants everybody to know it. Okay, so York gives them something to talk about for a while, and it's clear right off the guy knows the side streets, the bars without sobriety scanners, the places where the music is live and the women are hot to try old things. All interesting enough, it being slow time in the bar, too early for the bleary-eyed hardcore to turn up after all-night sessions at the tables, the songbird and her pickup band on a break, coupla guys lined up to do some of that *Karaoke*.

Mickey listening with one ear, Nikkei and the guy talking bands of a loud sort, which Mickey didn't have much tolerance for since his six months in stir. Still, he took it as a good sign the guy hadn't moved over a seat or shown any interest in exchanging names. But then he goes and mentions PhenomiCon. Real casual about it, too, like a tribe and a half of Indians showing up over the top of the hill when the wagon train is least expecting them. Seems a musician buddy of his had gone to the con and had been missing since. And the guy's thinking maybe his buddy got himself disappeared into one of those Virtual Network role-playing games the whiz kids were rumored to run in the sub-basements.

So now he had Mickey's serious interest, and Nikkei was tuned into it, too, swiveling in his seat to turn Mickey a wary look, Oriental features saying, "What's this shit?" In answer, Mickey snapped for the 'tender, ordered everyone another round. Idea being to keep the guy at the wheel, let him take the corners at his own speed, see just where this story about the disappeared musician was going, and find out whether or not the name scrawled over the finish line was going to read "Vanderloop."

Of course, the victim could only be Vanderloop from the way the guy was explaining things, too coincidental to be anyone but, and that spelled concern in caps. Because it was possible the guy had tracked them from New York down to AC by the false eyedees Bhang had them using at the con. Which meant the guy was way smarter than he looked.

Normally Mickey and Nikkei would have clammed up then and there, taken the time to figure some place where they could just off the guy without a lot of blood or unnecessary fuss; but the Vanderloop fuckup had been preying on them so much that they felt compelled to hang in for the count. After all, no amount of cash or credit, games or dames, was going to cancel out the sorry fact that the future cops who'd ridden to Vanderloop's rescue had shot holes in the flawless—well, perhaps spotty—Formica-Tanabe reputation for professionalism. Guys in play-suits with guns that could slag metal; then that weird after-mission debrief with Charlie Cola, where more was going on than met the ear . . . It was all just too *muy misterioso* to let lie there unattended.

So Nikkei had finally said, "You know, you're not going to believe this, but we were at that same convention. We thought it would be fun to dress up as aliens and mingle with the fringe. We even registered under phony names just for outlaw's sake. Besides, from what we heard, it was easy to pick up women."

"And that the women you could pick up were easy," Mickey'd added, yucking it up.

This had put the guy at ease some, and they'd given him their best listen, hoping maybe he'd let drop information of a usable sort: whether, for instance, this "musician" had enemies who might have wanted him disappeared. To which the guy'd said, no. Not an enemy in this or any other world.

"But maybe you saw my friend," he finally got around to saying.

And Mickey'd said, "Could be. What's he look like? I mean, you have a photo or anything?"

They watched closely as the guy pretended to pat himself down, pull out his wallet, run the whole now-where'd-I-put-that-thing number. A minute later pulling out the 2-D he'd had close at hand all the time and sliding it along the bar for Nikkei to see.

Nikkei studied the shot for a moment and swiveled in Mickey's direction. "What do you think," smiling cruelly, "did we see him?"

Mickey took the head shot between two fingers. Vanderloop, natch. Right down to the lost look and goofy hair. He stroked his chin. "Does look kinda familiar."

The guy's excitement showed. "I was talking to some costumers who said they saw him in one of the main floor rest rooms around noon."

"Yes, that was it," Nikkei said. "The rest room. Not that I usually remember the faces of people I bump into in rest rooms." Mickey played along, saying, "Just what *do* you remember about people you bump into in rest rooms?" Limp-wristed and end-user delivery for laughs.

But the guy didn't laugh. "I've got some other shots," he was saying, no routine now, pulling out papers, photos of friends, food coupons, status cards, music charts, all kinds of pocket litter from pants and trouser pouches. Ultimately turning up two additional wallet-sized shots of Vanderloop—one of them taken in the Magic Kingdom, for chrissakes—which he passed along to Nikkei.

By then, though, Mickey again wasn't paying attention. Because what caught his eye was the photo of Charlie Cola he'd spied mixed in with the rest.

The primitive photo-iridescent postcard Eddie had bought from the one-eyed street vendor showed an unlogged section of Amazon forest when you looked at it one way, a treeless expanse of raw red earth with superimposed grinning skull when you looked at it the other. In blue script across the bottom ran the line: "Just getting the bugs out!" Eddie took a cautious sip from his beer and contemplated the few sentences he'd written on the reverse side, lifting his eyes once in a furtive glance to see if the sorcerers seated across the room were still checking him out.

The taller of the three, employing unsettling hand and eye movements, had already succeeded in raising Eddie's body temperature a degree or so. Or so explained the campesina in the filthy polka dot dress when she had brushed past Eddie's table some fifteen minutes earlier. ''Those three monkeys over there,''—the woman's voice hushed but seemingly thrown into Eddie's ear— ''they have the scent of the money pouch you have strapped to your ankle and they mean to possess it.'' Eddie had fought an urge to reach down and feel for the pouch, kept his hands clasped around the cool taper of the faux-glass beer bottle instead. ''Those three can see through things—clothes, flesh, and bones,'' the woman continued. ''Watch their hands and eyes; they will bring the heat of midday inside the cantina, but only you will feel it. Then they will make you drink, drink, drink until your bladder is bursting. And as soon as you go outside to relieve yourself they will have your money. Your life, too, if you resist.''

Eddie wanted to ask her how she knew about the ankle pouch—no way it showed under the baggies he was wearing— but she'd moved on, out through the saloon doors, out into the blinding light, the dusty street, leaving him to gasp at the initial blast of heat, thinking for a moment the fan over his head had stopped. Looking up, though, he found the wooden blades rotating. And the gaze of the three sorcerers fixed on him. But it wasn't until the men began to rub their fingertips together that Eddie had broken a sweat, more instantly drenching than the one he'd broken on arriving in Dos Lagunas, leaping off the back of the Mercedes interbust truck, fine red dust and bloated bloodsucking flies swirling about, feeling the jungle heat of the frontier village lower itself onto him.

Eddie read what he'd written to Asia:

The long road to Dos Lagunas has been paved with—delete that: The road to Dos Lagunas isn't paved at all. In fact, it's scarcely more than a rutted gash through South America's only surviving jungle, joining a hole in the riverside vegetation of the Nacuyali with the village itself. A local merchant owns and operates the single vehicle that ferries goods and the occasional visitor back and forth between the two. There are otherwise no links to the outside world—no phones, faxes, telex machines, no Globo or Manchet TV. I'm going to ask the merchant to hand deliver this card to the captain of the next riverboat he drives down to meet. If it reaches you, tell

Brax thanx again for the money. No sign of Lucky yet; but I suspect the people here wouldn't say even if they had seen him. Now all I have to do is find Sean.

Eddie backhanded sweat from his brow and poured the final inch of beer into himself. Only the memory of the campesina's warnings kept him from slaking his sudden thirst with another bottle. The three sorcerers glowered, snapping brown fingers in time to warbling pre-Turn noise issuing from an old cassette tape player.

The Cantina Frontera wasn't the only bar in Dos Lagunas, but of the half dozen Eddie had visited in the past few days the Frontera took the prize for sheer funk and blood-loss potential. Built with hand-hewn timber and roofed with thatch, it was the sort of place where the bullet holes and bloodstains in the duckboard floor were initialed and the sneering shrunken heads that decorated the walls had been given nicknames. Business was transacted in American dollars, hallucinogenic drinks were available on request, and the electricity was provided by a noisy gasoline-powered generator. But while the beer and whiskey were largely backyard brewed—*arracachas* lager and *ahipas* brandy—the tables and chairs and mirrors had been imported at considerable expense from a Hollywood set-design company that specialized in breakaway furniture and glass. The clientele was mostly mestizo, with a medley of scar-faced Anglos, tattooed Asiatics, and pure-blood Amazonian Indians, their language a pidgin of Spanish, Portuguese, English, and Japanese. Prospectors, deserters, bandits, former guerrillas, mercs and terrorists, smugglers, and embezzlers—the self-disappeared. And nearly all of them strapped, if not with physical weapons left over from the drug wars, then with psychic talents acquired in the shaman camps that pocked the surrounding forest.

Opinion varied as to whether Dos Lagunas was situated in Brazil or Peru, rumor being that the border ran straight through the Cantina Frontera, as if that in some way accounted for the bar's surfeit of deadly face-offs and skirmishes. Pretty much picked clean of personal possessions along the way, it had cost Eddie four days of hard traveling to get there: by small plane, bus, boat, and interbust truck. The pouch on his ankle held what remained of the funds Brax had sent, after money changers and pickpockets working the Manaus airport had lightfingered the cash Eddie'd carried into the country. "An ankle pouch won't do you much good," the Pakistani shopkeeper who sold him the thing in Manaus had warned. "Not if you're serious about going to Dos Lagunas."

Steamed after the airport rip-offs, Eddie had scowled. "Maybe I should carry my money up my ass, huh?"

But the shopkeeper had only shaken his head. "That won't help much either. Save yourself the heartache: simply give everything away as soon as you arrive."

His clothes had been stolen during an overnight bus ride through the Japanese-owned black cattle towns of the interior that supplied Wagyu beef for Tokyo and New York, but Eddie wasn't aware of the theft until well on his way down the Nacuyali. Sick and sunburned, he'd discovered that thieves had not only pried open his bag but had left their own clothes in place of the ones they'd stolen—The flea-filled baggies he was wearing now had come from the cache. It was sometime during the boat trip that his passport disappeared as well. But Eddie had come to realize that arriving in Dos Lagunas stripped of one's identity, voluntarily or by quirk of fate, constituted the only proper way to arrive. And should Lucky turn up here, oh, how he was going to owe Eddie large for the trip.

Eddie, however, had followed the Junknowitzes' instructions to the letter. He had left a crosshatch of marks behind the wooden sign directing travelers to the Hotel Rama. He had awaited Sean's signal—a soda can, upside-down on the stucco wall that ran behind the Tienda Sol. He had tacked a hand-written note to the Sol's cork bulletin board, amid a yellowed paper jumble of coded messages, wanted posters, and reward notices. He had waited again. Deciphered, Sean's response had specified the Cantina Frontera. *Choose a table in the center of the room*, the note read. *I want you sitting where I can see you.*

Eddie remembered Sean from the few times he'd visited Lucky in New York before the war—Gulf War II. Three years older than Lucky, taller, more muscular and fair-headed, Sean was a loner whose dark eyes and large mouth seemed set in an expression of disquiet, mirroring some inner torment that was never articulated. He enlisted in the Marines, and had volunteered for the Middle East when things were just heating up—the world's final setback before the Turn, the one from which the U.S. and the Soviet Union had emerged as a kind of bilateral global peacekeeping force. Eddie had seen him only once after the war, and recalled thinking at the time that whatever had gone down in those oil-rich Arab lands—*between Iraq and a hard place*, as the saying went—had freed the beast that had looked out of Sean's eyes years be-

fore, freed it to inhabit the dark spaces the war had hollowed out.
Talk of troubling, sometimes violent incidents involving Sean
would reach Lucky through his parents or his older sister: reports
of broken relationships, crimes committed, sentences served, ep-
isodes the Veterans Assessment Council had labeled sociopathic,
midnight moves that were taking Sean further and further south,
off the map of normal byways into the lawless zone of the exiled.
Into what the Brazilians termed the *inoperância*—the tropical
breakdown, the tropical entropy.

Thinking about it now, mopping magically conjured sweat
from his forehead and the back of his neck, Eddie wondered how
many other Seans were self-disappeared in the tangled environs
of Dos Lagunas.

Lucky once said that Sean was only dangerous when he needed
to be, when he felt he was being lied to or taken for a fool. He'd
chosen the jungle because he could live off the land. The barbed
wire enclosing his compound was simply meant to discourage
visitors. He did, however, communicate with his parents and
brother from time to time. The monthly disability credit transfers
were received by an e-mail box in Manaus.

Eddie decided one more beer wouldn't hurt, and had his hand
raised for the Frontera's hunchbacked waiter when someone took
sudden hold of his wrist.

"You don't need that," Sean said, slipping into the chair
opposite Eddie's. They studied one another for a long silent
moment, Eddie taking in Sean's shoulder-length curls, the ritual
scars that lined his broad forehead, the tattoos encircling thick
wrists and bulging arms. "Feeling the heat, huh?" the veteran
said at last.

Eddie's eyes indicated the sorcerers. "Those three guys over
there. They've been working some kind of hocus-pocus." He
plucked the drenched sleeve of his shirt away from his bicep.

Sean turned to regard them; he was grinning when he swung
back around. "Who told you it was them?" Sean's smile revealed filed teeth.

"Some old woman."

"She's the one you need to worry about, not these characters," Sean said, jerking a thumb. "Maria Escondida. One of
the most adept *brujas* in Lagunas. Plants a suggestion in your
head, leaves her three assistants behind to dazzle you with a bit
of the *mal ojo*. Were they snapping their fingers?"

Eddie nodded, fingers attempting to mimic the sorcerers'
moves. "And this kind of thing."

"Razzle-dazzle, Eddie."

"You remember me?"

" 'Course I do. You and Lucky used to themer together, right?"

"So how come you left me sitting here sweating?"

"Had to be sure it was you. Or maybe you think I should buy every note somebody leaves on the board for the real item."

"No, it's just—"

Eddie slapped an American twenty on the table and stood up, announcing to the bartender, "We're outta here, Ribs." The sorcerer's apprentices glowered, then grinned, exchanging words with Sean in the same guttural Indian dialect Eddie'd heard used on the Nacuyali.

"You look more like Lucky than I do," Sean commented when they were outside, heading for the shade on the opposite side of the main street. Sheathed on his belt, Sean wore a huge Dundee blade. "Now suppose you tell me what the hell you're doing down here, Eddie. The note said you'd seen my folks, so then you must know I've got a mail drop arrangement with some people in Manaus."

Exhausted, Eddie blew out his breath and went down on his haunches in the shade. "I had to see you personally. About Lucky. He disappeared almost three weeks ago and a couple of us, his friends, have been looking all over the place for him. He told this woman friend of his he was heading down to see you."

"No chance," Sean said. "He would have checked it out with me first. Besides, I haven't heard from him in two or three months." The veteran paced while Eddie filled in the details of Lucky's disappearance.

"Gotta have something to do with this guy Vanderloop," Sean said when Eddie had finished. "You find him, you'll find out who grabbed Lucky by mistake."

Eddie held Sean's angry gaze. "Three weeks, Sean. If it was a mistake, why hasn't Lucky been released? Another thing— Vanderloop's nowhere to be found, either."

Sean gritted his teeth. "For a long time I've been thinking about going back to the States, Eddie. Just to give it another try. I guess Lucky's my good reason for finally doing it."

Harley awoke in a bed of cotton-quilted wildflowers, blue rose for a pillow, daisy-petal headrest, satin sheets and pure cotton coverlets ripe with artificial floral scents—none of which had touched off her allergies. Though the scents were what had woken her, what Phipps, when he'd seen her to the room the previous evening, had called the bed's aroma alarm. Shaking her hand at the door, very proper. "I've programmed the aroma alarm for seven, unless that's too early for you . . ." No, no, seven's fine, she'd told him, eager to please. Why not six, five? Phipps had so much to teach her, she had so much to learn, the more time she could spend in his presence the better.

The bedroom's window wall of on-off glass went to transparent mode as she sat up and propped her head on the blue rose, lilies and daffodils at her feet. The smart ceiling's astrodecor faded to white. The wall overlooked a shrub-forested hillside, an expanse of ocean beyond, some low-profile island out there in deep green water, bright blue sky streaked with cirrus clouds—Harley Paradise in paradise.

The room belonged to Phipp's youngest daughter, but was normally occupied in August only, when the Hagadorn family vacationed together. Filled with stuffed animals, matching furniture, holo-poster art, the latest in electronic gadgets, it was exactly the bedroom Harley would have liked to have grown up in. And now here she was, installed like one of the kids.

Growing up . . .

The room took up the top floor of a three-story, six-sided tower that was linked by wooden catwalk to the western wing of the main house, Meadow Suite, with its severely sloping roofs and wraparound decks. Phipps had designed much of it himself, from the central hallway's double-helix banister to the duck ponds' aquarium windows. Nuclear-submarine deck plating in the showers, pre-Turn infrared car-wash heaters to warm the floors, rain and wind sensors to control the skylights. The kitchen aerospace cabinet refrigerators could accommodate over three hundred pounds of vegetables—essential when the roll call for a typical party might list more than a thousand names.

The house was on Martha's Vineyard, a triangle of *uber* real estate off the southern coast of Cape Cod, where away from the few coastal towns you would hardly know the island was inhabited. Except for the no-entry signs and anti-intrusion devices positioned at the entrances to the unpaved driveways. As if poison ivy, deer ticks, and biting blackflies weren't enough to discourage trespassing. Martha's Vineyard, where—Harley had come to realize—all the money, trees, and open-topped jeeps had gone. Houses with shingles weathered gray by the salt air; winding roads where the tops of slender oaks met overhead to create tunnels of moody shade; miles of untrashed beaches where the tyfin signs could have read, THANK YOU FOR NOT WEARING CLOTHES; suntanned yacht persons, featured players, and celeb offspring who seemed untouched by the sociopolitical changes the Turn had ushered in. Who seemed even beyond fashion.

They'd motored up in Phipps's yacht, which she had thought totally huge until he had taken her by helicopter to see the one he'd recently purchased: a Japanese-built passenger liner formerly called the *Crystal Harmony*. Fifty-thousand tons of pre-Turn luxury, with an estimated worth of five hundred million world dollars. Satellite dishes, fantail skeet-shooting range, Vegas-style casino, Jacuzzi-equipped suites larger than Harley's apartment in Queens, specially commissioned statuary and paintings by renowned Japanese, Thai, and Indonesian artists.

Harley was one of fifteen people who made up Phipps's personal entourage—not counting the ex–action figures and Rio-trained watchmen who'd provided protection. The rest were Japanese translators, mostly, and calligraphers who specialized in *kanji*, *hiragana*, and *katana*.

Phipps apparently had plans to utilize the ship as a first-of-its-kind nautical science-fiction theme park, staffed by character actors costumed as extraterrestrials. And he kept insisting that she would make the perfect "hostess" for the ship—overseeing themer policy, greeting visiting VIPs, living out a sort of parade-queen/mascot fantasy.

Harley had simply to imagine herself as a "Minnie Mouse for Marsketeers." That was, once the "software" had been installed—the thousand or so themers.

Harley had done very little talking, a lot of attentive nodding. She knew that her work for the Gender Bias Council was highly regarded, but Phipps wasn't judging her on that. "I'm going by what I read in your eyes" was what he'd said. "I'm aware that you perform an important function with the council, but our little organization is involved in equally important enterprises around the world, and I'm hoping you'll think seriously about joining us."

A job offer was the last thing she'd been expecting, but she'd tried hard to take it in stride. Why else, though, would she have been invited to tour the vessel? Why else would someone like Phipps Hagadorn have taken an interest in her to begin with? Although to be headhunted by the best of them was not the worst thing in the world.

Unless she chose to listen to what SELMI had to say on the subject. Not that she had much choice, really, considering she was paying for the sessions regardless of whether or not she heeded the AI's advice.

AND WHAT ABOUT THE TIME YOU PLANNED TO DEVOTE TO THE ANTI-GLOSSNOST MOVEMENT? the machine had written when Harley confessed to petitioning the Gender Bias Council for personal time off so that she might spend a week in the Vineyard as Phipps's houseguest. Harley was not, however, to be deterred.

She had written back: *I seem to recall your thinking that Lucky's decision to take a leave of absence was a good idea. And whatever's good enough for Lucky Junknowitz is certainly good enough for me.*

The rectangular screen was quick enough in answering: I FIND NO FAULT WITH YOUR REQUEST FOR PERSONAL TIME, HARLEY, ONLY THE USE OR PERHAPS I SHOULD SAY *MISUSE*—TO WHICH YOU PLAN TO PUT THAT TIME.

Like running off to Antarctica or somewhere was making good use of personal time, was that it? Besides, she didn't see how SELMI could call spending her days with Phipps Hagadorn a misuse of time.

WHAT I KNOW OF PHIPPS HAGADORN SUGGESTS THAT HE MAKES PRODUCTIVE USE OF HIS OWN TIME—AND CONSISTENTLY TO HIS OWN ADVANTAGE.

What you know of him, Harley had entered.

She suspected that SELMI was jealous; worried about losing her to someone whose wisdom hadn't been written in but earned in the real world. Only jealousy could account for the machine's personal attacks, character assassinations directed against one of the world's most influential economists and brilliant thinkers. SELMI had even hinted that Phipps had ulterior motives in recruiting her to hostess for the *Crystal Harmonic*, as it was going to be rechristened—that there was something suspect about the purchase of the vessel itself. That Harley needed to watch her back when Phipps said things like, ''I like who I am when I'm around you, Harley.'' As if she didn't know a line when she heard one. And then there was the not-so-small matter of Phipps's wife and family. Like she was some Marla Rice, some Donna Maples or somebody.

SELMI just needed to hear some of Phipps's other ''lines''— the quotes from mystical Sufi texts that rolled off his tongue, the parables on maximizing corporate opportunities, his views on the restructuring of businesses to function more like living cells. ''Diversification is pre-Turn,'' he'd told her. ''The shibboleth of

the New Age is Globalization.'' And he went on to speak of
Gurdjieff, flexibility of mind and body, the need to cultivate an
awareness in which all scenarios were embraced.

He had so much to teach her.

Although some of what Phipps said, just some of it, had
started to sound like the not-doing, lean-into-the-turns mantra
intoned daily by Junknowitz and company. Especially when the
talk turned to job satisfaction, travel, and personal growth. Not
that Lucky or any of his posse could possibly fit into the Hagadorn world with the ease Harley had.

Just thinking about Ziggy and the rest of them gave her a
headache she was certain would last all morning. For the past
two weeks they'd been pestering her with calls about Lucky,
whether he might have checked in with her from the road. Just
before she'd left New York, in fact, there'd been a message from
someone named Bullets Strayhand, who was apparently looking
for Lucky on some business connected with the Theme Park
Advisory Group. Like she was his personal answering service or
something!

Harley climbed out of bed thinking of Lucky, and cursing
herself for it. Recalling their cute Hostage Day meet, Harley
dressed in yellow as the occasion called for, Lucky lost in the
crowd, leaning his long frame against the very pole Harley had
chosen to wear the ribbon she'd brought along. The ribbon going
right around Lucky's geek neck, Harley oblivious to Lucky's
choking gasp, laughing with friends, pulling the satiny ends tight
so she could tie a perfect bow, almost garroting Lucky in the
process. ''Oops, Harley,'' one of her friends said, spying Lucky,
''looks like you've caught something.'' As a result she'd had her
own captive to release—but one she wasn't sure she wanted to
let go quite so soon. Something about that long trim bod, the
large sparkling eyes and bushy brows, the mussed hair and Silly
Putty look. Plus he was funny, disarming, resourceful.

And then there was Lucky the themer, who reminded her of
any number of cuddly-animal mascots for whom she'd nursed
mad crushes the summer she attended Dynamic Cheerleaders
camp in the Poconos, learning Side Hurdler jumps, Double
Hooks, and Hanging Stag pyramids.

Harley could still summon a sigh for him. In the end it was
only that Lucky lacked ambition. And what she wanted was a
life of adventure, the terms of which translated to new things,
important people, exciting situations she just couldn't see Lucky
being able to provide.

Whereas important people flocked around Phipps. The ones, for example, who had been showing up at Meadow Suite these past few days. Foreign high-Q types arriving from the airport in the a-cell stretches Phipps sent to meet them, some of whose names she recognized from the financial screens of the compunews service she subscribed to. Lots of lingering handshaking, back-clapping, European double-cheek kissing, hours of quiet after-hours conversing going on in the main house. Almost as if something top secret were in progress.

How Lucky's friends would hate it.

Standing at the window wall, inhaling the sea breeze, gazing out over the tangled growth, the ribbon of pristine beach, Harley couldn't help but wonder where Lucky was just now, and just what he was up to.

TWENTY-THREE

LUCKY'S NIGHTMARE FOUND him a subway rider in Tokyo or somewhere, packed by push and shove in among illegal aliens and vagabond themers, slim things with oyster eyes and warts that talked, trapped in a runaway car tearing through what had to be the world's longest tunnel. Jostled, cursed at, elbowed by large creatures, kneed by smaller ones, he kept reaching for a strap that wasn't there, searching vainly for some chrome pole to grasp, a friendly shoulder to lean on. Too much to ask for an emergency cord within reach when in fact *there was no subway car*! Just this pillared comic-book crowd and that long dark tunnel which had engulfed them . . .

A moment later someone was screaming, but just who in that sudden, searing light it was impossible to tell. Then the screaming stopped and he heard someone mutter, "Never fails, even on this trip I end up standing next to the joker, a regular hole card, this one."

"Maybe the human forgot to wear his medication," from elsewhere in the white light.

"Rapid breathing, tongue hanging out, I'd wager a case of first-time-fade fatigue, case of stretch pants."

The crowd laughed.

He brought a hand to his face, his own five-fingered one he hoped, realized it was *his* tongue that was hanging out, that he himself was the object of the snide comments and laughter, and commenced screaming again. "I'm blind! I can't see!"

"Definite case of stretch pants," the now familiar voice repeated.

"Sir," followed a far softer one after a long moment of fumbling about, "perhaps if you'd just open your eyes . . ."

Choking back the scream, he walked his fingers up and over

272

the smooth terrain of his face, pressed his fingertips gently against drawn eyelids only to have them roll up like cartoon window shades. The light torpedoed him, but squinting he could make out that the soft voice belonged to an apparently female life-form with eyes like cherry cough drops and feathers where hair should have been. A wide-eyed quick scan of the arrival lounge revealed even more wondrous blends of flesh and bone, costume and cover—some bored god playing Mr. Potato Head with its creations. But he understood them to be his fellow travelers. In the Trough.

"Now, isn't that much better?" the feathered Adit attendant was asking.

He tried on a sheepish smile, a kind of yeah, heh-heh, silly-me look, which wrested a collective sign of relief from the alien group—a smirk or two besides—until it occurred to him he hadn't the slightest notion of who he was or exactly where it was he had arrived.

A flurry of hand gestures and wing flapping answered the panicked screams that escaped him. "Sir, if you'll only calm down—"

"Tell me where I am and I'll think about calming down!"

The attendant pecked at something under her wing, emerged composed. "We've arrived at Adit Staph, sir, our final destination."

"Staph?" There was something undeniably right-sounding about it. He squared his shoulders under the weight of the cape and cleared his throat, tried to sound at least as composed if not as professional when he said, "Staph, of course. And I'm, I'm, I'm . . ."

Hearing the mounting distress in his voice, the attendant trained a device on his forehead and announced, "We want to thank you for choosing Singularity Flings, Professor Vanderloop."

The words ran amok inside him, touching off the mental equivalent of hooters, sirens, pinball bells, flashing signs, holiday fireworks. "And I, Professor Vanderloop, wish to thank you as well." Somewhat urbane here, the Old World count at your service, clicking the heels of his grav boots, and bowing from the waist with a slight flourish of the cape.

The attendant's cherry eyes blinked with birdlike urgency. Just loud enough to be heard, she said, "You did remember to wear your medication, didn't you, sir?"

"Never leave home without it," he avowed, catching sight of

two large and rather menacing-looking beings in security uniforms who were fast approaching, moving against the tide of recent arrivals crowding the Adit lounge.

"We had a report of a case of thick shakes," the one with the longer tusk began.

"No, everything's fine, Officer," the attendant promised. "Professor Vanderloop here was just feeling a bit confused from the trip. We experienced some rumble-strip turbulence during our transit fade through Cephate Four, and I'm sure you know how that can be—especially when you're standing in the rear . . ."

The security officers relaxed some, but weren't yet convinced. The smaller fixed him with a gimlet stare. "Sure you're all right there, Professor?"

"Oh, absolutely." He struck his chest in a hearty gesture. "Never felt better."

The officers traded questioning looks. "Then what are you doing on Staph?" This from the one he was already thinking of as Major Tusk.

"What am I doing here? Why, why, I try to make it a point to visit Staph at least once a year."

Major Tusk tapped a five-jointed digit against the side of his helmet. "Thick shakes, no question about it." Lowering his voice to add, "Humans just aren't built for Trough travel. No matter what anyone tells you. The thick messes with their brains. Move 'em in ships is what I say."

The second officer gestured that the Adit attendant should make herself scarce. "What is it you do, Professor, that brings you here every year?"

"I, well, that is, on this occasion—"

"Spit it out, Professor, or it's back to New Bedlam on mass transit."

Something told him that wouldn't do, wouldn't do at all. "I'm here to deliver a talk on . . . aboriginals," he found himself saying an instant later.

Again the officers traded looks, though puzzled ones now. "Aboriginals?" Major Tusk said. "You mean Staph's abos?"

Staph's abos, he thought. "Exactly. Though I prefer to refer to them as the Aboriginals of Staph."

Tusk looked to his partner for suggestions. "What do you think, some kind of religious ceremony?"

The second officer shrugged. "I didn't hear anything. But when does anybody tell us what goes on? Things like this come up, they expect us to make a judgment call. Talk on abos, sounds damned irregular to me."

"Are you here as observer or as participant, Professor?" Tusk wanted to know.

"Oh, a participant, to be sure." Though he wasn't at all. "Observation is important, obviously, but participation is crucial to a true understanding of the principles."

Minor Tusk asked if he was a member of the club.

"Lifelong. I've been dying to make this trip."

Tusk's sharpened features contorted. "But you're a human. I thought it wasn't allowed or something."

"Why of course it's allowed. Free will, officer. You know us humans."

Tusk turned to his partner. "What do we do with him?"

Minor Tusk shook his massive head. "Hell, show him to the sleds, I guess."

Escorted out of the arrival lounge, he was hurried through a maze of seamless, windowless corridors into a kind of locker room where members of the Staph group were being fitted for metallic-looking flight suits and helmets—twin helmets, in a few cases. Some of the room's self-circulating holos read, "Did you remember to cancel your subscriptions?" Others: "It's not too late to change your mind," and "Accretion insurance information available on request."

An all-hands robot helped him out of his cape, soft boots, blouse, and trousers, then proferred a gaudy green wearever with pleats and multiple pockets, which he was asked to slip into.

That much accomplished, the same two security officers rushed him through a final corridor to a brightly lit staging area where the newly attired travelers in his group were being loaded, one to a vehicle, into phone-booth-sized coffins outfitted with transparent canopies. Lined up pointed nose to tail in some sort of anti-grav slipstream, the already occupied coffins were riding an invisible spiral that ascended to an iris exit thousands of feet above the staging-area floor.

The single-seat crafts, the lazy helix of their ascent, the cacophony of voices and accents stirred memories, a flush of sudden misgiving he might have surveyed were it not for the resolute hold of his escorts, the countdown urgency of the continuous-loading procedure. He was shown to a waiting vehicle, cautioned to lower his helmeted head, and helped down into a padded bathtub of a seat, where an activated harness field held him fast.

"Now about this talk," Major Tusk said, supporting himself on the small ship's still-raised canopy. "I take it you want it to go out over the communications net."

"Talk?"

"Thing is, we've got to know if you're planning to begin inside, or wait until you're outside."

"Outside?"

"In the thick, Professor—outside. You going to start now or wait for the tide?"

"The tide? Is it coming in or going out?"

This set the officers and a few nearby service personnel laughing. "Hole card," Minor Tusk said by way of explanation, slowly shaking his big head back and forth. Then: "It only goes one way, Professor."

His heart began to beat a tattoo against his sternum. The sense of foreboding increased and he squirmed against the harness field.

"Hey, buddy, can't you read?" one of the attendants yelled.

He followed the tip of the thing's wing to the craft's poor excuse for an instrument panel where a holo flashed: "Caution: do not attempt to stand up. Make certain all valuables and keepsakes are safely secured under the seat. Keep hands and feet inside the vehicle at all times and make certain the harness field is activated." Something inside him snapped; his brain rained memories—

"Told you," Major Tusk said as the canopy was lowering, "case a' thick shakes."

"Stretch pants."

Lucky recalled his tongue and railed his fists against the canopy. "There's been a mistake! I'm not who you think I am— who I said I was! Get me off this goddamn ride! I didn't even buy a ticket!"

He strained to press his face to the transparency as the coffin ascended through the lower loops of the coil, the security officers and stewards well below him now, various appendages waving good-bye, good luck, fuck off. Lucky slammed a hand down on the console communicator square.

"Did you wish to begin your talk now?" a female voice asked.

"I don't have any *talk*!" Lucky screamed toward the pickup, veins in his temples throbbing, face going redder than the blunt tail of the vehicle up front.

"But so many of us are eager to hear what you have to say about the Aboriginals of Staph, Professor."

"I've never even *met* the Aboriginals of Staph! And I'm not—"

What was the use, he thought, gloved hands thrown up as far as the harness field allowed. No one was going to pay attention to him anyway. If he had a tusk maybe, or wings, or a head full of stalked eyeballs, then they'd listen. But not to a human, not in this part of the goddamned galaxy. "I'm a member of a protected species!" he yelled nonetheless.

A fine way to begin his trip home. And after a flawlessly executed escape from that Sheena Hec'k, too. But could he have lucked into an Adit with a tour group booked for Alpha Centauri or the dark side of Earth's moon maybe? No way, Jose. He had to crash one—probably the only one—where the travelers were hooked on amusement rides, or sight-seeing tours or whatever the hell the crafts were headed for.

Well, at least there were no posted restrictions barring patrons with heart conditions, bad backs, inboard offspring . . .

He gazed straight up at the ceiling's irising egress, saw coffins slinking through it like dust motes.

But there had to be some way to stop the ride. Every car in every ride in every park he'd ever been in, from Gilligan's Island to Thebes World, had a cut-out switch of one sort or another, so why should things be any different on a ride in the Trough, on Staph?

With painful effort he raised his feet and began to boot the underside of the instrument console. He toed fragile-seeming connections, heeled others, slammed both feet against the audio dimples, leaving behind dents and smudges but failing to arouse even a hint of concern from the vehicle's safety sensors. His own coffin was high in the helix now, perhaps tenth in line from the circular portal.

"Outside," Major Tusk had said, "in the thick." Which Lucky supposed meant the void, deep space, vacuum. But why'd they call it the "thick" then? Why not the thin? And what was all that about the "tide" only going one way? He regarded the lineup of vehicles in front of him. Fourth in line now . . . third . . . second . . .

"Know soon enough," he muttered aloud as the gate irised, blinking him in . . .

The first thing Lucky glimpsed was a forever line of cruciform lights he took to be stars, a Great Arc constellation at the leading edge of the Big Bang. For there were no other lights in space save those. There was something distinctly unheavenly about the swirling, black terminus of the dotted line Lucky's ship was following—and you didn't need the IQ of an astrophysicist to figure out what it was, either.

Lucky had enough remaining wherewithal to realize he'd fallen in with a group that out-machoed even the diehardest of hurricane surfers, hands-up roller-coaster fanatics, edge-of-darkness skydivers. A group only interested in talking waves of star-stifling proportion, bottomless downhills, free-falls that lasted an eternity. Their grail ride, their black mass: the cosmic ultimate loop-dee-loop. A suicidal plunge into the light-rending maw of a black hole!

Lucky thrashed. He hurled imprecations at the ruined communications ports. He flailed, kicked, punched at everything and anything within reach. But it was only when he removed his helmet that the craft reacted.

"Warning," an obviously staggered synth-voice managed from the heads-up display, "cockpit life-support gases are nearing depletion. Shift to helmet life-support feed in twenty seconds and counting. Expiration estimate without helmet: one hundred and eighty seconds. Scheduled singularity burn: six hundred forty-nine seconds. Singularity event horizon ETA: two thousand three hundred and fifty-nine seconds. Evaluation: life-support termination. Expiration of vehicle occupant. Breach of contract. Reminder: no refunds."

Lucky waffled. He donned the helmet, he took it off, he put it on and removed it again. Was there a chance the ships were constructed to *withstand* the tidal forces generated by the collapsed star? Was this really some sort of amusement-park ride after all?

"Warning: In the event of a contractual breach by vehicle occupant, immediate action will be taken by Singularity Flings, in full accordance with guidelines set down by Black Hole Trough Amusements. Occupant has thirty seconds to comply."

"Come on," Lucky grated, "do something, you piece of space trash! I dare you!"

"Occupant has twenty seconds to comply."

"Your mother was a Melitta coffee maker!"

"Occupant has ten seconds to comply."

"I've seen better chips in a Tijuana restaurant!"

"Occupant has five seconds to comply."

"Just say no to silicon!"

"Occupant has failed to comply."

Lucky wheezed as the console belched a gas cloud full into his face. He had a final curse left in him before he lost consciousness.

"Lemme be sure I've got this straight," Charlie Cola said, rising halfway out of his deck chair. "This guy, this, this Indian had my picture? A picture of me?"

"And one of Didi," Dante told him, "although she was apparently somewhat out of focus." He paused to sip at his strawberry daiquiri while Charlie shook his head in disbelief. "Not your best angle either, from what Mickey tells me. But he says you were dressed to the nines. Standing on a movie line or something."

No need to puzzle it out, Charlie thought. The theater on West Forty-fourth, that stupid-ass musical, the goddamned camshafting star-stalkers he'd figured were after shots of Jason Duplex and Meena D. And that one lensman. The Indian. Charlie put his head in his hands and let out a groan. "I told you they were watching me. I told you."

Bhang remained silent for a long moment, watching the waves roll in, a barefoot couple dressed in white out for a low-tide stroll along Charlie's portion of Westhampton Beach. When Dante had phoned from the City two hours earlier, Charlie had told him, "Look, no more trysts, no more of this secret-agent crap. You have something to tell me, you come out to the house. Otherwise I don't want to hear it." Now Bhang was sitting right here on the rear deck and Charlie still wasn't sure he wanted to hear it.

"You know, you ought to think about moving to Cyprus. You'd like it."

Charlie lifted his head. "How about we compare beaches some other time? Right now I want to know what a Peer Group agent's doing following your people down to Atlantic City."

"Peer agent?" Dante looked at him and laughed. "You're wearing that one out, Charlie."

Charlie frowned in anger. "You've got things sussed, is that it?"

Dante shrugged. "I don't know from sussed, but I'm thinking clearer than you are. For starters, Charlie, why would a Peer agent bother to go after my boys?"

"That's what I want to know."

"Yeah, but you're not getting the whole picture here. Okay, it's a hundred proof we were being watched, a second sure thing the Peer Group engineered the abduct at PhenomiCon. So they had to know about Mickey and Nikkei all along, didn't they?"

"I suppose."

"Damn right you suppose. But I'm telling you Mickey said this guy, this Indian, was interested in learning what happened to his friend, Charlie—his friend, you understand? The guy my boys mistook for Vanderloop. The fucking guy the Agency's Peer Group took into the goddamned Trough with them." He took a swallow from his glass and ran a hand over his mouth. "You see what this means?"

Charlie got up out of the chair to close the glass slider that opened on the sunken living room. Dante had been told about the battles Charlie and Didi were having over the house alterations; in fact, they'd been arguing when he arrived. Charlie returned from the door after taking a wary look around and pulled his chair closer to Dante's, leaning forward to say, "I still want to know how this Indian found them."

Dante answered in the same whisper. "Fair enough. Problem is, I'm not certain myself. I've been thinking someone could have eyedeed them at the con. I had them registered under bogus names, but that doesn't rule out some whiz kid coming up with photos, tracking them to the hotel and down to AC."

"Okay," Charlie said, "so explain what this guy's doing with my picture."

Dante sniffed. "Well, the interesting part's not that he had it—you said yourself you were feeling stalked. What's interesting is how he laid it out. Or how he didn't, really. Just let my boys get a peek at you while he was supposedly rummaging around for headshots of his missing friend."

"You think he meant it as a smoke signal or something?"

"I do indeed."

"But what's he saying? What's he want, for Christ's sake?"

Dante pursed his lips. "It's possible—*possible*," raising a cautionary finger, "that this guy and whoever he works with is onto the truth about your little operation over at Quick Fix." At this Charlie closed his eyes and cursed. "Somehow they got your number. Don't ask me how, but they did. They might have even found out about Vanderloop and decided to snatch him themselves."

"For what?"

"So they could substitute one of their own people at the con."

The meaning of it struck Charlie between the eyes. Dante was suggesting that some group had infiltrated a spy into the Trough!

The Bronx Adit had been even busier than usual since the arrival, only the day before, of three top-ranking execs from Black Hole Trough Adventures. Something very important was in the works, but Charlie assumed he had less chance of learning what that was since the Vanderloop fiasco. Now a spy to add to things. He was in over his head, he was drowning . . .

"I told you the Agency had competition on this one," Dante was remarking. "But I'm only saying it's possible. Maybe they're trying to see how things work. Maybe they're hooked on the same Aussie puzzle that got Vanderloop in trouble with the Agency to begin with. Maybe they're all confused about what went down at the con—their guy getting double-snatched and all—first by my boys, then by the Peer Group."

Charlie opened his flabby arms to the sky. "When the Agency finds out about this, they'll have my fucking head."

Dante shook his head once more. "No reason they have to find out." He waited till he had Charlie's full attention to add, "You told them the Peer Group screwed up, right?"

Charlie nodded. "I said they moved too fast and grabbed the wrong person. Bunch of middle-management types are in a panic about it. From what I gather, they're still trying to sort things out."

"So you're back in their good graces."

"For now. But they're asking where the hell Vanderloop disappeared to, and they're not going to wait forever for an answer. Another Peer Group's being readied—this time from Terminal Abductions, not those clowns that run Technical Assist."

"Then we certainly don't want to spoil things at this juncture." Dante grew pensive. "What about we furnish the Agency with the name of the asshole who got himself snatched. That'd count for something, wouldn't it?"

"You've got the name?"

Dante grinned. "What am I running here, some chicken-shit operation? Of course I've got the name. You feed it to the Agency first chance you get. Try to sound pissed off about it, too. Tell them they better get some janitors down here to clean up after the mess the Peer Group left behind, 'cause all kinds of people are asking all kinds of questions about this missing guy."

"That might work," Charlie mused. "but that still leaves us with the Indian."

"Yeah, but that's an easy one to manage."

Charlie sat up straight. "No Marseilles Solutions, Dante. I won't have it."

Dante aimed a finger at his own chest. "What 'Marseilles Solutions'? I'm talking Agency directives, Charlie: A problem arises, it gets dealt with however it has to, so long as the Agency's cover is maintained. Am I right or am I right?"

Charlie returned a tight-lipped nod.

"So we take each problem as it comes, and first on the list is this Indian parading around with your picture in his wallet. I propose we let Mickey and Nikkei arrange for him to check into the hardwood Hagadorn. You know, to kick the oxygen habit."

Charlie swallowed hard. "They've already blown one job, Dante . . ."

Bhang waved a hand. "This they can handle, believe me."

"But suppose this Indian does have a line on Vanderloop? Suppose all this smoke-signal stuff is just his way of offering to deal?"

"Suppose it is. Okay, so we received his message when he flashed your picture. Now we send his people a message that they've stuck their noses into something that bites, and bites hard."

It emerged that Staph wasn't a planet at all, but a deep-space wagon wheel built and maintained by a Black Hole subsidiary known as Singularity Flings, for the express purpose of providing a suicide launch platform for members of the galaxy-wide Short Timers Club. The actual planet Staph lay some hundred billion miles away—even at that distance the closest world to the collapsed star known as Evening Tide—its indigenous population of sentient quadrupeds dead for many a millennium, its current population chiefly scientists, clerics, and waitresses.

What happened was that the Founders of Black Hole, having opened an Adit in Staphspace, had incorporated into the lore, legends, and Romanesque architecture of the downside evolving race a riddle: oral and glyphic hints to the effect that on some unnamed day in the distant future the Staphites could expect a "window" to appear in their piece of the heavens, through which they might pass en masse into a kind of promised land for the fleet and four-footed—providing, of course, that certain moral criteria included among the cache of clues had been satisfied. The Founders had been into such things then, jaunting about via the transspatial tunnels their tamed singularities shaped, leaving evidence of their passing here and there, performing experiments of a kind, goading planetary races down one path or another, beckoning some of the stars, sentencing others to the cruelest of evolutionary journeys, for reasons only the Founders themselves understood. But this particular riddle—the one their spectral agents had left Staph to decipher—had somehow been forgotten during the shake-up that transfigured the Agency. The Staph experiment was abandoned, the nearby Adit closed. No one, however, had thought to tell the Staphites, whose entire history, whose technological advancements and unsurpassed ethical achievements all hinged on the promise of that heavenly window, the compelling prophecy of group ascent.

What the Founders had helped to create, in fact, was a planetary race of remarkable refinement, unified almost from the start, neither divided by war nor ravaged by misunderstanding, but focused instead on the fulfillment of a divine covenant, each and every individual contributing his or her share to the cause of enlightened evolution. Even after the Staphites had devised a means to leave their world and venture into near space, their journeys were never undertaken with a thought to colonize or conquer, but simply to spread the word of peace, to fulfill their part of the bargain, to demonstrate to those godlike entities they believed were monitoring them that they were keeping to the path with heart and were prepared to go to any lengths—even, as it were, to meet their gods halfway.

The eventual, perhaps inevitable discovery of the collapsed supergiant Evening Tide was to prove their downfall. For, after the equivalent of a century of argument and debate, it was decided that the sinister gravitational sink was indeed the window the legends and ancient glyphs foretold. And so the Staphites had crowded themselves into ships that had been standing at the ready and flown into the depths of Evening Tide's swirling atomic storm, believing to the last that they were about to meet their creator gods, when it was the cosmic reaper, the black death, that had accepted them into its gloomy occult fold.

That, in any case, was the story as Lucky heard it from Metallica, the med-tech in charge of supervising his recovery aboard the wheel, who explained it all from the foot of the bed, at the edge of the clinic hover mattress—a kind of diagnostically formatted spread-sheet. This only after Lucky had fessed up to his ignorance regarding the planet and its hapless aboriginal race. A bit of post-travel delirium, he'd explained to Metallica, who scolded him for having neglected to wear a travel derm.

He was still in the clinic now, still numb from the paralyzing effects of the nerve gas his craft had belched, although scarcely too numb to be struck by Metallica's almost disconcerting love-liness. That she had made him forget entirely about Sheena was in itself telling; for even Sheena's fiery mane and ripe-fruit mouth couldn't compare to the planes and angles of the tech's silver-hued face. Then there were those peach-pink lips, that wonderful confusion of snow white hair, the tigress torso under the breast-and hip-hugging uniform, the angelic hands . . . God, he was such a sap for the feminine form! Why, there probably wasn't an ounce of intelligence behind those amber eyes.

"So members of this, uh, Short Timers Club have been com-ing here for thousands of years to throw themselves into a black hole?" Lucky asked as Metallica was studying the spread-sheet's holo readouts."

"The notion seems to appeal to the existentially desperate, Professor," she told him from across the small wedge-shaped room.

He hadn't bothered to disabuse anyone of the idea that he was Miles Vanderloop, what with his intracranial ticket implant read-ing that way and all.

Returned to the Staph wheel by the aggravated AI who mon-itored the suicide-crafts, Lucky hadn't been in the clinic five minutes when the chief of security had made an appearance, advising Lucky of his rights and questioning him about some group that called itself the Disk Dives, which of late had been infiltrating members into the Short Timers Club. Lucky, woozy under an IV drip of nerve-gas antidote, had denied affiliation with any group whatsoever. And as for his having ended up in the singularity line in the first place, well, that was just the result of a misunderstanding between him and the security officers who'd escorted him in from the Adit. Had they asked to see his club membership magic marker? No. Had they even asked to check his ticket? No, again. And *of course* he'd come to observe rather than participate. Why, he was human, wasn't he? A card-carrying member of a protected species. The tusked security officers had no right letting an Adit-dazzled traveler through to the sleds no matter what species he or she belonged to. Espe-cially one with so obvious a case of temporary amnesia, fade fatigue, stretch pants, whatever the hell they wanted to call it—regardless of his failure to wear a dermal patch. Why, he had half a mind to bring legal action against Singularity Flings *and* Black Hole Travel Agency.

Lucky sat up on the hover mattress to have a look around. The gaudy green wearever was long gone; Metallica or someone had outfitted him in a long, silky teal blue robe with a bright red sash. "Funny," he said to the tech's back, "nobody sounded existentially desperate. The ones I arrived with, I mean."

"They seldom do," she told him. "Most Short Timers are in fact staunch reincarnationists."

"Assuming Evening Tide leaves enough pieces to put back together." Metallica offed the display and started back across the room, her short skirt revealing the muscular curve of her thigh. Ah, nurse fantasies, Lucky thought, fingering his Vanderloop-coded medical bracelet.

"They refer to it simply as the Nineteenth Hole," she said. "Evening Tide."

"The 'nineteenth hole'?" Lucky hung his head and laughed.

Metallica inclined her head to regard him. "Because it's the nineteenth singularity counting out from galactic center along the Cephate spiral."

"I think I'm finally getting the hang of these mighty-mite contraptions," Lucky said around a smile. "It's like they have a thing about puns and colloquialisms and stuff." Metallica's bafflement showed. "You know, like on the one-way flights, just before the burn for the black hole? They oughta serve 'light cuisine.' "

Metallica's eyes narrowed. "Light cuisine? I'm not sure I— oh, I see. Very amusing, Professor. You're fitted for a tongue twister, then?"

"Among other things," Lucky answered, naming a few of them: hearing aids, odor eaters, dream machines.

"But your marker indicates that you're from Foxal."

"I'm from Earth, Metallica. Terra. Adit Navel, whatever it goes by out here. Blue, white, and brown place, third from Sol with a big ol' moon, you musta heard of it."

Metallica blinked. "Naturally I've heard of it. But I thought Terra was classified a tertiary world. How is it you're here?"

He smirked. "We'd need about a week and a half, Metallica."

"And this," she said, reaching out a hand to touch Lucky's maybe-not-so-lucky saucerette medallion. "How did you come by it?"

"Come by it? More like walked into it. But that's another long story." He watched her a moment, wondering if she could

be the friendly ear he was searching for. "If you want the truth,
I was headed to Earth when I took a wrong Adit out of Bedlam,
er, New Bedlam."

"And you'll fade to Terra when you leave Staph?"

"Well, I'll tell ya, little lady," Lucky unable to resist doing
his John Wayne impression, "I aim ta try, all right."

The tech wrestled with some decision. "I have something to
show you," she said, and prized from a sheath-like pocket inside
her short jacket a ten-inch taper of milky-white crystal, which
she deftly inserted into a mattress-side device. "I'll leave you
alone with this, Professor."

No sooner did she exit the room when a holo resolved in
midair at the foot of the spread-sheet. In translation, Lucky read:
"A Report to the Coordinating Committee with Regard to
Project Head Start." The projection faded, only to be replaced
by a full-color depiction of an Earthlike planet, opened as if
equatorially hinged, with a dollar sign emerging from its core.

The corporate logo of AzTek Development Consortium.

The company that employed Lucky's erstwhile roomie,
Rashad Tittle.

Lucky sat openmouthed through the remainder of the fifteen-
minute report. Metallica reentered as the final projection was
derezzing. "Strange what we learn when we're far from home,"
she said, sheathing the crystal.

Lucky turned to her, still agape. "I, I don't believe it . . ."

Metallica displayed her first sly-side grin. "Believe it,
Professor—"

She barely got the word out when the hatch slid open and the
Tusks, Major and Minor, burst into the room. With them, though
a step behind, came Sheena Hec'k. "That him?" the Major
asked, gesturing.

Sheena folded her arms and nodded. "That's him, all right."

The Tusks decided to put on a show for the two women, each
of them taking hold of an arm. "Well, now, Professor Vanderloop," from Minor this time, "guess you're not the fade-
fatigued innocent after all."

Lucky threw Metallica an imploring look, but she only showed
him her back.

"And the name isn't Vanderloop," Sheena snarled, activating
the twin-pack confinement field. "It's Lucky Junknowitz."

TWENTY-FOUR

TO THE LASTING astonishment of some twenty thousand fans of stage magic, a few of whom reportedly paid up to five thousand dollars for front-row seats in the Tokyo Harbor amphitheater specially constructed for the event, Erik Vogon, performing then and always under the name "The Awesome Vogonskiy," had caused to disappear from full view, and for a full fifteen minutes, the whole of the Japanese luxury cruise liner *Crystal Harmony,* along with a half-dozen tugs and smaller craft which happened to be in close proximity to the vessel at the time. On another occasion—and once again for fifteen minutes—Vogon had worked a freeze-frame on Angel Falls in southern Venezuela. And on still another, playing to the one thousand billionaires who had flown to Easter Island from nations worldwide to take part in what had been billed as "the illusion of this or any other lifetime," The Awesome Vogonskiy had engineered a total solar eclipse.

Physicists, investigators of the paranormal, Vegas magicians working with albino tigers and leggy women assistants—all had their explanations, their separate theories to advance. Vogon was accused of employing airborne psychotropic agents to induce mass hallucinations; of somehow hypnotizing the members of his audience as they were passed through theater weapons scanners; of entering into a conspiracy with his fans, who were encouraged to issue exaggerated reports to the media. To all of which the charismatic Vogon would reply that the illusions he performed could be executed by anyone who had a working knowledge of optics and a clear understanding of audience dynamics—particularly of those audiences predisposed to a willing suspension of disbelief. He denied employing hallucinogens or hypnosis, although he readily admitted to being an avid practitioner of mind-control techniques. "For what else is the creation of an illusion," he would often put to his legions of critics, "if not mind control of a kind."

To complicate matters further, the offstage Erik Vogon was a conservative thinker who considered himself a rigid scientist. Born in Moldavia of Greek Orthodox parents, Vogon had attended a host of Soviet and European universities, earning degrees in engineering, psychology, and applied laser technology. He was a member of CSICOP, the Committee for the Scientific Investigation of Claims of the Paranormal, long before he turned his hand to magic, and remained one of the committee's most outspoken debunkers and chief contributors to *The Skeptical Inquirer*. Too, it was Vogon who had a standing offer of ten million dollars for anyone who could furnish material proof of a mysterious visitation or disappearance—extraterrestrial, ghostly, or otherwise.

The stage show Brax and Asia attended at the Orpheum Theater paled in comparison to Vogon's media-event dazzlers. But what separated the show from the seasonal extravaganzas that typically enjoyed brief Broadway runs was Vogon's willingness to *explain* how he worked each card or conjuring trick, each instance of levitation or disappearing-animal illusion, showing precisely how and when he had palmed a card, made use of a false-bottomed table, or programmed the theatrical spots for maximum distraction. Not even those professionals in the house who paid strict attention, however, believed for a moment they could benefit from the explanations, since it had to be granted that Vogon's hands were indisputably the fastest in the business; that the man possessed an astounding memory; that, indeed, there was something almost superhuman about him—*non*human, some were wont to say. Especially in that he was able to provide his fans with just the show they wanted.

Vogon was an enormous man, over six and a half feet tall, who saw no shame in wearing his well-fed girth proudly. With his white tangle bib of beard, shock of gray hair, heavy-browed gaze, and flaring wizard's eyebrows, he was a return to the classic image of the conjurer, after too many decades when there'd been no telling apart magicians from rock stars or Hollywood celebs. He was wearing Chinese silk pajamas and curl-toed slippers when he admitted Brax and Asia into his backstage dressing room after the show. Russell Print, chief editor of Sony-Neuhaus's science fiction division and Brax's longtime friend, had secured the appointment.

"So how is old 'Rush'?" Vogon asked after a stiff handshake as he sipped champagne from a glass with a fluted stem, his broad face wrinkling under the pancake makeup. "Still turning out that outer-space trash?" He offered Asia a glass of the bubbly, appraising her openly, frankly interested.

"Careful," Brax said, trying to sound friendly, "I sometimes write that trash."

Vogon scowled at him. "A writer? Russell led me to believe this interview had to do with a personal matter. After all, Mr. Koddle, I've books of my own to write."

"It is personal," Brax was quick to assure him. "It's about a missing friend of ours." Including Asia in his gesture.

While Brax took him through the story of their fruitless search for Lucky, the talks with Professor Jacobs and Marshall Stack, Eddie's journey to Mexico and Brazil—he was due back in New York that very evening—Asia studied Vogon's diminutive dark-skinned assistant, Tumi, who was occupied in the wardrobe closet. During the audience mind-reading portion of the show, when he had been on stage, the man's skin had appeared deep brown. But here, up close and out of the effects of the spots and strobes, it seemed closer to purple than brown, and was mottled in places, as if from scars or skin grafts. Asia hoped the champagne glass was concealing her eyes, but the moment Tumi turned and caught her scrutinizing gaze, he countered with a look that pulsed through her like a sexual shudder. She sat frozen in place, instantly flushed and gasping, skin tingling, legs quivering—coming! Coming as she sat there, *coming*—

"Are you all right?" Brax asked in response to her sharp intake of breath.

She swallowed and found her voice, managed a long exhale as the warmth poured out of her. "Yeah, Brax, I'm okay. Just a chill or something . . ."

"A chill? Christ, I'm sweating to death in here."

Asia saw a look pass between Vogon and Tumi, who lowered his gaze and immediately excused himself from the dressing room. The magician quickly took up the slack, saying, "Now, about this friend Lucky—or perhaps we should say this unlucky friend—you're certain you've checked with everyone who knows him?"

Brax's gaze lingered on Asia for an instant before he turned to face the outsized magician. "We've even checked with people who *don't* know him. But Professor Jacobs thought you might have an idea or two we haven't tried."

Vogon drained his glass and refilled it; Asia, confused and still shaking from her spontaneous orgasm, declined his offer to enliven hers.

"Let me begin by stating that there are no mysterious disappearances. No more than there are ufos, ghosts, yetis, Elvis sightings, Bermuda Triangles, or second assassins. Such thinking is a remnant of pre-Turn fascination with the so-called occult—when we *expected* the paradigm to loose these things. Now it's our control over nature that makes us long for them. The more sure our control, the more forcefully this deeply buried need to believe in the supernatural asserts itself. And if you think things were bad before the Turn, just wait five or ten years." He snorted into his glass. "Perhaps it won't even require five or ten years. Perhaps by next year or the year after everyone will be seeing ghosts in their home videos, aliens on every street corner."

"They already are, if you subscribe to the *Video Examiner*," Brax thought to point out.

"Ah, the tabloids," Vogon said, spreading his giant hands. "The tabloids and I are fast friends. And do you know why? Because while they think they're promoting a mindset, they're actually reducing that mindset to the level of mere entertainment. My second best friends in the debunking business are these idiotic insurance companies offering policies for abduction and stigmata and the like. I don't think they had a clue the idea would catch on. And yet it's staggering to note just how much money people will spend to take out a policy when instances of a financial settlement are almost nonexistent. We have a need, you see, a need to believe."

Brax showed Asia a quick glance; they'd agreed beforehand not to reveal anything about her connection with Altamont Insurance. Asia was certain now, however, that Bullets Strayhand was a product of Vogon's training. A better question, of course, was who'd trained that Tumi?

"This disappearance nonsense especially. It irks me to no end. Every day you hear people claiming that their friends or lovers have disappeared. But just because a case is consistent with previously reported cases doesn't mean it's genuine. And I suppose you have the names of prominent celebs of unassailable character who are willing to lend their support to this claim?"

"Well, no, not exactly. In fact, there are just the five of us—"

"Frankly, I'm surprised you've come to me at all, since the findings of experts who are critical of the 'facts' will only be minimized or ignored. As will conflicting versions or details of the actual disappearance.

"Your friend, for example. Unknown to you, he might be one of these policyholders. You say he left his job. Perhaps he's engineered his own disappearance, hoping the beneficiary named in his policy can negotiate a substantial settlement."

"Lucky's not the charlatan type," Brax said.

"No, of course not." Vogon tried to keep the condescending tone from contorting his features. "However, the first thing I have to ask myself when someone approaches me with a story about a ufo sighting or a mysterious disappearance is, does this person really believe what he or she is saying, or does he or she think I'm dense enough to accept whatever it is I'm told." He set his eyes on Brax. "Which are you, Mr. Koddle? Do you honestly believe that your friend has 'disappeared,' or are you just trying to see if you can convince me?"

Brax bit back whatever it was he had in mind to say and shrugged. "We just want to know where he is, Mr. Vogon. We're worried and we want to know he's okay—wherever the hell that is, Earth, the moon, the goddamned twilight zone for all we care."

While obviously moved by Brax's sincerity, Vogon seemed mildly bemused as well. "Let's discount the latter two possibilities, then. Or shall I enroll you, Mr. Koddle and Ms.—Boxdale, is it?—among the ranks of those who purport to believe in Atlantis, psychic surgery, contact between extraterrestrials and primitive tribes, space-time portals by which we might all travel to distant worlds."

Asia held her tongue, but Brax said, "Do you have any ideas how we can find our friend, Mr. Vogon, or are you just going to sit here and pontificate?"

Vogon's gut-shaking guffaw rattled the dressing room. "All right, you two, since I can see that you're evidently serious about this." He held up cigar-thick fingers. "One: Stop relying on telephone calls, electronic bulletin boards, whatever it is you're using to let him know you're looking for him. Two: Stay out of the Virtual Network. Whether your friend is self-disappeared or has been abducted, word on the Network is only going to succeed in driving him or his abductors deeper underground. And finally: Make up a joke."

"A joke?" Asia said, calm enough now to let some of her impatience show.

"Precisely. Circulate a joke about your friend and I promise you it will reach him. Perhaps once he knows you're looking for him, he will try to contact you. I'm sure, in any event, that he will turn up in due time.'' Vogon folded his massive arms—his signal the discussion was over.

Brax was strangely silent as they made their way to the stage door and out into the tourist crowd and evening traffic din of Times Square.

"Well, what about it," Brax said at last, "can you think of a joke we can use? Something about getting 'lucky' at Phenomi-Con, maybe.''

"I think The Awesome Vogonskiy's something of a joke, if you ask me.''

Brax slipped an arm around her shoulders. "Hey, what happened to you in there, anyway?''

Asia shook her head. "I don't think I want to talk about it just yet.''

Brax let it go, saying, "I don't know, maybe Vogon's right about the joke. The usual methods aren't getting us anywhere. But you know what keeps nagging me? This thing about portals in space-time. Professor Jacobs mentioned the same thing.''

"So'd Bullets when I talked to him," Asia said. "But then so has every other one of you science-fiction writers for the past I don't know how many years.''

"Yeah, I suppose—''

Brax stopped short on the sidewalk, precipitating a chain reaction of pedestrian collisions that stretched halfway down the block. "Christ, *now* I remember it!'' he said as angry walkers were angling around him. "Bixby Santiago,'' he added, turning to take Asia by the shoulders.

Asia's fine brows V'ed. "I probably shouldn't ask, but—''

"One of the Worlds Abound authors. He wrote about some intergalactic corporation or something that had opened up portals on Earth, and were abducting people, 'Adits,' Santiago called them, leading to somewhere called the 'Trough.' No planetary assaults, no spaceships, just XT executives slipping in and out of these singularity-powered doorways.''

"I remember," Asia said, scrolling through her memory of the long days and nights she'd devoted to helping Brax sort out the series characters. "Santiago's book was called *Edge of Space.*''

If there was one area of Manhattan where the camera-shy could still turn when struck by a sudden attack of surveillance syndrome, Little Asia had to be it. A world unto itself covering dozens of square blocks on the East Side, from Canal Street south to the Seaport, the place had only grown more populated, more labyrinthal since the Turn. More deadly, as well, with the arrival of Japanese boryokudan and organized-crime figures from Hong Kong, Jakarta, and HCM City. The crooked streets and camera-free alleyways were a prize to be won, an empire to be claimed by those most cunning and ruthless, for with them came a clientele that cried out for protection, designer drugs, and black-market data.

Willy, consequently, wasn't exactly turning cartwheels over Nikkei Tanabe's suggestion that they rendezvous there to discuss Lucky's disappearance. As if the seedier side of Atlantic City hadn't been bad enough. But something had come up that Willy should hear, the broad-faced Japanese said. Something that couldn't be entrusted to the phone or modem. And besides, Nikkei knew a restaurant that served the best sushi in town.

It was Asia Willy would have asked along for company, but she and Brax had already left for Erik Vogon's magic show, "The Future of Illusion," when Nikkei's call came in; so Ziggy was the one he was stuck with. Ziggy, who, for most of the tube ride downtown, wouldn't shut up about the stupid house fly he'd caught in the loft.

"Not just some stupid house fly," Ziggy was saying now. "I had the thing looked at by a guy at the Museum of Natural History. We're talkin' a *dermatobia hominis,* amigo."

"Well why dint you say so?" Willy showed elaborate concern, with a no-loss-of-forward-momentum sidewalk about-face. "An actual dermaphobia Dennis the Menace, huh?"

"Dermatobia hominis," Ziggy countered, spitting it out like Daffy Duck. "A human botfly, to you. Their bites inject larvae into the skin, which, like, hang around feeding off you for forty days, then pop up as inch-long maggots. Real *Aliens* shit."

Willy stopped to check a street sign—an old painted number crowning a rusted pole. Corner of Pell and Lum Yen, Nikkei had told him over the phone. The restaurant to look for was The Dreamy Lotus. No sense asking anybody in the crowd for directions, though, not where English was at best a third language. "And so, what, this botfly showed up in your room?"

"Materialized is more like it. Flew right out my wall screen."

People were turning curious glances at Ziggy's ensemble of grape-colored shirt and sun-yellow pants, brighter than some of the storefront neon and fiber-optic displays.

"I still don't see the big deal," Willy said over his shoulder.

"The big deal's that botflies aren't indigenous to New York."

"So it migrated up from Mexico or somewhere. Species of plants do that all the time."

"Yeah, but Willy," Ziggy reached out a hand to arrest his friend's determined stride, "these botflies are also found in Australia, and the dude onscreen was a bushman—an Aborigine."

Willy thought before speaking. "Another videogeist captured by your VDRs, I suppose."

Ziggy's eyes darted about. "Yeah, if you must know. But I don't see that that matters any. Not with a synchronous event of this caliber."

Willy put his tongue in his cheek. "The Aborigine and the botfly. If this is another one of your RGO updates—"

Ziggy closed his eyes and shook his head. "You're boutique sometimes, you know that? It's like your brain's only picking up one channel. You tell me about this musical instrument you find in somebody's basement that plays mood music and do I question you? Do I doubt you? No, I listen." He tapped the side of his head. "I listen for clues."

Willy sighed in exasperation. "All right. Why don't we just skip the quiz-show portion. Exactly what clue did I miss?"

Ziggy's expression softened somewhat. "Lucky was wearing Professor Vanderloop's name tag at PhenomiCon, right? And all of a sudden, nobody knows how, both of them disappear. But Brax says Vanderloop was probably going to talk about this group of Australian Aborigines that are supposedly missing from their reservation." He bunched his shoulders. "So I think one of those missing Aborigines is trying to send us a message, Willy."

Willy had nothing to say for a moment. Then: "Let's just see what these two guys have to say."

Ziggy hurried to catch up with him. "These same two guys who use phony names at cons, Willy? Same ones who hang around the high-roller crowd in Atlantic City and have a thing about using the phone, huh?"

"Look," Willy shouted without slowing down, "I never said they were boy scouts, and I don't like being down here any more than you do. Maybe we should have all gone to see the magician. But this guy Nikkei didn't sound on the air when I talked to him. And, anyway, they admitted to using aliases at the con."

"Still, Will . . . Little Asia?"

Willy lengthened his stride, going out of his way to avoid a gang of headbanded Tongs lounging on the corner. "They want to treat me to some sushi. That's the way they are. Besides, I left word for Eddie where we'd be, so maybe he'll show up and bring Sean along." Willy laughed. "That make you feel any better?"

"I'm not sure," Ziggy was willing to admit, allowing a laugh himself. "But I'm telling you, all these disappearances—Lucky, Vanderloop, the Aborigines—they're all connected. And somebody sent us a botfly for proof."

The Dreamy Lotus was just across the street, a ground-floor corner place you entered through a poppy-flower doorway. If there were windows they didn't look out on either Pell or Lum Yen. The sign above the doorway was hand-painted and needed touching up.

"Hope the food's better than the ambience," Willy said as they were crossing the street.

"Told you the guy wouldn't be stupid enough to come alone," Mickey Formica commented as he and Nikkei, down the block a ways, observed Willy and Ziggy entering The Dreamy Lotus. "Brought along one of his homeboys."

"Yeah, but he was stupid enough to bring along someone who wears yellow pants. A regular potato." *Kono imo* was the actual term Nikkei used—a dweeb.

Mickey fell silent for a long moment. He wore yellow pants from time to time, and couldn't figure whether his partner had simply forgotten or was sending him an insult by proxy. "Okay, so I'm not worried either," he said finally. He nevertheless felt for the handgun strapped to his ribs under the beige rayon jacket. "How's it go down?"

Nikkei tapped him into motion and they hurried along the sidewalk in the direction of the restaurant. "The elder brother who controls The Lotus has been given the script. Tonight it's regulars-only, and no one will care very much about what we do. First, though, we all sit down and order some food."

"A script," Mickey said. "Let's just hope everyone's off book."

Nikkei snorted. "Try the tuna. I understand it's very good here."

"I'm not down for fish, man. Ever since your people started opening up sushi shops in Harlem."

Nikkei looked at him askance. "So next time we'll do this in Little Italy."

"Suit me," Mickey told him, well into his pimp roll now.

Damn kudzus, he thought. Messing up his home turf like that. "So, my man, what are you going to have them order?"

"It doesn't matter what they order. Fugu is what they'll be served."

Mickey raised his eyebrows and whistled. "That's that tiger puffer blowfish, last I heard. Toxic shit if the cook doesn't know his way around."

"You heard correctly. Very toxic."

"So I guess Mr. Bhang doesn't want to have a talk with them first, huh?"

Nikkei ignored it. "We'll take them out the back way when it's done."

Mickey aimed a look at him. "And you ain't the least interested in knowing what this is all about, Nikkei? Whether the guy we almost snatched was Vanderloop or this Junkywitz, how the Injun got Charlie Cola's photo and all?"

Nikkei shook his head, and said firmly: "We're just here to deliver a message."

In the loft, after a free ride in from LaGuardia from a Russian cabbie, an out-of-work biotechnician Sean had somehow pegged as a fellow vet, Eddie read the short handwritten note Willy had left them. He was glancing at the time display on the wall opposite Willy's Murphy bed when Sean returned from the bathroom. "We must have just missed them," he offered.

Sean's eyes scanned the note. "Nice group of roomies, Eddie. You come back from South America, and instead of welcoming you, two of 'em are off seeing a magic show and the other two are out eating raw fish."

Nurturing Brazilian amoebas or something, Eddie's stomach lurched at the mention of sushi. "No," he managed, "they're good people. You'll see when you meet them. Anyway, Willy and Ziggy went out to talk to someone about Lucky."

"Lemme see that." Sean snatched the note from Eddie's hands.

Eddie was adapting to the abuse, the sarcasm, and the petty violations, not that he was enjoying it any. Lucky's unexplained disappearance had Sean angry—apparently one of the only emotions he could summon when he felt things had slipped beyond his control. A holdover reaction from the war, he'd explained to Eddie during the jet jump from Brazil, and perhaps his primary reason for exiling himself in Lagunas, and choosing to live behind walls of thorny forest and concertina. Eddie ventured he was one of the few to have ever seen the inside of the jungle hideaway. Sean confessed how he couldn't be around other people because his instincts just wouldn't let him dismiss the lies, the manipulations, the bullshit way people had of dealing with one another. How when confronted with bullshit he would say so, and how his saying so would often lead to violence.

Eddie saw the way it worked when they had stopped over in Manaus so Eddie could secure a replacement passport and Sean could collect his e-mail messages and send off a letter to his folks, and one to his sister, too, even though they hadn't spoken in years—Lucky's disappearance prompting a memory of better times. They were in the airport bar when someone had commented on Sean's forehead scars, the ones he claimed he couldn't talk about because they hadn't been put there by steel of any sort. The man in the bar had pushed, pushed some more, successful in bringing a couple of friends into it as well, only to fall the bloodied victim to Sean's copoeira defense. The man's cohorts somehow knew enough to stay put, seeing that martial voodoo in Sean's eyes, his way of looking at them, those finger motions that chilled the heart.

Although violence wasn't all Sean had talked about. There was Antarctica, one place he had considered living after the war. McMurdo, Erebus City, Grahamland, he'd thought, somewhere between the Weddell and Bellinghausen Seas, where the weather was mildest. Continuous night from April to September, the curious appeal of knowing that just about everything in the world lay to the north . . . Trouble was, Antarctica was short of hiding places, and everybody seemed to know everybody else's business—which wasn't true in Lagunas. Even if you did have to cope with river blindness, leishmaniasis, assassin bugs, vipers, piranha, electric eels, giant catfish, botflies, and urethra-lodging toothpick fish.

And Sean had his considerate side. For example, he waited till they had cleared customs to show Eddie the weapon he'd smuggled through: some state-of-the-art ceramic handgun, a stranger to the airport scanners. But even then Sean was worried about being ripped off for a ride into the Bronx, despite Eddie's assurances that every licensed a-cell was security-cam-equipped, and that the transactions seldom involved cash. And so had begun the search for a cabbie Sean could trust . . .

Now the vet was staring fixedly at Willy's note, fingertipping the coarse recycled kenaf paper as if to determine its composition. "How long would it take us to get down there?"

"Little Asia?" Eddie rocked his head back and forth. "If you're willing to grab the first cab this time, we could be there in about twenty minutes. We might even beat them, assuming they tubed down."

"Then let's do it.'

Eddie didn't move. "Uh, about the gun . . ."

Sean adjusted the weapon at the small of his back, then cut his eyes to Eddie. "Don't go Twenty-One on me, man. This is still New York."

Bullets Strayhand emerged from behind a garbage dumpster parked in the street to give the poppy entrance to The Dreamy Lotus a closer look. One thing the master had always told him in cases like these: Just follow your nose . . .

His nose in the present case having dictated that he follow Willy Ninja over the several other flakes who floated with Lucky Junknowitz. Bullets couldn't explain why, save that in the beginning Willy'd struck him as regular cast, a working-stiff white-trasher. Then, after Atlantic City, he was certain he'd made the right call. He could still see the three of them sitting at the bar, Willy and the two plain-as-rain wiseguys he thought he was kidding. Bullets, out of the lights and the TV flicker, ordering shots of ersatz brandy for the *mama-san* who came with the table, hadn't heard much of the conversation; but even the little he heard was enough to tell him that Willy had chosen the wrong boys to scam. Fact was, if cases at Altamont hadn't been keeping him so busy, Bullets might have stuck with the pair—a tall black and a fireplug of a Japanese—just to see what they were all about. Not that he expected to discover a link to the Junknowitz case, but just to keep his hand in, stay in touch with what was happening on the street, what the opposition was doing for laughs. Retro to his days on the force, before vice had led him over into crimes of the inexplicable sort, the "nut 'n' honey cases" as some guys in the precinct called them, before his special training in the art of true detection at the foot of the master, Erik Vogon. But Junknowitz came first, because he'd promised Asia—even if she had lied to him about expecting a claim to be filed by Lucky's beneficiary. Hell, even if she might be in collusion with this Junknowitz character to milk a settlement out of the company. Bullets knew from the start he was doing Asia a solid, but damned if the fucking case wasn't turning out interesting enough to wrap him up.

Just following his nose.

The evening had offered several options: Eddie Ensign flying in from Rio or somewhere with policy benefish Sean in tow—maybe the brothers had pulled a switch, leaving Lucky down south? Asia and Koddle off to quiz the master himself. Then there was Marshall Stack, who'd sounded evasive on the phone; the witch doc Bulaful, who insisted he was over his gripe but whom Bullets wasn't ready to rule out; and Harley Paradise, on-the-go miz from the Gender Bias Council, who still hadn't returned his calls. One of them knew where Junknowitz was hiding. It was just a matter of sniffing out the right path.

In the end, of course, he'd settled on Willy again, tailing him down to Little Asia—an eyes-closed easy chore when your target was partnered to a guy wearing pants the color of California sunshine—watching him disappear into the plaster facade of The Dreamy Lotus. Bullets knew Little Asia from his days on the Jade Squad, and was thinking he would close the lead some, when who should show up but the two wiseguys from Atlantic City.

The real payoff, however, was yet to come. Bullets was loitering near the poppy-door by then, wondering why a regulars-only sign was posted, when out of a cab came Eddie and a drawn-tight soldier who had to be Sean. A problem at the door, but the two had forced their way in.

Not a moment before Bullets heard the first of several gun-shots.

TWENTY-FIVE

CHARLIE COLA FORCED a smile as Molly led the Quick Fix Adit's most recent VIP arrival through the stockroom and on into the front of the store. "And have a pleasant stay, sir." Charlie's mouth was beginning to ache from sustaining the grin. He collapsed the smile as soon as Jesus pulled the door shut, and sat there massaging his jaw for a moment before telling young Powell, "Make sure you get him to the airport without any problems." Adding as Jesus hurried off: "And don't let him leave the store without carrying something—a turkey dog, or a bag of those soy crisps!"

Agency reps—the lot of them frequent fades, recurrent relocators—had been stepping out of the freezer Adit at the rate of one a day for the past week, coming out of the cold demanding to be sped off to Kennedy-Monroe or LaGuardia, delivered to some Wall Street address or a posh uptown hotel. A human arrival, this latest, sporting a Black Hole Trough Adventures ID. Tall and rather distinguished-looking in a suit somebody or other must have had custom made in Italy—the kind of fine-hand linen Dante Bhang might wear to a Nosotros El Grupo luncheon. Charlie guessed what was going on, but refused to think about it. Didn't even want to know—not that anyone was offering. Just wanted to be left alone to mind the store, shepherd travelers in and out, verify documentation, ticket them through Calcutta Travel, send along his reports. Probably the first time ever he was happy about being left out, too. But that was fine, that was okay by him, even if it meant doing without the self-bestowed quarterly bonuses, the home upgrades, the Trough vacation. He could live with it. And Didi'd have to live with it, as well. That, in fact, was exactly how he would put it to her when she came at him: *Didi, you can live with this.* Meaning there were worse alternatives to being working class, Westhampton cast members. Like having some Agency Probe take a sudden interest in the Vanderloop fiasco and decide to show up on Earth. To get to the bottom of things, as it were. And it had come down to Charlie fearing just that each time the Adit indicators lit up to announce the imminent arrival of some Black Hole bigwig.

But he hoped that by furnishing the Agency with the name of the mistakenly disappeared Earther he had minimized the chances of a Probe-directed investigation. "Musician who goes by the name of Lucky Junknowitz," he had reported, admittedly uneasy about having to take Mickey Formica at his word. Of course Charlie'd neglected to mention that Junknowitz might be a Terran operative, inserted into the Trough by an as-yet-unidentified group who had substituted their agent for the also missing Miles Vanderloop. But then, had anyone included him in the Sumatra op—the possible rustling of a clan of Australian Aborigines? And besides, as Dante'd said, no one in the Agency would need ever know about the downside competition. Especially now that Bhang's people were enabled to deal with the lensman who'd cam shafted Charlie that night in front of the theater.

"Christ on a crutch," he complained to the air, reaching for the packet of aspirin he kept in the top drawer of his desk.

The danger of exposure and compromise; the existence of a group with its own hidden agenda; the reliance on losers like Mickey Formica and Nikkei Tanabe to carry out a character assassination . . . Additional headaches he didn't need.

He had, however, received one piece of good news through Adit contact Mussh Kunwar, to the effect that the Peer Group responsible for the abduct mix-up was having some trouble tracing the current whereabouts of Lucky Junknowitz. He laughed when he heard it, had said out loud, "Good, good, keep fucking up." Just so long as everyone kept fucking up in the Trough and not in his backyard. He wanted Quick Fix to emerge unscathed, he was even coming to feel somewhat proprietary about the place. It was amazing, in fact, how he was actually beginning to relish the smell of light-bulb-grilled turkey dogs.

Now if he could only rid himself of the suspicion that he was still being watched, stalked like some Jason Duplex. One thing was certain, though: he'd erred by involving Dante Bhang in his affairs. The next time a problem arose he would handle it himself, right from Quick Fix, using his own crack staff. Molly, Jesus, Labib, Sanpol—whomever it took.

*   *   *

Sobek was on Avonne, tracing the whereabouts of the Yg-gdraasian mercenaries, when he received orders from Light Trap to abandon his probe into the misrouted arms shipment and investigate the matter of a misplaced—and, as it would emerge, misidentified—abductee.

The intended target was a human named Vanderloop, whose inquiry into the disappearance of a group of indigs from his tertiary-indexed homeworld was endangering an earlier priority operation that had been overseen by Terminal Abduction. Some Black Hole division chief had ordered a surveillance, then given the go-to for an abduction and transfer of the target to al-Reem for handling. Some unknown higher-up in the Agency, however, had meddled with the orders and handed the operation over to Technical Assist—the same division that had failed in its attempt to employ the Yggdraasian mercenaries in a preemptive strike against Eternity Tours. Since then, the subtle approach having failed, the Agency had commenced corporate raids against both Eternity Tours and its ally, the AzTek Development Consortium.

As if this weren't enough, the tertiary world in question was the one that had figured in the intelligence report passed on to Eternity Tours by Ka Shamok: Earth, Adit Navel.

The puzzle was continuing to assemble itself.

And there was more. Not content to rely simply on the inept-itude of the Technical Assist division chief, the Agency unknown—Ka Shamok's contact, surely—had stipulated that the Peer Group tasked with the abduction should turn the target over to the care of a recently demoted Black Hole guide who had been a principal player in the Avonne muddle! In turn, this Sheena Hec'k had been ordered to travel *by ship* to al-Reem. Through a wrest area, no less.

The 'Reem-bound freighter Hec'k and her charge had boarded at Sierra had been attacked and destroyed. Sobek had hoped it had ended there for the both of them, but subsequently learned that several hundred survivors had been rescued by an Edrian warship and conveyed to Edri itself, Hec'k and the Earther among them. Planetside, apparently passing themselves off as representatives of Black Hole Trough and Adits, the two had gotten the indigs worked up over some tourism promotion scheme, and had earned themselves passage on a diplomatic ship to New Bedlam station.

Sobek was on New Bedlam now, awaiting a fade to Staph,

where Hec'k and the Earther had last been seen. The Probe was still trying to sort through the on-station events that had led to their Adit jump to Staph, but from what had been pieced together he surmised that the Earther—magic-markered with an open ticket—had faded alone and in flight. Something Hec'k hadn't mentioned when informed that her charge was not Miles Vanderloop but some hapless, innocent musician named Lukki Junkedwits. Sobek could only imagine what subterfuges the improperly-profiled nanites were working on the Earther's body and brain. That Hec'k had violated her orders by intending to use the Adits for transport was another matter. In any case, she had followed Junkedwits to Staph, perhaps in pursuit. And once more Sobek could only hope for the best—and the worst: that Hec'k had chased her escaped charge directly into the black heart of Evening Tide. He thought it wise nonetheless to learn what he could from whomever had had dealings with the fugitives on Staph.

To learn something about the Agency worm who had set all these events in motion, however, would probably require a fade to Earth for a long talk with the Adit franchiser who had monitored the movements of the Peer Group sent in by Technical Assist, and who may have been to blame for at least some of the confusion that surrounded the case. There was some suggestion, in fact, that the franchiser—one Charles Cola—had planned to hold Vanderloop for ransom.

And just where, Sobek wondered, was the intended target, if this Lukki Junkedwits was the one the Peer Group had abducted by mistake? Sobek realized that the path to Ka Shamok's spy led straight through Black Hole Technical Assist, but Charles Cola was the key to setting off on the right foot—even if that meant burrowing into every file, every data document and financial statement the franchiser maintained.

Silvercup understood that she had threatened her own security by allowing the Earther to view the info-crystal data. But in that she was only following Fealty directives: disturb, disquiet, destabilize. It was time to move on anyway, to slough her identity as Metallica and go to ground or Sweetspot. As her WitSec chaperon Lister had said shortly before his death on Gilgit, the trick was in not waiting for a problem to arise, but relocating even when things couldn't be better. To keep everyone guessing.

She wondered briefly what would become of the Terran with large, lovely eyes and the lucky medallion. Was he even aware of what it was he possessed? And now to go along with it, the

knowledge that his homeworld had been targeted by Black Hole
for inclusion in the Trough. Another small victory for the
founders, Black Hole's Sysops. For if there was a world that had
no need of the Trough, it was Terra, the galaxy's idiot savant.

Silvercup looked ahead and saw the Terran in her future. And
another being whose confederacy could tip the balance of power
in the Fealty's favor, should that one awaken . . .

But time enough to dwell on these things later, she told herself. Time to fade now, far from Staph, back into the world of
light.

When she returned to New York from Meadow Suite, Phipps
Hagadorn's oceanside retreat, one of the first things Harley did
was schedule an appointment with SELMI. The decision-support
system rightly deduced that its hazel-eyed, brown-haired, exquisitely proportioned client had come to gloat about the experience, but refused to let on.

I can't tell you how wonderful it was, Harley was entering,
five or so minutes into the session. *The weather, the food, the
evening get-togethers on the deck. I met so many interesting
people. I can't begin to tell you . . .*

TRY, the screen insisted.

Rhapsodic Harley, faceup on the couch with smart-pad in
hand, took a starting breath and entered: *Let me see . . .*

She typed names in a rush: headliners, prominent people,
featured players and their trophy spouses. She had to think hard
for some of them, struggled vainly for others. The machine
meanwhile provided onscreen photos, holos where available,
along with pertinent data culled from dozens of computer news
and info-tainment services.

TAKUMA TANABE:CEO:MITSUBISHI/NAGOYA AEROSPACE
RICHARD RYMER:PRES:UNIVERSAL STUDIOS:MP DIRECTOR
NABUKI MARISAWA:CEO:NIPPON FIBER OPTICS/KYOCERA
TIMOTHY ALSTON:CEO:IBM:VIRTUAL NETWORK DIVISION
DAMIR LINDH:CORP VPRES:ROYAL DUTCH SHELL GROUP
ERIK VOGON:STAGE MAGICIAN:CSICOP BOARD OF DIRECTORS
ASTERIA CUSHMAN:CEO:QUICK FIX CONVENIENCE STORES, INC
ULF WEIGEL:CORP VPRES:MANAGING EDITOR, *VIDEO EXAMINER*
JASON DUPLEX:OSCAR-NOMINATED SCREEN ACTOR
ARBOR SLOCUM:CHAIRPERSON:THEME PARK ADVISORY GROUP
VLADIMIR ARTEMOV:CONTROLLER:UNITED SOVIET COM-ECON

FATIMA BEBE:SPEC PROJ SUPERVISOR:VIDEO OB RESEARCH GRP
ENZO FAMULARI: *SEARCHING . . .*
JIANG DING:CEO:CHINA MOTORS

That's it, Harley entered minutes later. *Simpson something or other. Said or maybe Saif something. Somebody Frost . . . But I know that half of them were with Fortune Fifty corporations. Citibank, Lotus Development, Morgan Stanley, you know the ones.*

CROSS-REFERENCEING YIELDS SEVERAL INTERESTING CONNECTIONS, HARLEY, the screen displayed. WOULD YOU LIKE TO SEE THEM?

She frowned, asking herself how they had gotten over into this. Entered: *If you must. Although I'd prefer not to waste my fifty minutes watching your circuits play.*

SELMI promised to keep it brief. Instantly, photos of Jason Duplex and Richard Rymer came onscreen.

BOTH INDIVIDUALS ARE EMPLOYED BY MATSUSHITA-UNIVERSAL STUDIOS, BUT A SECOND LINK IS PROVIDED BY *ZONE DEFENSE*, A FILM DIRECTED BY RYMER IN WHICH DUPLEX STARRED.

Harley showed the cameras an impatient look. *I already knew that, SELMI.*

TAKUMA TANABE, CHIEF EXECUTIVE OFFICER WITH MITSUBISHI/NAGOYA, IS THE FORMER PRESIDENT OF NIPPON YUSEN KABUSHIKI, WHICH ONCE OWNED THE CRUISE SHIP *CRYSTAL HARMONY*.

I told you Phipps bought the ship. He's renaming it the Crystal Harmonic.

ERIC VOGON AND VLADIMIR ARTEMOV BOTH MADE *CELEB MAGAZINE*'S WORST-DRESSED LIST LAST YEAR.

Really, SELMI, you're getting to be a regular gossip.

CHECKING ALL CURRENT DIRECTORIES, I FIND NO LISTING FOR ENZO FAMULARI. PERHAPS YOUR RECALL IS FAULTY.

Harley sat up, typing: *My recall isn't faulty. Enzo's with the Aztec Development Corporation.*

SELMI took a moment to reply. CHECKING ALL CURRENT DIRECTORIES, I FIND NO LISTING FOR THE AZTEC DEVELOPMENT CORP. A column of alternative possibilities scrolled across the screen: ASTEK, ASTEC, ASTECH, ASTECK, AZTECH . . .

Harley shrugged and entered: *What can I tell you? Enzo told me he worked for Aztec. I don't see why he'd lie. Besides, I'm sure it's an actual company because Lucky's roomie works for it, too. And don't go putting Lucky's face onscreen,* she added before SELMI could do just that.

WERE YOU SURPRISED TO FIND ARBOR SLOCUM IN ATTENDANCE?

Was I. But it seems she's known Phipps for years. In fact, she worked for him just before they offered her the position on the Theme Park Advisory Group.

IS SHE AWARE THAT YOU AND LUCKY ARE LOVE INTERESTS?

WERE love interests. And no, in any case. But she did ask about him. Apparently he was supposed to be back at his job by now. I told her that I hadn't seen him in weeks, and that she should probably try putting out the word in Antarctica.

THE PHYSIOLOGICAL CHANGES THAT ACCOMPANY YOUR ENTRIES LEAD ME TO CONCLUDE YOU HAVE DECIDED TO ACCEPT PHIPPS HAGADORN'S OFFER OF A POSITION WITH PHOENIX ENTERPRISES. AM I CORRECT?

You are. Harley responded brightly for the cameras, finally over into something she wanted to discuss. *I start Monday as a kind of hostess for the* Harmonic's *maiden voyage. Phipps keeps stressing that the ship's themers are going to be a very hard-to-handle bunch, but by that I guess he means demanding, because of having to wear all that make-up and such.*

SELMI offered no immediate response.

I know you probably never thought I'd leave the Gender Bias Council to work in the private sector. But this is going to be important work, SELMI. Phipps is trying to tap into a whole new market: people who've never experienced a theme park. And he has hinted that the Crystal Harmonic *might be only a beginning for me. He's even thinking of using me as a kind of spokesmodel in the ad campaigns.*

ARE YOU AND MR. HAGADORN ONLINE ROMANTICALLY?

Absolutely not. And why do I have to keep repeating myself? Phipps is married, happily married. This is just business.

THEN I SHOULD CONGRATULATE YOU.

You certainly should, Harley told the machine with a flurry of fingers. Then she smiled for the cams. *And won't Lucky be surprised when he sees my face in an advertising display. It's almost like being a celebrity.*

Lucky's efforts to fight the confinement field were futile. He would no sooner stop walking than the forces that ruled within the twin-pack would literally lift him off his feet and deposit him a meter or so from Sheena Hec'k's shapely posterior as she continued her search for an open Adit out of Staph Station.

"Will you at least listen to me?" Lucky was asking now. "After all we've meant to each other." He was back in his caped crusader getup, his meager possessions stuffed into the outfit's cummerbund, an anti-stretch-pants derm pasted on the wrist that had worn the medical bracelet a short time before.

Sheena whirled, her abrupt move driving him to the perimeter of the field. "Don't try that tongue tide on me, Junknowitz. And what makes you think you've meant anything to me? You're an assignment, that's it."

Lucky spread his hands in a gesture of entreaty. "Look, I was just trying to get your attention. But as long as I have it, lemme just tell you about Metallica's holo-show, okay?"

She glared at him. "I'm not interested in any holo-show. Especially Metallica's."

"Funny," Lucky said, winging it, "she didn't like you either."

Sheena's mouth opened. "She said that?"

"Maybe not in so many words . . . But she said she thought you were entirely too competitive."

"Competitive? I'll show her who's—wait a minute, she didn't even know me before I walked into that clinic."

"Burst," Lucky revised. "You burst into the clinic. That's probably what tipped her off. First impressions, you know. Anyhow, she whispered it to me while the Tusk Twins were dragging me out: 'She's awfully competitive, isn't she?' Just like that."

Sheena snorted a laugh. "She should talk. Lady Broad Shoulders. You're lucky she wasn't your physical therapist."

Lucky adopted a dreamy look. "My fantasy for the trip home . . ."

Sheena's green eyes narrowed. "Who said anything about home? My orders are to turn you back over to the Peer Group as soon as we fade to New Bedlam."

"But I'm not Vanderloop!" Lucky shrieked in spite of himself. "You know that now."

Sheena was shaking her head. "Not for me to fix, I told you before. Now you can be someone else's problem for a while." When Lucky hadn't reacted a half minute later, she added, "I'm sorry, Lucky, but—"

"—there's nothing you can do." Lucky held her gaze. "It's

not something I would ever say. But I guess I understand what it means to be so hung up on keeping a job that you'll do anything you have to, even if you know that what you're doing is totally fucked up.''

Sheena's nostrils flared. ''I don't have to take this from you.'' She turned and set off down the Adit concourse, the twin-pack field insuring that Lucky kept up.

''Guess you kinda have to take it, though, don't you?'' he said to her back. ''Unless of course you want to turn me loose.''

She whirled on him again. ''You're completely addled, you know that? Completely addled.''

Lucky summoned every ounce of sincerity he had in him. ''I'm only asking you to listen to me for five minutes. If what I tell you doesn't change things, then, fine, I'll come along like a good puppy.''

Sheena folded her arms across her chest. ''Nothing you tell me is going to change things.''

''Earth,'' Lucky said. ''The holo report was about Earth—Project Head Start. It was compiled by a company called the AzTek Development Consortium for I don't know who, but the plan calls for Earth to be opened up for tourism.'' He didn't bother to add that his own back-home roomie had been employed by the same alien corp. Or that he, Lucky, was the ''Informant Zero'' mentioned in the project report.

''This agency you work for,'' Lucky continued, ''this Black Hole, has already made its decision. No one's supposed to know. But somehow the group that hired AzTek to survey Earth found out.''

Sheena studied him. ''That can't be right. The Agency would never be so careless with data concerning a tertiary world.''

''Black Hole doesn't permit mistakes, huh?''

''No, they don't.''

''Then what the hell am I doing here, Sheena? What is Lucky Junknowitz doing here when Professor Miles Vanderloop was the one the Agency was after?''

Sheena's ''I don't know'' was a long time coming. And all that long while she was asking herself just how Metallica had come into possession of the info-crystal in the first place. Had it been given to her by a member of the Short Timers Club who didn't want to deliver the bad news? Another Earther, perhaps. Her father came suddenly to mind. What kind of life had he led before arriving on Foxal? Had he been involved in intrigue of a similar sort? Had he returned *home*? . . .

"And I don't care what you tell me about Black Hole," Lucky said, "there's no way I'm gonna believe I'm the first mistake they made."

The HuZZah incident on Avonne had already squirreled into Sheena's thoughts, but what she said was, "So which is it you're concerned about, Lucky, Black Hole or Earth?"

He sniffed. "You need to ask, huh? When Black Hole is about to make my planet the next goddamned hot spot along the Trough—the object of some tourist invasion? Package it up the way they've done to . . . you tell me how many other worlds."

"Tourism isn't the worst thing," Sheena started to say.

"Hey, don't try to sell me on tourism, okay? 'Cause I've got a working knowledge of what it's *already* done to Earth."

Sheena inclined her head. "Then maybe Earth's long overdue."

Lucky scowled. "I'm not saying we don't deserve some flak, but, Christ, Sheena, it's *our* homeworld and that alone gives us the right to ruin it in our own way. Even if Black Hole *has* been influencing things, that still doesn't give them the right to decide shit like that."

"The Agency doesn't need the right."

"See, that's just what I'm saying. You're working for slime. Earth's at least half your homeworld, too, if what you told me about your father is true."

"Of course it's true."

"And Foxal, your mother's world, is that some protected place, a tertiary world, or have the tourists already conquered it?"

"It's a playground," Sheena said with faint distaste. "But it wasn't always like that. Not when I was growing up."

"And the other worlds, Edri, Kammu, Staph . . . Shit, I can't figure why you'd want to keep working for an organization like Black Hole."

Sheena put her hands on her hips. "And just what exactly do you see me doing?"

Lucky flashed on the many arguments he'd had with Harley over the same issue. He wished he could take hold of Sheena's shoulders, shake some sense into her, but the confinement field didn't permit contact unless it was damped way down. "I see you fading to Earth and helping me prevent this from hitting the fan."

Sheena laughed in disbelief. "Completed addled!"

"Okay, then how's this?" Lucky said quickly. "I see you

coming to Earth to find Miles Vanderloop. Because, because finding him will, uh, land you a better job with the Agency. A raise, increased benefits, whatever it is you want out of life. And your dad,'' he added in a rush, ''you could learn some things about your dad. You said he never told you why he left Earth—or Foxal. Those have gotta be questions you've asked yourself.''

Sheena was regarding him curiously—wavering, Lucky hoped.

''And I suppose it's your plan to show me around.''

Lucky beamed. ''I know the place, Sheena, ocean to ocean, pole to pole. Whether it's Vanderloop or your father, I can help find him. Hell, Vanderloop's probably an alien anyway.''

''You're an alien,'' Sheena told him for the nth time.

''Well, an XT, then. Somebody from somewhere in the Trough.''

Sheena was thinking about it, foot tapping the concourse floor, tongue moving around in her cheek. Maybe it was time to tender her resignation. Then she exhaled and shook her head. ''It would never work.''

''Why wouldn't it work?''

She looked at him. ''For one thing, Earth is still classified a tertiary world, and you can't just fade to a tertiary world without special permission.''

''But we've got open tickets.''

Sheena shook her head again. ''We'd need authorized visitor's permits issued through Black Hole Trough Administration.'' She pointed to her head. ''Here. Magic markered.''

''And there's no way to get those?'' Lucky sounded desperate all of a sudden.

''Of course there are ways, but . . . I don't know, Lucky.''

Despite the field he reached for her, only to be repulsed, harshly reminded. He nursed his hand and watched Sheena's expression change. ''Come on, Sheena, it's the least you could do after all the Agency's put me through. After what it's put *us* through.''

Sheena's smile gathered slowly, like a mounting breeze. Then her hand went to her belt and hovered for a moment above the twin-pack remote . . .

ABOUT THE AUTHOR

Jack McKinney has been a psychiatric aide, fusion-rock guitarist and session man, worldwide wilderness guide, and "consultant" to the U.S. military in Southeast Asia (although they had to draft him for that).

His numerous other works of mainstream and science fiction—novels, radio and television scripts—have been written under various pseudonyms.

A self-described "ambulatory schizophrenic," he currently resides in Manhattan and Annapolis, Maryland.

ROBOTECH

by

JACK McKINNEY

The ROBOTECH saga follows the lives and events,
battles, victories and setbacks of this small group
of Earth heroes from generation to generation.